SCOUT
★ STORM DOG ★

JENNIFER LI SHOTZ

#1 *New York Times* bestselling author

HARPER

An Imprint of HarperCollinsPublishers

For Emmett and Amelia

The Scout team is a proud supporter of The Sato Project, a dog rescue organization in Puerto Rico.

This book is a work of fiction. Names, characters, places, and incidents are either the product of the author's imagination or are used fictitiously, and any resemblance to actual persons, living or dead, business establishments, events, or locales is entirely coincidental.

Scout: Storm Dog
Copyright © 2019 by Alloy Entertainment

alloyentertainment
Produced by Alloy Entertainment
1325 Avenue of the Americas
New York, NY 10019

Library of Congress Control Number: 2019933497
ISBN 978-0-06-280264-4 (paperback)
ISBN 978-0-06-280263-7 (hardcover)
19 20 21 22 23   PC/BRR   10 9 8 7 6 5 4 3 2 1
❖
First Edition

1

SCOUT WAS WORRIED. He ran his snout over Matt's heavy suitcase, sniffing and snorting, his tail sticking straight out behind him and his ears perked forward. His brow was furrowed in concentration, as if he was trying to figure out where Matt was going.

"It's okay, Scout." Matt laughed as the dog nudged the lid of the suitcase open and stuffed his head into the neatly folded pile of T-shirts. "Relax, pal. You're coming with me." Matt wrapped his arms around his dog's chest and gave him a hug. "You don't think I'd go to Puerto Rico without you, do you?"

Scout responded by licking Matt's eyebrow.

Satisfied, Scout spun around three times and, after some rearranging of the blankets, plopped down next to the suitcase on the bed. He dropped his head onto his paws, still watching Matt.

"How's the packing going?" Matt's mom called from the kitchen. "We're wheels up at fourteen hundred hours."

"On it!" Matt called back down. He turned to Scout and shook his head. "How many times has she already asked me that this morning?" Matt questioned the dog, who stared at him blankly in response. "Military parents." Matt sighed.

Matt shoved a Reno baseball cap and a pair of flip-flops on top of his clothes and zipped the suitcase shut. He looked around his room, at his fishing rod leaning in the corner, the kayak oars hanging on the wall, and the photo of his whole family at his sister Bridget's high school graduation just a few months earlier. It was the last photo he had of the four of them. Now that Bridget was off at her first semester of college in California, she and Matt only talked via the occasional text. After Bridget had left, Matt's dad had shipped out too, for what Matt hoped would be his last deployment to the Middle East. They managed to FaceTime once a week, depending on his dad's schedule.

It had just been Matt, his mom, and Scout all summer, though Matt kept himself busy kayaking and rock climbing with Dev, Amaiya, and Curtis. Matt had been looking forward to going back to school with his three best friends in a couple of weeks, but plans had changed—as they so often did in his family.

If you had asked Matt to name the very last thing he imagined doing for his seventh-grade year, it would have been spending it in Puerto Rico with his mom and dog. Matt still wasn't sure how he felt about it—other than knowing it was the right thing to do. That was because the upheaval in Matt's life was nothing compared to what a lot of other people were going through in Puerto Rico. Just a few weeks earlier, a powerful hurricane had crashed through the island. Matt had seen the frightening images in the news: houses ripped from their foundations, tall trees snapped in half, cars flipped on their sides . . .

The island was devastated.

More than half of it was still without electricity. Tens of thousands of people were without clean water. Just as many people had no home to return to. Fallen trees blocked roads, making it hard for rescue crews to get through with food and water.

That's where Matt's mom came in.

National Guard troops from all over the country were headed to Puerto Rico to help, and she was leading the way. That's because she wasn't just Matt's mom— she was Colonel Tackett, in charge of the entire Nevada Army National Guard base. She would be heading up the response teams that were converging at the National Guard base in Puerto Rico. They were going to help in any way they could—they would find people who needed assistance in remote areas, distribute food and medical supplies, clear debris, rebuild businesses and homes, reopen roads . . . whatever needed doing.

When Matt's mom got word of her deployment, Matt had a decision to make. With his dad and Bridget gone, he couldn't stay alone in their house on base. His mom had spoken to Dev's mom and then gave Matt the choice to spend the first semester of seventh grade living at Dev's house. Matt was tempted—hanging out with his gangly, goofy, hilarious friend 24/7 would be a ton of fun. Plus, he had quickly felt more at home here in Nevada than in all the other states he'd lived in during his twelve years, mostly thanks to the closest friends he'd ever had.

But the more Matt thought about staying at home,

the more a little feeling started to tug at him. Matt had always felt as though he were a part of something bigger. Like the decisions he made weren't just about him.

After a couple of days, that wiggly feeling in his gut grew into a certainty, and his decision became clear.

I can't help from here, he thought.

Matt wanted to go with his mom and help out as much as he was able to. He knew he wouldn't be allowed out in the field with her troops, but maybe he could help in smaller ways—plus, he could still be with Scout.

Matt's mom was taking Scout to Puerto Rico too, in case her team needed him for a search-and-rescue operation. After all, Scout was the best dog they had. In the eight months since he'd joined Colonel Tackett's K-9 team, Scout had proven that he was the best of the best. He'd been rough around the edges at first—a little undisciplined and a *lot* stubborn. But then a dam burst and a flood crashed through Silver Valley. Scout had saved a lot of lives that day, including Matt's and his sister's. And if that weren't enough, Scout had also saved Matt, his dad, and his friends when they'd gotten stuck on a mountain in the middle of a terrifying wildfire.

Scout was the star of Colonel Tackett's team, but he

was also an important part of their family now. He didn't just live with the Tacketts, he was also Matt's shadow, protecting him all the time.

So it was decided: Matt would join Scout and his mom, and live with them at the National Guard base in Puerto Rico. They didn't know how long they would be there—at least several weeks, if not several months. All the schools on the island were still closed, but if they opened in time, Matt would probably start the school year there as well.

It would be a big change, but Matt was ready.

The doorbell rang downstairs, and Matt heard his mom greeting someone. A herd of elephants stomped upstairs and toward Matt's room.

"This is NOT happening," Dev bellowed from the hallway. Dev had not stopped giving him a hard time ever since Matt had made up his mind to go.

Matt grinned. "It's happening."

Matt turned to see Dev filling the doorframe. Amaiya ducked under Dev's arm and walked into the room.

"I can't believe this is really happening," she said with an exaggerated frown.

"Me neither," Curtis said from behind Dev.

Dev plopped into Matt's desk chair. "It's not too late

for you to come live at my house," Dev said. "My mom is a seriously good cook."

"No offense," Matt said, "but your room is too much of a mess."

"Ouch," Dev replied.

"I mean, he's not wrong." Curtis shrugged.

Amaiya turned to Matt. "Feel free to take me with you."

"I'd take you all if I could," Matt said.

Excited by all the new company, Scout hopped down off the bed and ambled over, plopping down on the rug at the center of the room.

"Scout!" the kids cried out.

"We're gonna miss you too, buddy!" Amaiya said.

"Gimme a kiss," Dev baby-talked, leaning down to rub his nose against Scout's. The dog obliged him with one big, wet slurp across the cheek.

As Amaiya rubbed Scout's ears, her expression grew serious. "What's it going to be like in Puerto Rico?" she asked Matt. "I went there once on vacation and the beaches were so beautiful, but now . . . It's awful what the storm did."

"Yeah, it's a mess," Matt said. "My mom said roads are still flooded or blocked with trees and stuff. Lots of people still don't have water or electricity."

"Sounds a little scary, man," Curtis said.

It did sound scary, but Matt wasn't afraid. He'd be living on base, where there were generators and supplies, so he wasn't worried about himself. He didn't know what to expect, but he knew that his mom and her team were the best and could handle anything.

The room got quiet. No one knew exactly what to say.

Matt looked around at his friends, sprawled around his room.

He was going to miss them.

"I'll be back so soon, you won't even know I'm gone," Matt finally said to fill the silence.

"Know you're gone?" Dev shot back. "I'm sorry—are you still here?"

Amaiya tossed a shoe at Dev, who caught it and chucked it back at her. She ducked and it hit Matt's closet door.

"You guys had better get out of here before you destroy the place," Matt's mom said from the door. Curtis jolted upright, and Amaiya and Dev sat up straight too.

"Sorry, Mrs. Tackett!" they said at once.

"I'm just kidding." She laughed. "At ease, people."

Matt always found it entertaining when his friends were intimidated by his mom. Sure, she had incredibly straight posture, wore her dark brown hair pulled back in a tight ponytail, and usually had on camouflage. But she was just . . . his mom.

"Well," Amaiya said, getting to her feet, "we should go anyway. We just came to say good-bye."

The kids gathered in a group hug while Matt's mom watched from the door.

"Bye, guys," Matt said.

"See you on the other side," Dev said, clapping Matt's hand in an upright shake.

"See you on the other side."

Dev, Amaiya, and Curtis filed out past Matt's mom. Scout watched them go and sat down by Matt's knee.

"I know this is hard, Matt," his mom said. "But you're handling it really well. I'm proud of you."

Matt shrugged. "Thanks, Mom. It's not really that hard, though. I mean, I'll miss them, but I'll see them again soon."

"You will. I know I promised you that we're staying in Nevada, and I meant it. We are not leaving Nevada. This is just temporary."

"Mom," Matt said with a huge eye roll. "You told me. Like, a thousand times."

She chuckled. "I just want to be sure you know that

I keep my word. We asked a lot of you when we moved here, and I don't take that for granted." She shot him a grateful look. "And I love seeing you with your friends, seeing how happy you are here. This is our home now."

"Then I don't mind leaving for a while, because I know we'll be back."

Matt's mom wrapped him in a tight hug. "Plus," he mumbled into her shoulder, "people need our help. We can't just stay here when we could be down there doing something. It's—" He pulled back and looked at her, trying to find the right words. "It's just . . . our duty, I guess."

"That's my boy," Matt's mom said, beaming at him.

At the word *boy*, Scout lifted his head and raised his ears. He looked from Matt's mom to Matt and back again.

"She wasn't talking to you, boy." Matt laughed. "She was talking to *me* boy." Matt dropped to his knees and took Scout's face in his hands. "We're in this one together, Scout."

In response, Scout wagged his tail, raised his snout, and let out one loud, excited bark.

2

MATT PRESSED HIS FOREHEAD AGAINST the plane window, trying to get a good angle on the land below. There had been nothing to see but clouds for what felt like hours. Now they were past the Gulf of Mexico, past Cuba, Haiti, and the Dominican Republic, and they were beginning their descent. Matt was getting his first sight of the island of Puerto Rico.

It was beautiful. From above, Puerto Rico was a rich, lush landscape of green hills rising and falling into shady valleys, of treetops and narrow roads winding through mountains. There were cities and crowded residential areas, and on one end of the narrow island was a thick patch of forest. All this was ringed with stunning pale beaches.

But as the plane got lower, Matt saw that the beaches were layered with debris and tree limbs. The hillsides were dotted with splintered homes with their roofs torn off, the gaping holes covered by blue plastic tarps. Bright teal, hot pink, and golden yellow houses were knocked off their foundations, as if they had just been picked up and moved a few feet over. Toppled utility poles were split in the middle like broken toothpicks and lay across highways that had chunks of asphalt gouged out of them.

Huge patches of land were still totally submerged by the floodwaters, which had risen fast from the storm surge and the rain that had lasted for days. Boats lay sideways on land where they had been washed ashore. The forest looked like a giant had walked right through it, stomping on trees and knocking them pell-mell into one another, leaving footsteps of flattened greenery behind.

As the plane prepared to land, they flew over a wide zigzagging wall—a fortress set on a spit of land surrounded by water. Matt squinted into the sunlight. He thought back to everything he'd read about the island in the last few days. He recognized the massive structure as El Morro Fort, a sixteenth-century military base built to protect this tiny island in the Caribbean Sea.

Matt was still taking it all in as soldiers greeted him,

his mom, and Scout on the tarmac and led them to a jeep. Scout clambered into the back seat next to him, leaning on Matt as they bumped along. The drive to the base was only a short distance, but it was a slow trip. The road was still covered in a foot or more of water, and the soldier driving the jeep steered it carefully around small mountains of debris. Downed electrical poles, tangled power lines, and piles of wood shards littered the sidewalk.

Matt saw people in T-shirts, shorts, and tall rain boots wading slowly, trying to go about their daily lives. They carried backpacks and stepped around sodden mattresses, torn sofas, rusted washing machines, and strips of corrugated metal siding. He looked up and thought he was imagining things, but it was all too real. There was a bent and twisted bicycle dangling high up in a tree.

Matt had never seen destruction like this before, but there was something familiar in the people. It was their hunched shoulders and their dazed expressions as they adjusted to their new reality. It was the same way Matt and the people of Silver Valley had looked after the terrible flood had crashed through their town. Like they couldn't quite connect what they were seeing with what they knew—things just didn't add up.

But this was way, way worse.

Matt rolled down the window. He wanted to feel and smell the air. It hit him like a briny slap. Scout hopped over Matt's lap to put his front paws on the armrest, stuck his head out the window, and sniffed wildly at the air. Matt felt the dog's body shaking with intensity and excitement. Scout was on high alert, taking in the overwhelming number of new scents and sounds—thousands upon thousands of them all pouring into his senses at once.

Scout was ready to get to work.

3

ON ONE SIDE OF THE HIGHWAY, a long stretch of beach raced alongside the car. The late-afternoon sun sparkled off the water. Matt blinked. They turned onto a smaller road, and soon the jeep slowed as they passed a huge sign, taller than the vehicle. WELCOME TO CAMP MADERA, it said in capital letters.

They drove slowly through the base, which spread out around them like an open field. Hills rose in the distance, providing a stunning backdrop to the buildings lined up neatly, row after row. The base was alive—there were soldiers everywhere. Troops marched in formation or stood at attention, eyes locked on their commanding officers. Others ran laps around a track in small packs.

Men and women in camouflage hustled by, rushing from one barrack to another. Trucks rumbled past.

It felt like home to Matt.

Through the car window, Scout's eyes flitted from one soldier to another, and his ears flicked to the left and right as he took in every sound. He sniffed at the air and pawed at the car door, ready to get out and stretch his legs.

The jeep lurched to a stop in front of a tidy two-story house. Matt had lived on enough bases to know that this was where the colonel lived—and that's who they were here to see. Matt and his mom climbed out. A tall man with gray hair, dressed in camouflage from his ankles all the way up to his cap, walked toward them. He was straight-backed and stern, with a deadly serious look on his face. Up close, Matt could see that he was much younger than his hair—and his posture—made him seem.

Scout hopped out and sniffed at the ground, following a scent across the dirt and over to the man's boots. The man ignored the dog at his feet. Matt was about to call Scout back—this guy didn't look like someone who would find a curious dog cute—but all of a sudden, the man opened his arms wide and burst out laughing.

Matt's mom did the same, and next thing Matt knew, they were wrapping each other in a giant hug.

"Colonel Ric Dávila!" she exclaimed.

"Colonel Trisha Tackett!" he replied in a deep, loud voice.

A woman about Matt's mom's age appeared next to them, and suddenly his mom was hugging her too.

"Sonia!" his mom said.

"Ah, Trisha, it's so wonderful to see you. Thank you for coming."

"How could I not come?" his mom said. "I'm just sorry it's under these circumstances." She turned to Matt and waved him closer. "This is my son, Matt," she said. "Matt, you don't remember meeting them, but this is Ric and Sonia Dávila, some of my oldest and dearest friends."

"Matt!" Sonia exclaimed in a way that made Matt want to get back in the jeep and hide. "Look at you! The last time we saw you, you were just a chubby little baby!" She pulled him into a hug.

Matt cringed at the attention—and the reminder of his chubby baby days—but tried not to let his squirminess show.

"Hi," Matt said. "It's nice to see you again."

Colonel Dávila held out a hand to Matt. Matt bit his cheeks to hide his pain as Ric closed his hand in a knuckle-busting grip. "It is great to see you again. Your mom tells me you're quite a brave young man."

Matt felt his cheeks turn red. "I don't know . . ."

"Modest too!" Ric let out a laugh that rattled Matt's bones. "You're just like your parents, that's for sure."

Before Matt could reply, two kids appeared at Ric's side. One was a very excited young boy, about five or six years old, who was bouncing on his toes. The other was a girl Matt's age. Except for their age gap, the two kids were carbon copies of each other, with their wavy black hair and deep brown eyes. The girl stood calmly by her parents, and after a quick glance at Matt and his mom, she spotted Scout sitting at Matt's knee. Her eyes lit up.

"Matt," Sonia said, "this is my daughter, Luisa, and my son, Emanuel."

"Nice to meet you, Emanuel," Matt's mom said. She dropped to her knees and held out her hand to the boy, who grabbed it and pumped it up and down.

"Nice to meet you, ma'am," he said, his voice a higher-pitched—but equally loud—version of his dad's.

"I've heard you like to cook with your dad," Matt's mom said. Emanuel nodded vigorously. She stood up

18

and held out a hand to Luisa. "Luisa," she said, "I've heard so much about you, about how well you're doing in school and how you want to be a veterinarian."

Luisa turned bright red, just like Matt had a second ago.

"Welcome," she said softly. She had a serious demeanor. *Is she shy?* Matt wondered. Her eyes flitted up to Matt's face for a second, then she looked down at the ground.

"Who's that?" Emanuel asked, pointing at Scout.

"That's Scout," Matt said. "Come here, buddy." He led Scout over to Emanuel, who eyed the dog warily. "It's okay. He's really sweet. Just let him sniff your knuckles for a sec so he gets to know you."

Emanuel held out a clenched fist and turned his head away, as if he couldn't bear to look. Scout sniffed his knuckles. Then his wrist. Then his elbow and all the way up to his armpit. Emanuel couldn't take it—he burst out giggling and put both hands on Scout's head.

"He likes to be scratched right behind his ears." Matt grinned. Emanuel gave it a try, and Scout let his tongue roll out of his mouth, happy at the attention. Luisa stepped over and knelt on the ground next to Scout.

"Hi there," Luisa said, her face brightening and her voice suddenly animated. She held out a hand and Scout licked it, then took a step closer and started sniffing at her hair. Luisa sat very still and let the dog check her out. After a moment, she ran a hand over his silky brown-and-white fur. With that, Scout seemed to make up his mind about her. He plopped down on the ground and laid his head on her lap.

"Oh, sorry!" Matt blurted out, tugging Scout's collar to get him off her lap.

"It's okay," Luisa said without looking at Matt. "I don't mind."

"He's not usually *this* chill with new people," Matt said. "He must really like you."

Luisa lowered her face to Scout's. He sniffed at her and pressed the top of his head to her cheek. Matt could see that she was really comfortable with dogs—it made sense that she wanted to be a vet, if animals took to her that quickly.

"He's beautiful," Luisa said. "Is he yours or is he a working dog?"

"Both," Matt said. "He's kind of . . . different from the other National Guard dogs. He gets special privileges."

"You can say that again." Matt's mom laughed. "This dog has us all wrapped around his paw, and he knows it."

"From what I hear," Sonia said, "he's earned it."

Luisa looked up at Matt, her eyebrows raised. "How did he do that?" she asked.

"Well . . ." Matt felt his cheeks go hot again. "I guess he kind of saved my life. A few times. And some other people's too."

"Oh," Luisa said in surprise. Before she could ask for details, her dad wrapped a firm arm around Matt's shoulders.

"Listen, Matt," Ric said. "Our home is your home now, okay? You and Scout. No need to knock—you just come and go as you need."

"Okay. Thanks."

"Your mom, Sonia, and I will be busy. There's a lot of work to be done."

The group grew quiet as the real reason Matt and his mom had come to Puerto Rico settled back over them all. "But tomorrow morning, bright and early, Luisa's going to show you around town," Ric went on.

"Oh, thanks," Matt said, looking over at Luisa. She looked away, seeming uncomfortable. "But that sounds like a lot of trouble—"

"Luisa's happy to do it," Sonia said.

He wasn't so sure about that.

"In fact, she can start right now and take you next door to your quarters," Ric said. "Luisa, do you mind?"

Luisa shook her head.

"Then come back for dinner," Sonia said. "Ric made his famous arroz con pollo."

With a nod, Luisa led Matt and Scout to their quarters—a cozy apartment in the building next door to the colonel's house. There were two bedrooms, a sparse living room, and a small kitchen.

"Here you go," Luisa said.

Matt wasn't sure what to make of her. She was nice enough, but she definitely seemed more comfortable with dogs than she did with humans.

"It's great," Matt said.

"What do you think, Scout?" Luisa said. Matt noticed that she smiled at the dog.

Scout had begun a perimeter check, sniffing his way around the room, sizing up the furniture, and putting his front legs on the windowsill to look outside.

"Seems like he likes it," Luisa said with a little laugh.

"I hope so." Matt smiled. "I sure do."

4

MATT WOKE UP THE NEXT MORNING to a quiet house. For a split second he didn't remember where he was. The light filtering in through the window was brighter. The curtains were whiter. The lumps in the mattress were bumpier. Out of habit, he dropped his left arm off the bed. The warm, furry creature with the wet nose and dog breath lying on the floor next to his bed was the only thing that was the same.

Matt's brain began to wake up along with his body, and he remembered.

He and Scout were in Puerto Rico.

Matt blinked a few times and sat up in bed. He'd tossed and turned throughout the night, woken by the unfamiliar sounds—the chirps and clicks and croaks from the island's nocturnal creatures. Scout looked wide awake, like he'd lain by Matt's side all night, protecting him. When the dog saw that Matt was awake, he dropped his head back down onto his paws with a sigh, his watch over.

Matt looked around at the small room, which had just enough space for a twin bed and dresser. Outside the window, he heard two women speaking in the familiar cadence of the military—short, declarative sentences, followed by quick responses. It sounded like the conversations he heard every day back home, but these two soldiers were speaking Spanish.

Matt checked his phone and saw that a text had come in from Dev overnight.

See what you're missing? Attached was a selfie of Dev in climbing gear. He was holding the phone at an angle above his head, and Matt could see that he was attached to a cliff, with rocks dropping away beneath him.

Nice! Matt wrote back.

Matt and a slow-moving Scout wandered through the empty apartment. He was used to being in a new place, by himself, with nothing in particular to do—that's what it meant when your family was in the military. His mom was long gone for work, but she had left a note taped to the bathroom mirror. *Love you, honey. Go to Luisa's for breakfast. See you tonight. —Mom*

Matt and Scout headed outside and to the Dávilas' house next door.

They stepped into the kitchen and saw Luisa—well, some of her. The top half of her body was inside the fridge, digging around for something in the way back. A covered pot bubbled on the stove, and an open back-pack and huge canvas tote bag sat on the kitchen table. Luisa backed out of the fridge and turned around with her arms full of leftovers.

"Oh—" she said, startled to see Matt and Scout. "I didn't hear you come in!" She dropped everything on the table.

"Sorry!" Matt held his hands out in front of him. "I just—" He eyed the bags. Luisa was clearly packing up to go somewhere. "I thought we were going to— Are you—"

"I was just going—"

"It's okay, I was just—"

"You can have breakfast—" She pointed at a box of cereal and a gallon of milk on the counter and then at a bag of kibble by the sink.

Scout looked from Matt to Luisa, confused. He swiped at Luisa with one paw, trying to get her attention.

"Good morning, buddy," she said, crouching down and letting him sniff her face while she scratched his back. "Do you want breakfast?" Scout tipped his head to the side in response.

It was amazing how well Scout responded to Luisa. Matt guessed it was her tone of voice, which was sweet but firm. It wasn't baby talk, like lots of people used with dogs, but it wasn't the way she spoke to people either. It was like she had a specific way of talking just to Scout. He recognized it as the way the vet or K-9 trainers back home addressed the animals—like they spoke on a dog frequency that only a few humans knew about.

Luisa held Scout's face with both hands and scratched him under the collar. He sat down, closed his eyes, and totally relaxed. She rubbed the top of his head, in the little dip between his eyebrows. He thumped his tail on the ground.

"I know I'm supposed to show you around today," Luisa finally said. "But I have to go. I'll be back, though. Soon. Sort of."

"Um, okay," Matt said, trying to mask his surprise. He dumped some kibble into a bowl for Scout, who wiggled away from Luisa and hurried over. He scarfed down the food, crunching loudly. Matt poured himself some cereal and milk.

"Where are you going?" Matt asked, trying to sound more casual—and less curious—than he felt.

"Nowhere," Luisa said as a timer dinged. She turned off the stove and lifted the lid on the pot. The starchy scent of freshly cooked rice wafted over to Matt. Luisa picked up the pot and poured the rice into a big bowl, then fanned it for a second and said something to herself under her breath in Spanish. Matt didn't hear her clearly—and his Spanish was only so-so anyway—but he got the impression that she wanted the rice to cool down faster. She was really acting like she had somewhere to be.

For someone who was going nowhere, Luisa sure was in a hurry and gathering a lot of supplies.

"Oh yeah, *nowhere*," Matt said half jokingly. "I love that place." Luisa turned around slowly, but before she could speak, Matt's phone chirped. It was a text from his mom. *Have fun with Luisa today! Cell service spotty so stay close to base. See you tonight.*

He held out the phone so Luisa could read it too. "Looks like our parents still think we're hanging out."

27

"I know, I'm sorry. I just really have to do this thing . . ." She trailed off.

"You're going somewhere your parents don't know about," Matt ventured. Luisa didn't respond, which he took as an indication that he was right. "I'm not going to tell on you, if that's what you're worried about," Matt went on. "But I do need to get Scout outside so he can get some exercise . . ."

Scout was a working dog—he didn't do very well when he was stuck in the house all day. Since Matt's mom didn't want to take Scout out on a mission until she had assessed the situation on the island, it was up to Matt to keep him exercised and happy.

Luisa pressed her lips together, as if she was weighing whether or not she could trust him. "I'd rather go alone."

"You're going to carry all that stuff by yourself?"

"I can get it," she said.

"Well, whether you tell me where you're going or not, I know you're doing something you're not supposed to. So . . ." Matt shrugged. "You kind of have to trust me either way. I promise I'm a good helper."

She thought about that for a second. "Okay . . . Fine. But do you swear you won't tell anyone?"

Matt knew from experience that when you kept a secret, it usually didn't end well. The last time he had been asked to keep a secret, Dev, Amaiya, and Curtis had ended up trapped on a mountain with a wildfire closing in on them . . . and Matt, his dad, and Scout had raced up the burning hillside to save them. Keeping secrets was not Matt's most favorite thing to do.

But he didn't really have a choice right now. If he said no, then Luisa would just leave without him. And if something happened to her while she was off doing whatever it was, he'd feel terrible.

But if he said yes, then he was just getting into the same jam he'd been in with his friends. What good would that do anyone?

His mind ran in circles, but he tried to slow it down. *There's a solution,* his dad always told him. *Focus on the solution, not the problem.*

"I'll keep your secret, but if you or anyone else is in trouble, the deal's off. Got it?"

"Got it." Luisa stuck out her hand and they shook on it. She dropped a tub of rice and the leftovers into the tote bag and pointed at it. "You can carry this one."

"No problem. I can fit some stuff in my backpack too, if you want."

"Sure." Luisa handed Matt the bag of kibble, a few cans of tuna, and a box of plastic trash bags. Matt filled his own pack, then hoisted the tote bag onto his shoulder. He clipped a leash to Scout's harness, and they headed out the door.

"So where are we going?"

"It's easier if I just show you."

5

"HE SEEMS LIKE A REALLY GOOD DOG," Luisa said as they walked across the base.

"He is."

"Can I walk him?" Luisa asked.

"Sure." Matt handed her the leash. He watched as she stuck her hand through the loop, then wrapped the leash around her wrist and grabbed it a few inches farther down. She knew exactly how to hold it.

Scout was busy trying to take stock of the entire base all at once, through his nose. His snout skimmed the ground, and his head swiveled back and forth, back and forth, as he led them down the sidewalk and around the closely set buildings. Every time a jeep drove past, one ear flicked toward the sound. He sniffed his way past the exchange, the administration building, the mess hall. Luisa and Matt walked along behind him.

"Do you have a dog?" Matt asked. "I didn't see one at your house, but you're so good with him."

"Oh, I wish." Luisa smiled for real, for the first time since Matt had met her. "I really like dogs," she said with a shrug.

They headed through the main gates, where the guards waved at her as she passed. Scout started to turn right, into the bushes on the side of the road.

"Scout, this way. Come, boy," Luisa corrected him in that perfect tone she had for him. Scout immediately spun around and headed left.

"He really responds to you."

"Does he not usually listen to commands?"

"No, he's really well trained, but sometimes he just has . . . strong opinions."

"So you're saying he's stubborn?"

Matt laughed. "Yeah, I guess so."

They walked toward town. The road was mostly clear, but tall mounds of rubble rose on the shoulder. It looked like emergency crews had managed to clear a path but had no way to get rid of the debris yet. Ric had said at dinner that their area was in pretty good shape, but based on what Matt had seen on the way from the airport yesterday, he could only imagine how bad things were elsewhere.

Luisa seemed to know what he was thinking. "It gets worse," she said with a sad shake of her head. "You'll see."

"Are you from the island?"

She nodded, then shook her head.

"Sort of. My parents grew up here. I was born here, but then we moved all over the place—you know how that goes."

"Yeah. I do."

"But then my dad got this job a few years ago, so we moved back for good."

"Is it a cool place to live?"

"It's amazing. I don't know, it's the only place that's ever felt like home to me."

"I get that." Matt thought about Silver Valley. The town in Nevada was the first place that had ever made him feel that way.

"It's not like the U.S.—we kind of do our own thing here. But it's been . . ." She trailed off. "It's been really hard. Since the storm. It's like we're all trying to get back to normal, but what does that even mean?"

33

Matt waited for her to go on.

"I know we'll be okay," she said firmly. "But I just don't know when."

Scout stopped in his tracks, and his body shifted into alert mode. His head was high, his ears stood straight up and pointed forward, his tail curved above his back, and his muscles were flexed and ready to propel him into action. He stared at something off in the distance. Matt looked down the road.

About forty feet ahead, three dogs clustered together in a small pack. They had frozen too, and they were looking right back at Scout.

"Scout, stay," Matt said. Scout whined but made no move to charge ahead.

Luisa tightened the slack on Scout's leash. "Scout's found our first stop," she said with a smile. Luisa opened her arms wide and called out to them. "*¡Hola, chicos! ¡Chiquita, Guapo, Tío!*" The dogs bounded toward her, their tongues dangling from their mouths. They were mid-size, smaller than Scout, with tall, wide, pointy ears that looked too big for their heads—heads that looked a little too big for their bodies. They weren't like any breed Matt had seen before.

Luisa dropped to her knees, and the dogs fought for space on her lap. She laughed and cooed at them in

Spanish. After they'd said their hellos to her, the dogs migrated over to Scout, who stood still—calm and cool, like the alpha dog he was—while they sniffed him. "Scout, meet Little One, Handsome, and Uncle. At least that's what I call them."

"Nice names." Matt laughed. Once they'd sized up Scout, the three dogs bounced around him playfully. They tripped and stumbled all over each other, then stretched their front legs out and lowered their chests to the ground, their rumps in the air and their tails up high. Their mouths were open in big, goofy smiles, and their tails wagged so hard they created a breeze. They were letting Scout know that they wanted to play, and Scout obliged, ducking and bobbing with them, then sniffing their bellies when they rolled onto their backs and stuck their paws in the air. "Are they strays?" Matt asked.

"They're *satos*," Luisa said with a nod. "It means 'street dog' in Spanish. There's a lot of them around here."

"They're so sweet. Are they all like that?"

"It depends. Some of them are kind of wild, and lots of them are too scared to go near people. But mostly they're really cute like these guys. And hungry."

"How many are there?" Matt asked.

"I don't know, hundreds. Maybe thousands?" Luisa

must have seen Matt's eyes bug out. "It's just the way it is here," she said. "We're used to them."

"Do they just, like, roam the streets?" Matt couldn't quite get his head around the idea. He tried to picture Silver Valley with hundreds of dogs wandering around while people just went about their day.

"Yeah. A lot of them live on Sato Beach." She pointed in the direction of the water. "The storm made things even worse for them."

"Do people adopt them?"

"Some. And there are rescue groups that take them back to the U.S. for adoption. But there are just so many satos, they can't possibly all find a home. So I try to help them out when I can."

She spoke matter-of-factly, but Matt heard the note of sadness in her voice. She turned to the dogs and pulled out the container of rice. The dogs pounced on the food, tails wagging. "We have to go, guys. *Hasta luego.* I'll be back soon."

Scout tore himself away from his fans and left the trio of dogs to their meal. Matt, Luisa, and Scout set off again, heading toward town. Matt looked over his shoulder at the dogs chowing down.

"You could adopt one," he said.

Luisa let out a laugh but shook her head. "My parents are not exactly dog-friendly. And even if they would let me have one, they would *never* let me adopt a sato." She paused. "They think they're all dirty strays."

"That stinks."

"Yeah."

Matt tried to imagine Scout wandering the streets or living on a beach with a bunch of other dogs, with no one to feed him or care for him. Scout had been a runaway puppy, but he hadn't been homeless for very long, Matt knew. He'd been rescued by a family and trained to be a search-and-rescue dog. But Scout was one of the lucky ones—it wasn't the satos' fault they didn't have homes or people to care for them. They were just dogs like Scout, who wanted to be loved. What if every one of them could bring a person as much joy as Scout had brought Matt and his family?

He knew Luisa was doing as much as she could to help the satos, but he wished they could do even more. Every dog deserved a home. But he had no idea how to make that happen, and until he figured that out, the best thing to do was to help them one by one.

"Let's get going," Luisa called back to Matt, who'd paused in the road.

"Coming!" Matt called, racing to catch up.

6

LUISA WALKED QUICKLY, and Scout bounded along beside her. Matt scrambled to keep up with them both. They reached town and walked along the main street, with its small cafés and shops. Three-story houses were lined up in tight formation, and were all the colors of the rainbow. One house was bright turquoise, the next a deep brick red, then sunny yellow, electric blue, and hot pink. Almost every house shared one detail, though: blue tarps tied to their roofs. Matt guessed that first responders had handed out the tarps after the storm.

As they walked, Matt saw kids playing in the street and old ladies sitting in front of the buildings. Two young girls ran over and called out Luisa's name. They wrapped her in a hug and spoke to her in Spanish. Luisa knelt down and talked to them, and Matt heard her say "Scout" at the end of a sentence. Scout walked over to the girls and sat down while they petted him and giggled. The girls waved at Matt, and he waved back.

Luisa started walking again, and a mom with a baby on her hip smiled and waved from the front door of a house. A shopkeeper came out of a small grocery and said *hola*. As they passed a small café on the corner of the main street, Luisa popped in and came out holding two bottles of Coke. She handed one to Matt.

"They're warm," she said. "There's still no electricity here."

"Thanks," Matt said, happy to drink the syrupy-sweet liquid.

Matt kept expecting Luisa to turn into a doorway and reveal her big secret. But she powered ahead until they reached the end of the main road on the edge of town, and then kept going. Matt's head began to spin with possibilities of where they were headed.

Finally, after what felt like an hour, Luisa turned onto a small paved road that angled gently uphill. As they climbed, the area around them turned a lush green and grew thick with trees. It was as if they'd stepped onto a different planet. They crested a small rise and Matt stopped to look out. Scout paused too and doubled back to stand by Matt's knee. Together they scanned the skyline.

The view was breathtaking. Below them, spreading out in every direction, was an ocean of green, a hilly forest that rose and fell like waves crashing toward the horizon.

But floating on this sea was an endless array of debris—split trees and jagged trunks. Matt could see clearings flooded with water and clusters of homes with their sides peeled off and tarps on top. From this elevation, though, he could also see a lot of houses with their roofs still intact, sprinkled throughout the destruction. It was as if the storm had touched down on some buildings and torn them apart, but randomly missed others.

"Where are we?" he asked.

"We're almost there," Luisa replied. "Come on."

They continued uphill until Matt was huffing and puffing. Scout, on the other hand, was barely panting. He acted as if they hadn't just walked for miles and climbed a long, gradual slope. They rounded a curve and a small building emerged from the foliage.

"We're here," Luisa said, pointing to a long, low building across the road. Matt would have walked right by without noticing it. It was windowless. Long, heavy tree branches still lay across the roof, and strips of tar paper had been ripped off and hung down the sides of the building. From where they stood, it looked half destroyed, abandoned.

Scout was going nuts. His nose was on overdrive, and he skittered back and forth in front of the building, inhaling every inch of asphalt and dirt, every patch of grass. He sniffed the walls, the downed trees, even the drainpipes, and slowly made his way toward the far end.

"What is this place?" Matt asked.

"Follow Scout and find out."

Scout had stopped at the corner of the building and was looking back at Matt, as if he was waiting for a sign that it was okay to proceed.

"Go ahead, buddy," Matt said. Scout shot off around the corner, his tail up and his back legs flying out behind him.

An ear-shattering clamor broke out as they walked around the building, and Matt nearly jumped out of his skin. It was an orchestra of barks. Dozens of dogs were howling and yipping and snapping and yowling all at once—some in high-pitched squeaks, others in deep bass bellows. Matt covered his ears, and Luisa laughed.

It was a sight even more overwhelming than all the barking: long rows of rusted, bent, open-air cages, at least twenty, each one the size of a small room and holding two or three dogs. Matt took it all in, and the pieces began to click into place: Luisa's secret was that she was sneaking off to an animal shelter. Suddenly it all made sense—the food, the stop to play with Chiquita, Guapo, and Tio along the way, her friendliness with Scout.

Matt turned to Luisa. "This is what you're hiding?"

She nodded.

"Are these . . . satos?"

"Mostly," Luisa said.

"Are they here because of the storm?"

"Mostly," Luisa repeated. "People have been rounding them up and bringing them here. It's just so crazy out there. It's not safe for them right now."

Matt pictured the jagged wreckage and knee-deep water and rusting furniture lying by the side of the road. It wasn't safe for anyone—dogs or humans.

"So that's why it's a secret," Matt said. "You can't tell your parents you come here . . ." He thought back to their earlier conversation. ". . . because they don't want you to get a dog."

"Exactly," Luisa said with a sigh and a sad smile. "But I'm still trying to help the satos as best I can."

And there were so many satos in this shelter. Some had big, round eyes and scrunched-up, fluffy eyebrows. Others had wide, pointed ears sticking straight out from the sides of their heads, like the dogs they'd met earlier. Some of the dogs were short, with stubby little legs and coarse fur. Others were long and lanky, like Scout. Many were stocky, with muscular legs and barrel chests.

And every single one of them was staring at Matt and Luisa with a look of such hope, such longing, that Matt sucked in his breath. Each and every one of them needed a home.

Scout ran along the front of the cages, stopping at each one to sniff through the bars and jump up on his hind legs to greet the shelter dogs. His tail was wagging wildly.

"Come on. Let's head to the back." Luisa pulled Matt away by the elbow and led him to a small, unmarked door on the back side of the building. The screen was practically hanging off its hinges. She pushed it open with a loud creak and they stepped into a dim interior with low ceilings and a pungent smell of animals. Lots and lots of animals.

Inside were smaller cages, filled with more dogs and a few cats. They lay on their sides. Their ears twitched at the sound of the door, but they barely lifted their heads to see the newcomers. These were clearly the injured or sick ones.

"Scout," Matt said, "stay." He didn't want Scout to startle any of the animals. Scout sat down and took in all the sights and scents and sounds of this strange new place. Matt scanned the room too. The rest of the long, open space was lined with metal supply shelves. They were looking pretty bare, except for a couple of fifty-pound bags of kibble, a bunch of old blankets, and a sprinkling of medicines and first-aid items.

But that was it.

In the center of the room were four stainless steel exam tables, each one with a different dog on it, waiting to be cared for.

For all of this, there were two staff members in scrubs.

"¡Hola, Luisa!" said a man with a surgical mask over his face. He didn't look away from the dog on the table, who he was trying to convince to swallow a pill.

"¡Hola, Alberto!"

44

"*¡Luisa, llegaste!*" said a short woman with her hair pulled back in a ponytail. She waved, but then bent back over the exam table and cooed to the dog in front of her. "*Mi cariño,*" she whispered as she used tweezers to pull something from the dog's paw. "*Muy bien.*" She patted the dog on the head and carried her back to a cage, then came over to Matt and Luisa.

"*Hola, Dr. Correa,*" Luisa said. "This is my friend Matt."

"It's nice to meet you." Matt shook Dr. Correa's hand.

"*¿Hablas español?*" she asked him.

Matt shook his head. Beside him, Scout wagged his tail at the veterinarian.

"*Hola,*" she said, placing a hand on Scout's head. "You're a handsome fellow, aren't you." She sized him up. "Is he a working dog?" she asked Matt.

"Yes. Search and rescue for the National Guard," Matt replied. "How could you tell?"

"It's in his bearing. See how he holds his head"—she straightened her neck and gently stuck out her chin—"and keeps his eye on me, but his nose is still working overtime."

Matt studied Scout as if he were seeing his dog for the first time. He was so used to Scout, but now that Dr.

Correa mentioned it, he could see what she was talking about. Scout was . . . self-possessed. Aware. Attuned to what was happening around him but also focused on the person talking to him. It was like he had heightened senses.

"It's okay if he wants to wander around," Dr. Correa said. "You can release him. He can go play with Jorge."

"Okay, Scout," Matt said. At the command, Scout hopped up and headed off to tour the room on his own.

"How's it going today?" Luisa asked the doctor. "Any supplies come in?"

Dr. Correa frowned. "No. Not a drop." She let out a long sigh. "We have enough food for another day—two at the most. I just hope the trucks can get through soon."

"I brought whatever I could find." Luisa pulled her backpack from her shoulders and unzipped it. Plastic baggies tumbled out, packed with food Luisa had made earlier and the leftovers of the amazing dinner Ric and Sonia had prepared for them last night. There were baggies of savory chicken and rice, crispy chicken skin, even a couple of sagging carrots. Matt emptied his backpack and then the heavy tote bag, pulling out the fresh rice and everything else that Luisa had jammed in there.

"This will feed a lot of our guys today!" Dr. Correa

exclaimed. "Thank you both." She wrapped an arm around Luisa's shoulder and gave her a squeeze. "I don't know what we'd do without you." She looked up at Matt. "It's just me and Alberto here," she said grimly. "We wouldn't make it through the day without this one."

Luisa looked down at the floor, shy at receiving so much praise. "You guys do all the work," she said softly.

"We're a team," Dr. Correa corrected her.

"¿*Doctora Correa?*" Alberto called her over.

"Pardon me," the vet said. With a wink at Matt and Luisa, the vet headed off across the room.

Matt stared at Luisa, unsure what to say.

"What?" she asked. "It's so run-down—is that what you're thinking?"

"What?! No!" Matt said. "Not at all. I was thinking that this place is amazing, actually. I can't believe they're here helping all these animals. I can't believe you're helping too."

She shrugged. "I don't get paid or anything"—she waved a hand around the shabby room—"obviously. But I do what I can."

Matt knew that Luisa didn't have to come here. She didn't have to trek through the ruins of the island, steal food from her parents, and sneak off to help. She could stay on base where it was safe, where there was food and electricity and everything she needed. But she didn't choose to do that. Matt was impressed. "It's amazing what you're doing," he said. "Really."

Luisa looked shy again. "I want to be a vet, so I want to help." Her eyes lit up. "But you haven't even seen the best part yet."

"What's that?"

"Not what, but *who*," Luisa said, and flashed a broad grin. "This way."

7

LUISA LED MATT TOWARD THE BACK of the room, where a fat mutt—Jorge, Matt guessed—and Scout were chewing on opposite ends of a knotted length of thick rope. She scooted past them and stepped around a desk. There, in the farthest corner of the room, in the center of a giant beat-up dog bed, lay the cutest dog Matt had ever seen.

"Matt," Luisa said, "meet Rosita. Rosita, meet Matt."

At the sound of Luisa's voice, the dog whimpered excitedly and her face lit up in a tongue-dangling grin. Her whole body wagged into the cushion. She got to her feet somewhat awkwardly, and Matt saw that her left front leg and back right leg were wrapped in bandages.

"No, honey, don't get up," Luisa cooed. But Rosita

wasn't interested in that advice. Even with her injuries, she was a wiry, bright-eyed ball of energy. She stepped off the cushion and trundled unevenly toward Luisa, practically vibrating with delight.

Rosita was small—she weighed maybe fifteen pounds—with short black fur and a terrier's frame. But her head was something else entirely. It was huge and round and looked like it belonged on a dog twice her size. She had saucer-like brown eyes and, topping it all off, a pair of tall, pointy, slightly mismatched ears that would have fit nicely on a bat. Patches of white fur dotted her chest. One of her front paws was white, the other black. Her back feet were the exact opposite. She had short, skinny legs and a big plump belly.

Rosita looked like a dog patched together from many different dogs, and yet there was something proud about her as she limped along, her head held high. Matt had to laugh—somehow Rosita managed to be both regal and goofy at the exact same time.

Luisa sat on the floor and held out her arms to greet the dog. Rosita climbed onto Luisa's lap and swatted at her with one paw, as if to give her a high five.

"Mi querida," Luisa said softly. "How are you feeling today?" Luisa lowered her face so their noses touched,

and Rosita licked her cheek. She leaned into Luisa's chest. The dog's whole body relaxed as Luisa gently scratched her sides. They stayed like that for a moment. Rosita had her eyes closed, and Matt thought that if she were a cat, she would have been purring.

As she snuggled into Luisa, Rosita opened one eye and turned it on Matt. She sized him up while he held out a hand for her to sniff. She ran her snout over his knuckles, across his palm, and around his wrist. Rosita must have decided that he was worthy of her attention, because she licked his hand and closed her mouth around it in a playful—and possessive—nibble. Matt found himself smiling at her, and he was ready to swear on his life that Rosita had just smiled right back at him.

"I can't—" He laughed. "This is seriously the cutest dog I've ever seen."

"I know." Luisa ran a thumb over Rosita's forehead and grinned down at her. "She's also the sweetest."

Scout broke away from Jorge and wandered over. He nudged his way between Luisa and Matt and took in Rosita, reigning like an injured queen on the throne of Luisa's lap. He gently touched her with his nose, sniffing at her bandage. Rosita sat still, granting him permission to perform his inspection. After a moment, she rolled onto her back and kicked her paws into the air, letting Scout sniff her tummy.

Scout exhaled sharply through his nostrils and sat back. Rosita slid off Luisa's lap and tucked herself between Scout's front legs. Scout stood over her like he was her bodyguard.

"Look at these two!" Luisa exclaimed. "It's like they've known each other forever."

"Scout knows a good dog when he sees one," Matt said.

Rosita looked up at Scout, then at Luisa, then over at Matt. She yipped once, as if she was trying to get their attention. Scout looked down at Rosita and licked the top of her head.

"*¿Sí?*" Luisa laughed. "What is it?"

Moving surprisingly quickly, Rosita hopped up and click-clacked across the floor toward the front of the shelter. She stopped and looked back over her shoulder at the three of them. She barked once and took another few steps, then looked back at them.

"I think she wants us to follow her," Matt said.

"Yeah," Luisa replied. "She does this all the time. Rosita, stop. Come back here, silly." Rosita looked toward the front of the building, then back at them, deciding whether to listen to Luisa or not. "Rosita," Luisa said firmly, *"ven aquí."* With a sigh, Rosita toddled back toward them and plopped down next to Scout, who curled himself around her. Luisa shook her head. "Every time I come here, she says hello to me for a second, then heads straight for the front door."

"Maybe she thinks you're her ticket out of here?" Matt asked.

"Maybe. It's like she wants me to take her somewhere, but I have no idea where. Plus she's not well enough to leave yet."

"What happened to her?" Matt gestured at Rosita's bandage and cast.

Luisa frowned. "It was bad. Someone found her trapped under a big tree branch after the storm. She had a broken leg and lots of cuts, and she hadn't eaten for days. Luckily she was able to lick rainwater off the ground around her." Luisa looked away for a moment, like the words were hard to get out. Matt waited until she was ready to talk again. "She was so weak when she got here. She couldn't eat. I had to spoon-feed her. We didn't think she was going to make it."

Rosita pricked up her ears.

"Sí, señorita," Luisa said. "I'm talking about you."

Rosita nudged at Luisa's hand with her snout. "Oh, sorry, am I not petting you enough?"

"She looks like she's healing really well," Matt said.

"Dr. Correa said she's never seen a dog recover so fast. That's because Rosita's a fighter." Rosita was also starting to gnaw on a thick friendship bracelet on Luisa's wrist. "Stop it," she playfully scolded the dog. "That's mine."

"Was she a sato?"

Luisa shook her head. "We don't think so. She has good teeth and some meat on her bones. So she wasn't starving before she got trapped. And no one here recognized her from Sato Beach. We think she might belong to someone." Rosita lay back down, rested her head on Luisa's hand, and put one paw over Luisa's wrist.

"You mean . . ." Matt was adding it all up. "Are you saying Rosita got lost in the storm—that she got separated from her family?"

Luisa nodded sadly.

"That's so awful . . ." Matt thought about what Luisa was saying. What if he and Scout got separated in the middle of a terrifying storm? What if his dog was out there somewhere, wondering why Matt wasn't by his side? Rosita's family had to be missing this quirky little pup. "Is there any way to find her family?" Matt asked softly.

Luisa shook her head. "She doesn't have a microchip or tags, and so far no one has come looking for her. And the island is a mess—it's not like we can just walk around putting up flyers."

Matt reached out a hand and gently rubbed Rosita's soft belly. "For now she just needs to get better, right?"

"Exactly," Luisa said.

Rosita began to doze off. Luisa gently, lovingly rubbed one of Rosita's ears between her fingers until the dog was out cold and snoring.

Luisa pulled her hand away carefully so she wouldn't wake up the little pup. "We should get to work," she said. She walked over to the metal shelves and grabbed two pairs of rubber gloves, handing one pair to Matt and snapping the others on her own hands.

"You ready to clean out some cages?"

"Absolutely," Matt said. "Show me what to do."

"It's dirty work, though." She raised an eyebrow, challenging him. "You sure you're up for it?"

Matt was totally up for it. He had come to Puerto Rico for a reason—to help in whatever way he could. He hadn't predicted that "help" meant cleaning shelter dog cages, but if that's what needed doing, that's what he would do.

"I'm sure," he responded.

They scrubbed each cage one by one, swept giant clumps of fur off the floor, and played with the dogs who pounced on their legs, eager for some attention.

Hours passed in what felt like a minute. Every so often, Matt or Luisa would look up to find Rosita—now wide awake—standing by the screen door, scratching at it with one paw and staring at them. And every time they caught her, they would scoop her up and take her back to her bed.

The third time Rosita scratched at the door, Matt picked her up and held her in his arms. "You're determined, aren't you," Matt said with a shake of his head.

Luisa looked over from the cage she was wiping down with a rag. "It's like she has somewhere to be," she said. Before Matt could reply, Luisa's phone buzzed in her pocket. She looked at it and gasped. "It's so late!" she cried. "We have to hurry! We barely have enough time to get back before my parents know I'm gone."

They stashed away cleaning supplies, said quick good-byes, and rushed to leave, but not before pausing over Rosita's bed.

"I'm sorry we have to go, my sweetie." Luisa leaned down and kissed the top of Rosita's head. Rosita whimpered. She knew Luisa was leaving. "But we'll be back soon." Luisa looked at Matt. "Every time I go, I feel so awful leaving her here."

"I know. But she's going to be okay."

"I love you, Rosita," Luisa whispered.

"Bye, you funny little dog," Matt said, scratching the soft spot under Rosita's chin.

Scout nudged at Rosita with his snout.

Matt forced himself not to look back at the big brown eyes staring after them as they ran out the door.

They hustled down the road, and Scout walked ahead of them. The sun was dropping and the sky was turning a hazy gray. Neither one spoke—they were too focused on hurrying home. But about a mile down the hill, Scout froze in his tracks. He raised his head, spun around in the road, and looked past Matt and Luisa, back in the direction they had just come from.

Matt stopped too. "Scout, what is it?" He turned to look behind them, but there was nothing there.

"Scout, we're in a hurry!" Luisa said.

In reply, Scout barked once, twice. Matt and Luisa followed his gaze toward the hill and squinted into the late-afternoon light. That's when Matt heard a rustling in the trees that lined the road. He and Luisa exchanged a worried glance.

"Who's there?" Luisa asked loudly.

Scout ran toward the sound. "Scout, stay," Matt cautioned him. Scout stopped and stared into the brush, his ears back.

The rustling grew louder. Matt swallowed the lump in his throat.

Something dark and low to the ground emerged from the shadows between the leaves and branches. Luisa sucked in her breath, and Matt's heart pounded in his chest.

The blur let out a familiar bark.

It was Rosita.

She had followed them.

8

MATT HAD A BASIC KNOWLEDGE of Spanish, but he definitely did not understand a single word that came streaming out of Luisa's mouth. He could only guess— from the shocked look on her face and her hands waving in the air—that she was really, *really* surprised to see Rosita. Luisa ran over and snatched up the dog from the ground, squeezing her tightly.

"Ay, Dios mío." Luisa exhaled, pressing her cheek to Rosita's furry snout.

"She must have raced after us when we left," Matt guessed. "What a little escape artist."

Rosita sniffed at Matt's face and gave his cheek a lick.

Scout pranced beside them, looking up at Rosita like he was excited to have his friend back.

Luisa shook her head and scanned the darkening sky. "We don't have time to take her back. We have to get home fast. What are we going to do?" Her face was screwed up with worry. "I can't take her to my house. My parents will never let her stay. But if I take her back to the shelter, I'll get home so late and they'll ask where I've been, and then . . ." She trailed off and buried her face in Rosita's fur. "You rascal," she said lovingly. Rosita shot her an innocent *who, me?* look.

Matt could see that Luisa loved Rosita the way he loved Scout. They belonged together as much as he and Scout did.

Maybe this wasn't a problem. Maybe it was an opportunity.

"Let's take her with us," Matt said without hesitation. "She can stay with me and Scout."

Luisa looked unsure. "It's not that simple, Matt."

"Isn't it, though?"

Luisa considered what he was saying. "Then what?"

"I don't know," Matt admitted, "but we'll figure it out."

Luisa gave Matt a skeptical look, though she had no

choice but to agree. She nodded and they set off for the long walk home.

Lucky for them, they made it back to base with seconds to spare. As Luisa settled Rosita into Matt's apartment, the front door opened and Matt's mom walked in. With barely a glance at them, she heaved her pack off her back and onto the floor with an exhausted sigh.

"Hey, honey," she said. "Hi, Luisa."

"Hey, Mom."

"Hi, Colonel Tackett."

Scout ambled over to greet her, stuffing his snout in her palm and leaning against her legs while she gave him a good scratch.

"Hey, Scout."

He sniffed at her pants and gear and the tens of thousands of new smells she had brought in with her.

Matt's mom took off her hat and pulled her hair out of its bun. She rubbed her face with both hands. She still hadn't noticed Rosita . . . yet.

"How'd it go out there?" Matt asked, trying to figure out the best way to tell his mom about this new pup. His mom was the biggest dog person he knew—she'd built her whole career around working with K-9s—but he didn't know how she'd feel about a surprise dog in her living room.

"It was tough." She shook her head. "We're just trying to start with the basics. You know, water, fresh clothes, a hot meal. There's a lot to do." She finally looked up at Matt. "I'm just glad we're he—" Her eyes fell on the scruffy black-and-white dog in Luisa's arms.

"Mom—"

"Um. Matt—" Matt's mom blinked once. Twice.

"I can explain—"

She took a deep breath and exhaled slowly, getting her reaction under control. "Why is there a new dog in my house?" she asked more calmly.

"Mom, this is Rosita."

"Rosita?"

At the sound of her name, Rosita wagged her tail, which made her whole body wiggle.

"Doesn't that mean . . ." Matt's mom squeezed one eye shut as she tried to remember the translation. "'Little rose?'"

"Yes," Luisa piped in.

Matt's mom didn't say anything as she studied the little dog. Matt held his breath and waited.

"She's cute," his mom finally said, much to his

surprise and relief. She stepped over to get a closer look. "She's so bright-eyed. And look at those ears!" As if she knew what was at stake, Rosita batted her eyelashes at Matt's mom and wagged her tail some more.

"I think she likes you," Luisa said, a hopeful note in her voice.

"You do like me, don't you?" Matt's mom asked Rosita in a singsong voice. "But that doesn't explain why you're here, now, does it, girl?"

"Yeah, so—uh, well," Matt began. "Rosita kind of followed us home."

"Is she one of those street dogs?" his mom asked. "There are so many here."

"No," Luisa said. "At least, I don't think she's a sato. I think she had an owner but they got separated during the storm."

"That's awful." His mom lifted up Rosita's ears and looked inside, then opened her mouth and checked her gums. She peered under the bandages on Rosita's legs. "And I agree with you. She seems like a dog who's been taken care of. She's not jittery like a lot of strays. She's very alert—you see how she's listening to every word I say?"

Matt and Luisa nodded.

Matt's mom ran a hand over Rosita's head and scratched her behind the ears. "You still haven't answered my question, though." She held Rosita's face in her hands. "What are you doing here, little one?" She looked from Matt to Luisa and back again. "She's not talking, so maybe one of you should?"

"It's my fault—" Matt and Luisa both blurted out at once.

Matt's mom chuckled. "I see. Have a seat, you two. And spill it."

Matt and Luisa confessed the whole story to his mom—how Luisa volunteered at the shelter, how Rosita always tried to escape, and how she had followed them home. Rosita sat on the floor at their feet, listening to their conversation as if she knew her fate was in their hands. Scout lay next to her, his head down on his paws.

"Please, Colonel Tackett," Luisa said. "My parents will never let me keep her."

Matt's mom was quiet for a moment, taking it all in.

"Here's what we're going to do." She put an arm over Luisa's shoulders. "Rosita can stay here with us tonight— Matt will take care of her."

Matt nodded energetically.

"I'll talk to your parents first thing tomorrow

morning," his mom went on. "I'll explain everything you just told me and then we'll all put our heads together and figure out how you can keep Rosita. Okay?"

Luisa sniffled and fought tears. "I'd do anything for Rosita. She's different. She's kind of . . . magical."

Matt's mom smiled. "That's what Matt said about Scout when I wanted to put him on the first plane back to Mississippi. And guess what? Matt was right. I think you are too."

"Thanks." Luisa gathered her things and got ready to leave. But just as she opened the door, a black blur whizzed past her ankles.

"No!" Matt and Luisa shouted at the same time.

But there was no time to react. It was too late.

Rosita had escaped again.

9

SCOUT SHOT OUT THE DOOR AFTER ROSITA, and Matt and Luisa were fast on his tail. They sprinted across the base. The smaller dog ran in an uneven gait, but her injuries didn't seem to slow her down one bit. She dodged Scout and scooted around him with surprising agility.

"Get her!" Luisa called out to Matt.

"Catch her!" Matt called out to Luisa.

They ran after Rosita, Matt breaking left and Luisa breaking right. It wasn't so much that the tiny dog was fast—it was that she was smart. Every time Matt caught up to her, she sensed him closing in and turned on a dime, redirecting and slipping out of his reach. Luisa and Scout didn't have any better luck.

"How is she doing this?" Luisa shouted to Matt.

"I have no idea!" he called back.

"She shouldn't be running like this—she's not even healed."

"Doesn't seem to be stopping her."

Matt scanned the area around them but didn't see the dog. He and Luisa stopped to catch their breath, when out of the corner of his eye, Matt saw a dark flash in a narrow passageway between two buildings.

"There she is!" Matt shouted to Luisa. "Go around the building!"

Luisa ducked left. Matt went the other way. Scout got to the back of the building a second before them.

But Rosita was gone.

Scout took off at a fast trot, his nose skimming the ground. He turned a corner and was quickly out of sight.

They raced after him. Just as they reached the corner where he had turned, a man stepped out in front of them, blocking their path.

With one hand, the man gripped Scout by the collar.

In the other hand, the man held a very guilty-looking

Rosita. She had her head down and peered up at Matt and Luisa like she knew she'd been busted.

Luisa sucked in her breath and held it. Matt was about to thank the man when he realized who it was.

It was Luisa's dad.

And he did not look happy.

Matt and Luisa reflexively snapped to attention, standing shoulder to shoulder, their backs straight and their arms at their sides.

"Dad!" Luisa squeaked.

"Colonel Dávila!" Matt gulped.

"You looking for this?" Ric said, one eyebrow up and his lips pursed. He held Rosita out in front of him as if he were holding a pile of dirty laundry.

"Um, yes," Luisa said.

"Yessir," Matt said.

"What is this dog doing here?" Ric asked. Matt couldn't help but notice that Ric barely ever blinked.

Matt swallowed hard.

"Dad, it's my fault . . ." Luisa began.

But before she could finish, Matt found his voice. "That's my dog. I mean—for now. I'm just taking care of her. Her name is Rosita. My mom was going to talk to you about her . . ."

Ric fixed a hard stare on Matt. Matt's insides churned and he thought he felt his blood actually freeze in his veins.

He was starting to see what Luisa meant about her dad being slightly stern.

"I see," Ric finally said. He released Scout and put his hands under Rosita's armpits. He held her up and inspected her with a critical look in his eye. He was holding her face close to his when Rosita's tongue darted out of her mouth and licked Ric's nose with a quick slurp.

Matt fought to keep a straight face. At his side, he felt Luisa shaking with barely contained laughter. Ric handed the dog to Matt and wiped his nose on the sleeve of his camo jacket.

Ric looked from Matt to Luisa and back again, locking his eyes on Matt's.

"This dog's stay on my base is entirely conditional upon her behavior. If she's not trained, she goes. We can't have dogs running around here. It's not safe."

"Yes, sir," Matt said. "I'm sorry, sir."

"Keep her on a leash, son." Without waiting for a reply, Ric turned stiffly on his heel and walked away.

The minute he was gone, Luisa groaned. "That was close."

"Too close," Matt said. "But on the upside, at least we don't have to hide her from your dad?"

"True, but you heard him. If we're going to get my parents to love Rosita, she's going to have to be *really* well trained."

"Yeah. I got that impression."

"If she has an owner, she'll probably have some training, right?" Luisa asked.

"Hopefully," Matt replied. "But we're going to have to see what she knows—"

"And teach her what she doesn't," Luisa finished. "We can train her on the field behind the mess hall. Tomorrow morning. We start at oh seven hundred hours."

"Copy that, Colonel."

10

THE SUN WAS BARELY UP, but the base was already empty and quiet as Matt and Luisa began Operation Train Rosita. Nearly all the troops were out on assignment. They passed a lone soldier, who smiled at the sight of the tiny, odd-looking dog on the end of Scout's very long leash. Rosita wore one of Scout's old collars, which was huge around her little neck.

"She doesn't seem to be hurting after all that running last night," Matt said. "That's good."

"Dr. Correa said she needs to get some exercise. It'll help her get stronger, but that was probably a little *too* much. She's supposed to take it kind of easy."

Rosita didn't seem to be concerned about the doctor's orders. She tugged on the leash, walking as far ahead of them as it would allow her to. Scout stuck close to her side, slowing down when she did and waiting patiently when she stopped to sit down and rest, panting, every now and then.

"He's so sweet to her," Luisa said.

"He's a little overprotective." Matt laughed.

"He's looking out for her, that's all."

They watched the dogs walk—Rosita bobbing up and down on her short legs in an uneven but determined gait, Scout with his long, lean body trotting along in relaxed, perfect, athletic rhythm. They reached the field and Matt, Scout, and Luisa stopped. Rosita kept ambling ahead until the leash was pulled tight and she couldn't go any farther. She plopped down and rolled herself around on the grass, tangling herself up in her leash.

"Rosita, come!" Matt called out, making his voice sound extra positive and encouraging.

Rosita looked over her shoulder at him, as if she were trying to be sure she'd heard him correctly.

"Rosita," Matt repeated. "Come!"

Rosita stood up and turned to face him.

She sat down.

Matt and Luisa burst out laughing.

"It's a start," Matt said.

"You trained Scout, right?"

"Sort of," Matt said. "He was trained when he moved in with us, but he couldn't really focus. He was all over the place—a little nervous and a lot stubborn. So I worked with him to get him to listen to me. But I also had to learn how to command him the right way."

"What do you mean? Isn't a command a command?"

"Nope. It's not just what you say but how you say it." Matt put a hand on his belly. "You have to speak from here. And you have to really mean it. Not in an angry way—in a convincing way."

"Can you do it with Rosita?"

"I can try." Matt studied the small, scruffy dog with the ears pointing off in different directions, her dark fur sticking out all over. Her steady gaze was on him. Matt walked back to Luisa, while Rosita stayed where she was. "Do you have those treats?"

Luisa dropped one small nugget into his palm.

"There's one thing," she said.

"What's that?"

"I don't think Rosita speaks English."

"Duh." Matt felt silly for not realizing that sooner. "But . . . I don't know commands in Spanish."

"It's easy. *Ven* means 'come.' *Siéntate* means 'sit.'"

Matt took a deep breath and exhaled. "Rosita," he said, his voice kind but firm. Her ears flicked in his direction, and she tipped her head slightly to the side. She was paying a different kind of attention now. "Rosita, *ven.*"

She blinked at him once. Twice. Then she hopped to her little feet and pranced toward him, her tongue hanging out of her mouth and her tail sticking straight up in the air.

"Good girl!" Matt said. He held the treat out between his fingers. Rosita sniffed at it, weighing her options, seemingly gauging whether Matt was serious about this offer or not. Then she gently, delicately took it between her teeth and tugged it from his hand.

"She did it!" Luisa said. "*¡Muy bien, Rosita!*" She crouched down and gave Rosita a good scratch on her ribs. Luisa looked the happiest that Matt had ever seen her. Rosita sniffed for treats in Luisa's pocket. Luisa pulled out a few and placed them on her palm for Rosita to eat.

Rosita gently nosed Luisa's hand, picking up each and

every treat, then licking Luisa's palm over and over, like she was giving Luisa a bath. Luisa giggled. "Oh, Rosita, thank you! Ready to get back to work?" Rosita wagged her tail.

They ran through the command a few times, and Rosita nailed it over and over.

"Let's try it without the leash," Matt suggested.

"Are you sure that's a good idea?" Luisa looked nervous as Matt unhooked the leash from Rosita's collar.

"I think she knows better now, don't you, Rosita?" The dog cocked her head. "See? She agrees."

"If you say so," Luisa said.

"Do you want to try a command?"

"Sure." Luisa looked down at Rosita and took out a treat. Rosita spotted the tiny bit of food. Her eyebrows shot up and she took a couple of excited steps backward, yipping at Luisa in a croaky voice.

"From here." Matt gestured at his gut. Luisa nodded.

"Rosita," she said, her voice strong, *"siéntate."*

But Rosita didn't have time to respond.

Matt felt the ground vibrating before he heard the sound. It was a familiar sensation—he'd spent his entire life on a military base and could practically tell what make and model truck was turning the corner and rumbling in their direction.

Scout's ears twitched at the sound. He was otherwise unfazed.

But not Rosita. She wasn't used to giant double-axle trucks carrying heavy equipment lumbering toward her. Her whole body went taut, and her eyes grew huge with fear. The fur on her tail stuck out and she spun around to see the truck, barking and growling like she was facing off against a wild animal.

Matt knew what she was about to do.

"Rosita!" he called out in a warning tone, taking a step toward the dog.

"No . . . don't do it, Rosita!" Luisa pleaded.

Scout barked and positioned himself between Rosita and the truck, which was still a good distance away.

But Rosita was spooked. With a round of frantic barks, she bolted in the opposite direction of the truck, past Matt and Luisa, toward the base's main gate. She stopped only long enough to frantically paw at her collar, slipping her neck out of it, then dashed off again.

"Rosita!" Luisa cried, her voice high-pitched and strained. "No! Get back here! *¡Ven! ¡Ven, Rosita!*" She took off running after the dog, but like the night before, being chased just made Rosita run faster. Luisa slowed to a walk and watched helplessly as Rosita disappeared behind a building. She picked up Rosita's collar and buried her head in her hands. Scout shot past her like a bullet—racing after Rosita.

Everything had just gone from bad to worse.

11

"SCOUT—STOP!" Matt shouted. "Come back!" Scout skidded to a halt and reluctantly, with a long look toward the spot where Rosita had disappeared, turned and trotted back toward them. Just like Scout, Matt's every instinct was to run after Rosita as fast as he could, but he knew that wasn't a good idea. They didn't know which direction she had gone or whether she had already made it out the front gate and onto the main road. Scout would be able to keep up with her, but Matt and Luisa would never be able to keep up with *him*. And Matt didn't want his dog out there on his own.

Slowly, the reality of the situation dawned on Matt.

This was bad. Really, really bad.

This wasn't just about whether or not Rosita could live with Luisa and her family. This was about whether the dog got injured again or lost. If that happened . . .

"Luisa, I'm so sorry," Matt said, sounding as miserable as he felt.

"It's not your fault."

"Of course it's my fault. I'm the one who took the leash off her. I'm the one who told you it would be okay to bring her here in the first place—"

"And I'm the one who didn't take her back to the shelter because I was afraid of my parents," Luisa said, cutting him off. "Not you."

Matt clamped his mouth shut. He hadn't thought about that, or about how Luisa might be feeling. "You couldn't have known that she was going to bolt."

"Exactly. And neither could you. Right?"

He exhaled. "Right."

Scout looked from Matt to Luisa and back again as they talked. Matt dropped his hand to Scout's head and ran his fingers through his dog's silky fur. It helped him think clearly.

Don't focus on the mistakes, was what his dad would say. *Focus on the mission.* But what was the mission?

"I know what we need to do," Luisa said. It was like

she was reading his thoughts. "There's a reason this keeps happening."

"A reason?"

"Yes. There's a reason Rosita keeps running off. I think this dog wants to go home—back to her owner. And there's nothing we can do to stop her."

Matt knew Luisa was right, but somehow he didn't feel any better.

"Okay," he conceded. "But still, if she gets off base, if she's on the street . . ."

Matt didn't have to finish the sentence. Luisa understood better than he did what was at stake for Rosita.

"We have to go after her," Luisa said with a grim nod. "And make sure she gets to where she wants to go."

Matt saw a flicker of sadness cross Luisa's face. He knew how hard it was for her to even consider giving up the dog she loved so much. And though they'd only met a short time ago, he already knew Luisa well enough to know that she would never let that stop her from doing what was right.

She collected herself. "But the island is a wreck," she said, "and we have no idea which direction Rosita's going, or if she even knows where she's going. So. Where do we start?"

Suddenly, Matt's misery lifted. That was where they had the advantage. Rosita could outsmart them, but she could never outsmart Scout's nose.

They wouldn't chase her—they would track her.

"We start with this." Matt took Rosita's collar from Luisa's hand. It was the perfect scent item. "And that guy." He pointed at Scout, who sat with his head high, his ears on point, his eyes gleaming.

Scout barked impatiently. He was already on the case—and ready to find his friend.

Matt and Luisa ran back home for supplies. Matt filled his backpack with water bottles, snacks, kibble, and a flashlight. He scanned the fridge, which was empty except for a squeeze bottle of mustard, a loaf of bread, and a family pack of sliced ham. He snatched up the ham and tossed it into the pack.

He grabbed Scout's K-9 vest from its spot by the front door and ran outside to meet Luisa.

"Ready?" he asked.

"Ready."

Matt slipped the reflective vest over Scout's head and pulled it taut around his puffed-out chest, buckling it snugly underneath. He looked down at his brave, smart dog, who had saved so many lives—Matt's sister and father, his best friends, and even Matt himself. He looked up at his new friend Luisa, whose face was filled with determination to find the dog she had saved once before.

Matt couldn't have imagined two better partners for this mission.

He held Rosita's collar under Scout's nose. Scout sniffed it once, twice, again. When he was done, he sat down and locked eyes with Matt, waiting for his next command.

Matt beamed at Scout.

"Scout, search! Find Rosita."

12

SCOUT HAD LOCKED ON TO ROSITA'S SCENT, and he was in a hurry.

He beelined off the base and made a right, in the opposite direction from the shelter. Luisa and Matt had to double-time it to keep up. When Scout looked back every few minutes to make sure they were following him, Matt was pretty sure he saw an impatient look in the dog's eyes.

Matt knew Scout was just as worried about Rosita as he and Luisa were. Dogs were usually pretty quick to make friends with each other, but Scout and Rosita's relationship felt different. They had bonded so quickly— they were like a big brother and little sister.

The road began to narrow, and they passed through a small residential area with more houses than stores. Soon they were on an isolated stretch of road, with no buildings at all, just thick trees. Morning birds chirped in the trees.

Scout's nose grazed the ground as he ran. Every so often, he raised his head and sniffed at the air, then dropped it back down again to keep tabs on Rosita's scent. He showed no signs of slowing down.

"How does it work?" Luisa asked. "When he smells the collar?"

"The scent item?"

"Yeah. The scent item. Like, how does he know to find that exact smell? Can't dogs smell a million things at the same time?"

Matt laughed. "Not quite a million, but yeah, a lot. People can smell about a hundred things at once, but dogs can smell like ten thousand or so."

"'Or so'?" Luisa's jaw hung open. "But what does Scout do with them all?"

"He . . . sorts them, I guess you could say."

"And he can find the *one* scent you want him to find?"

"Yeah." Matt knew how impossible that sounded. "It's sort of gross, but we're kind of like a walking snowstorm—except the 'snow' is made of microscopic flakes of our skin. They're called rafts, and they're on all our clothes and float off our bodies and fall on the ground. And every one of us has a specific smell. So he smells Rosita's scent on her collar and then he can separate that from the other nine thousand nine hundred ninety-nine, and he picks it up and follows it."

"And he just ignores all the other scents?"

"He's trained to stay focused on that single one. So basically, if you need to find someone fast, Scout is better than a dozen people."

"Have you had him since he was a puppy?"

"No. He was a stray when he was a puppy. Well, first he was in a dog-fighting ring, actually."

Luisa sucked in her breath. "That's awful."

"But then he was rescued by the most famous K-9 search-and-rescue dog in Mississippi and trained to be a police dog."

"So what was that thing your mom said about wanting to send him back?"

Matt recalled the day Scout had arrived, scared and defiant, at the Reno airport in a crate. "He was picked to be on my mom's National Guard K-9 team, but she didn't think he could do the job and she didn't want to keep him."

"I can't imagine Scout not being able to do any job," Luisa said. "Look at him—he's amazing. So why didn't she send him back?"

"I convinced her not to. There was something different about him. Something she wasn't seeing, but I saw it." Matt smiled. "And then Scout saved my life. Like, more times than I can count. Plus, he saved my friends and my dad and my sister. He's just . . ." Matt searched for the right words. "He's not like anyone I've ever met. He's so much better and braver and more loyal than anyone could ever be."

Luisa sighed and gestured toward the road ahead— the road they were following to find the dog she loved. "I think I might have some idea what you mean."

They walked on in silence. Matt breathed in the dampness and the smell of dirt and trees that filled the air and seemed to be coming out of the ground they walked on.

"Dogs can travel crazy far to get back home," Matt said after a little while.

"Yeah, I know," Luisa said. "But if that's what Rosita is doing, then that's a good thing."

"How so?"

"Because if she's willing to travel that far, it means

there's someone she really loves," Luisa said simply. "And there's someone who really loves and misses her."

She was right. That didn't stop Matt from feeling a sharp pang at the thought of not seeing Rosita anymore, but he took comfort in the idea of her reuniting with her people.

She deserved that.

13

THE PATH ANGLED SLIGHTLY DOWNHILL, and a small cluster of houses appeared in the distance. As they drew nearer, Matt's feet began to slip. The pavement was muddy. Soon, his feet weren't slipping anymore—they were submerged in dark, dirty water up to his shins—and the road wasn't a road at all. It was a river, with houses rising out of it on either side. Scout's nose skimmed the surface as he tried to keep hold of Rosita's scent on the water.

The houses were in terrible shape, way worse than the ones in town. Their sides were ripped off, and their roofs were missing. Windows were broken. Matt peered in and saw refrigerators floating on their sides in living rooms where three feet of water lapped at the walls.

Doors dangled by a single hinge. Inside a small grocery store, Matt saw that the shelves lay tilted and angled on top of one another like fallen dominoes. The ceiling had collapsed onto the register.

The buildings were dark, and not just with a lack of electricity. They were empty—uninhabitable.

A chill went through Matt. "This is bad," he said.

"This is the way it is everywhere." Luisa's face was drawn. "It's not so bad in town. There's more people to help with repairs and stuff. But it's quiet out here."

"Why isn't anyone helping? Why aren't my mom and your dad and their teams here?"

"They can't be everywhere at once, I guess."

"Where did all the people go?"

Luisa shook her head. "To their families'. Their friends'. Wherever they can."

They passed by the deserted houses and trudged along. The road rose up and the water receded, but their feet were soaking wet. Matt's sneakers squished with every step. Scout shook out his fur, sending a spray of water in every direction, and, with a quick look back over his shoulder at Matt, continued on.

Matt thought back to the news stories he'd heard about the storm while he was home in Nevada. The coverage had been constant at first—there was overhead footage of flooded neighborhoods and front-page photos of desperate moms carrying their babies through waist-high water. He'd even seen one image that had haunted him for days—an apartment building with the entire front wall ripped off. But the rest of the building was fine, and people sat in their apartments, on their furniture, looking out where the wall used to be.

But then it had stopped. Or maybe it didn't so much stop as fade . . . off the front page, out of the broadcast, and from people's minds. From Matt's mind. Within a week or two of the storm, the news reports got shorter. They became updates. Then they disappeared completely.

Soon the news was about regular things—sports, politics, local happenings—that Matt could afford to tune out. He was free to think about other things—anything. But the hundreds of thousands of people there, in Puerto Rico, couldn't put the storm out of their minds. They were too busy living it.

Matt felt terrible for not knowing just how awful it really was.

"They're just—they're not talking about it back home," he said. "They're not showing people how bad it is."

Luisa looked pained. "We're used to that."

"That doesn't make it okay."

"No, it doesn't."

"Can I ask you, Luisa—"

"What?"

"It's okay if you don't want to talk about it."

She stopped and turned to face him. "You want to know what it was like? During the hurricane?"

Matt felt bad for asking. Why would she want to relive what was probably the worst night of her life?

"I'm glad you asked, actually," Luisa said softly. "It feels better when I talk about it, you know?"

Matt nodded. They started walking again as Luisa spoke.

"It was awful," she began. "It came in the middle of the night, around one or two A.M. The wind—I've never heard anything like it. At first it sounded like screeching or shrieking, but it got louder and louder until it was more like a train going right over us. And the rain was like bullets on the windows—hitting over and over and over, *ping ping ping*." She paused and took a breath. "It went on for hours. It felt like it would never end—the noise just wouldn't stop. It made my ears and head hurt. Our whole house was shaking so hard I thought it was going to just break apart. My mom, dad, Emanuel, and I—the whole time we held on to each other in the dining room. All we could do was pray that the walls didn't get ripped off and we didn't get sucked out of the house by the wind." She choked up and had to wait a second before continuing. "You could hear the trees snapping and slamming into things outside. I kept waiting for one to hit our house."

"No one should have to go through that," Matt said.

"But we got really lucky," Luisa said. "We had some broken windows, but that's all. Not a lot of water got in—I have no idea how. It was so much worse for so many people."

Matt looked up at the clear blue sky above them. It was hard for him to imagine such a violent storm hitting this beautiful place.

"Walking out of our house the next day," Luisa went on, trying to keep her voice steady. "When it was finally over . . . it was like we had landed on another planet." She closed her eyes for a second, like she was replaying it in her mind.

"But it's not like it ended when the storm ended," Matt offered.

"Yeah." She sounded sad. "I couldn't sleep for the first

few nights after. I'd fall asleep and then, like, jolt awake a few minutes later, thinking that I was in the middle of the storm again. It got better after a while but . . . I don't know. The hurricane made me . . . different."

"I'm sorry, Luisa." Matt felt like that was all he could say. There were no words that would soften her memories. He was just glad that Luisa had shared everything with him, like he was a true friend she could trust. Because after the crazy twenty-four hours they'd had with Rosita, he thought of her as his friend, too.

"Thanks," she said simply. "I mean it."

"No, thank you," Matt said. "And I mean it."

14

THEY WALKED ON. Midday was turning into afternoon, and the day was hot. Matt's wet feet were developing blisters from rubbing in his shoes, and he felt like he was walking through a heavy steam shower. But they kept going.

As the trees on either side of the road got taller, they passed a lone house set back from the road. It was badly damaged and as desolate and lifeless as all the others they'd passed. Matt saw the remains of a small shed behind the home. It had nearly caved in on itself and was nothing more than a leaning pile of plywood and hinges and corrugated metal—a house of cards that was barely standing.

As they neared the house, Scout came to a halt.

"Wait." Matt held out a hand to stop Luisa.

They peered into the distance and strained their ears for any sign of what Scout had sensed. At first there was nothing, but then Matt and Luisa heard it at the same time—a quiet, high-pitched cry, so faint they could have missed it.

"What was that?" Luisa's eyes grew wide.

Matt recognized the sound at the exact moment Scout shot off toward the shed.

"I think it's Rosita," Matt said. "Scout found her!"

Scout ran in a frantic circle around the shed, barking and yawping. Matt heard the whimpering more clearly now. It was definitely Rosita—and it was definitely coming from inside the wreckage of the shed. Scout's ears went forward on his head, and he was electrified by a desperate drive to get to his friend.

Through a gap in the crisscrossed wood, Matt caught a glimpse of Rosita's black-and-white fur, her pointed ears, and her frightened eyes.

"Rosita!" Luisa gasped, her voice breaking. "It's okay, sweetheart—we're here!"

The structure was fragile—one brush against it could have sent the whole mess toppling down onto the little dog. But before Matt could stop him, Scout darted right toward the center of the pile, his head disappearing into a crevice. He wedged his front half through a narrow opening barely as wide as his shoulders.

With one loud, creaking groan, the whole thing shuddered like it could barely hold itself up any longer.

"No!" Luisa screamed, frightened for not just one, but two dogs.

"*Scout,*" Matt said firmly, trying not to sound as panicked as he felt. "Get out of there!"

But Scout had found Rosita, and he wasn't about to leave her now. He was not going to let her get hurt.

"He's not going to listen," Matt said.

"So we have to help him."

They dropped to their knees on either side of Scout, trying to figure out their next move. Matt squinted through the cracks and saw Rosita shaking with fear. She had stopped whimpering, and she had locked her big brown eyes on Scout.

The shed shook and swayed above them, and Matt and Luisa reflexively ducked and covered their heads.

"Scout," Matt sounded a warning to his dog. "Whatever you're doing in there, you need to do it fast. Come on, buddy!"

A hunk of tin roofing material slid off the top of the pile and clattered to the ground nearby, sending up a splatter of mud.

"You should get out of here," Matt said to Luisa.

"No way," she replied, wiping wet dirt from her face. "I'm not leaving her in there."

Matt knew from the steely look in her eye that there was no point trying to talk her out of it. And it was the same reason he wasn't going to leave either—neither one of them was going to abandon their dog.

Matt peered into the center of the pile again and saw that Scout had his mouth closed around the back of Rosita's neck. He was going to carry her out by the scruff.

"He's got her!" Matt said.

Luisa looked worried. "When they come out, this whole thing is coming down," she said. "We need to try to stabilize it."

They hopped to their feet just as Scout began backing out of the opening. His shoulders reappeared, then his neck.

The shed began to shake. It tipped toward Matt and Luisa, leaning farther and farther, until it threatened to come crashing down. Matt's hands flew up to catch it.

The rough surface smacked into his palms and bent back his wrists. He leaned into the weight, planting his feet wide apart for leverage. Out of the corner of his eye he saw Luisa doing the same. She grimaced and her face turned red with exertion.

"Scout—*hurry!*" Matt shouted through gritted teeth.

With a grunt, Scout leaped backward, clearing the structure and landing a couple of feet away, Rosita dangling limply in his jaw.

The dogs were safe.

Matt and Luisa locked eyes. As if on cue, they began to count down.

"Three—"

Matt took a sharp breath in through his nose.

"Two—"

He exhaled through his mouth, trying to calm the surge of adrenaline pumping through his arms and legs.

"One!"

Matt and Luisa hurled themselves backward as the teetering mountain of wood crashed to the ground with a thunderous noise. Matt landed hard on his back, knocking the wind out of him. He felt the sting of a thousand tiny slivers of wood pelting him on the arms and face. When it was over, he sat up and opened his eyes. His mouth was filled with mud, and blood pounded in his ears.

Scout and Rosita were a few feet away. Rosita had tucked herself into the nook under Scout's chest, and Scout was licking the top of her head.

Matt turned his head to the right, where Luisa was on her back too, with her hands covering her face.

Everyone was safe.

He closed his eyes, waiting for his heart rate to return to normal. After a moment, Matt felt heavy pressure on his chest and something warm and scratchy on his face. Scout had planted both front paws on Matt's rib cage and was licking his cheeks.

"I'm okay, buddy." Matt sat up and wrapped his arms around his dog in a grateful hug. "Thanks for checking on me, though." He pulled Scout in and lay his head across the dog's neck, breathing in the familiar scent of Scout's soft fur.

"Matt."

"Yeah?" Matt replied without raising his head.

"Matt."

Matt looked up. Luisa had gone sheet white, and her bottom lip trembled.

She pointed at the spot where Scout and Rosita had just been sitting together. There was nothing there.

Rosita was gone.

Again.

Neither of them spoke. What was there to say? They were hot and exhausted and frustrated, and there was no sign of the dog who had just given them the slip for the third time.

Matt wanted to be mad at Scout for letting Rosita get away, but he knew it wasn't his dog's fault. Scout had only turned his back on her so he could make sure Matt was okay.

Rosita was on a mission, and all they could do was follow her as best as they could.

15

IN THE DISTANCE, something lay across the road. They got closer, and Matt saw that two fallen trees blocked their path entirely. The giant trees were tangled up in each other, one lying diagonally across the other. Even on their sides, the trees were way taller than Matt.

"They must have been growing right next to each other," Luisa said. "One fell and brought the other down with it."

Scout scrambled up onto the thick trunks, assessing the situation. The top tree wobbled under his weight. It didn't look safe.

"Scout, off." Reluctantly, Scout got down and walked

to Matt's side. Matt and Luisa inspected the pile. He kicked at the lower trunk with his wet foot. The whole thing tottered, and the top tree threatened to roll right off. Matt and Luisa jumped back.

They'd had enough things fall on them today already.

"We can't go over them, that's for sure," Matt said. "They're not stable."

"Does Scout think Rosita went over them?" Luisa asked. "Or maybe under." She checked under the trees for a gap, but there wasn't even enough room for a mouse to wiggle through.

Scout had moved to the side of the road. He looked over at Matt, pawed at the ground, and whimpered. He wanted them to follow him.

"He's still tracking her scent." Matt looked at where his dog wanted to go and realized that they were on the edge of the forest. Scout wanted to leave the road and head into the woods.

Matt scanned the horizon. The forest went on as far as he could see. But something wasn't right. Matt knew from years of hiking and camping with his dad that a forest should be cool and damp, because leaves on the trees blocked the sunlight.

But this time, there were no treetops. There was no dappled light. Matt breathed in the smell of wet dirt and tree sap, but the light was too bright and the air was too hot. He squinted, running his eyes up and up and up the tree trunks until he reached the top—and saw that there was nothing there.

The trees were stripped completely bare.

It was as if someone had plucked every single leaf off every single branch. Matt blinked a few times, as if maybe he wasn't seeing clearly. But it was real, and it was mind-blowing. The 155-mile-an-hour winds from the hurricane had ripped the leaves off but left the trees upright.

And that was just on the trees that were still standing.

Huge swaths of fallen trees leaned on each other and lay sideways at sharp angles.

Scout was sniffing busily at the air, trying to reorient himself in this world of new odors.

"Where are we?" Matt asked.

"El Yunque forest," Luisa said quietly.

"It's big, right?" he asked.

"Yeah. Like, really, really big."

Matt closed his eyes and pictured the map he'd

studied before coming to Puerto Rico. El Yunque was a huge forest on the eastern end of the island—but it wasn't just any forest. It was a rain forest, which meant it should have a thick canopy of trees, a vibrant array of greenery and wildlife, and a rich palette of colors. But it was wiped out, washed out, absent of color—and strangely, uncomfortably quiet.

There was no chirping or cawing. There was no rustling in the underbrush. There was no snuffling and grunting of an animal on a quest for food. When the storm had blown through and clobbered the forest, it had destroyed the habitats of the animals and birds that lived there. Matt felt like he was sneaking around someone's house when they weren't home.

"The animals." Luisa gasped. "Where are they?"

"I think they're . . ." Matt strained his ears to be sure he wasn't imagining things. But he wasn't. "I think they're gone."

Scout's sharp bark snapped Matt out of his shock. The dog had run into the forest and stopped, and now he was staring at Matt and Luisa impatiently. His tail was up and curled over his back, his ears were at the sides of his head, and every muscle in his body was flexed. He was ready—he just needed the humans to keep up.

"Let's go," Matt said. "He's got Rosita's scent again."

But Luisa didn't move. She ran her eyes across the devastation and shook her head. "I don't know."

"What do you mean? It's fine. Scout knows what he's doing."

"But the forest?" She pressed her lips together. "We don't know how bad it is in there. What if it's not safe? What if we can't find her? What if we can't find our way back?"

Matt weighed Luisa's words carefully. He peered between the trees, took in the thickets of debris and tangled branches. He tried to envision how much worse it could be deeper inside the empty, broken forest.

For a second, Matt's imagination went rogue and he had the strange sensation that they were the last three living creatures in the forest—and on Earth. He zoomed out of El Yunque, up into the sky, and looked down on them from miles above the still, silent planet—totally empty of a single heartbeat, except for theirs.

Scout whined and barked at him again. Matt shook his head and chased the images away.

Scout took off a few yards into the woods, then stopped and looked back.

That was all Matt needed to see. He turned to Luisa.

"Scout is never wrong. It'll be okay. I bet Rosita's owner lives near the forest and this is just a shortcut to get to their house."

"Okay." She still looked nervous. *"Vámonos."*

"Go, Scout," Matt called out. Scout bolted ahead through the trees, and they wended their way through the forest behind him. Matt had been confident that Scout wouldn't lead them astray, but after they had trekked a couple of miles, he had to admit that these silent woods were creepy.

They carried on, and soon Matt noticed that they were in slight shade. He looked up and saw that the canopy wasn't totally destroyed now that they were farther in. Though there were still downed trees and broken limbs everywhere, for the most part the trees here had held each other up—and kept more of their foliage intact.

"Did you hear that?!" Luisa stopped in her tracks and raised a finger.

"I did!"

There it was again. A single bird chirped high above them. Another bird responded from a few yards away, its lilting song floating over their heads. Soon it was a chorus of birds, calling and responding, chattering back and forth.

It was a beautiful sound. It had seemed so strange, and now it felt like a real forest again. Matt exhaled and felt the anxious tension leave his body.

Matt and Luisa—and even Scout—had a new spring in their step, as if the signs of life around them had given them a much-needed shot of energy. His tongue dangling out of his mouth, Scout ran ahead of them. Matt and Luisa hustled along behind him.

Luisa pointed into the distance. "Look!"

Matt followed her gaze and saw a stunning sight: a splashing, crashing, spilling, glinting waterfall, cascading down into a pool of clear water.

"Whoa!"

"Pretty, right?"

"It's amazing. Are there just waterfalls in the middle of the forest like that?"

"Yep." She held her arms out, gesturing at the once lush, now broken landscape that surrounded them. "El Yunque is—was—really special. My dad and I used to come here on the weekends and wander around."

"Used to?"

"He's so busy now that he runs the base."

Matt nodded in recognition. "I hear you."

She shot him a sideways glance. "Your mom must be pretty busy too. And your dad—how often is he gone?"

"A lot." Matt was used to his dad being deployed, but that didn't mean he liked it. He changed the subject. "What did you guys used to do here?"

"We'd hike. Find waterfalls like this one and swim." She chuckled at a memory. "We got to see a Puerto Rican parrot once—that was amazing. They're really rare and no one ever sees them, but it just flew right by us."

"Cool."

"Yeah. And we'd always try to stay as late as possible so we could hear the *coquíes* come out at night."

"The cookies?" Matt wasn't sure he'd heard her correctly.

"*Coquíes*. Like ko-keeze." She rolled her eyes at him. "We seriously need to work on your Spanish."

"Yeah, yeah, I know. But what are *coquíes*?" He over-pronounced the word just to annoy her.

She ignored him. "Puerto Rico's famous frogs. They're literally everywhere. Have you really not noticed them yet? They're, like, the loudest animal ever."

"What do they sound like?"

Luisa sucked in a breath of air and paused, then burst out laughing before she could make a sound.

"Come on!"

"Okay. Hang on." She took a deep breath and held it for a second. *"Kohhhh-KEE!"* Her voice shot up high on the last syllable.

Matt cracked up laughing. Scout spun around and came racing back toward them, ready to pounce on whatever strange creature was making noises at Matt.

"It's okay, Scout," Matt said between chuckles. "It's just Luisa imitating a frog."

"Kohhhh-KEE! Kohhhh-KEE!" she peeped at Scout. He cocked his head, one ear rotating forward and the other moving backward. *"Kohhhh-KEE!"*

"I've heard those!" Matt caught his breath. "They're crazy loud at night. I just didn't know they were frogs."

"They're not just frogs," she said with a wicked gleam in her eye. "They're *flying* frogs."

"What? No. Frogs don't fly." At least, Matt hoped they didn't.

"They're tree frogs. They have sticky feet and they jump from tree to tree, way up there." She pointed straight up. They tipped their heads back to look.

Matt realized with a start that it was late afternoon already. The sun had moved across the sky.

"And if we don't hurry," Luisa said, "you're going to start seeing them go by really soon."

"In that case . . . let's go, Scout," Matt said. "Time to hustle. Find Rosita!"

16

SCOUT RAN AHEAD. Matt and Luisa moved along steadily without speaking, focused on getting as far as they could before the sun went down. They lifted their feet high with each step, trying not to trip on the tangled forest floor.

The day had been hot, and the late afternoon felt even hotter and stickier, like the warm air had gathered and settled around them. Matt was sweaty and grimy—and itchy. *Slap!* He swatted a mosquito on his arm and another on his neck. They were always worse at twilight.

"Ugh!" Luisa smacked one on her ankle.

Matt willed himself forward, but the forest seemed endless. Were they even making progress? How was it possible that they hadn't found Rosita yet? Where was she? A tiny drumbeat of fear started to rise in his chest as something scrabbled by in the brush near his feet. He jumped, then heard a strange cry directly above him— an angry screech that rattled his bones. He flinched and took a step back, bumping right into Luisa.

"What the heck was that?"

"A monkey."

"Great."

A monkey. A really hostile-sounding monkey. That was *not* what Matt had expected to encounter that day.

He had to admit it: This was way harder than he'd thought it would be. Matt closed his eyes for a second, letting the sounds of the forest wash over him. The squawking and cooing, the rustling, and even the screeching blended together and became a symphony that grew louder and louder until it was booming, threatening to overwhelm him.

And one thought ran through it all.

This was a terrible idea.

Matt and Luisa tramped steadily forward, keeping one eye on the twisted underbrush and the other on Scout's back as he ran ahead of them. Scout kept up a quick pace, easily hopping over piles of debris that Matt and Luisa had to skirt around or gingerly step up onto and scramble down without bringing the whole thing crashing down.

Matt bit his bottom lip so he wouldn't blurt out the dark thoughts running through his mind. Every now and then, Luisa's arm flew out and she gripped Matt by the sleeve of his T-shirt, holding him back. Matt would freeze, and she would point to a strange plant tangled up on a fallen tree branch or creeping along the forest floor. She didn't have to explain herself. Matt understood that these were poisonous plants that he needed to avoid at all costs. He was grateful that she was there to stop him in time, or he'd have been in serious trouble.

The air grew thicker and damper, until Matt felt like someone had draped a warm, wet blanket over his skin. It was hard to breathe. The sky was pressing down on them, and suddenly the air became electric, full—about to burst.

Luisa looked up. Flat gray clouds had formed overhead. *"Ay, Dios mío,"* she muttered under her breath.

"What?" Matt followed her gaze.

"Rain."

"Wait, wha—" Matt didn't have time to finish. Before he could blink, the sky opened, and a wall of water came down so hard that Matt's skin stung. The rain was so heavy Matt had to shield his face with his hand, and he was soaked through to the bone within seconds. Peering out, he spotted Scout cowering by a tree. "Scout, over here!" Matt shouted over the loud rain. "Come, buddy!" Seeming relieved to hear Matt's voice, Scout stayed in a low crouch and made his way over to Matt's side.

Matt dropped to his knees on the wet ground and wrapped an arm around Scout's chest, pulling him in close. The dog was shaking. Matt had never experienced a sudden deluge like this, and he was slightly freaked out. He could only imagine what Scout was thinking.

"There!" Luisa called out, pointing off to their right. There was a rocky rise in the land. Two trees had fallen and their tops had landed on the hill, forming a small shelter underneath. Luisa ran for it, dragging Matt by the arm. Their feet slipped on the muddy ground and piles of wet leaves. Matt hit an especially slick patch and felt his feet start to come out from underneath him. He windmilled his arms wildly before managing to right himself, just as Luisa fell to her knees and hopped back up.

Scout reached cover first, and the three of them squirmed their way into the shallow alcove. It was tight, but the tree trunks a few feet above their heads protected them from the full force of the rain. Scout shook himself out as best he could, whipping Luisa in the chin with his tail.

"Ouch!" She held out a hand to protect herself. With a yowl, Scout sat down between them and ducked his head, watching the rain come down just inches from their faces.

"This is insane." Matt tried to wipe his face on his wet sleeve, but he only succeeded in spreading the water around.

"It's a rain forest." Luisa wiped her eyes with both hands, flicking water off. "This is what rain forests do."

"Right." Matt took a few deep breaths to calm himself. The situation had gone from bad to terrible in a matter of seconds. He felt trapped by the rain, suffocated. They were confined to this tiny alcove—and for who knew how long? What would conditions be like after it stopped?

How much worse could it get out there?

An awful thought occurred to Matt, a creeping dread that spread through his body.

Rosita.

Where was she? Was she out there in the forest—alone? Had she been able to take cover quickly enough, and was she as surprised and frightened as they were? He pictured the small, wiry black dog hiding under a branch, trembling and wet and wondering why no one was coming to get her.

Matt looked over at Luisa and could tell from her pursed lips and furrowed brow that she was thinking the same thing.

"She'll be okay," Matt said.

Luisa shook her head. "How do you know?"

Matt didn't know. But he hoped. "Because she's Rosita."

Scout leaned into him, and Luisa leaned on Scout. Matt's heart rate slowed to match Scout's, and soon they were breathing in unison. Just having his dog by his side helped Matt feel calmer. Scout was soaked, but he was still strong and sturdy under his wet fur.

The rain came down as if it would never end, so dense it was impossible to see more than a couple of feet away. Just as Matt began to calm himself down, he felt a soft vibration. He realized it was coming from Scout.

He was . . . growling?

Matt felt Scout's growl as much as he heard it, but before he had time to react, his ears rang with a harsh sound that nearly made him jump out of his skin. It was

Scout, up on his feet, barking right in Matt's ear at full volume—an aggressive bark followed by a deep, threatening rumble in his throat.

"Scout!" Matt's heart and adrenaline were pumping. "What the—"

"What is it?" Luisa's eyes were wide-open with fear. "What does he see?"

"I don't know." Matt looked around frantically, trying to catch any hint of what Scout was sensing. Scout had spun around and backed halfway out of the small enclosure. The fur in the center of his back stood on end, and he was looking at something over Matt's head. His steady stream of barking and growling got louder and more intense.

That's when Matt saw it.

It happened in slow motion.

Matt turned his head to see what Scout was focused on. The hair on the back of his neck stood up, and his arms came alive with goose bumps. He saw it, felt it, and knew it all in the same instant, with a recognition that was so clear and startling, it was as if he'd known it all along.

There, right above his head, wrapped around the fallen tree trunk that had provided them shelter, was a snake.

17

IT WAS A GIANT TAN BOA constrictor with brown spots, winding silkily around the tree. It had to be at least six feet long.

Matt and Luisa screamed at the same moment and shot backward out of the alcove so quickly they fell into the mud outside. Matt's hands slipped in the wet dirt as he scuttled like a crab in reverse, getting as far away as he could. He didn't care that the rain was pelting his head and face—he just wanted to put as much distance between himself and the snake as possible.

He and Luisa came to a stop side by side, a few feet from the downed trees. Scout still had his head in the alcove. He lowered the front half of his body into a crouch, oblivious to the rain on his back. He snapped his jaw and bared his teeth.

The snake raised its head, its beady black eyes on Scout.

Matt knew that Scout was not going to stand down until Matt and Luisa were safe. It was exactly what he had done when they had encountered a bear on Mount Kit. That day, Matt had been scared that Scout would be so protective of him and his dad that he would go for the bear—and incite the bear to attack in response. Matt had given Scout firm commands to get him to back down and let the bear walk away.

That's what he had to do now, he realized. He didn't want Scout to make this snake strike.

"Scout!" Matt shouted over the rain and the dog's barking. "Come!"

Scout ignored him.

Matt waited a beat before trying again. This time he focused his mind and took a deep breath into his belly. When he gave the command again, he spoke from his gut, his voice authoritative and firm.

"Scout—*come*!"

Scout's barking slowed, but his growl only deepened. With his eyes still locked on the snake, he took a hesitant step backward.

"Good boy." Matt's voice was firm but soothing.

Scout took another step. Then another. Soon he was standing between Matt and Luisa, his whole body shaking with rage.

"Nice, Scout." Matt put a hand on his dog's neck and scratched his wet fur under the collar. He felt Scout's growl still rumbling in his chest. "It's okay. You can calm down."

The snake flicked its tongue and seemed to consider them for a long moment. Matt held his breath. Luisa didn't move a muscle.

Finally, with a swirl around the tree branch, the snake slowly slithered away.

Matt watched it go, making sure it was really clearing out and not just getting a better angle on them. But it writhed right onto the ground and disappeared into the underbrush.

"Is it safe to go in there?" he asked, pointing to the spot under the downed trees.

"It's not coming back," Luisa said. She grabbed Scout's head and turned his face to hers. "I think you made enough noise to scare him off for good. Thank you, Scout." She wrapped her arms around him and pulled him into a tight hug. Scout grunted. "Plus, snakes really aren't after people. We're not very easy to eat. Or very tasty."

"You're hilarious," Matt said. "Can you be hilarious while we're not getting rained on?"

"Sure."

They scrambled under the trees and leaned back, both letting out a sigh of relief.

"That was terrifying," Matt said.

"Seriously," Luisa said. "But I guess this is their home, not ours."

"How long do these crazy storms usually last?"

"Shouldn't be much longer." She peered out from under the overhang. "Looks like it's winding down now, actually."

"Good, because we need to find Rosita fast."

No sooner were the words out of Matt's mouth than Scout was up on his feet again. Matt flinched and quickly scanned the trees above them. There was nothing there. He exhaled, his heart thudding hard in his chest.

Matt studied Scout. The dog wasn't barking or growling anymore—he was listening carefully, his ears up and turned to the sides, his brow furrowed and his eyes darting back and forth. Matt strained to hear something—anything—above the slowing rain and loud drops of water falling from the leaves and hitting the ground in a loud, uneven rhythm.

And then, there it was. It was faint and inconsistent. Matt heard the sound, but it disappeared just long enough for him to wonder if it had really been there at all. Then it started up again.

He looked at Luisa. She was staring out from under the trees and trying to figure out which direction the noise was coming from. As she did, a smile broke out on her face.

They recognized the sound at the same time.

It was Rosita barking.

"She's here!" Luisa cried. "She's close, isn't she?"

"Yeah, she's that way." Matt pointed off to the left. Rosita's bark rang out louder, but this time it sounded like it came from the right. "Ugh, maybe not."

Scout looked confused by the direction of the sound too. He whined and sniffed at the air, but he was having trouble picking up Rosita's scent after all the rain had washed everything away.

Rosita let out a new round of barks, but something

was different. Her tone had changed. Her bark grew higher, more shrill, with an edge of desperation. Matt's chest tightened with worry.

Rosita was afraid. More than afraid—she was terrified. He could hear it in her voice.

They darted out of the enclosure together, following the sound as best they could. Scout headed one direction, and Luisa ran in a slightly different one. Matt split the difference, and together they tromped through the wet forest, slipping and stumbling as they went.

"Anything?" Luisa called out from the trees.

"No."

Scout barked.

"Coming, Scout!" Matt shouted. He turned and nearly crashed into Luisa. Scout barked again, giving them a clear direction to follow. They reached him at the same time and saw the big dog skirting what looked like a small pond.

And right in the middle of it stood Rosita, soaking wet and trembling from scruffy head to stumpy tail.

"Rosita!"

Scout ran through the water toward the dog but froze in his tracks a few feet from her.

"Scout? What is it?" Matt was confused—why wasn't

Scout going to get Rosita? What was Scout seeing that he couldn't see?

"She's okay—is she okay?" Luisa took a step into the water too, then pulled back immediately.

That's when Matt realized that it wasn't water at all, and it wasn't ground, either. It was something else entirely—it was a deep pit filled with a thick mass of dirt, sodden and crushed leaves, splintered tree branches, sharp sticks, and rainwater, all churned together into a sludge that looked treacherous.

Rosita stood at the center of it, balanced on a narrow tree branch that stuck out of the mud at an angle, her four paws gripping it tightly. Her feet threatened to slip right off, and if she lost her balance, she would fall directly into the darkness that surrounded her on all sides.

"Scout, come!" Matt commanded his dog. Sensing that he was in danger, Scout did as he was told. He backed up carefully, his paws making loud slurping sounds.

Matt took a step into the water and immediately understood why Scout had stopped and Luisa had pulled back. It was thick and goopy—heavy—and it suctioned around his foot so fast that it felt like hands grabbing him from deep within the earth. If he took another step, he would get sucked in—and he wasn't sure he'd be able to get himself out.

Matt jerked his foot back. There was no way to walk to Rosita, and Rosita definitely couldn't come to them.

They would have to figure out another way.

18

THE RAIN HAD STARTED UP AGAIN. It fell in sheets, harder than before, if that was even possible. It pounded Matt's face with such power that it hurt and forced him to shut his eyes. He and Luisa shielded their eyes with their arms and wiped their faces as best they could, trying desperately to see Rosita through the wall of water.

The tiny dog was still at the center of the pit, but she was scrambling to keep her balance on the dripping-wet branch. The mire around her was growing deeper by the second as the rain poured down.

They had to get her. And fast.

Scout clearly felt the same way. He kept his eyes on Rosita as he skittered back and forth on the bank of the pit looking for a way to get to her. With a sharp bark, Scout hurled himself forward into the swirling muck pit.

It was a disaster.

Within seconds, Scout's legs had disappeared under the surface and he had sunk up to his chest.

"Scout!" Matt cried. "No, no, hang on, buddy! I'm coming!"

Scout tipped his head back to hold his snout up for air. The rain beat down on him, but he couldn't swipe at his face with his paws, which seemed to be stuck in the mud. Scout's body strained as he tried to pull his legs out and move forward, backward . . . any direction.

Matt took a step into the pit toward Scout.

"No—Matt, no—" Luisa cried. "Don't do it. Look how far Scout sank already!"

"I can't just leave him there!" But Matt knew she was right. Desperation rose in his chest, and he cast his eyes around for something—anything—he could use to help Scout. But before Matt could find anything, Scout suddenly lurched forward, his left front paw rising above the surface with a giant *slurp* sound. With one leg free, Scout was able to wriggle his body enough to gain some traction. He pressed forward, trying to get closer to Rosita.

She watched him head her way, and her whole body

began to shake with excitement. Rosita extended her snout toward Scout, stretching her neck and swiping a paw in the air, as if she was reaching out to him. But he was still too far away.

Matt looked up at the sky and saw a solid mass of clouds above. The rain showed no signs of abating, which meant it was a bad idea for Scout to forge ahead. The thick mud was only going to get worse. Matt had to get him back.

"Scout—come!" Scout's ears flicked at the sound of Matt's voice, but he continued pushing against the mud, trying to move forward. Matt took a full breath and closed his eyes. *Dig deep,* a dog trainer had once told him. *Speak with conviction.* "Scout—*come here, now!*"

Scout's whole body reacted to Matt's command. His head popped up, and—with one sad look at Rosita—he slowly turned himself around. Every step required great effort as he tugged one paw up and out of the sludge, then plunked it back down, then pulled up the next and plunked it down. He trudged toward Matt and Luisa, finally planting his front paws on the wet ground and pulling his back half out. He shook himself violently, sending a spray of mud and leaves out into the rain.

Scout looked at Rosita. She whimpered and let out

a few terrified yips, sliding on the branch and trying to chase after Scout. She fell sideways and landed in the muddy goop.

"*¡Ay, Dios mio!*" Luisa's hands flew to her mouth. "I don't know if she can make it!"

With a wild look in her eye, Rosita had rolled onto her belly. Her legs were quickly under the surface, but she had summoned something fierce and scrappy from deep within herself. Struggling, Rosita scooted forward one inch, then two. She got close enough to the branch to reach out one front paw and latch on to it with her claws. Then she dug the other paw into it and scratched and scrabbled at it until she had pulled herself up to safety.

Matt and Luisa gasped with relief.

Rosita shook herself off and, without missing a beat, picked up right where she had left off with her high-pitched barks and cries.

"Talk to her, okay?" Matt said to Luisa. "Just tell her it's going to be okay—she listens to you."

"Okay." Luisa took a deep breath and exhaled. "Rosita," she said in a soothing tone. "*Tranquila, mi vida. Todo va a estar bien.*"

Matt was practically blinded by the rain, and his feet were getting sucked into the wet, muddy ground.

Frustration mounted and threatened to burst out of him, but he forced himself to take a slow, deep inhale through his nose and let out an even slower exhale through his mouth. It was what his dad had always taught him to do when he was afraid or stressed or unsure how to proceed.

Immediately Matt felt his heart rate come down and the knot of anxiety in his chest begin to loosen.

And it was something else his dad had always taught him that helped him figure out what to do next. *Work with what you've got, Matt-o. When the mission is going south, you can't just ask everyone to wait a sec while you run out for supplies. You've got to take the only things you've got—your own brain and whatever's right in front of you—and use them to your advantage.*

Matt spotted a long tree branch lying nearby. It was in pretty good shape, not splintered like so many of the others. And it lay by itself, not tangled up in a pile of heavy, wet debris. He snatched it up by the wide end and dragged it over to Luisa and Scout.

Luisa seemed to get what he was trying to do. "You're going to make a bridge?"

"Yep." Matt was trying to maneuver the heavy branch toward the pit so he could swing the end out over the surface toward Rosita.

Luisa shook her head. "She'll never be able to walk on it. She'll fall off."

Luisa was right. But anything wider and it would be too heavy. Even if Matt and Luisa could drag it over to the mud pit, it would sink the second they laid it on the surface.

They needed width and stability, but not weight. Matt squeezed his eyes shut, trying to picture just what would fit that description, out here in the middle of nowhere.

Think! It's here—it's right in front of you. You just have to find it.

Matt opened his eyes. He had it. One big branch would be too narrow and heavy, but two branches side by side would be wide enough together—and light enough individually to stay afloat.

He ran around, peering through the rain, until he found a branch that was similar in size and heft to the first. He dragged it over and he and Luisa positioned the two logs tightly together, extending all the way to Rosita from the bank where they stood. They knelt on either side and braced the trunks.

Rosita stopped whining and watched them with big, round eyes. She swiped at the wood with one paw, then pulled back.

"Come on," Matt called out, barely able to control his emotions enough to speak calmly. "Rosita, go on—get on the tree and come over here."

"You can walk on it!" Luisa whistled gently. "Rosita— *¡ven aquí!* It's okay—we got you."

But Rosita was shaking too hard to move, and now she was covered in thick, wet mud. She looked at the bridge they had made for her, then at Scout, then at Matt and Luisa. She whimpered sadly.

Scout barked once—sharp and shrill.

Rosita couldn't do it. She didn't understand what they wanted her to do—or if she did, she was too terrified to do it.

Matt couldn't fight his frustration. "Rosita, you have to come here, now—"

He caught a blur of motion out of the corner of his eye, and suddenly the tree trunks jerked under his palms. A brown-and-white streak—Scout—was stepping quickly and lightly across the makeshift bridge toward Rosita. Before Matt could find his voice, Scout had reached Rosita and, in an instant, snatched her up by the scruff and turned back around. Moving gracefully and quickly—as if he were just taking a walk and not racing along a wet, slippery tightrope—Scout brought

Rosita back and hopped onto the ground. Scout gently laid the little dog at Luisa's feet and began to nudge and lick her with his nose.

Matt couldn't help himself. He scooped up the muddy Rosita, cradling her in one arm while he wrapped the other around Scout's neck and pulled his dog in. Luisa gave Scout a kiss on the top of his head and held out her arms for Rosita. Matt handed her over, and Luisa cuddled the small dog, softly cooing into her ear.

They stayed there, ignoring the rain, for a long moment. Relief washed over Matt. Luisa closed her eyes and pressed her cheek to Rosita's. They were all covered in mud, and they were sopping wet, but they were now all together and safe.

Matt looked past Scout and took in the sky in the distance. It wasn't just gray with rain clouds anymore. It was getting dark as the sun went down, turning inky and opaque.

Matt turned to Luisa and realized he could barely see her. "Luisa," he said. She looked in the direction he was pointing. "It's getting dark. We don't know where we're going. We'll never find our way out of here at night."

She nodded and swallowed hard. Matt saw a flash of

fear cross her face, but she kept her composure. "So we stay."

Matt knew she was right. "We stay." He hated the thought, but he didn't see any way around it.

His stomach felt queasy, and his arms and legs had gone numb.

He'd camped out a thousand times, and even been in some scary situations—like a flood and a wildfire. But this was a rain forest. A devastated rain forest, where no one else had any reason to be—where they were utterly, totally alone.

He was in way over his head this time. He had no big ideas, no way to fix this, and no backup plan.

Matt felt about as low as he ever had. He swore to himself that when they saw the light of morning—*if* they saw the light of morning—he would get them safely home and never, ever do anything like this again.

But first, they had to get through the night.

19

IT WAS SO DARK NOW THAT Matt couldn't see his own hand in front of his face. He, Scout, Rosita, and Luisa huddled together, leaning back against a stack of boulders that were angled just enough to provide them with cover. It wasn't perfect, but it would have to do.

After the heat and humidity of the day, Matt hadn't expected to be cold. The rain had stopped, but now that the sun had gone down and he was soaked to the bone, the chill had set in. His clothes were heavy with water, his skin was covered in goose bumps, and his fingers were puckered and pruny. Luisa's jaw was tight and her lips shivered as she wrapped her arms around herself and leaned into Scout for warmth. They were all chilled through and through.

Scout lay between them, seeming like he wasn't sure who to look out for first—Matt, Rosita, or Luisa. Rosita was tucked safely at his side, curled into the curve of Scout's hip. Scout sniffed at her and licked her head every few minutes. In between, he tipped his head back and looked up at Matt, as if checking to be sure he was still there. Matt scratched Scout's neck and under his chin, running his fingers through his dog's soft, damp fur. Scout turned to Luisa on his other side and placed a paw on her leg. She leaned down and rested her head on his, draping an arm over his body.

Matt reached across Scout and patted Rosita's belly. She grumbled with satisfaction, happy to be snug and safe again. Matt thought about this tiny, odd dog and how far she'd traveled that day just to be with her family, wherever they were.

Out here, adrift in the deep forest and the inky blackness, he remembered what it felt like to want to go home really, really badly. He got why Rosita was so determined, and how much she was willing to go through just to find her loved ones again.

All around them, the sounds of the forest cawed and

tapped and hummed, like a symphony warming up. Some animals were winding down for the night, and others were just getting started. Matt listened intently, trying to sort out the sounds—but soon he couldn't hear much over the rising chorus of the *coquí* frogs.

Coquí! Coquí! began one.

Coquí coquí coquí! replied another.

The rest of the frogs hidden in the trees all around them took their cue, and soon the night was booming with their calls. Matt couldn't help but laugh, despite their current terrible situation.

"I told you that's what they sounded like," Luisa said with a chuckle.

"You do a good impersonation."

"Thanks. I've had years of practice."

Matt closed his eyes and listened to the frogs' melody. It was relaxing, like the sound of waves crashing on the beach.

The gurgle of Matt's stomach interrupted the music.

"Hungry?" Luisa asked.

"Not really. You?"

"Sort of. I know I should be, but I don't feel like eating. Not that we have any food anyway."

Matt thought for a second. "Wait—I do have food!"

He turned on his flashlight and dug around in his backpack. Everything inside it was wet, but he closed his hand around two sealed granola bars and the pack of ham he'd thrown in there at the last second.

"Carbs *and* protein!" Matt handed one bar and the ham to Luisa. He ripped open the wrapper on the other bar and broke off half, then split that in two. He gave one piece to Rosita and one piece to Scout. They both ate it in one gulp.

"Ham?" Luisa held out the package to him as she chewed and swallowed the meat.

"Thanks. I bet these guys would like some." Matt took the packet from her and pulled out a slice. He fed it to Scout and Rosita, who were more than happy to eat it. "There you go, guys." He forced himself to eat some too.

Fed and comfortable—and protected by Scout—Rosita dropped her head onto her paws and closed her eyes. Scout licked his lips, and his eyelids lowered halfway. He wasn't asleep. He was resting, but his senses were still on patrol. Matt could see his ears flicking with each sound, and his nostrils twitching as he kept tabs on every scent that floated by on the air.

Matt closed up the ham packet and dropped it back into his pack. The food had taken the edge off his nerves, and with one arm lying across Scout's stomach, he leaned back against the rock and closed his eyes. Like a movie in slo-mo, the long day played out in his mind: all the destruction and damage they had seen, trekking in the heat and rain, getting lost in the forest, the stress of finding Rosita . . . Exhaustion hit him hard, and before he knew it, the sound of the frogs was fading into the distance, growing softer and softer until Matt had fallen deeply asleep.

There were dogs howling in Matt's dream. They were loud—so incredibly loud—and Matt just wanted them to stop. "Quiet!" he commanded them. "Scout—shush!" But it was like that dream that plagued Matt, when his alarm clock was beeping but he couldn't turn it off no matter how many times he hit Snooze, or even after he had unplugged it. Scout and the other dogs wouldn't listen, and the howling continued.

It was a wild sound, sad and fierce all at once. There were so many of them—how many different voices was Matt hearing? The dogs joined together, hitting different notes but their calls overlapping and rising together, then falling off and starting over again. Matt grew agitated, determined to make the sound stop.

He fought to wake himself up, struggling against the

weight of sleep and the fogginess of the dream. Slowly he pushed up, up, up into a drowsy wakefulness. For a confused moment, he didn't remember where he was or why. He felt cold and damp. The air was thick and smelled of dirt, and his back hurt from the hard surface behind him.

It came to him slowly. He was in the forest. With Luisa. And the dogs.

The dogs.

Matt snapped into alertness and his eyes shot open. He tried to adjust his vision to the darkness that surrounded him as it became crystal clear why he couldn't get the dogs to quiet down in his dream.

It was because they weren't in his dream. They were real.

And the wild dogs were howling all around them. The air was filled with their calls. Scout was standing up, a soft growl emanating from his chest. Matt fumbled around for Rosita. She was trembling, and he pulled her onto his lap to comfort her, holding her tight.

"Luisa?" Matt whispered into the darkness.

"I'm here," she replied. "They're satos—but not the nice kind. What do they want?"

"I don't know."

Scout's growl grew louder.

"Scout, stay," Matt said, reaching up and grabbing hold of Scout's collar. He didn't want Scout to take off into the dark, after some unknown dogs they couldn't even see. He would be outnumbered—plus, he was on their turf and they would have the advantage. No way Matt was going to let Scout put himself in that kind of danger.

Matt felt Scout crouch down low and heard his growl grow deeper and fiercer. He was preparing to defend them. The dogs kept howling, but the tenor of their cries changed. They got louder, and there was a note of something harsher, more menacing.

Matt blinked into the darkness, willing his eyes to adjust. As the faint light of the moon reached the forest floor, Matt saw something that made his blood run cold. Something glinting and bright. Something terrifying.

Eyes.

Five pairs of eyes were arrayed around them in a half circle, blinking at them from many directions at once.

The wild dogs were closing in.

A sharp pain burst in Matt's chest, and he realized that fear had stopped him from breathing.

"Matt . . ." Luisa whispered, her voice shaky.

Matt ran through the options of what they could do. Scout could fight, and he might even stand a chance against more than one of these dogs. But there were just so many of them—how would Scout fare? Matt didn't want to find out. "Scout," Matt said slowly and firmly. "I need you to stay. You hear me? *Stay.*"

The eyes got closer. Then closer.

Scout's growl became a snarl. He took one step forward, closing the distance between himself and the other dogs.

The dogs moved in again.

They were so close Matt could hear them panting. He, Rosita, and Luisa were already pressed against the rock behind them. They were trapped.

Matt's heart pounded in his chest. Luisa reached out and grabbed him. He squeezed her hand back. Rosita trembled in his arms.

This was it.

The dogs were poised to attack.

20

MATT SCRAMBLED TO HIS FEET. Luisa rustled around in the dark and stood up, holding two shards of a splintered tree. She handed one to Matt.

Matt placed Rosita on the ground and tucked her behind his legs, where he could protect her.

"Stay there," he whispered to her.

Rosita, thankfully, stayed put.

Scout had positioned himself as the first line of defense against the wild dogs. He paced back and forth in front of Matt, Luisa, and Rosita. Matt held the wood straight out in front of him like a sword, while Luisa raised hers over her shoulder, ready to swing. The dogs were within arm's reach, but Scout wouldn't let Matt or Luisa get any closer to them.

But Matt was just as protective of Scout.

"Scout—you need to stand down, buddy. You hear me?"

But it was too late. Scout was beyond the reach of Matt's commands. He was operating on pure animal instinct, and he and a husky black dog with bulging muscles in his legs—who seemed to be the leader of the pack—were practically nose-to-nose. They crouched down and snarled at each other, spit flying from their bared fangs.

The alpha dog made the first move. He snapped at Scout, nipping his cheek. "No!" Matt screamed. Scout didn't seem to be hurt. He pulled back and repositioned himself, poised to attack as soon as he saw an opening.

Something exploded in Matt when he saw Scout in jeopardy, and one thought filled his mind: No one was going to hurt his dog. He leapt forward, swinging the stick at the other dog. "Get out of here!" Matt shouted. "Get out—go—leave us alone!" The wood whizzed by the dog's face but didn't make contact. The dog growled at Matt but took a skittish step backward.

Scout was to Matt's left, and Luisa was behind Scout. One of the other dogs, a lean, copper-colored hound, took a step toward Scout. Before it could get any farther, Luisa ran toward it, bringing her branch down like a hammer. She just missed the dog, but it was enough to get it to back off.

Matt swung the stick in front of the dogs' faces. Scout snarled low and deep at them. Luisa waved her branch up and down.

The pack retreated in unison, but they didn't leave. They stood firm in their formation, leaving Matt, Luisa, and their dogs cornered.

"Why won't they leave us alone?" Matt asked.

"They want something," Luisa replied. "They're not just here to fight. We weren't threatening them."

"But we don't have anything." Matt's mind was racing. And then it clicked, and he felt so stupid for not realizing it sooner. What else would a feral dog in the middle of a forest after a terrible hurricane want but one thing: food. "Ham!"

"What are y—" It took Luisa a second too. "Ham! Give it to them— where is it?"

Matt fumbled in his backpack for the meat. He was so nervous that he dropped it, and the alpha dog took an aggressive step toward him. Scout opened his mouth and clamped it shut around the dog's neck so fast it seemed impossible. The dog cried out in pain.

"Scout—no!" Matt waved the stick over his head.

"Let him go, let him go, let him go . . ." Scout released his hold on the dog and stepped back. "Look here," Matt said to the hound, and opened the packet of ham. The smell of the meat traveled to the dogs. "Look what I have. Is this what you want?"

The animals' entire demeanor changed. They went from ferocious to frantic in the blink of an eye. Their eyes followed the food, their heads moving side to side.

Matt felt a pang of pity for them. They weren't there to hurt Matt and his friends—they were hungry. Who knew how long it had been since their last meal? They were animals, doing what animals do: surviving.

"You want it, you can have it!" Matt said. He cocked his arm back and released the package in a perfect arc over their heads. It disappeared into the darkness, and so did the dogs. Moving as one, they turned and sprinted toward the meat, which had landed with a soft thud about forty feet away.

After a moment, Matt and Luisa heard them barking and baying at each other, fighting over the small feast. Scout barked after them, then paced and swatted at the ground as his fight response faded and his heart rate came back down.

Matt dropped to his knees at Scout's side and wrapped his arms around the dog's chest. "You're amazing," he said into Scout's fur. "Thank you."

Luisa knelt down too. She ran a hand down Scout's back and scratched him behind the ears. "You're like a one-dog army." She looked up at Matt. "Let's get out of here before they come back."

"Okay." Matt swallowed hard. He didn't relish the thought of heading out into the woods in the dark, but they couldn't stay there—he knew that much. "Rosita, come—" Matt stepped toward the rocks where he'd left her. "Come on, girl, we need to get go—"

He froze.

"What?" Luisa asked, her voice rising with worry. "Is she okay?"

"I—I don't—" Matt spun around, looking at the piles of broken trees, the rocks covered in leaves and mud, the sludgy ground all around them, as the moon peeked out from behind a cloud.

But she wasn't there.

Rosita was gone.

"Where is she?" Luisa choked back tears.

Matt didn't know. And he couldn't bring himself to speak out loud the terrifying questions blaring in his mind.

Had Rosita run away again while Matt was distracted?

Or had she been snatched by one of the savage dogs?

21

MATT FELT SICK TO HIS STOMACH.

He stood there, in the spot where Rosita had just been, burying his face in his hands. He was paralyzed.

Matt wanted so badly to do something—to run after Rosita and pick her up and save her from the endless dark forest that dwarfed them all. But he couldn't do that, because he had no idea where she was, or which way she had gone, or even if she was still alive.

He had no idea what to do, and he hated himself for that.

"I don't think the dogs got her," Luisa said quietly. Matt wasn't sure if she really felt that way or if she was just hoping that saying it out loud would make it true.

He didn't reply, because he knew there was nothing he could say to make either one of them feel better. The *coquíes* had picked up singing where they had left off, but Matt barely noticed.

Scout sniffed at the ground by Matt's feet. He moved in a circle, grazing the ground with his nose and exhaling sharply to clear his nostrils. But the rain had come down so hard and so steadily that Matt didn't know if Scout would be able to catch Rosita's scent. Had it been washed away completely?

The thought topped off Matt's despair. He didn't know if he could possibly feel worse. Matt raised his head to watch his dog move in ever-widening loops. At first Scout didn't seem to be heading in any particular direction, but soon he took a sharp right and headed into the trees.

"Is he taking us somewhere?" Luisa asked.

"I'm not sure," Matt said.

And what difference did it make? They didn't have much choice but to follow Scout—where else would they go? They couldn't just sit there, doing nothing.

Using the flashlight, Matt lit up the woods around them. The beam was a burst of brightness in the dark, hurting their eyes and turning everything in its path a bright, flat white. Blinking nervously, Luisa headed off after Scout, her feet squishing into the soaked, soft ground. Matt walked behind her, keeping a lookout for tangled piles of debris—and snakes.

Scout was still moving along at a steady pace, but he didn't seem to be following any particular scent. He seemed to be trying to reorient himself, pausing from time to time to look up at the trees or turn his head in the direction of a particularly loud *coquí* call.

Matt started to notice how uncomfortable he was. His clothes were heavy with rain and stuck to his body. His shoes squirted out water with every step he took. His skin was clammy. Luisa's hair was plastered to her face, and she shivered, but she didn't complain.

Matt couldn't believe he had gotten her into this terrible mess.

"This was a really stupid idea," he said. "I'm sorry."

Luisa stopped and turned to face him. "What was a stupid idea?"

"This." Matt waved his arms at the woods around them. "It's all my fault. I should have listened to you when you said we shouldn't come into the forest."

Luisa shot him a sympathetic look. "Stop."

Matt wasn't sure how to respond.

"Matt, stop. This isn't your fault."

"Of course it is."

"Actually no, it's not. This was my decision as much as it was yours. You didn't make me follow Rosita—I wanted to."

"I guess. But I told you we could trust Scout."

"And we can," she said. "So far he's saved us from a snake and a pack of hungry dogs. Oh, and he carried Rosita over a flaming pit."

Matt had to laugh.

"Okay, so it wasn't flaming," Luisa went on. "But he still saved her."

"I guess." Matt wasn't convinced. Anything Scout had done to save them was done in spite of Matt's bad judgment—as a way of trying to correct his bad decisions. Wasn't it?

"If it makes you feel better," Luisa said, "I know these dogs."

"How so?"

"I mean, I know what they can do. Rosita is an island dog. She's tough—look how much she's already been through. She knows how to survive."

Matt wanted so badly to believe her, but he couldn't stop picturing Rosita, small and soaked and shivering, struggling to make her way through this broken and unkind landscape.

"I know," he said. "She's amazing."

Just then, Scout came to a sudden stop ahead of them. His head rose up, and Matt noticed a familiar shift in the dog's body language. The muscles in his legs grew taut. His ears rotated back on his head, and his tail curled up in a C over his back.

He had caught a scent.

"Is it Rosita?" Matt asked, his voice rising. "Scout— can you find Rosita?"

In response, Scout shot off into the woods at full tilt.

22

MATT FORGOT ALL ABOUT HOW WORRIED he was. He forgot about being chilled to the bone. He forgot about the blisters on his feet and the fact that they were in the middle of nowhere.

All he thought about was following Scout.

Scout bounded ahead, his back legs flying out in the air behind him as he sailed over fallen trees and piles of rocks. When Scout was almost out of sight, Matt looked out for the tip of his tail floating in the darkness, or a flash of light against Scout's reflective vest.

Matt and Luisa ran as fast as they could behind him, trying to keep up—and keep upright. They climbed small, rocky rises and stumbled down the other side.

They ran on the tightrope of a narrow path that wended through the dense trees, then trailed off into dirt. They skirted small, empty buildings—tourist stops under normal circumstances—with busted walls and no roofs. The ground was slippery and Matt's flashlight beam bounced unevenly as he ran. His lungs hurt and his heart pounded in his ears.

But Scout wasn't going to slow down or wait around for them. He had Rosita's scent, and he wasn't going to stop until he found her. Matt had never seen his dog like this. Usually, even under the worst and most dangerous circumstances, Scout would slow down and let Matt catch up to him.

Not this time.

The light of Matt's flashlight dimmed as the sky started to lighten. Soon the very air had a pinkish cast to it, and the trees and vines and rocks began to fade into view, as if a curtain had risen to reveal them. The forest woke up along with the light, and soon a loud conversation between birds began above their heads. If Matt had been paying attention, he would have noticed a dozen cries and calls and squawks he had never heard before.

But he was too focused on Scout. Dawn made no difference to the dog, who was following his nose more than his eyes as he moved at the same crazy pace. Soon the sun was fully up and Matt began to notice more and more light between the trees, and not just above them. The forest was thinning out.

Scout powered ahead and stepped through the edge of the tree line and out onto a small road. Matt and Luisa stumbled out after him. With their feet on solid ground again, they bent over and put their hands on their knees to catch their breath.

Scout didn't wait around for them. He ran off down the road without a backward glance. Matt and Luisa exchanged a hopeful look and jogged after him. As he ran, Matt checked his phone—there was no service. He winced at the thought of how angry his mom was going to be, but he couldn't worry about that right now. He would explain everything later . . . and hope she understood.

The road rose and fell in gently sloping hills. They climbed a steep incline and rounded a curve, and in the distance saw a small town—nothing more than a cluster of houses and a couple of stores, really. They made their way toward the old wooden structures. There were holes in the roofs and boarded-up windows, but even the damage couldn't diminish the absolute beauty of this spot.

Matt had traveled a lot with his family and he'd lived in a long list of places across the U.S., but he'd never seen anything like this. He spun around in a circle and took in the 360-degree view—over the treetops—from the hill where they stood. Lush, undulating greenery spread out around them like a carpet at their feet. Other hilltops peeked out above the foliage and into the brilliant blue sky, and in the far distance, flashing and sparkling in the morning sun, was the ocean.

A morning breeze brushed Matt's face. The day felt fresh, new—hopeful.

They followed Scout toward the buildings. An elderly lady stepped out of a house and began sweeping her front steps.

"*Buenos días,*" Luisa said.

"*Buenos días,*" the lady replied. She shot them a strange look—which, Matt figured, made sense, since they had just emerged from the forest and probably looked like they'd slept under a rock . . . which they essentially had. "*¿Están bien, niños?*"

"*Sí,*" Luisa reassured the woman. They chatted in Spanish, and soon the woman's husband came out to join them. A middle-aged man stepped out of the house next door to join the group too. From the few words of

Spanish that he recognized, Matt could tell that Luisa was telling them about their night in the forest and also describing Rosita. They patted her on the shoulder and clicked their tongues with concern.

Scout had continued down the road, quickly moving past the houses and a small *mercado,* where a woman was stacking fruit on a table outside. A low pyramid of spiky soursop sat next to a pile of guavas, a couple of pineapples, and some waxy starfruit. It wasn't a plentiful display, and Matt could tell that the townspeople were doing the best they could with the food they had available to them—or that they could pick themselves—since the storm.

Scout raced past the fruit stand without pausing to sniff at it. He continued on, running his nose over the ground, ignoring everything else. He wasn't just moving fast, he was moving with purpose—his whole body was animated and alive.

"*¡Gracias!*" Luisa said to the assembled group. "Matt!" she said excitedly, turning to him. "They know who—"

"Look!" Matt interrupted her. He pointed at Scout, who had come to a halt in the middle of the road.

His whole body wriggling with barely contained excitement, Scout sat down and looked down the road at Matt.

"Scout?" Matt called out. "Did you— Are you—"

Scout's tail began swishing back and forth across the ground. He opened his mouth and his tongue dangled out the side. He was relaxed, happy—triumphant.

"Yes!" Matt pumped a fist in the air.

"He found her?"

"He found her!"

They took off running down the street. Worried thoughts fought their way into Matt's mind—Was Rosita okay? Was she hurt? Had she made it here on her own?—but one fantastic, familiar, delightful sound blew all those fears to bits.

It was a happy, hearty bark.

Rosita's bark.

23

A BLACK-AND-WHITE BLUR ZOOMED INTO the road. Matt barely had time to register it when suddenly it was streaming in circles around his legs. From somewhere at the center of the dark flash of movement, Matt heard a joyful yipping.

Scout hopped to his feet and did a funny, skittering dance, his tail going so hard it whapped Luisa in the leg.

Matt and Luisa dropped to their knees right in the middle of the street, holding out their arms. The blur became a bouncing dot as it jumped from Matt's lap to Luisa's and back again. It slowed to a steady wriggle, and finally Luisa was able to wrap her arms around Rosita, who stood up on her hind legs and planted her front paws on Luisa's shoulders. Rosita stretched her neck to reach Luisa's face, which she promptly and vigorously began licking. Luisa squeezed her eyes tightly shut so Rosita wouldn't lick her eyeballs.

"Rosita!" Happy tears spilled down Luisa's cheeks. She grabbed Rosita under her front legs and held her out so she could look her in the eye. Rosita's short back legs dangled in the air. "I knew you'd be all right. You're one tough pup."

"Are we happy to see you," Matt said, poking the dog gently in the belly. "You scared us!"

Rosita let out a long yawping sigh in reply. Scout barked to get her attention, and Rosita wriggled out of Luisa's hands so she could focus entirely on him. She lay down at his feet and rolled onto her back. Scout nuzzled her belly and sniffed at her, trying to piece together, by scent, everything that had happened to her in the last few hours.

Seeing the two dogs together filled Matt's heart with happiness. For the first time since Rosita had run off the day before, he felt like he could really exhale. Luisa wiped her tears on the back of her hand and grinned from ear to ear. Satisfied that Rosita was safe and sound, Scout lay down on the ground next to the smaller dog.

Rosita climbed halfway up his side, her front paws on his chest. She yipped at Scout and ducked her head, trying to get him to play.

"*Hola*," a soft voice said from behind them. Matt and Luisa turned to see a young girl, probably about nine years old. Matt could tell from her red eyes that she'd just been crying. She smiled shyly at them and gave them a little wave. "*Yo soy Isabel.*"

"*Hola, Isabel,*" Matt said. "*Yo soy Matt.*"

"*Yo soy Luisa.*" Luisa gestured toward Rosita. She spoke to Isabel in Spanish and translated the girl's replies for Matt. "Is this your dog?"

Isabel nodded. "Yes. That's Paleta." Tears filled her eyes again. "That's my dog." At the sound of Isabel's voice, Rosita—Paleta—scrambled off Scout and ran over to her, wagging her tail so hard it practically lifted her back end off the ground. "She's been missing since the storm. I thought—" At this, Isabel burst into tears. "I thought she was gone forever!"

Isabel picked up Paleta and squeezed her so tightly that the dog let out a little squeak. In turn, Paleta licked the tears from Isabel's cheeks, which made the girl giggle and squeeze her even tighter.

Luisa flashed a bittersweet smile. "She's back now,

right where she belongs. And she's not going anywhere this time."

Isabel closed her eyes and pressed her cheek to the dog's. "It's better than my birthday." She sighed.

Matt thought about how he'd feel if Scout disappeared into thin air. Just the thought of it was like a punch to the gut, and he wouldn't wish that fear and sadness on anyone. He also knew how amazing it would be if Scout just suddenly reappeared as quickly as he'd gone. That's what Isabel was feeling right at that moment—the roller coaster of emotions that ended in overwhelming relief and joy.

Matt felt two equally strong and clear—and contradictory—emotions at the same moment. He was ecstatic to play a small part in bringing Isabel and Paleta back together . . . but he was crushed that Luisa would have to say good-bye to the pup she had hoped would be with her forever.

Rosita wasn't going to be Luisa's dog after all—something Luisa had worried about all along.

There was a lump in Matt's throat. His heart was breaking for his friend, but he tried to focus on what he knew was right.

Rosita and Isabel belonged together. There was no other way.

He thought about Luisa's face when she looked at Rosita—the love and affection written there. He thought about how Luisa had described Rosita's injuries and how bravely the little dog had faced her time at the shelter, healing. He pictured Rosita's proud, sweet face the day he met her. He thought about how upset Luisa had looked every time Rosita had taken off and run away.

Now, at least, they knew where she had been going.

Luisa smiled at Isabel.

"All this time, she was trying so hard to get back home to you," she said.

24

ISABEL, LUISA, AND MATT walked side by side toward Isabel's house as Scout and Paleta ran ahead of them.

"The day of the storm, we were all hiding at my grandmother's house," Isabel said. "It was so scary—" She shook her head, as if to clear the memories.

"I know," Luisa said, putting her arm around the girl's shoulders. "It was terrible."

"There were no lights and it was so loud . . . everything was really confusing. Paleta was there and then all of a sudden she was just gone. The next day, when the storm was over, I couldn't go look for her. My mami wouldn't let me leave the house because it was too dangerous. I kept thinking that I would try to find her, but our town has been so bad . . . I couldn't leave."

Matt looked around. For the first time he noticed that there wasn't a single light on in any of the homes, and there was no sound other than people talking. There was no music playing, no talk radio or TV shows, no ding of a microwave.

"You still don't have electricity?" he asked in English. Luisa posed the question to Isabel in Spanish.

Isabel shook her head. "We almost ran out of water and food too, but a truck came and delivered some."

Matt couldn't wrap his head around everything this little girl had gone through. He didn't think he could handle half of what she'd experienced—especially if, the entire time, Scout was missing.

And what if Scout were missing but Matt was trapped—unable to go out and look for him because the whole world around him had been turned upside down?

"I cried every day," Isabel said. "I didn't know if she was okay—I was so scared that something bad had happened to her. I thought maybe . . . you know . . ."

She didn't need to finish the sentence.

"Did you take care of her?" Isabel asked Luisa, taking her hand.

Luisa squeezed Isabel's hand and nodded. "Someone found her after the storm. She was hurt pretty badly."

Isabel winced.

"They brought her to the shelter where I work," Luisa went on, skipping over the details of Paleta's injuries. "She had a broken leg, but we fixed her right up and she was never alone there, I promise. She had lots of other dogs to play with, and the doctor took really good care of her, and I played with her almost every day. We really loved—*love*—her."

Isabel stopped and turned to Luisa. "Thank you," she said. "Everything was bad. But now it's better because of you. Maybe things will feel more normal now, for my mami and papi, too."

"You have a very special dog—do you know that, Isabel? Because that's how I felt when I met Ros—I mean, Paleta. It was the first time I thought everything might be okay again." She took both of Isabel's hands and crouched down so she could look the girl in the eye. "Everything will be normal again, I promise. We will get our home back."

Isabel nodded solemnly, then wrapped her arms

around Luisa's neck. The girls held on tightly to each other, and Luisa stroked Isabel's hair. Scout and Paleta wandered back over to them. Paleta wedged her way between Luisa and Isabel.

"Awwwww!" the girls said in unison.

Scout sat down next to Matt, and Matt put his hand on Scout's head. He scratched the soft spot in front of each ear. Scout closed his eyes and let out a contented little wheeze.

Isabel stood up and pointed to a house across the street. "That's my house," she said. "My parents are going to be so happy to see Paleta—I want to surprise them. Can you stay here with her?"

Luisa and Matt nodded.

"I'll go get them, and they can drive you home." Isabel turned to her dog. "Paleta," she said, *"siéntate. Quieta."* Paleta sat, but whimpered as she watched Isabel walk away.

They stood in silence for a second. Matt didn't want to acknowledge what he and Luisa both knew.

This was good-bye.

He took a deep breath and got down on the ground. "Hey," he said. Paleta tore her eyes away from Isabel's back and looked up at him. She instantly broke into a happy dance, her mouth open in a smile and her tongue out. Scout walked over, and he and Paleta pressed their foreheads together. Luisa sat down cross-legged, and the four of them huddled up.

Matt didn't know what to say. He'd only known Paleta for a short time, but he already felt so attached to her—like she'd been with him for years.

"Hey, sweet girl," he said, holding Paleta in one arm and cupping her chin with his free hand. "Thanks for hanging out with me. You're an amazing pup, you know that?" Paleta responded by nipping playfully at Matt's hand and looking up at him while she gently gnawed on his thumb. "I'm going to miss you."

Scout snuffled at Paleta and licked her face a few times. He whimpered and whined, as if he knew that this was the last time he would ever see her. Paleta placed a paw on his head and left it there.

It was Luisa's turn. Matt got up and he and Scout walked a few feet away, giving them some space. Matt couldn't hear her words, but Luisa spoke to Paleta for a long while and rocked her like a baby. Paleta's lids got heavy and her whole body relaxed.

Something in Matt's chest clicked back into place as he watched them, and the heavy sadness he felt got lighter. Isabel wouldn't have to worry anymore. That was worth leaving Paleta behind.

Luisa came over, Paleta curled up in her arms. A thought occurred to Matt. "Hey," he asked Luisa, "what does *Paleta* mean, anyway?"

A huge grin crossed Luisa's face.

"What is it?" Matt couldn't help but smile back.

Luisa tried to say it out loud, but she couldn't speak while fighting her laughter. Finally, with a loud guffaw, she blurted it out: "Lollipop."

Their loud cackles bounced off the torn-up houses and splintered trees and caved-in rooftops, carrying all the worry and sadness in the world right up into the bright blue sky.

25

THE RIDE HOME WAS BUMPY AND LONG. Isabel's mom, Nayeli, had to steer them around busted couches and teetering piles of plywood and scrap metal. She had to drive their truck through puddles that rose up the sides of the tires. Even when they drove on a two-lane paved road, there were patches of missing asphalt that she had to avoid.

Matt got a cell signal as soon as they dropped down into the valley. He reached his mom and held the phone away from his ear as she let him know how worried she had been—and exactly how she felt about his extended absence.

When they pulled onto base, it was already lunchtime.

Matt's mom and Luisa's parents and brother were waiting for them outside Luisa's house. Isabel's mom held out her hand to shake Ric's, but instead of taking it he pulled her into a hug and thanked her for bringing the kids home.

"Your daughter saved our dog," Nayeli said. "We thought she was gone forever . . ." She trailed off. "Your kids," she said to Matt's mom and Luisa's parents, "traveled so far to bring her home. You have no idea how much joy they have brought back to my family."

Matt's mom and Sonia both had tears running down their cheeks, and Matt thought he saw something dewy in Ric's eyes too.

"Whatever you need," Ric said to Nayeli, "I am always here to help you." He ran to his truck and came back with a canister of gasoline. Nayeli held out her hands to say no, but Ric walked to the side of her car, opened the gas cap, and began refilling her tank.

Sonia held out a stuffed bag of groceries. Nayeli tried to say no to that too, but Sonia wasn't having it. She opened the passenger-side door and dropped the bag onto the seat, then came around the truck and gave Nayeli another hug.

"We're going to come to your town next to help you,

I promise," Matt's mom said, joining the women in their embrace.

"*Gracias*," the women said over and over to each other until they all laughed.

When Isabel's mom had driven away, the two families stood together silently.

"It's okay, Mom," Matt finally said. "I know you're angry. And you should be."

"I am," she said, her lips pressed firmly together and her hands on her hips. "But—and I don't know if Ric and Sonia will agree with me on this—I also understand why you did what you did. I don't like it, but I get it."

Matt nodded. His stomach churned, but somehow he gathered up the courage to raise his head and look Sonia and Ric in the eye. "Please don't be mad at Luisa," he pleaded with them. "I'm so sorry about this—I really am. But it's my fault, not hers. It was my idea to foster Rosita, because I thought maybe if you got to know her, you'd let Luisa keep her."

Ric and Sonia looked at their daughter, then at each other.

Once he had started, Matt couldn't stop. "Luisa didn't think it was a good idea, but I insisted. And then when we realized the dog had a family somewhere, I was the one who wanted to go after Rosita—I mean, Paleta."

Ric glared at him. Sonia looked away. Luisa stared at the ground.

A tiny giggle broke the uncomfortable silence. Emanuel, Luisa's little brother, pushed his way out from behind Ric's and Sonia's legs. "Wait." He giggled again. "The dog you found was named Paleta?"

It took every ounce of willpower Matt and Luisa had to hold back their laughter. Matt didn't dare look over at her. He knew if they made eye contact, they would both lose it.

"What does that mean?" Matt's mom asked. "Why's it so funny?"

No one answered for a second, until finally Ric opened his mouth to speak. But instead of a word, out came a snort so loud it took them all by surprise. Matt couldn't believe his eyes: Ric was laughing. And not just snickering. Tears ran down his cheeks, his whole body shook, and he couldn't speak or take a breath. Sonia couldn't fight it. Cracking up, she put a hand on Matt's mom's shoulder and managed to squeak out one word: "Lollipop."

Matt's mom doubled over, and soon they all stood

there cackling their heads off while Scout stared at them like they had lost their minds.

Matt's sides were sore from laughing.

"I'm sorry about Paleta," Matt's mom said, managing to keep a straight face. "I'm sorry you had to give her back. Luisa, I know how much you loved her."

"It's okay, Colonel Tackett," Luisa said. "She's where she belongs. She's supposed to be with Isabel, not with me." Ric and Sonia stepped over to Luisa, enveloping her in a family embrace. She cried softly into their arms.

Matt's mom reached over and hugged him tightly. "You're a sweet boy," she said into the top of his head. "Even if you make me completely insane."

26

THE DOGS INSIDE THE SHELTER WERE barking like crazy. They jumped up on their hind legs, their tails wagging wildly, and jammed their noses through the bars. Scout and Matt's mom went over to say hi to each and every one of them as Matt wondered what was going through the dogs' minds. He imagined it was some version of *Please please please can you take me home with you—I'll be a good dog!* or *Are your pockets full of kibble?*

He was less sure about what Ric and Sonia were thinking. He couldn't read the expressions on their faces as they stepped into the shelter and took in the stacks of empty food bags, tied-up bags of trash, piles of wadded-up newspapers . . . and dogs. More and more dogs.

"Puppies!" Emanuel shouted. He ran to the indoor cages and squatted down next to the lowest one. A fluffy white nugget of a dog hopped up and did a happy dance at the sight of him, and Emanuel squealed with delight.

"Here it is," Luisa said nervously, holding her arms out wide.

Ric pressed his lips together. Sonia crossed her arms and spun in a slow circle, running her eyes over every inch of the place.

"*Hola.*" Dr. Correa came over and greeted the Dávilas warmly. They chatted in Spanish, and the vet led them on a tour of the facility.

"Emanuel," Sonia said over her shoulder, "*vámonos.*" He scurried to her side, and the little white dog whimpered sadly as she watched him go.

"It's going to be okay," Matt said softly to Luisa.

"What if they never let me come back here again?" Luisa's eyes filled with tears. "That would be the worst."

Scout sidled up and leaned against Luisa's leg, looking up at her sweetly.

"See—even Scout says it's going to be fine," Matt said.

"I hope you guys are right."

Matt's mom came inside. "Those dogs out there are a great bunch," she said. "There are a couple I'd even consider for my training program."

"Really, Colonel Tackett?" Luisa's eyes lit up. "That's amazing."

Dr. Correa and Luisa's family circled back toward them.

"And we couldn't have done any of that without her help," Dr. Correa was saying in English. "She showed up rain or shine and did the dirty work like it was nothing." She turned and winked at Luisa. "Your daughter is very special," she said to Ric and Sonia. "She has a special gift with animals—not everyone has that. But every great vet does."

Ric and Sonia were quiet. Ric had his hands on his hips and was staring at the floor, deep in thought. Sonia walked over to the cages and held up her hand to a sleepy cocoa-colored puppy. The dog raised its head and sniffed at her knuckles, then gave them a lick through the bars. Sonia smiled and whispered an endearment under her breath.

Luisa and Matt stood shoulder to shoulder and waited.

"I'll leave you guys to it," Dr. Correa said. She headed back to a terrier-size brown dog with big bat ears and a swoop of black down her forehead, who sat waiting patiently for her on an exam table.

"That dog looks a lot like Rosita," Luisa said sadly.

Rosita. Just the thought of her sent a pang through Matt's chest. He couldn't imagine how it felt for Luisa to picture her sweet, goofy face.

"You nursed that dog back to health?" Ric asked Luisa. "What did you call her—Rosita?"

Luisa nodded.

"When did you do this?" Sonia asked, genuinely puzzled.

"I don't know," Luisa said with a guilty shrug. "You guys have been really busy. I have lots of time to myself without school, so I came here when you were working."

"Every day?" Ric asked.

"Pretty much."

"I want to come here every day and see the doggies too!" Emanuel piped in. Sonia shushed him.

"And you clean these cages?" Sonia asked.

"Yes. And I feed the dogs and wash their bowls and talk to them a lot." She shrugged. "Whatever needs doing, I guess."

"But—how? Why—" Sonia fixed her eyes on her daughter's face, as if she'd find answers there. "Why is this so important to you?"

Luisa took a deep breath and looked at Matt, her brow furrowed. *Should I tell them everything?* she seemed to be asking him. He nodded. She turned to her parents and began to talk.

"I feel at home here," she said. "It's, like, the best place in the world—there's just so much love. Dr. Correa and Alberto care about every single one of the dogs. And there are so many—Mom, Dad, every day there's a new truckload of animals. It's so sad. There aren't enough families for them all, but people should be adopting these dogs because they're the sweetest . . ." She looked at Matt for backup.

"They're amazing," Matt said. "Every one of them just wants to be loved, like Rosita and Scout." As if on cue, Scout tipped his head to the side, perked up his ears, and opened his mouth for maximum charm.

"But they're satos, right?" Ric looked through the screen door at the dozens of dogs outside. "Satos are . . . wild."

"They can be, Dad, but they're not all like that, I swear. Most of them just want a family, that's all. They're not dangerous."

Ric and Sonia looked at each other. Luisa steadied herself, waiting for them to make their pronouncement.

"We're very proud of you, Luisa," Sonia said. Luisa's eyebrows shot up. That wasn't what she was expecting to hear.

"You're a good kid, Luisa," Ric said. "Except for this ill-advised adventure with Matt here—" He jerked a thumb in Matt's direction. "Which I'm going to blame entirely on Matt, at his suggestion."

Matt knew that was Ric's way of forgiving him, and he was silently—and deeply—relieved.

"And you're gifted with animals—always have been," Ric went on. "We just didn't know how important this was to you."

"It's very generous, what you've been doing for these dogs," Sonia said.

"And brave," Ric added.

"You really think so?" Luisa asked.

"We do," Ric said. "And if this is what you want to do with your time, then we'll support you."

Luisa's face lit up. She threw herself at her parents and wrapped them in a hug.

"You too, Matt," his mom said. "I can see how much you care about these satos, so we'll figure out a way to help them. Who knows—the next Scout might be one of those dogs out there. And it seems like the rescue organizations can use all the help they can get, so let's make some calls."

Matt was overwhelmed, once again, with his mom's compassion. She always seemed to know what mattered most to him—and always seemed to find a way to support him. He wrapped her in a hug, and she kissed the top of his head. "Thanks, Mom."

"There's one more thing," Sonia said, looking at Ric for confirmation. He hesitated, then nodded slightly begrudgingly, as if he'd lost this one. "Luisa, is there a dog here that you really like? Because you can bring one home."

"*What?*" Luisa screamed so loud that Emanuel covered his ears. She hugged her parents again, then jumped up and down cheering. Matt high-fived her with a loud *slap!*

Scout hopped up on his hind legs and waved his front paws in the air. When he saw Matt and Luisa spinning around the room with glee, he let out a long, loud, happy howl.

27

MATT LEANED BACK AGAINST THE COUCH. Scout lay across his legs. There was barely enough room for Luisa, who was squished at the other end. In her arms lay the brown dog with the black stripe on her head—the one who had reminded Matt of Rosita. Luisa had named her Dulce. She was passed out cold and snoring very loudly.

"Seriously, Scout?" Matt groused, wrapping his arms around Scout and pulling the dog higher onto his lap, giving Luisa and Dulce more room. Scout quickly fell sound asleep, sinking heavily into Matt's thighs.

Matt couldn't imagine life without Scout. Wherever Matt went, Scout was there. Whatever Matt did, Scout made it more fun. Whenever Matt was in trouble, Scout saved him. Scout was his constant companion, his shadow, his protector—his best friend.

Every one of those dogs at Dr. Correa's shelter could be someone's best friend too, he knew. And every pup there deserved the chance to have someone who loved them back, unconditionally, the way Matt loved Scout.

Matt was going to do everything he could to help make that happen, while he was still in Puerto Rico and after he got back home.

Scout twitched and flapped his paws in his sleep, probably chasing Rosita in a dream.

Matt's phone buzzed on the coffee table. He stretched to reach it, which wasn't easy without being able to move the lower half of his body—or without waking up the dogs.

He swiped to answer the incoming video call. The screen flashed on to reveal Dev, Amaiya, and Curtis mugging for the camera and shoving each other out of the way. Matt could see water behind them, and a tower of boulders behind that. They were at the ravine, their favorite swimming hole, where the ten-foot jump into the water never failed to get Matt's heart racing.

"What's up, Matt!" Dev howled like a TV announcer. "How's everything?"

"Hey, guys," Matt said, waving into the camera.

"Come back, man!" Curtis shouted over Dev's shoulder.

"Matt! Save me from these two dorks!" Amaiya jokingly pleaded. "You're the only sane one!"

Scout raised his head at the sound of familiar voices. Matt turned the camera toward him, and Scout blinked at the screen nonchalantly.

"Hi, Scout!" the kids called out. Scout yawned in reply.

"Guys, meet Luisa." Matt tipped the phone up so his friends at home could meet his friend on the island. "And Dulce."

"Hi, everyone." Luisa waved at the phone. "I've heard a ton about you guys."

"Hi, Luisa!" Amaiya said warmly.

"Oh, hey," Curtis said shyly. Then, "Oh my God, Dulce's so cute!"

"Whatever you do, Luisa," Dev said drily, "run, don't walk, away from Matt. You hear me?"

"Why didn't you tell me this last week?" Luisa laughed. "Before he got us into a ton of trouble?"

Matt turned the phone back around. "Okay, that's enough out of you two."

"I'm just making sure she knows the truth," Dev said. "Just kidding, Luisa!" he shouted into the phone so she could hear. "Matt is the best—send him back, would you?"

"He's all yours," Luisa called out.

"Admit that you miss us, dude," Dev said to Matt.

"I admit it," Matt said. He hadn't had time to think about how much he missed his friends, although now that he saw their faces, he knew it was true.

But he had things to do in Puerto Rico, and he wasn't ready to go home just yet.

"So what've you and Scout and Luisa been up to?" Amaiya asked. "Anything fun?"

"Well," Matt replied with a mischievous grin, "who wants me to bring them home a sato puppy?"

ACKNOWLEDGMENTS

The butterball currently asleep on my couch was once a sato like Rosita, and my family and I are so lucky to have her. We named her Vida because she's full of life—and adds so much to ours. She also chews our things, steals my side of the bed, and suckers everyone into giving her too many treats, but we don't mind.

Brian and the goons, thank you for putting up with all this and loving me anyway. LYTS. Virginia Wing, we know you secretly love the dog, but we promise not to tell her. Thank you for so, so much. Kunsang Bhuti and Tenzin Dekyi, thanks for your endless kindness. Susan Friedman, thank you for all the books all these years! Three cheers to the Society for Animal Care and the amazing fourth graders who dedicate recess to helping our furry, scaly, and slithery friends.

Thank you to the Scout Pack: Margaret Anastas at Harper; Les Morgenstein, Josh Bank, and Sara Shandler at Alloy; Katelyn Hales at the Robin Straus Agency; and the Harper sales, marketing, and publicity groups.

Luana Horry, Hayley Wagreich, Romy Golan, and Robin Straus—forgive me for repeating myself, but you guys are truly the best. Thank you. Adriana M. Martínez Figueroa, thank you for the keen eye and thoughtful guidance.

Thanks to Animal Lighthouse Rescue, The Sato Project, and all the rescue organizations for your hard work. You bring joy to many people!

Love dogs?
You may also like...

COUNTDOWN

BASED ON THE DC COMICS SERIES

GREG COX

ACE BOOKS, NEW YORK

THE BERKLEY PUBLISHING GROUP
Published by the Penguin Group
Penguin Group (USA) Inc.
375 Hudson Street, New York, New York 10014, USA
Penguin Group (Canada), 90 Eglinton Avenue East, Suite 700, Toronto, Ontario M4P 2Y3, Canada
(a division of Pearson Penguin Canada Inc.)
Penguin Books Ltd., 80 Strand, London WC2R 0RL, England
Penguin Group Ireland, 25 St. Stephen's Green, Dublin 2, Ireland (a division of Penguin Books Ltd.)
Penguin Group (Australia), 250 Camberwell Road, Camberwell, Victoria 3124, Australia
(a division of Pearson Australia Group Pty. Ltd.)
Penguin Books India Pvt. Ltd., 11 Community Centre, Panchsheel Park, New Delhi—110 017, India
Penguin Group (NZ), 67 Apollo Drive, Rosedale, North Shore 0632, New Zealand
(a division of Pearson New Zealand Ltd.)
Penguin Books (South Africa) (Pty.) Ltd., 24 Sturdee Avenue, Rosebank, Johannesburg 2196,
South Africa

Penguin Books Ltd., Registered Offices: 80 Strand, London WC2R 0RL, England

This is an original publication of The Berkley Publishing Group.

Visit DC Comics online at www.dccomics.com or at keyword DC Comics on America Online.

PRINTING HISTORY
Ace trade paperback edition / July 2009

Library of Congress Cataloging-in-Publication Data

Cox, Greg, 1959–
   Countdown : based on the DC comics series / Greg Cox.—Ace trade paperback ed.
      p. cm.
   ISBN 978-0-441-01718-8
   1. Heroes—Fiction.   2. Gods—Fiction.   I. Title.
   PS3603.O9C68 2009
   813'.6—dc22

                                                              2009010402

PRINTED IN THE UNITED STATES OF AMERICA

10   9   8   7   6   5   4   3   2   1

Acknowledgments

As with my previous DC Comics novelizations, there's no way I could include all of the plot and characters from the entire fifty-two-issue series this book is based on. Sacrifices had to be made, and I hope that readers won't be too disappointed to find that certain scenes and characters did not make it into this adaptation. Readers who want the full story should definitely check out the original comic book series.

Needless to say, I once again have to thank all the talented writers and artists and editors who worked on the actual comics. I scoured their scripts, sketches, and final pages eagerly as I strove to capture the feel of their epic story in prose.

I also have to thank my own editors, John Morgan and Chris Cerasi at DC Comics and Ginjer Buchanan at Ace, for, among other things, waiting patiently while I had a suspicious kidney removed. I truly appreciated their concern and consideration during a difficult time. (Don't worry, I'm all better now!) Thanks also to my agents, Russ Galen and Ann Behar, who played an important part in making this book happen. And to my favorite comic book store, Captain Blue Hen Comics in Newark, Delaware, for keeping me well supplied in "research materials."

Finally, my girlfriend, Karen Palinko, deserves special honors for taking care of both me and our growing household of pets while I was recovering from surgery and trying to get this book finished more or less on time. She was truly a super heroine in her own right.

This novel was adapted from the *Countdown to Final Crisis* comic series, originally published in fifty-two weekly issues by DC Comics, from July 2007 to June 2008. The series was created by the following people:

EDITORS
Michael Carlin
Michael Marts

ASSISTANT & ASSOCIATE EDITORS
Elizabeth V. Gherlein
Jeanine Schaeffer

WRITERS
Tony Bedard
Adam Beechen
Paul Dini
Justin Gray
Sean McKeever
Jimmy Palmiotti

STORY CONSULTANT
Keith Giffen

COVER ARTISTS
Matt Banning
Ed Benes
Mariah Benes
Talent Caldwell
Claudio Castellini
Ian Churchill
Shane Davis
Rachel Dodson
Terry Dodson
JG Jones
Karl Kerschl
Scott Kolins
Adam Kubert
Andy Kubert
Norm Rapmund
Stephane Roux
Alex Sinclair
Tim Townsend
Pete Woods

PENCILLERS
Al Barrionuevo
Jim Calafiore
Dennis Calero
Tom Derenick
Manuel Garcia
Jamal Igle
Scott Kolins
Ron Lim
David Lopez
Carlos Magno
Mike Norton
Howard Porter
Jesus Saiz
Jim Starlin
Freddie Williams II
Pete Woods

INKERS
Dennis Calero
Keith Champagne
Wayne Faucher
Don Hillsman II
Scott Kolins
Jay Leisten
Alvaro Lopez
Mark McKenna
Jimmy Palmiotti
Andrew Pepoy
Jack Purcell
Rodney Ramos
John Stanisci
Art Thibert
Freddie Williams II
Pete Woods

38 AND COUNTING.

APOKOLIPS.

The torture chamber reeked of fear, pain, and blood. Humanoid bodies hung on meat-hooks from the vaulted ceiling of the subterranean chamber, buried deep beneath the smoldering surface of an alien world. The grandiose architecture blended the medieval with the futuristic, the high-tech trappings failing to conceal the primal horror of the scene. Glowing rods, embedded in the gloomy stone walls, cast a sanguinary crimson radiance over the chamber. Agonized whimpers escaped the lips of suffering wretches who had long since lost the strength to scream. A stooped figure in a hooded purple robe applied a scalpel to the bare skull of yet another prisoner, who was strapped onto a cold steel operating table. The harsh white glare of elevated spotlights threw the unfortunate victim's captivity into even starker relief. A worn leather gag muffled his cries of torment. His anguished eyes held no trace of hope, only dread. Blood from the incision trickled down the side of his head before dripping into an ornate basin at the hooded figure's feet. The steady drip of the blood punctuated the pitiful moans of the prisoners awaiting their turn. Desaad, chief inquisitor of the planet Apokolips, savored every whimper.

"What is the worth of a single life?" he reflected, moved to philosophize by the charnel house atmosphere of the dungeon. Bangs of stringy black hair drooped out from beneath the top of his hood. Cruel blue eyes peered from his sly, vulpine features. "How does one measure its power? Even the humblest of souls touches others, its ever-widening ripples spread across the universe, altering for better or for worse the destinies of countless beings on infinite worlds." He scowled in disappointment as the Lowlie upon the table inconveniently went into its death throes after only the briefest exploratory surgery upon the pain centers of its brain; Desaad had apparently miscalculated the wretch's ability to withstand the procedure without anesthesia. "And yet, for all the good and ill that life accomplishes, it perishes at last with an imperceptible whisper . . . as if it had never existed at all."

A deep bass voice intruded upon his soliloquy. A looming black shadow fell across the operating table. "Your analogy is depressingly nihilistic."

"A thousand pardons, master." Desaad laid his scalpel down beside the corpse of his latest experiment and turned to greet the source of the shadow.

Darkseid, supreme ruler of dread Apokolips, stood atop a stone stairway looking down into the dungeon. His craggy gray features looked as though they had been chiseled out of solid granite. Crimson eyes glowed like embers beneath his beetling brows. A somber blue cuirass encased his stocky frame. A wide metallic belt girded his massive torso. A matching blue helmet, gloves, and boots completed his imperial raiment. Over eight feet tall, he towered over the spindly torturer.

Although quick to apologize to his master, Desaad felt emboldened to speak further. "And yet, no disrespect meant, of course, do you refute its ultimate conclusion?"

"Were I hobbled by your limitations, I would say no," Darkseid conceded. He turned away from the doorway and Desaad scurried after him, hiking up the hem of his robe as he crept up the stairs to a war room one floor above. "Fortunately, my vision encompasses a greater horizon."

Darkseid contemplated a chessboard upon which were arrayed miniature figurines fashioned in the likeness of various inhabitants of the planet Earth. That seemingly insignificant world, separated from Apokolips by vast gulfs of time and space, had often figured in Darkseid's ambitious designs and machinations. That his plans for universal conquest were frequently opposed by Earth's myriad superpowered champions only made that world a more tempting prize. Joining his master before the table, Desaad identified the figures as representations of Superman, Captain Marvel, Black Adam, Eclipso, Harley Quinn, Donna Troy, Jason Todd, Klarion the Witch Boy, and many other Terran nuisances, both celebrated and obscure. He looked forward to the possibility of treating all or more of said personages to his singular hospitality. He licked his lips in anticipation of testing their individual pain thresholds. *What new campaign,* he wondered, *does the master have in store?*

"I see the time fast approaching," Darkseid revealed, "when existence itself shall be re-created and Darkseid shall be its architect." He plucked a tiny statue of James Bartholomew Olsen from the table and repositioned it upon the board. "But your venomous tongue speaks at least one truth, Desaad. Even the humblest soul touches others. . . ."

37 AND COUNTING.

GOTHAM CITY.

Arkham Asylum, home for the criminally insane, looked like something out of an old Basil Karlo movie. The forbidding Gothic edifice, with its sooty brick walls, slate shingles, and turrets, was located on the outskirts of Gotham, not far from the DiAngelo Sewage Treatment Plant. A noxious miasma wafted up from the river as Jimmy Olsen approached the infamous asylum, which usually housed any number of Gotham's most notorious homicidal maniacs. Iron rods barred the windows. Razor wire topped the spiked metal fence enclosing the hospital and its grounds. Gargoyles perched on the eaves of the old Victorian mansion. The red-haired cub reporter and photographer swallowed hard as he snapped off a couple of shots of the asylum's gloomy exterior with his new digital camera. Maybe this wasn't such a good idea after all?

Then again, he thought, *if I want the Chief to take me seriously as an investigative journalist, and not just a photographer, I need to follow a story wherever it takes me . . . even to Gotham and this creepy old place.*

Armed guards escorted Jimmy to a checkpoint outside the maximum security ward, where he was asked to strip down to his boxers. "Just a precaution, Mr. Olsen," a guard explained. A sign posted on the wall read:

NO
WEAPONS, COINS, UMBRELLAS,
PLANTS, BOTTLED WATER,
PLAYING CARDS, OR COOLERS
BEYOND THIS POINT.

Guess they're not taking any chances, Jimmy realized. Embarrassed by the strip search, he wished that he hadn't worn the boxers decorated with Superman's S-shield on them today. His press pass dangled on a cord around his neck. A chilly draft raised goose bumps on his exposed skin. "Maybe you guys could turn up the heat in here?"

"Sorry about that," a guard explained as he swept a metal-detecting wand under Jimmy's outstretched arms. Jimmy's wristwatch elicited a beep, but otherwise he was clean. "Mr. Freeze brings the temperature down in the entire building."

Right, Jimmy thought. *I forgot about him.* Not for the first time, he decided that Gotham had way too many scary villains. *This is why I live in Metropolis. Sure we get plenty of mad scientists, giant robots, and alien invasions, but we have Superman too.* Gotham just had Batman, who was almost as spooky as his foes.

Mercifully, the guards let him put his clothes back on before admitting him to the ward. Locked doors lined both sides of a long corridor that stretched down one entire wing of the former mansion. Closed-circuit TV cameras tracked Jimmy's progress as he made his way down the hallway. His footsteps echoed on the scuffed linoleum floor. The refrigerated air smelled of unwashed bodies and antiseptic. Sobs, cackles, and hysterical laughter escaped the inmates' cells. One prisoner (Two-Face?) argued vehemently with himself. Horizontal slits were cut at eye level into the sturdy iron doors of the cells. Jimmy could practically feel the lunatics' eyes upon him. He nervously fingered his wristwatch.

"What do 4-D beings look like?" a voice hissed at him. Crazed, dilated eyes peeked out through the slit in a door. "Could they be inches away from our 3-D world, ready to eat our chocolate cake?"

"I . . . *um* . . . hope not." Jimmy quickened his pace, the faster to get away from those manic eyes. *Who the heck was* that?

At last, he came to the end of the corridor, where Arkham's most dangerous inmate occupied a special cell of his own. The Joker squatted on the floor in front of Jimmy, behind a thick wall of clear, bulletproof plastic. A canvas straitjacket bound the evil clown's arms against his chest. His head was drooped forward, concealing his face, so that only his wild green hair could be seen. His bare feet, bleached white as chalk, emerged from the trousers of a bright orange institutional jumpsuit. His bleak cell was furnished with only the barest of necessities: a cot, a sink, a commode. Disk-shaped air holes in the plastic wall allowed Jimmy to hear the Joker chuckling quietly under his breath.

What's so funny?

Jimmy cleared his throat, but the Joker didn't give him a chance to introduce himself.

"Lookie, lookie, it's Superman's pal, Jimmy Olsen! The redheaded stepchild of the *Daily Planet*." His shrill, sarcastic voice made Jimmy's blood run cold. "Let me see the watch, Jimbo. Get Superman on the line. Nurse Ratched won't let me watch the World Series!"

Jimmy got the reference. Apparently, the Joker was a Jack Nicholson fan. He caught himself hiding his signal-watch behind his back, then attempted to get down to business. "I . . . I'd like to ask you a few questions, Joker."

His voice quavered only a little.

"I'd like to strangle your pink little neck until your eyes pop out of your head," the Joker said savagely, revealing the malice behind the mirth. He kept staring down at the floor, not even bothering to make eye contact with the young man whose life he had just threatened.

Jimmy's mouth went as dry as the Great Kahndaqi Desert. His face paled behind his freckles. Part of him wanted to turn around and catch the first train back to Metropolis, but the reporter in him was determined to stand his ground, just like Lois or Clark would. *Don't let him spook you,* he urged himself. *You can do this.*

· "It's about Lex Luthor," Jimmy said. "There's a rumor going around the underworld that you killed him—or tried to—after that big Crisis in Metropolis a year ago. But there are also stories that you and Luthor have been working together occasionally." He tried to fix the Joker with a steely gaze. "So what's the story, Joker? Are you in cahoots with Luthor? Or did you murder him?"

"Murder Lex?" The Joker looked positively stricken by the question. His lurid grin turned upside down. "Are you telling me Lex is *dead*?"

"I don't know," Jimmy admitted. Superman's archenemy hadn't been seen in months. Nobody knew if he was just lying low, plotting some campaign against the Man of Steel, or if he was truly dead. "Do *you*?"

"Poor Lex . . . dead? No! Say it isn't so!" The prisoner grew increasingly agitated. Leaping to his feet, he lunged at the plastic divider separating him from Jimmy. "Who could have done such a terrible thing? Was it *you*?"

Jimmy recoiled from the wall. "No! I . . . I was hoping you might know."

"Know *what*?" the Joker asked.

"Where Lex is. If he's really dead."

The Joker looked confused. "Do you know?"

"I'm asking you."

"Asking me what?" the Joker demanded. "If I'm in on the joke?"

Jimmy decided he'd had enough. "Okay, this was obviously a bad idea. You don't know anything."

"I know more than you, Jimbo!" The Joker pressed his face against the transparent plastic so that one of the holes circled his right eye like a monocle. His malevolent grin stretched from ear to ear. "You're a photographer. You have the all-seeing eye of the camera, but your lens cap is still on. You're out of focus. You can't see the Big Picture!"

"What Big Picture?" Jimmy challenged him.

The Joker's bloodshot eye nearly bulged through the circular gap in the wall. "Come closer and I'll show you."

"No way, Joker." Jimmy knew better than to get too near the murderous clown. Even bound and caged, the Joker was nobody to let your guard down around. "What's the Big Picture?"

"It's a universal conspiracy, Jimbo! It's all around us. Something's not quite right with the world. Haven't you noticed? Haven't you *felt* it?"

By now, Jimmy's goose bumps had goose bumps, but he tried not to let the Joker's unhinged ravings get to him. "You're crazy and locked away. How would you know?"

The Joker shrugged his shoulder beneath the straitjacket. "You're right.

I'm a conspiracy nut! And you know what else? Oh, this is the kicker. I *did* kill Lex! Or rather, I killed *a* Lex Luthor, but not *our* Lex Luthor. Doppelgangers gone wild, Jimbo! When Earths collide . . . *hah!*" His maniacal laughter escaped his cell as Jimmy turned away from the imprisoned clown. "You slay me! Let me slay you in return!"

"Freak show," Jimmy muttered. *Talk about a waste of time!* Out of the corner of his eye, he spotted an armored guard escorting Killer Croc to a vacant cell. The scaly green monster was over seven feet tall and looked more like his reptilian namesake than a human being. Slitted vertical pupils divided his bloodred eyes. Drool dripped from saurian jaws. His clawed hands were cuffed tightly behind his back, while heavy leather straps bound his arms to his sides. A ridged tail swept the floor behind him. Jimmy recalled that Waylon Jones suffered from a unique genetic disorder that had slowly transformed him into a human crocodile. The cannibalistic murderer towered over his captor.

"Keep moving, Jones!" the guard ordered through his protective faceplate. Croc's escort was decked out in full riot gear, for safety's sake. An electronic cattle prod goaded the prisoner forward. "Give me any more trouble and you won't get fed tonight! No raw meat for you!"

Jimmy considered snapping a picture, but then the Joker called out from his cell, distracting him. "So long, Jimbo! Be a sweetie and send me the obituaries!" He rocked back and forth upon the floor, convulsing with fiendish glee. His diabolical laughter echoed loudly. "Y'all come back real soon, ya hear?"

Uh-huh, Jimmy thought. *Like that's going to happen.* He fished his cell phone from his pocket. *Better touch base with Lois, and let her know this whole thing has been a dead end. . . .*

A ferocious roar suddenly drowned out the Joker's hilarity. The guard shouted in alarm. Twisted metal screamed in protest. Jimmy spun around to see Killer Croc break free from his restraints. The cuffs came apart, the leather straps snapping like rubber bands. Electricity crackled as the panicked guard jabbed Croc with the prod, but the high-voltage jolt only served to enrage the reptilian monster further. An immense green arm smashed the guard into the wall hard enough to crack the man's body armor. Hissing furiously, his tail savagely whipping the air behind him, Croc took hold of the hapless guard and bit the man's head off, helmet and all, in an explosion of blood and gore.

Holy cow! Jimmy thought.

It all happened so fast. One minute Jimmy was calling the *Planet*. The next, he found himself alone in the dismal corridor with a bloodthirsty carnivore. His cell phone slipped unnoticed from his fingers. He groped frantically for his signal-watch, desperate to summon Superman, but Croc was already lunging toward him. Frozen in shock, Jimmy could only watch in horror as Croc's blood-splattered jaws opened wide for him. Razor-sharp claws swiped at his face. . . .

And then things got *really* strange.

At the last minute, right before Croc's claws ripped off his freckles, Jimmy's neck *stretched* out of the way of the monstrous claws, elongating like taffy until it was at least five feet long! Seconds later, as Jimmy threw himself backward, his arms and legs stretched as well, so that the charging crocodile-man missed him entirely. The elastic limbs, extending far beyond his sleeves and trousers, flailed about wildly as the startled reporter tumbled clumsily onto the floor.

Huh? Jimmy thought. His tangled limbs looked like a pile of pink spaghetti. *Am I really doing this?*

Croc's momentum carried him past his intended prey. His claws and fangs meeting only empty air, he skidded to a stop and turned to look for Jimmy. A bewildered expression momentarily replaced the naked bloodlust on his bestial face. His slitted eyes blinked in puzzlement. "What the hell?"

Good question.

He lunged at Jimmy again, and the reporter kicked one leg up to defend himself. To his amazement, the leg extended halfway down the hall so that his heel connected with Croc's chin. The blow, which seemed to startle the monster more than damage him, only slowed Croc down for a moment. He eyed Jimmy warily as he stalked toward the fallen reporter, whose elastic limbs retracted in fear from the advancing saurian. Scooting backward on his butt, Jimmy found himself trapped against the unyielding stone wall behind him. There was no escape. . . .

"These people pump me so fulla meds, I can't even trust my own eyes anymore," Croc groused. Resentment permeated his gravelly voice. The creature's slavering jaws were only a few feet away from Jimmy now. "But I'll bet you taste fine. Maybe just a little rubbery . . ."

Jimmy frantically pushed the signal button on his wristwatch. In theory, the watch emitted a supersonic alarm that Superman—and only Superman—could hear anywhere on Earth. The Man of Steel would make short work of Killer Croc, but apparently he was occupied elsewhere. *Probably rescuing a sinking ocean liner,* Jimmy figured, *or saving the entire world from a killer asteroid.* Unfortunately, not even Superman could be in two places at once.

A vivid memory of the guard's head exploding between Croc's jaws flashed through Jimmy's mind. Closing his eyes in anticipation of the end, he wondered if his gory demise would rate page one of the *Planet.* . . .

This wasn't exactly how I wanted to make the front page.

A loud electric zap caught him by surprise, even as a bright blue flash penetrated his closed eyelids. Croc let out an agonized roar, only inches away from Jimmy. The reporter's eyes snapped open and he saw his attacker stiffening in shock as an entire team of Arkham security guards attacked him from behind with their stun rods powered up to the max.

Reinforcements, Jimmy realized. *Thank goodness!*

Multiple electrodes succeeded where that lone guard's cattle prod had failed. Amazingly, Waylon Jones managed to stay on his feet for a few minutes, despite the relentless galvanic barrage. Fiery blue sparks raced across his scaly hide. He twitched spasmodically like a frog in a science experiment. Smoke rose from his head and shoulders. The unmistakable scent of ozone suffused the air. Tiny hairs rose up all over Jimmy's body just from his proximity to the massive electrical discharges. Croc roared one last time before toppling face-first onto the floor. Jimmy had to quickly roll out of the way to avoid being squashed beneath the falling monster.

"Jeez Louise!" he exclaimed.

The guards ignored Jimmy as they hurried to secure the prisoner. "Cuff him before he recovers, boys!" their leader ordered gruffly. He scowled at the bloody remains of the unlucky guard. "And don't be gentle about it!"

"Jimmy? What's happening?" An anxious voice emerged from his dropped cell phone. "Jimmy. . . !"

Climbing unsteadily to his feet, he quickly retrieved the phone from the floor. "Lois? I'll have to call you back. . . ." He wasn't sure he was up to telling her the whole story, even if he understood it himself. Now that the danger was over, he felt drained, exhausted, and more than a little confused. *What was all that freaky stretching about?!*

The guards dragged Croc into a waiting cell. Satisfied that the monster was under wraps for the time being, their leader finally checked on Jimmy. A badge on his front pocket identified him as Lucas Sevick, Chief of Security. Jimmy wondered idly if he let his men call him "Chief," unlike a certain editor in chief he knew.

"Mighty brave, standin' your ground like that," Sevick commented. Glancing again at what was left of the unfortunate guard, he sounded surprised to find Jimmy still alive. "How'd you keep Croc from shredding you?"

Jimmy fingered his neck experimentally. It seemed to be in one piece, and back to its usual proportions. "Uh, I kind of thought he did." He glanced down at his arms and legs. They certainly felt like rubber at the moment, but they looked perfectly normal. *Did I just imagine them stretching like that? Maybe all that adrenaline was messing with my head. . . .*

He decided not to mention his inexplicable elasticity to Sevick. Jimmy was a visitor to Arkham, not an inmate, and he intended to keep it that way. The last place you want to sound crazy is a lunatic asylum. Jimmy couldn't wait to get out of the creepy madhouse.

If he hurried, he could still catch the six o'clock train back to Metropolis.

NEW YORK CITY.

"Shazam!"

Mary whispered the magic word. Once upon a time, this would have summoned an enchanted lightning bolt, transforming her into Mary Marvel, the World's Mightiest Maiden, but now nothing happened. No thunderclap boomed overhead; no flash of lightning lit up her private hospital room. Her everyday clothes were not transmuted into a super heroine's colorful costume. No symbolic thunderbolt adorned her chest. She was still just Mary Batson, an ordinary teenage girl.

Where did the magic go? she wondered for perhaps the thousandth time.

Ever since waking from a coma a few weeks ago, she'd said the word dozens of times a day. Sometimes she'd even wake herself up by shouting it in her sleep. But always with the same dispiriting results. *Nothing.*

She sat on the edge of her hospital bed, a small bundle of personal belongings packed by her side. With her auburn hair, blue eyes, and slim figure, she looked like the proverbial girl next door. She wore a bright red Windbreaker over a beige sweater and blue jeans. Bernice, her friendly physical therapist, appeared in the doorway. "Time to go, kiddo," she said cheerfully. "You must be excited, finally getting out of this place after all your recovery time."

According to the doctors, Mary had been in a coma for nearly three months. *Ever since that big battle with Black Adam, in other words.* Adam, the evil counterpart of Mary's brother, Captain Marvel, had declared war on the whole world, and the entire Marvel Family had joined forces to stop him. The last thing she remembered was Black Adam striking her hard enough to knock her all the way from Sydney, Australia, to northern India. She had crashed to earth in front of the Taj Mahal—and woken up in this Manhattan hospital ten weeks later. Her powers had been AWOL ever since, along with her friends and family.

"Yeah, sure." Clutching her bag, she joined Bernice in the bustling corridor outside. Doctors, nurses, patients, and visitors hurried past them as they strolled down the hallway. Directional signs pointed the way toward Checkout and Radiology. A loudspeaker paged doctors whose names Mary didn't recognize. Antiseptic suffused the air. A family of visitors, bearing flowers and gifts for a loved one, provoked a familiar pang in Mary's heart. "I have to ask you again, Bernice. Are there any messages for me?"

The physical therapist shook her head sadly. "We've been over that, honey."

"I know," Mary said. "It's just that I was here so long. I thought one of them would have called." She didn't understand. Where was her twin brother, Billy, and their best friend, Freddy Freeman? Why hadn't they come to visit her? The boys' continuing absence filled her with anxiety. Had something terrible happened to them? According to the Internet, which she had searched from her hospital bed, Black Adam had been defeated eventually, but neither Captain Marvel nor Captain Marvel Jr. had been seen or heard from since. Had they lost their powers too?

Feeling lost and abandoned, Mary let Bernice escort her to the checkout desk, where a gray-haired administrator presented her with a sheaf of documents. A plaque on her desk identified the older woman as Helen Powell. "I have your release papers ready to go, Ms. Batson."

"Thanks." Mary sat down opposite the older woman. She had been fretting about this moment for weeks. "But I—I'm afraid I can't pay. I have no money or insurance. . . ."

"Don't worry," Ms. Powell reassured her. "Your bill was settled by your brother."

"Billy?" Hope flared in Mary's heart. She knew that Billy had survived their clash with Black Adam because he had apparently arranged to have her transferred from Agra to New York, but she had started to fear that she was never going to see him again. "He's here?"

"Not anymore," Ms. Powell said. "He stopped by this morning just long enough to make the payment."

"But he must have left *something* for me," Mary insisted, more confused than ever. "A note, a phone number, anything?" She had already tried calling home to Fawcett City, only to discover that Billy's old number had been disconnected. Ditto for Freddy's. Both boys seemed to have vanished and left no forwarding address.

Helen Powell handed Mary a folded piece of paper. "Just this."

I knew it! Mary thought jubilantly. *Billy would never just disappear on me.* Her spirits sank, however, as she opened the note and read the terse message inside:

Mary. Don't try to find me. B.

"No," she whispered hoarsely. This wasn't like Billy at all. She desperately wanted to dismiss the note as a fake, but she recognized her brother's handwriting. Deep in her heart, she knew it was true. For some unfathomable reason, Billy had ditched her, perhaps for good.

I'm on my own.

Still in shock, she made it out of the hospital to the sidewalk outdoors. New York City rose up around her, huge and intimidating. The brisk fall weather was startling. It had been springtime when Black Adam had sent her crashing to earth like a fallen angel. *I missed an entire summer.* A cloudy gray sky vaulted above the towering skyscrapers. The lofty clouds called out to Mary, reminding her that once she had been able to soar among them. She couldn't resist trying the magic word one more time.

"Shazam!"

A boom of thunder raised her hopes, but a sudden cloudburst doused them a second later. Rain poured down from the sky, soaking her to the skin. Mary chuckled bitterly at the cruel joke Fate seemed to have played on her. The thunder was just thunder. There was nothing magic about it anymore.

Just like me.

Wet, cold, and alone, she left the hospital behind and began walking.

36 AND COUNTING.

METROPOLIS.

"Let me get this straight," Perry White growled. "I do a photographer a favor by sending him on a reporter's assignment—I send you all the way to Gotham City—and you come back with *nothing*?"

The surly editor in chief of the *Daily Planet* glared at Jimmy from behind his cluttered walnut desk. A fuming stogie was clenched between his teeth. Venetian blinds and a closed door concealed the interior of Perry's office from the bullpen outside. File cabinets and bulletin boards lined the walls. A mug of black coffee sat atop the page layouts on the desk. An old-fashioned manual typewriter occupied a spare desk in the corner.

Jimmy winced at his boss's irate tone. "Like I told Lois on the phone, Chief, there was nothing to get. The Joker just babbled like a crazy person."

"What about all that commotion I heard when you called?" Lois Lane asked. The *Planet*'s star reporter leaned against a filing cabinet by the door, sipping a cup of coffee. She had graciously offered to provide Jimmy with some moral support when he filled Perry in on his fruitless trip to Arkham. "What was *that* all about?"

"Oh, that," Jimmy mumbled. He wasn't sure what part of yesterday's close call bothered him the most: the fact that Killer Croc had almost eaten him, or how he had *stretched* out of the way just in time. *Probably that last part,* he decided, reluctant to divulge all the weirdo details to either Lois or Perry. He didn't want them to think that he had snapped under the pressure and hallucinated the whole thing. "Nothing . . . nothing important."

"Can we stay on point here?" Perry said impatiently. "I've still got a paper to put out, and we need a new angle on—" A sudden boom from outside the building cut short his tirade. The deafening blast rattled the window behind him. "Great Caesar's Ghost!" he exclaimed. The cigar tumbled from his lips. *"Now* what?"

All three journalists raced to the window, which offered a spectacular view of downtown Metropolis. Only seconds ago it had been a clear fall day, but now ominous black clouds obscured the sun. Bright golden flashes lit up the roiling clouds from inside. For a moment, Jimmy thought that maybe it was just a freak thunderstorm, but then coruscating bolts of shimmering yellow energy blasted down from the sky, wreaking havoc on the city below. A destructive beam tore through an elevated billboard for Sundollar Coffee, setting it ablaze, while another ray blasted apart a rooftop water tower. Gallons of spilled water instantly evaporated into steam, adding to the turbulent atmosphere. More beams lanced through the air, barely missing vulnerable skyscrapers and clock towers. Thunderous booms accompanied the devastating fireworks.

"Olsen!" Perry shouted. He stomped out the fallen stogie while still keeping his gaze glued to the fearsome spectacle outside. "Get down there with your camera!"

Jimmy was already out the door. Eschewing the elevators, he raced down the stairs to the first floor, thirty-seven stories below, and dashed across the lobby to the sidewalk outside, where he encountered a scene of utter pandemonium. Frightened citizens ran for shelter, looking back over their shoulders at the lethal pyrotechnics overhead. Their panicked cries were all but drowned out by the cacophonous din. Drivers abandoned their vehicles midtraffic as they joined the stampede on the sidewalks. Jimmy backed up against the Daily Planet Building's granite façade in order to avoid being trampled. He was anxious to capture the chaos on film, but first he took a moment to activate his signal-watch. *Superman probably already knows about this emergency,* he figured, *but it can't hurt to alert him just in case.*

Raising his digital camera to his right eye, he snapped off some quick reaction shots. Most everyone around him seemed to be running for safety, but he was startled to see a shell-shocked family of three standing frozen in terror right in the middle of the sidewalk. Baseball caps, disposable cameras, and souvenir T-shirts marked them unmistakably as tourists, new to the Big Apricot. A white-faced mother clutched a pigtailed toddler to her chest, while her husband stared aghast at the tumult all around them. Unlike the seasoned natives of the city, who knew what to do when Metropolis was under attack, as happened twice a week or so, the clueless trio looked like they didn't know which way to turn. They were practically asking to be collateral damage.

"Hey!" Jimmy shouted at the family, concerned for their safety. "You can't just stand there!"

Sure enough, a sizzling bolt of energy slammed into the skyscraper behind them. The southwest corner of the roof exploded, blasting a heavy stone gargoyle into pieces. Shattered rubble rained down from the blasted cornice, plunging straight toward the defenseless family, who were only seconds away from being pulped. Letting go of his camera, Jimmy instinctively ran to their rescue even though he knew it was already too late to save them.

Or was it?

To his amazement, he put on a sudden burst of speed that instantly ate up the distance between him and the endangered tourists. He grabbed on to them with both arms and whisked them down the sidewalk only a second before the plummeting debris crashed into the pavement behind him. Shards of broken masonry exploded into the air, leaving deep fissures in the sidewalk, but Jimmy had already carried the potential fatalities safely clear of the flying shrapnel. Over half a block from the smoking wreckage, Jimmy slowed to a stop and let go of the unscathed tourists, who looked dazed and confused by both their brush with death and their unexpected rescue.

"Mother of God," the woman whispered in shock. She stared at the shattered stretch of sidewalk where she and her loved ones had been standing only moments before. It took her a minute to fully grasp what had just occurred. She hugged her daughter like she never wanted to let go while gazing thankfully at Jimmy. "You saved us!"

"Wow!" the husband exclaimed. He scratched his head in confusion as he contemplated the distance they had covered in a matter of seconds. He looked at Jimmy. "How'd you do it, buddy?"

Jimmy had no idea. *What's happening to me?* he wondered. *Yesterday I was Plastic Man; today I'm the Flash?* He was at a loss to explain it. "Uh . . ."

"It's like those stories you hear," the father theorized, "about old ladies gaining super-strength to lift a car off a baby!"

"Yeah, that must be it," Jimmy agreed hurriedly, even though he didn't buy that explanation for a second. This was way too weird for that. But before he could give the unsettling mystery any more thought, a high-pitched keening, almost like a scream, drew all eyes upward. The scream grew louder by the second—and seemed to be heading right for them. "That sound! Something else is falling. . . !"

He barely got the words out of his mouth. The shrill keening gave way to an earth-shattering explosion as *something* slammed into the middle of Shuster Avenue with the force of a meteor strike. The impact felt like an earthquake, almost knocking Jimmy off his feet. Abandoned cars and trucks were tossed into the air like Tonka Toys, their windshields blown out by the shock wave. The uprooted vehicles crashed down onto the shattered asphalt and each other. Clouds of dust and pulverized concrete billowed up from the crash site.

Holy cow! Jimmy thought, his head ringing. *What* was *that?*

Thankfully, he didn't think that the unidentified falling object had landed on top of anyone. Plus, also on the bright side, the tremendous crash had kept the puzzled family from asking any more questions about how exactly he had saved them. Checking on the tourists, he was relieved to see them scurrying toward the lobby of the Planet Building. They'd be safer there than on the streets, even though the worst of the crisis seemed to have passed. Glancing upward, Jimmy saw the stormy black clouds dispersing. Sunlight and blue skies poked through the smoke from countless small fires throughout the city. As the ringing in his ears faded away, he realized that the thunderous booms had ceased as well. No more energy bolts stabbed down from the heavens. The sirens of racing emergency vehicles blared in the background. Whatever had transpired overhead, it appeared to be over.

Or so Jimmy hoped.

Holding a handkerchief over his mouth and nostrils to keep out the airborne dust and grit, he crept cautiously toward the lip of the enormous crater carved out by the *something*'s crash landing. The dust clouds began to settle, offering a clearer view of the devastation. As Jimmy made his way over the rubble, he had no idea what he expected to find at the bottom of the pit. A giant glowing meteorite? A crashed alien spacecraft? Bizarro? Here in Metropolis, anything was possible. Camera in hand, he peered over the edge of the precipice.

"Ohmigod." His blue eyes widened in shock. "Lightray!"

The battered figure lying within the crater was one of the New Gods, a race of vastly powerful alien beings who dwelt on the distant planet of New Genesis. Cosmic legend had it that when the primordial gods of antiquity perished in some bygone cataclysm, the universe gave birth to a new breed of gods who reigned from two eternally warring worlds, the heavenly New Genesis and the hellish Apokolips. Lightray, whom Jimmy had first met a few years ago, hailed from New Genesis. Eternally cheerful and optimistic, he had always struck Jimmy as the friendliest and least intimidating of the New Gods.

But what had happened to him now? Despite possessing literally god-like power and immortality, Lightray looked more dead than alive. He lay sprawled upon his back, the cracked debris beneath him fused to a glassy sheen by the heat of his arrival. His skintight white uniform, which was usually spotless from head to toe, was torn, shredded, and even scorched in places. The golden headdress that framed his once-handsome features was dented and barely holding together. One eye was swollen shut, and his lips were split and bleeding. His wavy red hair had been burnt and torn away in spots, exposing the raw scalp underneath. A formerly radiant smile now lacked several teeth. A leg was twisted at an unnatural angle. His breathing was ragged, and he seemed to lack the strength to even lift his head from the glazed concrete. He looked barely conscious.

Who could do this to him? Jimmy wondered. *Darkseid? Doomsday?* His affable manner notwithstanding, Lightray was no pushover. Along with the superhuman strength and endurance of a New God, Lightray also possessed the unique ability to harness all the various frequencies of the light spectrum. Jimmy had seen Lightray repel squads of vicious Parademons with the blinding beams that had inspired his nom de guerre. He could be a tough customer when he had to be. *So how did he end up beaten to a pulp?*

A familiar *whoosh*ing sound heralded the arrival of Superman. Jimmy's best friend, and Earth's greatest hero, descended from the sky. His bright red cape flared out behind him. His world-famous S-shield was emblazoned on the chest of his sky blue uniform.

"Sorry I'm late," he apologized. "I was out near Vega when I got your—" He spotted the brutalized figure at the bottom of the crater. "Great Rao! Is that Lightray?"

Jimmy knew that Superman and Lightray had often fought side by side against Darkseid and his sinister minions. "We heard what sounded like a battle going on above the clouds and someone screaming. Then he fell out of the sky." He watched helplessly as Superman touched down beside the wounded god. Kneeling, the Man of Steel confirmed that Lightray was still breathing. Jimmy figured he was probably using his X-ray vision to check for internal injuries too. "Superman, is he dying?"

"I'm not sure I even know what that means in the case of a New God, Jimmy, but whatever could do this to Lightray clearly isn't to be trifled with." Rising back onto his feet, Superman scanned the heavens with his super-vision. "I didn't see anything unusual when I descended through the atmosphere, but I'd better take another look." He launched himself into the air, raising a cloud of dust around the young reporter. "Stay here, Jimmy. Lightray knows you. Talk to him."

Me? Jimmy thought. He felt distinctly out of his league. "I don't know what I could say that would make a god feel better," he called down to Lightray, "but hang in there, buddy." Not wanting to let his friends down, he scooted down the sloped walls of the crater until he reached Lightray's side. "Superman's looking out for you, so you're in good hands. . . . Hey!"

Without warning, Lightray reached up and grabbed Jimmy by the wrist. "In–infinite . . ." he said weakly, coughing up blood. His blackened left eye, the one that wasn't entirely swollen shut, stared urgently into Jimmy's. He seemed desperate to communicate some vital message or warning. "Infinite . . ."

Jimmy tried to tug his arm free from Lightray's grasp, but, even bruised and bleeding, the god's strength far exceeded Jimmy's own. "Can't . . . get . . . loose . . ." Jimmy grimaced in pain as Lightray's fingers squeezed his captured wrist. "Let go. . . . You're hurting me!"

But the mangled god had only one thing on his mind. "Infinite," he wheezed once more. "Infinite . . ."

I don't understand, Jimmy thought. *What are you trying to tell me?*

Lightray's entire body started glowing, emitting a brilliant golden radiance that grew brighter and more intense by the second. The preternatural effulgence hurt Jimmy's eyes, forcing him to shut them and look away. A sensation like static electricity caused all the hairs on his body to stand on end, and there was a peculiar buzzing in his ears. The glow lit up the entire crater and radiated outward like a mushroom cloud. Jimmy heard startled shouts and gasps from the street above. "Get back!" he hollered, afraid that some sort of dangerous chain reaction was in progress. Had Lightray lost control of his inner luminosity? What if this was just the beginning of a divine meltdown? The whole city could be in danger.

"What's happening?" Jimmy pleaded. "Tell me how to stop this!"

Then, just as inexplicably as it had begun, the blinding glow faded away. The last of the discharged energy seeped into Jimmy's bones. Lightray's fingers went limp, releasing their iron grip on Jimmy's wrist. The god's arm dropped lifelessly onto the fused concrete. His ragged breathing fell silent.

"No," Jimmy whispered.

He opened his eyes. Bright blue spots danced in his field of vision. He wiped the tears away from his watery eyes. Lightray's real name popped into his mind.

Solis, he recalled. *His name was Solis.*

"Jimmy!" Superman suddenly landed in front of him. His own pupils looked dilated from the glare of seconds before, and he sounded alarmed. "That light was visible even from orbit! Are you all right?"

"I—I'm fine," Jimmy stammered. His blurry vision cleared as he gazed down at the motionless figure lying before him. Every last trace of Lightray's sunny personality appeared to have fled the bloodied carcass at the bottom of the crater, perhaps via the gaping hole in his chest. A faint glow, like the final embers of a dying fire, burned where the god's heart should have been, before fading away entirely. A glazed blue eye stared blankly into . . .

what? Infinity? "But Lightray . . . Solis . . . I think he's dead." Jimmy shook his head in disbelief; the very idea sounded inconceivable. "But how is that even possible?"

"I don't know," Superman confessed. He looked equally troubled by what had just transpired, which only worried Jimmy more. He was used to Superman always being on top of things. The hero's brow furrowed in concern. "What does it mean for the universe . . . when a *god* dies?"

NEW YORK CITY.

Hokus & Pokus Occult Curioso, read the sign above the entrance to the small shop, which was tucked away in a secluded corner of Greenwich Village, between a coffeehouse and a gay bookstore. Cabalistic symbols adorned the first-floor windows, next to a mounted palmistry chart. Fortunes Told, promised a smaller sign above the chart. Enter Freely—Unafraid.

Easier said than done, Mary thought. Without her powers, she felt uncomfortably vulnerable. Vaporous incense fogged the air inside the shop, where she sat on one side of a round mahogany table. The lights were turned down low, so that the glowing crystal sphere resting atop the table provided most of the illumination. Murky shadows hid the corners of the intimate parlor at the back of the store. Shelves lined with occult artifacts and paraphernalia could be only dimly glimpsed. An Oriental rug with intricate designs lay upon the floor. Weird, ethereal music played softly in the background.

Mary prayed that she had come to the right place.

"The faint residue of magic coats your aura," declared the exotic-looking woman sitting across from Mary. A band of indigo silk covered the woman's eyes; rumor had it that she had been blinded by the Spectre during the vengeful ghost's rampage two years ago. A slinky, low-cut purple dress displayed her womanly figure. Straight black hair hung past her shoulders. Silver glittered on her wrists, neck, and ears. Her smoky voice held an indefinable accent. "Until recently, you knew the power of the spoken word."

That's one way to put it, Mary thought. "I lost my power, Madame Xanadu, not my memory." She fidgeted impatiently. "If you can't help me . . ."

The other woman held up her hand to silence Mary's protests. Storefront psychics and fortune-tellers were a dime a dozen these days, but Madame Xanadu was the real thing. Although her origins were shrouded in mystery, everyone in the magical community heeded her counsel. The wizard Shazam, who had originally granted Mary and Billy their powers, had regarded the reputedly ageless oracle as a peer. It was said that when Madame Xanadu foretold the future, even the Phantom Stranger listened. . . .

"The boy you are searching for, your brother," she stated, "he is nowhere to be found, at least not by me." She lifted her blindfolded gaze from the crystal ball. "Let us focus on *you* for the moment."

"Me?" Mary said. She had sought out Madame Xanadu's Christy Street address in hopes of tracking down her missing sibling. "What about me?"

"Your future is cloudy, Mary, full of turbulent shadows, obscuring many paths." Luminous mists swirled inside the crystal ball. "You will be tested; that much I can discern."

"What sort of tests?" Mary asked anxiously. "Do I get my powers back?"

Madame Xanadu paused before answering. Despite her silken blindfold, she seemed to peer deeply into Mary's very soul. "Difficult to say. There is power in your destiny; that much is clear. The extent and nature of it is not. There are equal parts light and dark."

"That's not very helpful," Mary complained. She had come here for answers, not cryptic utterances. Not for the first time, Mary wished that the wizard was still alive to advise her; unfortunately, Shazam had been slain by the Spectre about the same time that Madame Xanadu had been blinded, during the infamous Day of Vengeance.

"You must be careful what you wish for," the mysterious fortune-teller cautioned her. "And heed me well: Above all else, you must stay away from Gotham City."

"Gotham?" Mary echoed in surprise. *Batman's hometown?* "What does Gotham have to do with anything?"

"It isn't safe for magic," Madame Xanadu said with maddening vagueness. She somehow sensed Mary's growing dissatisfaction. "Child, there's a reason we're not supposed to gaze into the future. To do so is cheating, and the laws of magic make it difficult to predict with a high degree of probability—especially where matters of mystic power are concerned."

"Great," Mary replied irritably. She rose from her chair, now convinced that this entire session had been a colossal waste of time. "I feel even more lost than I did before."

Madame Xanadu remained seated behind her crystal ball. She appeared to take no offense from Mary's griping. Perhaps she was accustomed to such reactions. "If you're lost in the wilderness, look for a guide."

That's what I thought I was doing, Mary thought, *but apparently I came to the wrong place after all.* She threw a couple of dollars onto the table before heading for the door. "Okay, then," she said sarcastically. "Thanks for clearing everything up."

A bell jingled above the doorway as she let herself out. *Talk about a dead end!* She seethed in frustration. As far as Mary could tell, she had only picked up one piece of concrete information from the entire reading.

Gotham City, huh?

35 AND COUNTING.

SAN FRANCISCO.

The setting sun cast a ruddy twilight glow over the lonely graveyard. Weathered stone monuments preserved the memory of those buried beneath the neatly trimmed lawn. A chilly breeze whistled through the skeletal branches of scattered willow trees. Crinkly brown leaves littered the grass. A spiked iron fence surrounded the cemetery, protecting the grounds from intruders. The gates would soon close for the night.

Donna Troy wasn't worried about getting locked in by mistake; if necessary, she could always fly over the fence. She was a strong and confident woman; the stars themselves glittered in her lustrous black hair and shimmering black leotard. The silvery flecks matched her wristbands, boots, and belt. A satiny black choker adorned her slender throat. Her clear blue eyes contemplated the name inscribed on the tombstone before her:

DONNA TROY.

Although she was immune to the cool fall weather, a chill ran down her spine nonetheless. Donna had seen and lived through much over the course of her convoluted existence, but it was hard not to be unsettled by the sight of one's own grave.

Years ago, while fighting alongside her fellow Teen Titans, she had fallen in battle against a berserk Superman robot. Her friends and teammates had duly mourned her, but death, for her, had not proved permanent. Revived by cosmic forces to play a key role in the defense of the universe, she now found herself walking the Earth once more . . . even as the engraved marble marker continued to commemorate her heroic sacrifice. *I suppose,* she mused, *I should arrange to have the gravestone removed.*

But that was not why she had come here today.

Tearing her gaze away from the disturbing tombstone, she glanced around the cemetery. She appeared to have the melancholy setting to herself, but suspected otherwise. "All right," she called out impatiently. "I'm here, just like you asked. Show yourself."

A dark-haired youth, only a few years younger than herself, stepped out from behind a tree. A black leather jacket, leather pants, and boots failed to conceal his athletic physique. A crimson domino mask was affixed to his face, but she recognized him nonetheless. She stiffened and crossed her arms over her chest.

"Jason Todd."

He smirked at the suspicious edge to her voice. "Hey, babe. Come here often?"

"Not really," she said wryly. "What do you want, Jason? And why here?"

He answered the second question first. "Seemed appropriate." He strolled over to her grave and knelt to inspect the tombstone. "After all, we're both supposed to be dead."

He's got a point, Donna conceded, *albeit a morbid one.* Jason had been working as the second Robin, replacing Dick Grayson, when he'd been murdered by the Joker several years ago. Like hers, his death had been neither ambiguous nor disputed; nevertheless, he had recently returned to carry on his career as a vigilante in Gotham City. Donna was a little fuzzy on the details of his rebirth, but she believed it had something to do with that "Infinite Crisis" over a year ago, when an alternate version of Lex Luthor had attempted to alter the very fabric of reality. Although Earth's heroes had ultimately foiled the villain's scheme, putting the universe more or less back to normal, not everything had ended up *exactly* the way it was before.

But what's a resurrection or two between friends?

"What do you want, Jason?" she repeated.

He shrugged. "Hey, can't one ex-sidekick get together with another for old times' sake? 'Once a Titan, always a Titan.' Isn't that what they say?" He rose from the grave and brushed the fallen leaves from his knees. "Besides, maybe I just wanted to talk to someone else who knew what it felt like to be living on borrowed time."

Despite his cocky demeanor, Donna sensed that he was deeply troubled and unhappy, and who could blame him? It wasn't easy finding out that you were supposed to be dead, that your friends and loved ones had all gone on with their lives without you. Even Batman, who had already trained a new Robin long ago. No wonder she detected a distinct note of bitterness in his voice.

"Go on," she encouraged him. Her tone softened a bit.

He took off his mask, revealing a familiar, if slightly older, face. Sullen blue eyes peered into hers. "Look at us, Donna. We don't belong here anymore. I wouldn't even be breathing if not for that psycho Luthor clone or whatever he was, and as for you . . . Hell, I've never been able to keep track of all the different identities and origins you've had. Even before you died and came back, your past has always been a tangle."

Thanks for rubbing it in, Donna thought. He wasn't lying, though. Donna had spent most of her life wrestling with conflicting memories and shifting personas. She had been a heroine, a harbinger, a wife, a mother, and a goddess. Although she originally joined the Titans as Wonder Girl, she had also been known as Darkstar and Troia. More recently, she had even assumed the role of Wonder Woman while her former mentor, Diana, took a yearlong sabbatical. Now she was simply Donna Troy again. *Whatever that means.*

"I suppose we do have some things in common," she admitted cautiously, still uncertain as to what exactly Jason expected from her. She hoped this wasn't just some elaborate pickup scheme; although the former Boy Wonder had grown to be an attractive young man, she had never thought of Jason that way. "You could've chosen a less . . . upsetting . . . meeting place, but if you really just want to talk, here I am."

"Now is no time for mere conversation," a deep bass voice intruded. A pillar of coruscating orange energy materialized before them, resembling the transporter effect on *Star Trek*, and an imposing alien figure emerged from the sparkling radiation. "The universe—and I—have urgent need of you!"

Over seven feet tall, the humanoid figure wore a bulky suit of futuristic armor. A flowing red cape was affixed to a pair of massive gold shoulder-plates. Electronic circuitry blinked upon his matching golden wristbands, while the elaborate silver and purple armor left only his head exposed. Florid pink skin and glowing red eyes testified to his extraterrestrial origins. A bristling black beard framed his lantern jaw, and rows of parallel cornrows traversed his cranium. His craggy face bore a dour, saturnine expression.

"Donna, watch out!" Jason immediately dropped into a defensive posture. He drew a Glock automatic pistol from beneath his jacket.

"Wait!" Donna grabbed on to his gun arm before Jason did something rash. She recognized the bizarre newcomer. "It's a Monitor! Let's hear what he has to say."

The Monitors, she knew, were a race of highly powerful beings who watched over the fifty-two separate realities that composed the Multiverse. They seldom took direct action themselves, preferring to manipulate events indirectly in order to fulfill their self-appointed mission of preserving order throughout the cosmos. Although their intentions were good, the appearance of a Monitor rarely boded well. They seldom appeared to lesser beings unless some manner of universal cataclysm threatened.

Please, she prayed. *Not another Crisis.*

"You are wise, Donna Troy," the Monitor said solemnly. "We have no time to waste on pointless displays of aggression. The fate of your reality, and perhaps all others, depends on us taking swift action to avert a disaster beyond all imagining."

Donna's heart sank. *I knew it. Here we go again.* The last Crisis had cost the lives of several valiant heroes, including some of her fellow Teen Titans. Who knew how many might perish this time around?

"Oh yeah?" Jason challenged the Monitor. He lowered his gun but did not put it away. "I've heard that before."

"Do not make light of the dreadful apocalypse before us." The Monitor ignored Jason's gun; Donna suspected that mere bullets posed little threat to him. "All that you know may perish—unless you help me find the one called Ray Palmer."

"Ray Palmer?" Donna echoed in surprise. "The Atom?"

A longtime member of the Justice League of America, the Atom had once used his size-changing abilities to defend humanity by microscopic means. In recent years, however, his life had been marred by tragedy; his mentally disturbed ex-wife, Jean Loring, had murdered some of the Atom's closest friends and later become host to an evil entity known as Eclipso. Crushed by guilt and heartbreak over what Jean had done, Ray Palmer had literally shrunk out of sight. As far as Donna knew, no one had seen him in years.

"Indeed," the Monitor confirmed. "Sources beyond your ken foretell that Ray Palmer shall play a crucial role in the coming struggle, but only if he can be located in time. For that, I require your assistance."

"Is that so?" Jason said sarcastically. "Why us?"

Good question, Donna thought. *This sounded more like a job for the Justice League. I barely know Ray Palmer—nor does Jason.*

"Though vast," the Monitor explained, "my knowledge does not grant me a full understanding of the emotions that drive humans such as yourself. Ray Palmer has hidden himself from the universe for reasons of his own; it may well be that I shall need your insights to grasp his past and future behavior." His enigmatic gaze swept over the humans. "Moreover, I have reason to believe that Palmer now dwells in a reality in which he does not truly belong, much as the pair of you now do."

Donna nodded. She thought she understood . . . sort of. "Set an anomaly to catch an anomaly, right?" She eyed the Monitor suspiciously. "Our meeting here today, Jason and I . . . That was no coincidence, was it?"

He shook his head. "I planted the idea in Jason Todd's mind to bring you together, and remind you of your unique status in the universe."

"What?!" Jason lunged at the Monitor. "You stay out of my head, you cornrowed freak!"

Moving at super-speed, Donna grabbed hold of Jason, restraining him. He fought furiously to break loose, but she was many times stronger than him. "Jason, please! This isn't helping!" She didn't think that Jason could actually harm the Monitor, but she wasn't going to let him provoke the powerful being into retaliating. Despite his preternatural return from the dead,

Jason was still just an ordinary human being with no superpowers. "Get control of yourself!"

"Like hell!" he snarled. His gun went off, missing the Monitor but tearing up the earth at the foot of Donna's tombstone. Were there still remains in the buried coffin? If so, the bullet had probably just shattered her skull. "I'm tired of being treated like a pawn in these lunatics' cosmic games! I'm not letting anybody mess with my life again!"

The sheer fury in his voice startled Donna. Jason had always been kind of a hothead, but this was something else altogether. *He's changed,* she realized, *and not for the better.* She deftly pried the gun from his fingers and tossed it onto a grassy sward nearby. *And since when did Batman's apprentices carry guns anyway?*

She knew the Dark Knight would not approve.

"Enough!" the Monitor said impatiently. "Such primitive histrionics only delay our quest. *I* am responsible for this universe, and *I* say we must get under way. Somewhere outside this reality, beyond even my own ability to detect, Ray Palmer awaits."

Jason stopped squirming against Donna's tight embrace, but she kept holding on to him just in case. "Uh-huh," he retorted. "And how do you know the Atom's not already dead?"

"Because if he is," the Monitor stated gravely, "then we all are."

34 AND COUNTING.

METROPOLIS.

Suicide Slum, in the bad part of Metropolis, reminded Jimmy of Gotham City after dark. Hookers and drug dealers loitered on the street corners. Winos camped out on the sidewalks. Broken bottles, fast-food wrappers, tabloid newspapers, and other refuse littered the pavement. Faded chalk outlines testified to the neighborhood's notoriously high murder rate. Graffiti defaced the ugly metal shutters and bars that protected the district's few legal enterprises after sundown. The occasional streetlights created meager oases of light amidst the nocturnal shadows. Dry, brown weeds sprouted up from cracks in the sidewalks, and greasy puddles filled the potholes. Empty storefronts sheltered squatters, crackheads, and who knew what else. Law-abiding folks knew better than to drop by at midnight.

Maybe this was a bad idea, Jimmy thought.

Surly-looking slum dwellers eyed the young reporter, who tried unsuccessfully to act like he belonged here. A platinum blonde hooker offered him an obscene suggestion. Avoiding eye contact, Jimmy nervously hid his expensive digital camera beneath his Windbreaker while he searched for the address scribbled on the anonymous note he had received at the *Planet* earlier today. The letter said that if Jimmy had questions about what had happened to Lightray, he would find them at 666 Hob's Lane, deep in the diseased heart of this urban jungle. The address alone set off warning bells in Jimmy's head.

Good thing I'm not the superstitious type.

666 Hob's Lane turned out be an abandoned brownstone that had obviously seen better days. The windows were either boarded up or broken, and yellow crime scene tape cordoned off the front entrance. The sooty brick walls looked like they hadn't been washed since the Great Depression, and no lights shone inside the decrepit building. A notice posted on the front door declared the brownstone condemned.

No kidding, Jimmy thought.

A homeless man wearing a ratty scarf and an ill-fitting parka leaned against the stoop of the building. His greasy white beard looked like it hadn't been shaved or combed since the Luthor administration. A crumpled paper bag held a bottle of fortified wine, which he sipped from religiously. "Hey, red," the vagrant called out to Jimmy, noticing his interest in the dilapidated brownstone. Slurred words suggested that he had probably been drinking all day. "You probably don't want to go in there."

"Yeah, you're right." Jimmy appreciated his warning. He hesitated on the sidewalk in front of the building. "I don't."

He took a deep breath to steady his nerves, then walked up the steps past the concerned Good Samaritan. Ducking beneath the police tape, he gave the front door a tentative shove. A broken lock admitted him to the foyer of the building, which looked just as unappetizing as its grimy façade and neighborhood. Dingy beige paint was peeling off the walls, and a couple pieces of rotting wooden furniture had been shoved into a corner. Scuff marks and cigarette burns marred the tile floor, which had been turned into a dumping ground for cigarette butts, empty syringes, rat droppings, and even less attractive waste. The entryway smelled like a wino's lavatory. Rats scurried away at his approach, cobwebs shrouded the ancient crown molding, and a water stain on the ceiling resembled the outline of Bialya.

Jimmy's nose wrinkled in disgust. *First Arkham, now this,* he thought crankily. *How come I never get assigned to Paradise Island or Atlantis instead?*

Sheer revulsion briefly replaced trepidation . . . until a phlegmy voice called his name.

"Olsen . . ."

"H-h-hello?" Jimmy stammered. The eerie voice seemed to be coming from upstairs. It sounded vaguely familiar, but he couldn't quite place it. "Who's there?"

The speaker declined to identify himself. "Second floor. Three doors down."

Jimmy peered dubiously at the murky staircase. Slivers of light from the street outside penetrated the boarded-up windows, providing just enough illumination to see by. Jimmy stalled at the base of the stairs, but he had come too far to turn back now. *If nothing else,* he thought, *maybe I can find out why I'm stretching and super-speeding sometimes.*

Those freaky incidents still baffled him. The first time it had happened, at Arkham, he'd thought that maybe he had just inhaled a dose of the Scarecrow's fear gas or something, but that second incident, when he'd rescued those tourists at the speed of sound, had forced him to face the truth. For a few, fleeting moments, he had actually possessed superpowers, just like Plastic Man or the Flash.

But why?

Maybe the answer lay upstairs. . . .

Hoping that he wasn't walking into some sort of nefarious trap, he cautiously headed up the stairs. The rickety steps creaked beneath his feet; Jimmy nervously recalled the Condemned notice. A moldy runner reeked of mildew. He grabbed on to the banister, which was slick and greasy to the touch. A cockroach scuttled across his hand.

Gross!

Making it to the second floor in one piece, Jimmy spotted a glimmer of candlelight coming from a room on the right. The flickering amber glow led him to an ajar wooden door that was barely hanging on to its rusty hinges. He pushed the door open all the way, and an overpowering stench, like raw sewage mixed with rotten eggs, assailed his senses. "God," he blurted, gagging at the fetid odor, "it stinks in here, like . . ."

"Sleez." The room's sole inhabitant identified himself. An obese alien with mottled green skin, a hairless dome, and pointed ears squatted on a badly stained mattress across from the door. Filthy brown rags clothed his corpulent frame. X-rated centerfolds plastered the walls of the creature's squalid lair, alongside cheesecake shots of scantily clad super heroines like Starfire, Isis, and Big Barda. "Former servant, aide, and counsel to Darkseid, now a doomed exile on this deplorable mudball you call home." Piggish yellow eyes glinted in the candlelight as Sleez leered at his visitor. His slimy face glistened like mucus. "Have you missed me, Olsen?"

"Definitely not." Jimmy finally recognized the voice—and the smell. The loathsome creature before him had been banished from Apokolips because of his boundless depravity, which was really saying something; you had to be pretty perverted to be too vile for Darkseid to tolerate. "I thought you were dead."

"Alas, no," Sleez chortled. "By sheer force of will alone I have survived in the hope of someday taking revenge on Darkseid."

"Your note said you had something to tell me about Lightray." That this loathsome toad, who looked like Yoda's degenerate cousin, had cheated death while the noble New God had not struck Jimmy as cosmically unjust. "So just tell me what you know, and don't try any of your skeezy mind-control games on me. I'm onto your tricks. I'll signal Superman if you even look at me funny."

Sleez gave Jimmy an appraising look. "Grown some hair on your freckled chest, have you?" He nodded, his lecherous face assuming a more serious expression as he got down to business. "Listen closely, Olsen. Darkseid can finally be destroyed if you—" His eyes widened in alarm. A note of panic sounded in his voice. "Oh no! He's here!"

"Who?" Jimmy asked anxiously. A resounding boom shook the deserted brownstone to its foundations. A blinding yellow glow penetrated the exposed brickwork. The pinups on the wall burst into flame. Chunks of plaster rained down from the ceiling, which looked ready to cave in at any moment. A horrifying thought occurred to Jimmy as a stony gray countenance surfaced from his memory. "Is it Darkseid?"

Sleez threw up his pudgy hands to shield himself from the falling debris. "No . . . there's no time." Oily perspiration ran down his face. "Run away. . . . DO IT NOW!"

Jimmy waffled, uncertain what to do. *How badly do I want this story?* "Greetings, Sleez."

A stentorian voice issued from above the disintegrating ceiling. Jimmy tried to make out the source of the voice, but the high-intensity glare was too bright. A sickening sense of déjà vu came over him; this was Lightray's final moments all over again. "No," Jimmy protested to no one in particular. "Not again . . ."

"No! Please leave me!" Sleez begged, but his frantic plea fell upon deaf ears. A sizzling blast of energy zapped the exiled demon in the chest. He let out a bloodcurdling scream of agony.

"So begins the end!" the mystery voice proclaimed.

The end? Jimmy thought. *The end of what?*

Another thunderous boom shook the heavens and the golden glow faded, leaving Jimmy alone in the dingy apartment with Sleez's charred and smoking corpse. Scorch marks surrounded the remains, while a gaping hole glowed dimly where Sleez's black heart had once resided. *Just like with Lightray,* Jimmy realized, his watery eyes still recovering from the blazing burst of light. He stared aghast at the slain god, feeling trapped inside some cosmic murder mystery beyond mortal comprehension. Sleez's note had promised Jimmy answers, but his death left yet more questions behind. His heart pounding, Jimmy rested his weight against the nearest wall. His teeth ground in frustration.

"What the hell is going on here?"

GOTHAM CITY.

Madame Xanadu was right, Mary realized. *I shouldn't have come here.*

Racing footsteps, accompanied by raucous hoots and whistles, pursued her as she ran frantically down a deserted city street. Sleeping office buildings offered the frightened girl no refuge. By day, this vicinity of Gotham was relatively clean and safe, but after dark the entire character of the neighborhood changed. The various businesses closed for the day, the office workers went home, and a more unsavory element took over the streets. Like the urban predators now chasing Mary by the lambent glow of the streetlights.

"Stop running, little girl!" a harsh voiced shouted at her. Heartless laughter came from the skinhead's fellow gang members. There were at least three of them, all gaining on Mary as she tried to get away from the tattooed thugs. Her wide blue eyes searched for sanctuary, but all she saw were locked doors and darkened windows. Metal shutters protected the coffee shops, copying centers, and Greek diners that, by day, catered to the professional crowd. Breathing hard, Mary urged her tired legs to keep on running. A painful stitch stabbed her side with every step. If only she still had the speed of Mercury . . . !

This was a mistake, Mary thought. She still wasn't entirely sure why she had defied Madame Xanadu's warning and caught a Greyhound bus to Gotham, just like she couldn't really explain why she had felt compelled to venture down these lonely streets at night. All she knew was that she had to do *something* to get her powers back, and Gotham City was the only lead she had. *What didn't Madame Xanadu want me to find here?* Mary had been willing to face any sort of mystical threat or ordeal to regain her powers, but now it looked like her reckless quest was about to come to a nasty end.

Her sneakers slapped against the pavement. Glancing back over her shoulder, she saw the punks closing in on her. They whooped and hollered like a pack of hungry wolves, eager to get their hands on their defenseless prey. Madame Xanadu had been wrong about one thing at least; there was nothing at all magical about these creeps.

But that didn't make them any less dangerous.

A four-story brownstone midway down the block caught her eye. Mary thought she spied a hint of movement somewhere within the silent edifice. She found herself strangely drawn to the building, much as she had felt driven to explore this neighborhood earlier. Desperate for any sort of shelter from the would-be muggers pursuing her, she sprinted up the front steps of the building. Her fists pounded against a pair of heavy wooden doors. "Please, somebody! Let me in!"

To her surprise, the unlocked doors swung open, almost as though something inside had been awaiting her. Not wanting to look a gift horse in the mouth, she dashed indoors. Her eyes hastily surveyed her surroundings, looking for a friendly face or maybe just a safe place to hide. Lights from outside exposed the lobby of what had obviously once been a very elegant address. Marble columns and floor tiles greeted her eyes. A grand staircase led to a mezzanine overlooking the ground floor. An unlit crystal chandelier dangled from the ceiling. The bare walls and floor had been stripped of any expensive furnishings or carpets. Scuff marks recorded the departure of heavy desks or sofas, and cobwebs hung in the place of draperies. Thick layers of dust suggested that the brownstone had been abandoned for months at the very least. Her footsteps echoed in the sepulchral silence of the empty lobby. Nothing stirred within the venerable walls, not even a rat or cockroach. The musty air smelled sour and rotten, like something had crawled inside the building to die.

What is this place? Mary wondered apprehensively. The desolate setting sent a chill down her spine, reminding her of the hidden subway tunnel that had once led to the wizard Shazam's timeless throne room. *Is this how Billy felt the first time the wizard summoned him?* As her eyes adjusted to the oppressive gloom, she made out more details of the lobby's interior decor, which seemed to have a distinctly Middle Eastern flavor. Elaborate arabesques wound around the marble columns and moldings. Faded mosaic tiles, embedded in the walls, depicted the gods of ancient Egypt. Arcane hieroglyphics, inscribed throughout the chamber, made the forlorn lobby feel like the tomb of some forgotten pharaoh. Mary frowned; not too long ago, the wisdom of Solomon would have allowed her to read the hieroglyphics with ease, but now they might as well have been written in Kryptonian. She was certain that she had never set foot in this building before, yet somehow the place felt oddly familiar. . . .

Her pursuers gave her little time to ponder the mystery, barging into the lobby after her. "Hope you're not lookin' for a phone in here, baby," the leader of the hoodlums said with a sneer. Serpentine tattoos coiled atop his shaved skull. Metal studs and rings pierced his eyelids, ears, and lips. Death-metal decals plastered his scuffed leather jacket. A tarnished steel swastika hung on a chain around his neck. Steel-toed boots stamped across the marble floor. " 'Cause this dump ain't had water or power or nothing since them ragheads moved out!"

Mary backed away from the snickering hoodlums. "Shazam," she whispered uselessly. Her fists clenched at her sides. *If I just had my powers back,* she lamented, *I'd teach these creeps a lesson they'd never forget.* She hated feeling so scared and helpless. *Mary Marvel would make short work of these losers.*

But she wasn't Mary Marvel. Not anymore.

Salvation came instead from an entirely different quarter.

"Ragheads?" a deep voice sounded from above. "I detest that term."

All eyes turned upward toward the mezzanine, which remained cloaked in shadow. *Who?* Mary thought. For a moment, she thought that maybe Batman had come to her rescue—this was Gotham City after all—but the voice's distinct Middle Eastern accent reminded her of someone else instead. *Oh no,* she realized in horror. *Not* him*!*

A pair of powerful hands grabbed on to the skinhead's shoulders, yanking him off his feet. The startled punk yelped in surprise as he dangled several feet above the floor. Wet, rending noises cut off his cries as he was literally ripped into pieces by his unseen assailant. Blood splattered the walls. The mugger flew apart in more pieces than Mary could count. She gagged as a bloody fragment landed at her feet. Severed limbs hit the floor. A head rolled down the stairs. Intestines snagged on the chandelier. If she could have afforded to eat today, she would've lost her lunch for sure.

Horrified by their comrade's grisly demise, the remaining skinheads fled the building as fast as their rubbery legs could carry them. Mary instinctively ran in the opposite direction, toward the back of the lobby. Maybe there was a rear exit or something? She only got a few feet, however, before she tripped over something lying in her path.

Or some*one.*

Tumbling onto the floor, she reached out to break her fall. Her fingers grabbed on to something dry and withered. Teeth rattled beneath her hand, and she felt the bony outline of a skull beneath her palm. Her fingernails poked through brittle, parchmentlike skin. *"Aaach!"* She yanked her hand back as she instantly grasped that she was touching a dead body. She rolled away from the corpse, only to bump into another body only a few inches away. Her eyes widened in horror as she scrambled away from yet more bodies, which seemed to be all around her. Almost a dozen corpses, in various states of decay, were strewn about the floor. Missing limbs, broken necks, and large brown bloodstains testified to the extreme violence that had ended the victims' lives. The smell of rotting flesh filled Mary's mouth and lungs. Desiccated faces held expressions of unimaginable horror, and mice had gnawed on the sundered remains. A spider emerged from a vacant eye socket.

"Who . . . ?" Her appalled gaze darted from body to body, each more mutilated than the one before. Random limbs were scattered like puzzle pieces. "Who *are* they. . . ?"

"Drug addicts, squatters, real estate agents." The dour voice conveyed equal quantities of scorn for all of the above. Mary glimpsed a shadowy figure perched on the balustrade running along the edge of the mezzanine. "People stupid enough to intrude upon my solitude." A snarl distorted his voice. "People like you."

Defying gravity, the figure hurled himself off the balcony and swooped down toward Mary. A shaft of light from an upstairs window exposed one of the world's most wanted fugitives: the genocidal super-man known as Black Adam.

There was no mistaking him. A powerfully built Arab man, he wore a tight black uniform that contrasted sharply with his golden boots, sash, and wristbands. Sleek black hair met in a widow's peak above his saturnine features. The golden thunderbolt emblazoned on his chest matched those worn by Captain Marvel and the rest of the Marvel Family, including, not so long ago, Mary herself. Indeed, Teth-Adam had been the wizard Shazam's original champion, back in the days of the pharaohs, until anger and ambition overcame his soul, transforming the heroic Mighty Adam into the dreaded Black Adam. Fresh blood dripped from his bare hands.

Those gore-stained hands came at Mary, eager to throttle the life from her.

"Adam! Wait!" She jumped to her feet. "It's me, Mary Batson!"

Her frantic cry got his attention. Pausing in midlunge, he touched down onto the floor and scrutinized the cowering girl before him. A cruel smile lifted the corners of his lips as he recognized Mary's mortal incarnation.

"Well, then," he said darkly. "Perhaps this day is not a total loss."

Mary shuddered. The last time she had encountered Black Adam, during his rampage three months ago, his titanic blow had put her into a coma from which she had only just awakened. He was the last person she wanted to face right now, especially with her powers missing. She was all too aware that he could tear her apart as easily as he'd killed all these other people.

"You seem afraid to see me, Mary," he observed.

"Well, y-yes." She realized now that this abandoned building must have formerly been the Kahndaqi consulate. Until recently, Black Adam had been the unquestioned ruler of that small Middle Eastern nation. No wonder this place had felt familiar. It reminded her of Adam's sumptuous palace in Kahndaq. "These bodies . . . the horrors you've committed . . ."

There had been a time, only a year ago, when it had seemed that Black Adam had reformed. His marriage to the beautiful Egyptian heroine Isis had softened his heart and quelled the murderous fury that had consumed him for over three thousand years. Along with her younger brother, Osiris, Adam and Isis had employed their supernatural powers for the betterment of Kahndaq. Mighty Adam had become his people's champion once more. But when nefarious foes struck back at Adam, killing both Isis and Osiris, the old Black Adam had returned with a vengeance, lashing out at the world. It had taken the combined efforts of Captain Marvel and the entire Justice Society to stop him. Eluding capture, he had been in hiding ever since.

"Horrors?" He angrily smashed his fist into a nearby column. Shards of shattered marble went flying. "The world stole my homeland and my family from me! You dare to judge me!" Rumor had it that Black Adam had been magically stripped of his powers, but apparently that was no longer the case. He gestured savagely at the corpses on the floor. "These others paid the price for disturbing me. That you too have worn the lightning bolt across your chest will not spare you their fate!"

He stalked toward her, his dark eyes gleaming balefully. "Teth-Adam . . . wait!" Mary pleaded. "I found you by accident, I swear! I haven't come to judge you. . . ." She swallowed hard as a disturbing possibility occurred to her. "I think, maybe, I was *sent* here somehow . . . for your help?"

"Help?" The sheer absurdity of her request gave Black Adam pause. He eyed her warily, as though suspecting that this might be a trick of some kind. "Where is your brother if you need help? Where is the noble Captain Marvel?"

"I don't know!" Mary confessed. "I've been looking for him every-where." She figured she had nothing to lose by telling the truth. Besides, if Black Adam had somehow regained his powers, wasn't it possible that he might know how to restore hers as well? "When I was drawn here, part of me hoped that it was Billy calling me, but maybe . . . I mean, we're the same right now, abandoned, alone, scared. Well, I am anyway." She chose her words carefully, not wanting to provoke the hot-tempered fugitive. "But, Adam, you're still connected to the magic. You're not helpless. Your powers make you strong. . . ."

"My powers?" Black Adam surprised Mary by laughing out loud. Gales of bitter hilarity poured out of him, causing him to quake from head to toe. Tears leaked from his eyes. "My powers . . . *hah!*"

Mary didn't get it. "Uh, did I say something funny?"

The immortal villain struggled to bring his laughter under control. "When I think of what my power has brought me . . ." He wiped a tear from his eye as his voice assumed a more somber tone. "No, that is not correct. When I think of what my power has *cost* me . . ."

Had he lost his mind, or just all hope of happiness? "They're not a curse," Mary insisted. "They're a gift!" Even after everything that had happened to him, she couldn't believe that Black Adam didn't appreciate having his pow-ers back. She would have traded places with him in a second. "I wish—"

"You wish?" he interrupted her. He seemed intrigued by her reaction. All traces of his unsettling hysterics vanished as he regarded her with a specula-tive expression upon his regal face. He stood astride the bodies of his victims like Anubis, the ancient Egyptian god of the underworld. "Make no mistake. Just as these unwary fools asked for death by coming here, so do you risk it by beseeching my aid."

Trembling, Mary stood her ground. "I don't want to die, but I can't live like this anymore." She remembered how terrified she had been when the muggers were chasing her; she never wanted to feel that weak and powerless again. "Please! I just want my old life back!"

"I fear that's impossible, Mary." Black Adam stepped forward and laid his palm upon her brow. He could have crushed her skull like an eggshell, but instead he spoke like a judge imposing a death sentence. "But I can ease your loneliness . . . with the company of the gods." He peered down at Mary's anguished face. Hot tears streaked her cheeks. She wrung her hands. "Is this truly what you seek?"

Mary nodded.

"So be it," he declared. "Shazam!"

Thunder boomed inside the deserted consulate. A bolt of eldritch lightning lit up the darkened interior, striking the floor of the lobby with explosive force. A mystical shock wave drove Adam and Mary apart, even as the crystal chandelier crashed to the floor. Billowing clouds of dust and smoke filled the air, obscuring Mary's vision, but she barely noticed the haze at first. Something far more compelling was taking place inside her.

As fast as lightning, supernatural energy coursed through her body. An ecstatic convulsion left her gasping. It was like the charge she had always felt when transforming into Mary Marvel, and yet strangely different somehow. More potent, more primal . . . almost intoxicating. The voices of ancient deities whispered seductively inside her skull. Her skin tingled with divine electricity. Closing her eyes, she luxuriated in the sheer euphoria of the moment. So overpowering was the sensation that it took her a second or two to realize that she was now floating several inches above the floor.

Holy Moley! she thought breathlessly. *I feel incredible!*

A rasping cough intruded on her rapture. Glancing down, she saw that Adam was pinned beneath the fallen chandelier. A few minutes ago, he could have easily tossed the massive conglomeration of crystals aside, but now he strained futilely to lift the wrecked chandelier off his trapped torso. He grunted between coughs, exerting all his might, but the glittering debris stubbornly refused to budge. His flushed face was scratched and bleeding.

"Here," Mary Marvel said, descending to the ground. Broken crystals crunched beneath her boots. "Let me help."

Reaching down, she effortlessly hefted the chandelier and hurled it away. It crashed loudly into a wall several yards away. A battered figure, clad in the simple linen garments of ancient Egypt, rose to his knees. Dust caked his flesh and clothes. No longer imbued with the power of an entire pantheon, the mortal Teth-Adam peered up at Mary through the fading haze. A bemused expression came over his narrow face. "By the gods, Mary," he said archly, "look how you've grown."

She gazed down at herself in surprise. Instead of the brightly colored cape and costume she had previously worn as Mary Marvel, a satiny black sheath now clung to her body, far more tightly than her old uniform ever had. A short black skirt exposed her bare legs. Jet-black gloves and boots matched her new outfit. Only the golden thunderbolt on her chest added a touch of color to her ensemble, which was clearly a feminine version of Black Adam's old uniform.

But not just her costume had changed. The slim young teenager now possessed the ample figure of a full-grown woman. Lustrous brown hair cascaded past her shoulders. Generous curves filled out the skintight silk dress.

It was a lot to take in. Momentarily speechless, Mary compared her striking black attire to Teth-Adam's humble garments. His own physique was noticeably slighter than before. His face was drawn and weary-looking. Smudgy purple bags shadowed his mournful eyes. The full enormity of what had just transpired gradually sank in. "You . . . you've given me . . ."

"All of it," he confirmed. Rising to his feet, he brushed the dust and ash from his arms and legs. Small cuts and bruises attested to the loss of his former invulnerability. "Not just my own power, but that of my late wife as well. You now possess the magic of Isis, along with the wizard's accursed gift."

Mary was baffled by his sacrifice. "Why?"

"I have lived long enough with the burden," he said acidly. "Over three millennia, to be exact." He looked accusingly at Mary. "Besides, this is what you wanted, is it not?"

I guess so, Mary thought. It was hard to see a downside to Adam transferring all his power to her. She certainly deserved them more.

Turning his back on her, Teth-Adam staggered toward the exit. Mary experienced a moment of anxiety as he moved to leave her behind in the ruined consulate. Smoke rose from the cremated remains of his victims, which had been reduced to ashes by the sizzling lightning bolt. She could still feel the wild magic surging inside her, changing her. Competing voices jostled for attention at the back of her mind. "Teth-Adam?" she called out hesitantly, uncertain what exactly this new power meant. "I . . . What can I do?"

Framed in the doorway, he glanced back over his shoulder. A rueful expression came over his haggard countenance. "If you see your brother," he said, with what might have been a touch of remorse, "tell him . . . I'm sorry."

Huh? Mary thought. *What does he mean by* that?

33 AND COUNTING.

METROPOLIS.

Holly Robinson trudged through the Greyhound Bus Station, doing her best to keep a low profile. To her relief, none of the other travelers making their way across the crowded terminal appeared to be paying any attention to the inconspicuous young woman wearing an open army-surplus jacket over jeans and a Hello Kitty T-shirt. A hunting cap was clamped tightly onto her head, the visor and earflaps helping to conceal her gamine features. Mirrored sunglasses hid her tired blue eyes. Her short red hair was now dyed a mousy shade of brown. A battered canvas travel bag, containing all that remained of her worldly possessions, was slung over her shoulder. Scuffed black boots carried her through the station, which felt oppressively warm. Overdressed for the temperature, she sweated beneath her thick jacket. Her butt ached from the two-hour bus ride from Gotham City. A pair of cheap wool gloves kept her fingerprints to herself.

Welcome to the Big Apricot, she thought.

A newsstand displayed a variety of daily papers. Holly paused to glance over the headlines. "EVEN GODS DIE!" proclaimed the front page of the *Daily Planet,* above a black-and-white photo of Superman bearing the lifeless body of some costumed alien named Lightray, but it was today's edition of the *Gotham Gazette* that made her heart miss a beat. "COP KILLER STILL AT LARGE!" her hometown newspaper lamented, above an unflattering mug shot of one Holly Robinson.

Oh, crap! She resisted the urge to flip the topmost paper over and instead crept furtively away from the newsstand, keeping her head low. Her finger pressed the shades farther up her nose, just to make sure they stayed in place. Spotting a bored-looking cop standing guard over the station, she took the long way around to avoid him. Her heart was pounding a mile a minute. Sweat trickled down the back of her neck. There were way too many copies of the *Gazette* floating around the station. At any moment she expected someone to look up from their paper and shout, "There she is! The cop killer!"

In fact, the truth was far more complicated. Not so long ago, Holly had prowled the East End of Gotham as Catwoman, filling in for Selina Kyle, the original Catwoman, while Selina was on her own version of maternity leave. Holly was not nearly the femme fatale that Selina was, but she'd thought she filled Catwoman's black leather boots reasonably well, until a run-in with two sadistic Russian super-villains exposed her secret identity—and cost an unlucky cop his head. Holly had not been responsible for the detective's grisly decapitation, but try telling an outraged G.C.P.D. that. With the entire police force out for her blood, she'd been lucky to get out of Gotham at all. . . .

Exiting the bus station, she wandered out onto the sidewalk. A cold autumn breeze drove her to pull her jacket closed. Busy pedestrians bustled past her, intent on their own errands. Car horns punctuated a steady rush of late afternoon traffic. She rested her bag on the pavement, giving her shoulders a break, while she tried to figure out which way to go. This was her first time in Metropolis, and the strange city stretched out all around her, vast and intimidating. The names and numbers on the unfamiliar street signs meant nothing to her. Born and raised in Gotham, Holly felt lost and alone.

Her spirits sank. In a moment of weakness, she extracted a cell phone from her pocket. An on-screen menu listed her most frequent contacts: Selina, Bruce, Dick, Karon.

Karon . . .

Her throat tightened and a solitary tear ran down her cheek. Karon's smiling face, spiky pink hair, and hip designer glasses surfaced from her memory. Holly's index finger hovered over the name of her girlfriend. She'd give anything to hear Karon's voice right now.

"No!" she whispered hoarsely as her better judgment overruled her longing. Holly's nocturnal clashes with Gotham's criminal underworld had already put Karon in the intensive care ward once. *Never again,* Holly vowed. She loved Karon too much to bring down any more heat on her. Holly may have left a certain glossy black catsuit behind in Gotham, but she knew that she was still bad luck for anyone who got too close to her. The best thing she could do for Karon, and all her other friends and loved ones, was disappear entirely.

She tossed the phone into a nearby waste bin. A scuzzy-looking homeless guy immediately pounced on the discarded piece of tech. *Help yourself,* Holly thought. *It's all yours.*

Hefting her heavy bag back onto her shoulder, she took off down the street toward nowhere in particular. The bus station turned out to be located in a somewhat seedy part of town, around the corner from a topless bar and a plasma collection center. Flophouses, soup kitchens, and liquor stores catered to a less than affluent clientele. Broken glass, crushed beer cans, and cigarette butts littered the sidewalk The area looked slightly cleaner than the East End back home, but only by a hair. She appeared to have traded one slum for another, except that now she was just as homeless as the winos and beggars slumped on the stoops around her.

You can do this, she reminded herself. *You've lived like this before.* She'd been a teenage runaway at thirteen, fleeing an abusive home environment, and had never looked back. *It only feels like your life is over. Think of this as a whole new start.*

Yeah, right.

"Excuse me, you look like you need a place to stay."

She rolled her eyes. *I should've seen this coming.* Pimps were always haunting bus stations looking for fresh meat, as Holly knew from personal experience. She'd worked the streets herself, as "Holly Gonightly," before Selina helped her escape that life.

"Sorry," she said brusquely, not even turning around to look at the speaker. "I don't do that anymore."

Part of her kind of hoped that the stranger wouldn't take no for answer. Her fists bunched in anticipation. Kicking a little bad-guy ass might be just what she needed right now. *Don't mess with me, bitch. I've been trained by Catwoman herself.*

A feminine chuckle greeted her refusal. "You mistake my intentions. I'm no predator, just a concerned sister."

Holly turned around and was surprised to behold a statuesque woman clad in a flowing silk robe. Auburn hair was bound up at the back of her head in a matronly fashion. Cool gray eyes peered from the woman's elegant features. Her narrow lips and strong chin reminded Holly of a priceless Greek idol Selina had once stolen from the Gotham Museum. A golden circlet crowned the woman's high forehead, while more gold glittered upon her throat, wrists, and ears. In her sandaled feet, she stood at least a head taller than Holly. The brisk fall weather seemed to have no effect on her.

"I have to admit," Holly conceded, "you don't look like the usual chicken hawk."

"Call me Athena." The woman's deep voice held a trace of an exotic accent. "I run the women's shelter across the street." She pointed at a nondescript redbrick building on the other side of the avenue. A surprisingly classy-looking collection of tapestries and ceramics was displayed in the first-floor window. Medusa's head, complete with serpentine tresses, was embossed upon a hanging bronze shield occupying a place of a honor within the exhibit. A freshly painted sign, mounted over the front entrance, identified the building as the Athenian Women's Shelter.

Holly recalled that Athena was the Greek goddess of wisdom. She was supposed to be tight with Wonder Woman these days. The graceful stranger certainly looked the part, but surely she didn't expect Holly to believe that she was actually *that* Athena?

Did she?

"I have a feeling that you'll find a place for yourself there." She raised her arm and, to Holly's amazement, a snow-white owl descended from the sky to alight upon Athena's wrist. "If not, you don't have to stay."

Although flummoxed by the unexpected appearance of the owl, Holly remained wary. She eyed her would-be benefactor suspiciously. "Really?"

"You have my word."

Holly considered the offer. The sun was sinking toward the horizon and it was already starting to get darker and colder outside. Her stomach grumbled irritably; lunch had been a bag of potato chips from a vending machine back in Gotham. *What can it hurt?* she thought. *Maybe I can get a warm meal out of this, then bail later if things get weird.*

Nodding, she followed Athena across the street. The sidewalk in front of the shelter was noticeably cleaner than the rest of the block. Stone gryphons guarded the front steps. Athena opened the door and stepped aside to let the younger woman enter. Holly kept her guard up, but wasn't too worried. Even if this was some sort of trap, she was confident that she could take care of . . .

Her jaw dropped.

For a moment, Holly thought she'd died and gone to lesbian heaven. The doorway opened onto a spacious lobby holding dozens of lithe young women in short linen tunics. Of every race and ethnicity, they milled about the palatial chamber, laughing and chatting amongst themselves, seemingly without a care in the world. More women lounged on scattered chairs and sofas, snacking on olives and wine. Holly tried not to ogle the other gals too obviously, but couldn't help noticing that they were all attractive and in excellent shape, without an ounce of flab or cellulite among them. Speechless, she wondered if she had accidentally wandered into an audition for *America's Next Top Amazon.* . . .

The lobby's decor matched the overpowering beauty of its inhabitants. Belying its humdrum outer façade, the building's interior was a masterpiece of classical Greek architecture. Pristine white columns supported the domed ceiling, which boasted shining gold filigree. Marble statues of willowy nymphs, muses, and goddesses occupied arched niches and alcoves. Olive trees sprouted from decorative ceramic urns. Perfume scented the air, which was invitingly warm and toasty, and a lyre played softly in the background. Holly lifted her shades to make sure she was seeing correctly. She shook her head in disbelief. Overall, this place looked more like a five-star hotel or spa than any homeless shelter she had ever set foot in before.

Who's funding this joint? Bruce Wayne?

Athena entered behind her. The owl hooted happily and soared out over the nubile throng. Curious eyes turned toward Holly.

"Welcome home, Holly," Athena said warmly.

So dumbfounded was the streetwise fugitive that it never even occurred to her to wonder how the other woman knew her name.

METROPOLIS.

Suicide Slum was only slightly less threatening in broad daylight. Pawn shops, liquor stores, taverns, adult video stores, tattoo parlors, and check-cashing venues made up the bulk of the local businesses. "SHOW OFF!" had been spray-painted onto the hood of a snazzy green sports car that someone had foolishly parked by the curb. Gangs of street toughs lounged on the stoops and sidewalks, laughing raucously amongst themselves while making rude comments to unlucky passersby. Most pedestrians hurried past them, eyes carefully lowered in hopes of avoiding a confrontation.

But not Jimmy. Dressed in his Sunday best, he strolled down Hob's Lane whistling a pop tune. Two of his priciest cameras dangled from his neck. His press pass was pinned to the lapel of a designer jacket. The rubber soles of his deluxe running shoes slapped against the dirty pavement. Jimmy figured he made a pretty tempting target, which was the whole idea. He had even considered donning a bow tie for the occasion, but that might have been pushing it.

His nonchalant air was just an act. A trickle of sweat, running down his temple, betrayed his anxiety. Walking around Suicide Slum like this was just asking for trouble. *I gotta be nuts,* he thought, but how else was he going to figure out what was up with his on-again, off-again superpowers? As nearly as he could tell, they only manifested under stress, like when he or someone else was in danger. *This isn't suicide,* he told himself. *It's a scientific experiment. Sort of.*

"S'up, fellas?" he cheerfully greeted a trio of tough-looking customers who were camped out on the stoop of a graffiti-covered crack house. Matching red bandannas and pyramid amulets tagged them as members in full standing of the Sphinxes, one of the city's most violent street gangs. Tank tops, baggy trousers, and spiky Mohawks made an intimidating fashion statement. They glowered at the towheaded interloper who'd had the nerve to address them so familiarly. "How about those Metros?"

"Metros suck, yo!" The punks jumped to their feet, all too obviously spoiling for a fight. Their eyes gleamed with bloodthirsty anticipation. Clenched fists gave away their intentions. "We're Yankee fans!"

"In fact," a second tough explained, "we're on our way to a game right now." He grinned maliciously. "Maybe we take your cameras, so we can get some pictures, and your money, so we can buy the tickets."

"And your shoes," the third hood added. "Just because."

They surrounded Jimmy on the sidewalk, cutting off any chance of escape. Nearby pedestrians hurried away in the opposite direction, doing their best not to get involved in the fracas. Part of Jimmy wished he could join them.

Here goes nothing.

"Oh yeah?" he challenged them. Raising his fists, he charged forward and kicked the nearest gang member in the kneecap. "You and what army?"

It wasn't the snappiest repartee, but it had the desired effect. "Hey!" his injured target blurted angrily. His face flushed red. A cocky smirk was instantly replaced by a look of genuine outrage. A metal chain rattled against his hip as he drew back his fist.

Jimmy gulped. *Okay, powers, do your stuff. . . .*

Tattooed knuckles flew at his face. Jimmy threw his head back, expecting his neck to elongate like before. Poised leg muscles waited eagerly for another burst of superhuman speed. Boy, were these antisocial bruisers in for a surprise when his astounding new abilities kicked in any minute now. . . !

Nothing happened—except that the punk's fist collided with his jaw.

The blow sent Jimmy reeling backward into an overflowing trash can. He crashed down onto the pavement amidst a heap of spilled garbage. Tasting blood in his mouth, he probed his front teeth with his tongue. Nothing was missing, thank goodness, but a couple incisors felt loose. A gong rang loudly inside his head. It took him a second to focus his blurry eyes.

And right about then, he thought to himself, *Maybe I should've told Superman I was coming here, just in case.*

The Sphinxes weren't done with him yet. Led by the snarling hood who had laid Jimmy flat, they converged on the fallen reporter with clenched fists and bellicose expressions. Jimmy scooted backward, only to bump into the overturned trash can. Outnumbered three to one, he suddenly wished that he had left well enough alone.

"O-okay guys," he stammered, trying in vain to talk his way out of a severe beatdown. "Sorry for the misunderstanding. Have a good time at the game. Popcorn's on me." He smiled weakly up at the sneering hoodlums. "Uh . . . go Yankees?"

"Go nothing, fool." The gang leader grabbed Jimmy's throat with murder in his eyes. His fingers tightened on the reporter's windpipe. "Nobody messes with me and keeps suckin' oxygen!"

Oh my God, Jimmy realized in horror. *This guy's playing for keeps!*

A tingling sensation rushed over his body. Before he knew it, needle-sharp spines poked up from his skin like the quills of a porcupine. The spines shot from his face and palms, spearing his attacker, who recoiled in pain and surprise. *"Yaaaahh!"* the hood shrieked as the barbs punctured his skin. Looking like he had just run face-first into a cactus, he scrambled backward into the arms of his fellow Sphinxes, who appeared equally frightened by Jimmy's bizarre transformation. Their startled eyes bulged from their sockets.

"Let's bounce!" a spooked hooligan exclaimed. Assisting their limping comrade, the gang members beat a hasty retreat. They booked down the sidewalk as fast their drooping trousers permitted. "Dude's a *freak*!"

Jimmy barely noticed their departure. He was too busy staring in shock at the quills projecting from his hands. For a second, he feared that he had permanently turned into some sort of human porcupine, then breathed a sigh of relief as the pointy spines retracted back into his flesh. Within seconds, they had vanished entirely. Only a scattering of fallen quills upon the pavement proved that he hadn't imagined the whole thing.

I don't understand, Jimmy thought. *Why'd they come out when that guy tried to choke me, but not when he slugged me? And why shooting spines, anyway?*

His experiment had been a success of sorts, but had left him even more confused than before. Gathering his things, Jimmy clambered to his feet and made tracks toward the nearest subway station. His jaw ached. A dizzying mix of fear and excitement had his brain awhirl.

What's happening *to me?*

32 AND COUNTING.

GOTHAM CITY.

No longer bound by gravity, Mary Marvel soared through the heart of a raging thunderstorm. She thrilled in the fury of the tempest and her new-found powers. The night sky serenaded her. The thunder roared like a symphony of drums, as though the very atmosphere were drawn tight over the planet and hammered on with the fists of gods. Turbulent winds caressed her, and driving sheets of rain baptized her rebirth. She could hear the dark clouds scrape against each other and the raw elemental forces cycling through the air around her . . . for *her*. Forty thousand thunderstorms happened every day, and right now she could feel ten thousand storms scattered between Gotham and Beijing. She was one with the lightning.

This is amazing, Mary exulted. *It's even better than before.* She twirled high above the city, exhilarated by the sheer bliss of being able to fly once more. All her prayers had been answered—and then some. *How on Earth could Teth-Adam walk away from a feeling like this?*

She wasn't just powered by magic anymore. She *was* magic. Her entire body was attuned to the mystical energies flowing unseen through the city below. She felt a subtle distortion in the ley lines and realized that something was seriously amiss. Perhaps that was why Madame Xanadu had tried to warn Mary away from Gotham before? As it turned out, however, she needn't have been concerned; with the combined powers of Black Adam and Isis at her disposal, Mary felt more than ready to deal with whatever occult menace awaited her.

Time to show the world that Mary Marvel is back—and better than ever.

She swooped down from the clouds toward an apartment building in Midtown. Her heightened senses drew her straight to the source of the disturbance. Five pregnant women, clad in matching white robes, knelt atop the roof of the building, chanting in unison. They faced each other from the five points of a pentagram. The pouring rain plastered their ceremonial robes to their swollen bodies. Thunderclaps punctuated the verses of their chant. Swirling fumes rose from a lit cauldron at the center of the pentagram. Freshly spilled blood traced the outlines of a five-pointed star. A nearby clock tower tolled midnight.

Okay, Mary decided at a glance. *This can't be a good idea. . . .*

"Stop!" she called out from overhead. "You don't know what you're doing!"

But they knew enough to raise a little hell, apparently. Before Mary could call a halt to the blasphemous ritual, fire and brimstone erupted from the cauldron, instantly incinerating all five congregants. The sudden flare-up blindsided Mary, who threw up an arm to protect her face from the bright orange flames. By the time she lowered her arm an instant later, the hellfire had died away and an honest-to-goodness demon stood atop the roof, surrounded by the smoking remains of the careless coven. The falling rain quickly extinguished the glowing embers.

Mary wasted little time mourning the reckless women; they had brought their incendiary demise on themselves. Instead she concentrated on the grotesque apparition they had foolishly summoned from the abyss. Curved horns crested the demon's skull. Fiery red eyes glowed like hellfire, and cloven hooves stomped against the tar-papered rooftop. Arcane markings tattooed his bestial features. All pretty standard, in other words. What was really disturbing was what the demon was *wearing.* To Mary's disgust, the creature appeared to be clad in a suit made up entirely of . . . dead babies?

Overlapping layers of emaciated infants squirmed all over the demon's leathery hide. Their shriveled, wrinkly faces were more hideous than cute.

Cyanotic blue skin was stretched tightly over their bony bodies. Scores of tiny, toothless mouths wailed incessantly, the shrill caterwauling quickly grating on Mary's nerves. They smelled like a hundred dirty diapers.

That's just gross, Mary thought, making a face. She descended directly into the demon's field of vision, hovering only a few yards above the rooftop. "So," she challenged the vile creature, "what's your deal?"

"Ha lo karno sako!" the demon snarled, baring its fangs. His guttural voice scraped at her eardrums. *"Devini morti! Formang'l al cii!"*

Mary didn't bothering trying to figure out the monster's infernal dialect. "Oh yeah, that's what I would have said."

"I am Pharyngula, the harvester of stillborn souls." He scowled, as though annoyed at having to repeat himself. "Forgive me; I have not spoken English in over six hundred years, and your peculiar idioms are unfamiliar to me. Long have I been trapped outside this sphere of existence."

"No doubt for the betterment of humanity," Mary guessed. She glanced at the steaming piles of ashes that were all that remained of the unfortunate coven. "Too bad those dimwits let you back in."

"Yes," Pharyngula agreed. "For you."

He flung out his arm and a flood of writhing fetuses shot across the distance between them. Dozens of grabby little hands seized her with unexpected strength. Tugging painfully on her hair, clothes, and flesh, they dragged her down toward Pharyngula until the demon's leering face was only inches away from her own. She felt his hot, sulfurous breath upon her face. The dead babies swarmed over her body, enveloping her in their greedy clutches. Her skin crawled beneath their clammy touch, and a forked tongue licked her cheek. "Hey!" she protested indignantly. "What do you think you're doing, you pediatric pest!"

"How do you say in English?" He racked his brain for the right words, grinning evilly as he came up with an appropriate translation. "I'm going to devour your flesh and suck the digested waste from your intestines!"

Yuck!

"No way!" Mary declared. She wasn't a just a frail, helpless girl anymore. If this revolting monstrosity thought she couldn't defend herself against a pack of stinking rug rats, he had a lot to learn. Calling upon the strength of Amon, she tore herself free from the avalanche of stillborn infants. She shook off their mewling corpses like a dog shedding its fleas, but her stomach still turned at the thought of the satanic sucklings crawling all over her. *You're paying for that,* she thought, glaring furiously at Pharyngula. *Big-time.*

A roundhouse punch connected with the demon's jaw. He went flying off the roof and plunged seven stories to the street below, where he smashed through the roof of a parked Mercedes. The loud metallic crash caused windows to light up all over the sleeping apartment building. A blaring car alarm woke up the entire neighborhood. Worried faces peered out into the night. The sirens and flashing lights of emergency vehicles converged on the scene, no doubt attracted by the pyrotechnic eruption of a few moments ago. The unleashed hellfire must have been visible from blocks away.

Mary hoped that Pharyngula had survived the fall. She wasn't done with him yet.

"Mortal harlot!" The demon rose from the crushed interior of the Mercedes. Howling in pain and anger, he shook a taloned fist at his attacker. The tip of one horn had been chipped off. A noxious green ichor bled from his nose. "I will consume your filthy human womb!"

Watch your mouth, Mary thought. Fists first, she dived toward her foe. His crimson orbs bulged in alarm as he saw her streaking down from on high. At the last minute, he ducked beneath her airborne assault, throwing himself facedown onto the mangled luxury car. Mary whooshed above his head, her gloved knuckles grazing the back of his skull. *Smooth move,* she conceded, *but don't think you're getting away from me that easily.*

Without even slowing down, she grabbed on to the chassis of an empty SUV and carried it up into the sky with her. Whirling in midair, she raised the huge, gas-guzzling vehicle above her head and took aim at the demon below. Visibly alarmed, Pharyngula frantically shifted gears. "Child, wait!" he pleaded. "I merely desire to inhabit this world again. I will eat only what I need to survive!"

"No deal!" Mary informed him. Her mission was clear: drive Pharyngula back to whatever purgatorial realm he hailed from. *Or kill him,* she thought with a shrug. *I'm not picky.* One way or another, he was going back to Hell.

She hurled the SUV at Pharyngula with the force of a catapult. Six tons of solid unibody construction smashed down on the demon, squashing him between the crumpled automobiles. Mary watched with satisfaction as an enormous fireball consumed both cars. The smell of burning gasoline carried the promise of barbecued hellspawn. She punched the air triumphantly.

Holy Moley! That felt great!

"DAMN YOU!" Torn metal shrieked in torment as Pharyngula clawed free of the flaming wreckage. His nauseating coat of babies was charred and smoking. Flames licked at the blackened flesh of the soulless brats. He tottered unsteadily upon his cloven hooves, a broken arm hanging limply at his side. His right eye was completely swollen shut. He spit out a mouthful of broken teeth and slime. "You have no right to deny me my rightful repast. Predator and prey alike, all creatures eat . . . and I am *starving!*"

Mary had no sympathy for the voracious demon. Launching herself at Pharyngula, she seized the monster's throat with one hand. All but demolished by her previous attacks, the outmatched demon was in no shape to fight back. "Sorry, devil day care," she quipped. "You may have a lot of mouths to feed, but you're not stuffing them with human flesh!"

Her fingers dug into his scaly neck. *Time to stop playing around,* she decided, *and finish this monster off for good.* She drew back her fist, ready to knock the demon's ugly kisser right off his shoulders. Mystical energy sparked and crackled around her clenched knuckles. *Say good-bye to your head, baby-snatcher.*

But before she could deliver the fatal blow, a blazing lightning bolt stabbed down from the heavens, striking both Mary and her defeated foe. A blinding flash of light briefly turned the night into day, and when the dazzling glare faded, no trace remained of either the girl or the demon. Only a smoking pile of rubble marked the site of their final confrontation. Bewildered cops and firefighters cautiously approached the shattered pavement. To their amazement, they found only a heap of blasted steel and concrete.

Mary Marvel—and her inhuman adversary—were gone.

METROPOLIS.

"**Help!**" a female voice cried out in the night. "Somebody!"

A second later, a scruffy-looking lowlife darted out of an alley, clutching a designer handbag in one hand and an open switchblade in the other. The eight-inch blade caught a gleam from the streetlight at the corner. The fleeing mugger smirked as he made his getaway.

Not so fast, Jimmy thought. He stepped out from beneath the shelter of a recessed doorway and directly into the path of the knife-wielding thief. Arms akimbo, he struck a heroic pose, the better to show off his homemade super-hero costume. A blue cowl concealed the upper half of his face. A blue A was emblazoned on the bright red tunic he wore over a navy blue sweater and trousers. A wide yellow sash circled his waist. Red gloves and boots, snazzily trimmed with yellow, completed the outfit. The color scheme echoed Superman's costume, perhaps a little too closely, but Jimmy didn't think of it as stealing. More like an homage. He admired his reflection in the window of a closed boutique.

"Oughta watch where you're going, dirtball," he warned the mugger, deliberately lowering his voice an octave. "'Cause you never know when"— he paused dramatically—"*Mr. Action* will be on the scene!"

"Mister who?" The mugger halted in his tracks, momentarily taken aback by the unexpected advent of the masked vigilante, but he quickly went on the offensive. "Out of my way, jerkface," he snarled as he slashed at Jimmy—that was, Mr. Action—with his knife.

I was hoping you'd try something like that, Jimmy thought. Sure enough, his torso stretched away from the striking blade. An elastic arm wrapped around the thief's knife hand, trapping it. Thorny spines protruded from Jimmy's knuckles only seconds before he slugged the flabbergasted mugger in the chin. Super-speed gave the punch enough *oomph* to knock the crook out cold with just one blow. He dropped onto the sidewalk like a sack of potatoes, his useless knife clattering against the cement.

"Hmm," Jimmy murmured to himself. "Maybe I should've drawn it out a bit longer." Ever since he'd decided to emulate Superman and use his mysterious new powers to combat evil, he had been looking forward to Mr. Action's big debut. He'd spent hours designing his costume, while trying to come up with the perfect super-heroic alias. Now that he'd finally taken on his first villain, it had been over way too soon. "Definitely gotta work on the banter too."

An attractive blonde, about Jimmy's age, emerged from the alley. A sexy off-the-shoulder gold lamé minidress and glittery disco belt suggested that she had been taking a shortcut home from a nightclub when the mugger had ambushed her. Although mussed up, she appeared more or less unharmed.

"Here you go, miss." Jimmy retrieved the stolen handbag and handed it back to the young woman. "Are you all right?"

"I think so." She stared at the vanquished mugger. Judging from her wide-eyed reaction, Jimmy guessed that she had seen him take down the crook with his powers. "Ohmigod, that was amazing!"

"Er, thanks," Jimmy replied, not quite sure what to say next. Superman always made this look so easy. "I'm, um, glad to have—"

Without warning, she threw her arms around his neck and planted a grateful kiss against his lips. The spontaneous embrace caught him completely off guard. Her warm softness pressed against him. The heady odor of her perfume flooded his nostrils. For a few seconds, he forgot about everything except the moist lips smooching his own. He was almost too dumbfounded to kiss her back.

Finally, after what felt like an eternity of bliss, the girl sheepishly pulled away from him. A fetching blush turned her cheeks pink. Jimmy guessed that he was just as red behind his mask. "I don't know what came over me," she offered by way of (non)explanation. "You're just so . . . adorable." Clutching her rescued handbag, she gave Jimmy a parting smile as she continued her trek home, sticking to the well-lit avenue this time. "Thank you!"

"Oh, uh, sure. . . ." Jimmy caught himself using his ordinary civilian voice, but the departing woman didn't seem to notice. She was a full block away before Jimmy realized that he had never gotten her name. This minor lapse did little to curb his euphoria, however. *Wow,* he thought, the taste of the nameless beauty still lingering on his lips, *this super-hero business is going even better than I dreamed!*

Frantic footsteps intruded on his rapture. Spinning around, he spotted the defeated mugger escaping back into the alley. *Drat!* Jimmy thought. *He must have come to while I was distracted.* He threw out his arms, but, now that he was no longer in danger, his limbs stubbornly refused to stretch after the thief. Jimmy pursued the crook, only to discover that his super-speed had evaporated as well. Within moments, the fleet-footed criminal had disappeared into a shadowy maze of back alleys. Huffing and puffing, Jimmy reluctantly abandoned the chase.

The mugger's escape took some of the luster off Mr. Action's debut. *Still,* Jimmy reminded himself, *I did get the girl her purse back. Not bad for a first try.*

He'd do better next time.

METROPOLIS.

Okay, Holly thought, *I could get used to this.*

She soaked luxuriously in a steaming hot tub, enjoying the Athenian Women's Shelter's well-equipped spa. She had the tub to herself, but she was not the only one taking advantage of the sumptuous facilities. Young women, clad only in towels or terry cloth robes, indulged in free massages and herbal treatments, coming and going at will. Holly's own robe was draped over a nearby bench. Windows of polarized glass let in the sunlight while keeping out prying eyes. Potted plants, marble columns, incense, background music, and ewers of fresh ice water added to the relaxing atmosphere.

It all seemed too good to be true, but Holly had yet to find the catch. Despite her lingering suspicions, she'd been at the shelter for days now, and no one had tried to sell her into white slavery or convert her to some creepy cult. Nor had she spotted any hidden spy-cams streaming video to pervs on the Internet. Granted, statues and shrines to the goddess Athena could be found on every floor of the shelter, but there wasn't any obvious brainwashing going on. Holly found herself in no hurry to leave such opulent accommodations. *Sure beats camping out in a soggy cardboard box. . . .*

"There you are!" A chirpy voice interrupted Holly's musings. She looked up to see a svelte blonde, about her own age and size, strolling toward the tub. She wore the same belted white tunic, which Holly had learned was called a chiton, that served as standard attire around the shelter. Braided yellow pigtails gave her a slightly comic appearance, as did the goofy smile plastered across her face. Not exactly Holly's type, but cute enough in her own way. A platter bearing a teapot and porcelain cup was expertly balanced atop the blonde's head. "I brought you some *gyokuro* Japanese tea." She knelt down and placed the platter at the edge of the tub. "Hope you're enjoying yourself, Holly."

"Oh, totally." Holly was mildly embarrassed that she didn't know the other woman's name. The blonde looked oddly familiar, but there were so many new faces here. By Holly's estimate, at least three dozen women currently resided in the shelter, all young, physically fit, and apparently unattached. The conspicuous absence of any single mothers or older women had struck Holly as curious, but it had been explained to her that, by Athena's degree, women with children and senior citizens were beyond the purview of this particular institution. Holly wasn't sure she entirely approved of that; still, as a newcomer and a guest, she didn't feel comfortable telling Athena how to run her own shelter. *At least not yet.*

"Great!" The blonde poured Holly a cup of tea. Her squeaky voice made her sound like she had OD'd on helium. "This place is a godsend. It saved my life and that of just about every other woman here." Making herself comfortable, she stretched out beside the tub, the better to converse with Holly. Her rosy-cheeked face shone with the fervor of a true believer. "I tell you, honey, before I got here I was a real mess . . . and trust me, that's the understatement of the year."

Holly sampled the tea. It tasted sweet and not at all bitter. "Thanks. This is delicious."

"Athena turned my life around," the blonde continued. "She taught me to love and respect myself for me, you know?" She let out a theatrical sigh. "I was the kind of girl that always needed a man, even if he was the worst possible example of the species. My last boyfriend was a real *maniac*."

Holly wasn't quite sure how to respond to this unsolicited confessional. "Uh, I'm not really here because of . . ."

"Honey, you don't have to talk about it if you don't want to," the blonde reassured her. "This is a pressure-free zone." She sat up and slapped her forehead. "Oh gosh, where's my manners? I didn't introduce myself." Smiling, she held out her hand. "I'm Harleen Quinzel."

Holly did a spit take. The teacup slipped from her fingers, spilling its contents into the tub. Taken aback by the name, Holly didn't even notice the dark tea infiltrating the swirling water around her.

Harleen Quinzel . . . ?

Harley Quinn!

The Joker's girlfriend!

Holly had never run into the notorious Harley Quinn before, but Selina had, and she'd had nothing good to say about the Joker's devoted moll, who was supposed to be just as bonkers as the Clown Prince of Crime himself. *Wow, Harley wasn't joking when she said that her ex was a "maniac." She just left out the "homicidal" part.* Holly scrutinized the blonde's features, mentally adding a domino mask, jester's cap, and white clown makeup. She compared the mental portrait to the outlandish face on Harley Quinn's Wanted posters. *It could be the same woman,* she acknowledged, *but what's she doing here in Metropolis when she should be in Arkham Asylum where she belongs?*

Holly's consternation must have shown on her face because Harley's sunny expression darkened momentarily. "Don't look at me like that," she pouted, withdrawing her hand. "I told you, I've changed. I'm a new woman." She smirked at Holly. "Besides, I'm not the one who spent her entire adult life sucking up to Catwoman."

Holly gulped.

She knows who I am?

31 AND COUNTING.

THE ROCK OF ETERNITY.

One minute Mary had been in Gotham City, about to knock that demon's block off. The next, she found herself . . . somewhere else.

Rough stone walls enclosed a murky tunnel that appeared to have been carved out of the solid rock surrounding her. The granite floor beneath her boots had been worn smooth by the passage of centuries. Torches sputtered in polished brass sconces. A cool breeze carried a whiff of incense. Compared to the raging thunder and blaring sirens she had just left behind, the hushed stillness of the tunnel came as a shock.

"Where . . . ?"

Disoriented by her abrupt shift in location, it took Mary a second to realize where she was. *Holy Moley*, she thought, *it's the Rock of Eternity!*

The mystical sanctuary, which existed outside time and space, had once been the home of the wizard Shazam, before the Spectre slew the venerable mage. Mary had often visited these tunnels before, but, without her powers, she had been unable to reach the Rock after waking up from her coma. It wasn't exactly the sort of place you could catch a bus or taxi to.

Yet here she was, without even trying. Mary looked around eagerly, hoping to find Freddy or her brother, but she appeared to have the dimly lit passageway all to herself. Even Pharyngula was nowhere to be seen.

"Hello?" Her voice echoed in the empty catacomb. "Is anyone here?"

A deep baritone answered her from the far end of the tunnel. "Just you and me, Mary."

"Billy! Cap!" Her heart leapt at the sound of that familiar baritone. She rushed down the corridor past a row of grotesque stone idols representing the Seven Deadly Enemies of Man: Pride, Avarice, Lust, Wrath, Gluttony, Envy, and Sloth. The leering gargoyles were not just statues, but the actual Sins, trapped in stone by the wizard's magic, but Mary was too excited to give the looming idols even a passing glance; after all, she had seen them many times before. Knowing exactly where she was now, she dashed through a framed archway into the cavernous throne room beyond. Jagged stalactites hung from the ceiling. A fuming brazier filled the grotto with the smell of incense. Magic mirrors, mounted upon the limestone walls, faced an imposing marble throne. Mary scarcely noticed any of these details, her attention riveted by the solitary figure standing beside the glowing brazier.

Her brother was waiting for her.

At least she *thought* it was her brother.

"Billy? Is that really you?"

She barely recognized him at first. Instead of his cheerful red and yellow uniform, Captain Marvel now wore a spotless white version of his traditional costume. Only the golden thunderbolt and trimmings remained the same. His revised garb was as chastely white as her own new look was black as night. And, like her, not only his apparel had changed. His short black hair had also turned snow-white and was now several inches longer. There was something different about his manner too. Even though her twin brother turned into an adult whenever he said the magic word, he had always kept his youthful exuberance and sunny disposition. But now the weight of the world seemed to rest heavily upon his broad shoulders. His wide face was etched with worry lines that Mary was certain she had never seen before. In a way, his austere, authoritative mien reminded her of the ageless wizard who had once presided over the throne room. The legacy of Shazam was stamped upon his features.

"It's me, Mary," he assured her. "After a fashion."

What did he mean by that? She longed to rush over and hug her brother, yet something held her back. He seemed so different, so reserved.

"Oh, Billy, what's happened to you?"

He came forward to greet her. "It's complicated, Mary. After Shazam died, the world of magic was thrown into flux. All the power he controlled, all the dark forces he held at bay, ran amok. The old rules were rewritten. Malevolent entities, long barred from the mortal plane, began to find their way back into the world."

"Like Pharyngula?" She glanced back at the Seven Deadly Sins, half expecting to see the baby-snatching demon petrified alongside them. "What happened to him anyway?"

"You needn't worry about him any longer," Captain Marvel assured her. "He's been banished back to the netherworld."

And good riddance, Mary thought. She tried to make sense of what she had just heard. "Does all this have something to do with why I lost my powers?"

Her brother nodded. "In order to heal itself, the power of Shazam drew upon the Marvels, taking back the gifts it had bestowed on us before. You and Freddy both lost your powers, while as for me . . . Well, the power needed a new vessel here at the Rock of Eternity. *Someone* had to fill the void left by the wizard's absence."

"You?" Mary guessed.

"Me." He smiled sadly, and for a moment, Mary thought she spied a trace of the boyish hero she remembered. "Unlike before, when I would wield the power of the gods, now I am the keeper of that power."

Just like the wizard used to be, Mary realized. "But you're still Billy in there, right?" She contemplated his snowy locks and grave demeanor. "You seem . . . different, like you've changed somehow. What's this power done to you?"

"I grew up," he said.

Something about that simple declaration struck her as immeasurably sad. "And Freddy?" she asked.

"The power still needs a champion on Earth," Marvel explained. "Freddy is on a quest to prove himself worthy of that mantle. If he passes his trials, if he survives, he will become the World's Mightiest Mortal." He looked somberly into Mary's eyes. "It may be some time before you see him again, if ever."

Mary was shocked by her brother's ominous prediction. *How can he say that so calmly?* she thought in dismay. *The Marvel Family always sticks together! Or we used to.*

"What about me?" she asked, feeling a lump in her throat. "Where do I fit into all these changes?"

"That's why I brought you here." He sat down upon the marble throne. "I'm afraid we have a problem. A big one."

Mary tensed. She didn't like the sound of this. "I don't understand. What do you mean?"

"I watched your battle against Pharyngula," he informed her solemnly. "Frankly, it left me concerned."

"Why? I was just doing what I used to do. I was fighting evil." *And doing a pretty kick-ass job of it,* she recalled with pride. *What's Billy's problem?*

"It's the way you went about it." He shook his head in disapproval. "I've never seen you so brutal, so savage. Even after Pharyngula had no more fight left in him, you didn't let up. You looked like you were on the verge of killing him."

So? she thought indignantly. *He was a flesh-eating demon, wasn't he?*

"Look at you, Mary," Captain Marvel said severely. "Even your uniform is darker than before." He eyed her new wardrobe with obvious concern. "What's happened to you?"

I could ask you the same thing, she thought. *In fact, I did.*

Still, she figured he deserved an explanation. "The power I have now came from Black Adam." She wondered briefly how Adam had managed to retain his powers after she and Freddy had lost theirs. Perhaps it was because he derived his strength from an entirely different pantheon of gods? "He surrendered it to me willingly."

"You *what*?" Captain Marvel lurched to his feet, clearly appalled by her revelation. Apparently his magic mirrors had missed that particular development. "Are you out of your mind? You have no idea what that tainted power could do to you!"

Mary bristled at his tone. This was *not* the joyful family reunion she had been praying for. She hadn't spent so much time searching for Billy just to be lectured to. "What was I supposed to do?" she shot back. "I woke up from a coma, I had no powers, and I was totally alone." An anger she had never dared acknowledge came pouring out of her. It was like it had been simmering inside her all this time, just waiting to erupt. An aggrieved inner voice egged her on. "I couldn't find Freddy; I couldn't find you. . . . What else was I to do?"

"Start a brand-new life?" her brother suggested gently. Overcoming his initial shock and outrage, he adopted a milder tone. He stepped forward and laid a comforting hand upon her shoulder. His icy blue eyes regarded her with compassion . . . or was it just pity? "Mary, did you ever think that maybe it was destiny that you lost your powers? That you weren't meant to have them forever?"

Mary couldn't believe what she was hearing. "You don't know that," she whispered hoarsely, getting more worked up by the moment. Her face flushed with emotion. "Did you ever think that perhaps my getting Black Adam's power was precisely what was *supposed* to happen?" Raising her voice, she slapped his hand away from her shoulder. He staggered backward, blindsided by the rebuff. "You don't know what it was like for me before, after you abandoned me in that miserable hospital." Painful memories stoked the seething resentment growing inside her. "I have power again, Billy. And I'm going to use it for good, just like before!"

She clenched her fists. *First Madame Xanadu,* she thought furiously. *Now my own brother!* They seemed determined to keep her weak and helpless, like she was still just a child who couldn't be trusted to fight evil on her own. *Well, I'll show them.*

She launched herself toward the ceiling. Shattered stalactites rained down onto the throne room as she smashed through solid rock like a human missile. Falling rubble knocked over the flaming brazier, spilling burning coals onto the floor. The shock wave generated by her blastoff cracked the magic mirrors, and the Seven Deadly Sins grinned evilly. Pride and Wrath looked particularly pleased. "And if you can't approve of that, then I'll pursue my destiny alone!"

"Mary! *Wait!*" her brother called, but Mary wasn't listening anymore. She was her own woman now, not just Captain Marvel's perky teenage sister. With the awesome powers at her disposal, she could easily find her own way back to the mortal plane. Her fists drilled a brand-new tunnel through the Rock of Eternity until she burst out into the timeless ether outside, leaving behind a gaping cavity in the floating stone spire. Spectral shapes and apparitions drifted like cloud formations through an empty gray void. Her brother's voice receded into the distance until it vanished altogether. "Maryyyyyyyy . . ."

She was alone again, but that didn't seem quite so bad anymore.

Look out, world. Here I come!

SAN FRANCISCO.

Titans Tower occupied an island in the harbor, not far from the Golden Gate Bridge. Jimmy could see the famous bridge from the top floor of the gleaming, T-shaped high-rise that served as the headquarters for the youthful champions known as the Teen Titans. One-way bulletproof windows offered a spectacular view of the misty bay below.

"Is this your idea of a joke, Olsen?" Robin asked. Batman's sidekick eyed "Mr. Action" dubiously. An ebony cloak was draped over Robin's dark red uniform. A few years younger than Jimmy, the slim, athletic teenager already had an impressive reputation as a crime fighter. His black domino mask failed to conceal his skepticism.

"Um, no?" Jimmy replied, slightly taken aback by the Boy Wonder's reaction. He had caught a red-eye flight from Metropolis just to make this appointment with Robin, who currently served as the leader of the Titans. To Jimmy's disappointment, none of the other Titans seemed to be around. *Guess they had other plans for the weekend.*

Robin still seemed unconvinced. He glanced around the high-tech conference room. A chrome silver round table held seats for the team's shifting membership, including a reinforced steel chair for Cyborg. A flat-screen monitor covered the far wall. "Seriously, is Lois Lane hiding with a video camera somewhere?"

"Listen to me," Jimmy insisted. "I'm not here for the *Planet*. I want to join the Teen Titans."

He had given the matter plenty of thought. As promising as his solo career as a super hero looked to be, he could only imagine the awesomeness he'd bring to a group dynamic. The only question had been figuring out what team would be right for him. The Outsiders were too angsty, the Doom Patrol was too weird, and as for the Justice League . . . Well, Jimmy was humble enough to realize that he probably needed to start out in the minors before working his way up to the majors. The Teen Titans, which had started out as a team composed entirely of the Justice League's youthful sidekicks, had struck him as the perfect place for Mr. Action.

Robin, on the other hand, seemed to have his doubts. "Jimmy, no offense, but—"

"I know," Jimmy interrupted him. "I don't blame you. I wouldn't believe me either. But give me a chance and I'll show you what I can do." He put up his dukes. "I'm not just 'Jimmy Olsen, cub reporter' anymore. I'm Mr. Action."

"Mr. Action?" Robin echoed. "Wow. I guess all the good names really are taken."

At least I'm not named after a bird, Jimmy thought. "Attack me," he challenged Robin. "Don't be afraid. I want you to attack me so I can show you my powers."

Besides, that's the only way they work.

But instead of testing him, Robin just sighed. "Okay, let's talk about what's going on here, Jimmy."

"I need you to take me seriously," Jimmy complained. What was Robin's problem anyway? *I bet he never treats Beast Boy like this!*

"I know you're tight with Superman," Robin said patiently. "Sometimes, when we have a close relationship with, say, a father figure who also happens to be famous . . ."

Jimmy saw where he was going with this. "This isn't about Superman!" Or Batman, for that matter. "I have powers. I don't know why or how, but I have them and I want to use them to help people!"

His sincerity seemed to convince Robin. "All right," the costumed youth conceded reluctantly. "I'll . . . attack you."

"Great!" Jimmy enthused. He adopted a martial arts pose he'd seen in a movie once. "Let's do thi—"

Robin's heel shot past his defenses, nailing him in the chin. The powerful kick knocked Jimmy backward onto his butt. The hard tile floor made Jimmy wish that they had sparred on a mat instead. *I didn't even see that coming!*

"I'm sorry!" Robin said, sounding even more mortified than Jimmy. "I thought you'd duck!"

Jimmy massaged his aching chin. "I don't understand. I should've stretched or something. . . ."

"I didn't hit you *that* hard," Robin said, not quite getting it. He reached down and helped Jimmy to his feet. "Are you okay? Do you need to visit the infirmary?"

Jimmy tried to make sense of what had just occurred. "Wait . . . this happened before in Metropolis. These guys in Suicide Slum attacked me, but it wasn't until my life was in danger . . ." A sudden realization dawned in his eyes. "Wait a minute," he accused Robin. "You held back."

"Of course I did," Robin admitted. "You think I want Superman pissed off at me when I send his pal back to Metropolis in a neck brace?"

Jimmy realized that he was fighting a losing battle. "There's no chance I can get you to attack me for real, is there?"

Robin shook his head. "I'm sorry, Jimmy. If it makes you feel any better, we're not really looking for any more Titans right now. We're cramped enough as it is."

Jimmy wondered if that was true, or if Robin was just being polite.

"Let's not have an *American Idol* moment," the Boy Wonder said sympathetically. "You're a photographer, and a damn good one. Don't discount the impact you make on people's lives." He shook Jimmy's hand. "Stick with what you're good at."

Jimmy appreciated Robin's attempts to soften the blow, but he wasn't ready to throw in the towel just yet. "No, Robin. All I want to do is help people."

Even if he wasn't cut out to be a super hero, he knew he'd been given these powers for a reason. One way or another, he was going to find out what they were for . . . or die trying.

30 AND COUNTING.

GOTHAM CITY.

An earsplitting explosion greeted Mary Marvel's return to the mortal plane. Descending from the night sky, she saw flames and smoke erupting from the uptown branch of the Gotham National Bank. The blistering heat from the fire could be felt even high above the city. Thick black smoke filled her nostrils. A glance at a clock tower informed her that it was nearly three in the morning. *Thank goodness,* she thought. At this hour, it was unlikely that anyone had been inside the bank when it blew up. *Probably no need to search for casualties.*

Sirens heralded the approach of police cars and fire trucks. Assuming that the authorities could cope with the blaze on their own, Mary scanned the scene from the air, looking for some clue as to the origin of the explosion. Foul play seemed like a safe bet; banks seldom exploded on their own, especially in Gotham City.

She wasn't the only one taking in the show. Her eyes lit up as she spied a lanky figure watching the fireworks from the rooftop of a five-story building across the street from the burning bank. Embossed purple question marks, sewn into the fabric of a dapper green suit, tie, and bowler hat, immediately identified the onlooker as Batman's longtime nemesis Edward Nigma, aka the Riddler. He lowered a pair of high-powered binoculars. A purple domino mask failed to conceal his avid interest in the spectacular conflagration. Intent upon the fire, he appeared unaware of the black-clad super heroine spying on him from above.

"Well, well!" She chuckled to get his attention. "What have we here?" After her infuriating reunion with Billy at the Rock of Eternity, she welcomed the opportunity to take out her frustration on a deserving target. "Explosions, alarms, and one big-name Gotham bad guy just begging for an ass-kicking!"

To her slight disappointment, the Riddler appeared unruffled by her arrival. "I would agree with your assessment, young lady," he said glibly, while brazenly attempting to look up her skirt, "although it appears I should make you aware of certain facts before you—*hey!*"

Swooping down from the sky, she nabbed him in midsentence. His bowler hat went flying, exposing receding brown hair, as she grabbed on to his collar and plucked him off the rooftop. Startled, he dropped his binoculars, which tumbled downward while she carried him high up into the air, hundreds of feet above his former perch. The lost spy-glasses crashed loudly onto the roof below.

"Before you jump to conclusions and turn me into street pizza, my dear," he said calmly, despite the fact that he was currently dangling from a great height, "although I sincerely hope that such a virtuous Girl Scout as yourself would never do such a thing, I must inform you that, as a duly licensed private investigator, I don't *commit* crimes any longer. I *solve* them."

"What are you saying?" Mary asked, irked by his persistently chipper attitude. "That you've *reformed*?" She raised a skeptical eyebrow. *That's what Black Adam said too. Before he pounded me into a coma.*

The Riddler stuck to his story. "Ask Batman if you don't believe me."

"I don't," she said confidently. "I saw you. You were at the crime scene *before* the police." She gave him a good shaking. "Riddle your way out of that one!"

"It's no mystery," he insisted. "Like you, I heard the explosion and came to investigate." Twisting in her grasp, he pointed down at the sidewalk far below. "Look! See that muddy trail leading away from the bank? It will most assuredly lead us to whoever's *really* behind this outrage."

Mary descended to the rooftop to get a closer look. To her annoyance, she saw that a trail of thick brown glop did indeed stretch from the rear of the bank to the mouth of a secluded alley a few blocks away. Given that there were no parks or gardens nearby, the large quantity of mud looked distinctly out of place. Maybe the Riddler was actually onto something.

Shrugging free of her grip, he dropped back onto his feet. "I was just about to follow it before your timely arrival," he continued, retrieving his hat from where it had fallen before. In his emerald outfit, he looked like a tall, skinny leprechaun. "What do you say, Mary Marvel? Care to play girl detective?"

Mary scowled. She had been looking forward to teaching this irritating clown a lesson. But what if he was telling the truth, and the real culprit was getting away as they spoke? "Okay," she said reluctantly, her hands upon her hips. "You've bought yourself five more unbruised minutes, but don't expect me to trust you, Riddler." Taking hold of his shoulder, she dived off the roof and zoomed toward the alley in question. His terrified yelp gave her a bit of satisfaction before they touched down onto the grimy floor of the alley. "Once a criminal, always a criminal."

He recovered his composure far too quickly for her liking. "You don't believe people can change, little miss Mary?" He scoped her out by the glow of the streetlights. "Then answer me this: What used to be bright and sunny, but is now black all over?"

She knew he was alluding to her recent makeover. "Point taken," she conceded. "But consider yourself warned. I might not be such a Girl Scout anymore."

"I'll forgo asking you for cookies, then," he quipped. "But about your new look, Mary, I have to say I'm not really a big fan." He looked down his nose at her sleek black dress and boots. "A little too Dark Knight for my tastes."

His cocky demeanor still nettled Mary, but she tried not to take it personally. Years of dealing with Batman had probably rendered the Riddler immune to intimidation; he couldn't have lasted long in Gotham otherwise. "Hey, there's something I don't need," she shot back. "Fashion tips from a goofball in a green derby."

"No need to get defensive," Nigma chided her. Bowing at the waist, he stepped aside to let Mary lead the way into the murky alley. "Ladies first."

Mary suspected that the Riddler's chivalrous gesture had less to with courtesy than with his own cowardly sense of self-preservation. *Sure,* she thought, *hide behind the bulletproof girl.*

With the police and firefighters still preoccupied with containing the fire, they had the telltale smears of mud all to themselves. As she marched deeper into the alley, leaving the streetlights behind, she wondered why someone would blow up a bank on purpose. To make a political statement, or just to destroy all evidence of a bank heist? And what was the deal with all this mud anyway? There weren't any mucky footsteps on the ground, only scattered clumps of slick brown goo.

"Intriguing," the Riddler observed, tagging along behind her. "Most intriguing."

Mary had no idea what he was finding so fascinating. Looking around, she didn't see any obvious clues, just a dirty alley full of rusty trash cans, empty liquor bottles, and a soggy cardboard box that was probably some wino's home address. Cigarette butts, fast-food wrappers, and beer cans littered the uneven pavement. Obscene graffiti and gang signs were spray-painted onto sooty brick walls. Rickety fire escapes climbed toward the rooftops, but nobody seemed to be using them to make a getaway. A stray cat hissed at Mary from the shadows. The less said about the smell, the better.

A glimpse of the Bat-Signal, shining brightly through the smoke-filled sky, prompted her to wonder why Batman was nowhere to be seen. *Probably dealing with some bigger emergency,* she guessed. *Maybe with the Justice League.* For all she knew, Gotham's premier vigilante was helping the League fend off an alien invasion at the moment. *I suppose not even Batman can be everywhere at once.*

Disappointingly, the trail led to a literal dead end. A high concrete wall, topped by concertina wire, blocked their path. A sizable heap of mud, large enough to fill a wheelbarrow or two, was deposited at the base of the wall. Bats Suck! was scrawled on the dirty concrete. Jokers Rule! Mary could easily fly over or smash through the barrier, of course, but that wasn't the point. Their quarry had given them the slip.

"End of the line," the Riddler remarked, stating the obvious. He slipped past Mary to examine the mound of mud. Extracting a customized green and purple pencil from his pocket, he poked the gunk experimentally. "Although, you know, I'm beginning to suspect that this isn't actually mud at all."

Mary eyed him suspiciously. Was he just stringing her along for some reason? "Okay, Sherlock, what is it?"

Before he could answer, the pencil was sucked from his grasp. He jumped back from the quivering sludge as it suddenly came to life before their eyes. The amorphous muck rose up from the pavement to take on a vaguely humanoid form. Beady red eyes ogled Mary from a crude approximation of a face. A pair of pulsating slits provided a mere suggestion of a nose. The mouth was just an open gash beneath the nostrils. Rows of jagged ceramic shards gnashed together like teeth. Broken pieces of pencil were spat onto the ground. A phlegmy voice answered Mary's question.

"Clay!"

Of course! Mary kicked herself for not figuring it out earlier. The being before her was one of Batman's most freakish foes, a malleable mass of malevolence that had once been an unscrupulous treasure hunter named Matt Hagen. Now better known as . . .

"Clayface!"

"You bet, honey!" the villain gurgled. Drawing the excess sludge back into his person, he expanded until he towered over both Mary and the Riddler. The self-proclaimed sleuth scurried behind Mary, shamelessly using her as a shield. Clayface oozed forward menacingly. "Too bad you and Nigma couldn't leave well enough alone!"

Clayface surged at them like a tidal wave, engulfing them in a flood of viscous muck, which clung to Mary like a sticky mixture of quicksand and wet cement. The loathsome avalanche tore the Riddler away from her. He flailed wildly, struggling to keep his head above the suffocating clay. "Mary!" he squealed like the rat that he was. "Where are you?"

"Here!" The squishy clay was everywhere, in her hair, on her face, enveloping her entire body. She swallowed a mouthful by mistake, and gagged in disgust. Clayface tasted worse than the mud pies she had crafted as a child. She coughed up the gritty sludge. "I'm here . . . and I'm not happy!"

That was putting it mildly. *First dead babies,* she thought, *now this!* The clay hardened around her like concrete, squeezing her tightly. Wet goo seeped into her gloves and boots. It felt cold and damp against her skin. *When did bad guys get so gross?*

"You should have stayed outta Gotham, babe!" Clayface gloated in her ear. "You ain't dirty enough for this town!"

"Is that so?" Mary said, her temper flaring. "We'll see about that!"

Enough was enough. Exerting her strength, she broke loose of Clayface's slimy embrace, sending broken chunks of clay in all directions. Bellowing wetly, the monster hurled a glutinous fist at her, but she deftly evaded the punch so that it splattered uselessly against the wall behind her. Taking to the air, she yanked the Riddler free as well and tossed him, none too gently, out of harm's way. The empty cardboard shelter cushioned his landing, which Mary figured was probably more than he deserved. "Atta girl, Mary!" he cheered her on from the sidelines. "Don't worry. I've got your back!"

Yeah, right, Mary thought.

She didn't waste another moment on her worthless partner. There was a bigger mess that needed to be cleaned up right now.

"Think you can sucker punch Mary Marvel, Clayface?" Calling upon the speed of Heru, as well as Isis's divine mastery of the winds, she flew circles around Clayface at faster and faster speeds, until she generated a whirling cyclone that sucked up every last clump of the monster's gelatinous substance, along with any nearby trash. Clayface raged inside the spinning vortex, but his profane threats were drowned out by the roaring whirlwind, which lifted him off the ground and sent him rocketing into orbit. "Wrong!"

Slowing to a more leisurely pace, Mary dismissed the turbulent winds. A canvas bag crashed to the ground in the tornado's wake. Coins, greenbacks, and expensive jewelry spilled onto the floor of the alley, immediately attracting the Riddler's attention. "Case closed, Mary!" he chortled gleefully. "I've uncovered the loot!"

"And I shot Clayface into outer space," she replied, unimpressed by her partner's dubious achievement. She landed nimbly on the pavement and wiped a few leftover traces of Clayface from her face and costume. Cut off from the monster's animating intelligence, the remaining clumps of clay flaked off her easily. One of her new outfit's many magical properties, she had come to realize, was its preternatural ability to repel dirt and other stains. *Guess the gods want me looking my best.*

"Outer space?" the Riddler parroted. He glanced up at the heavens. Mary noticed that the billowing black smoke was already beginning to disperse; apparently Gotham's Bravest already had the fire under control. "A bit extreme, don't you think?"

"Was it?" The question gave her pause; to be honest, she had hurled Clayface into orbit without even thinking about it. "Was that too much?" She felt a twinge of guilt. Despite his monstrous appearance, Matt Hagen wasn't actually a soulless demon like Pharyngula, just a bizarrely mutated human being. Maybe she should have gone easier on him?

Then again, an inner voice soothed her conscience, *it's not like he didn't have it coming.*

"No biggie," she insisted, more to herself than to the Riddler. "He's just dirt, and dirt will fall back to Earth sooner or later."

"Maybe," Nigma replied, not sounding entirely convinced. Unlike her, his once-dapper outfit was now liberally coated with damp clay. He wiped his filthy hands on his trousers and straightened his tie. "Certainly, Hagen has proved ridiculously durable over the years. And yet . . . I've spent enough time around Arkham to recognize when someone is out of control. And I'm *not* talking about Clayface."

Billy said the same thing about me, Mary recalled uncomfortably, *after I trashed that demon.* She shrugged, trying to pretend that the Riddler's snide remark hadn't hit a nerve. The smug former villain was the last person she wanted to confide in. "I admit that I don't really know my own strength anymore."

The Riddler smiled slyly, like she wasn't telling him anything he hadn't already figured out on his own. "If I may be so bold as to make a suggestion," he said, pushing his luck, "perhaps you should consider seeking a mentor? Maybe someone who specializes in magic . . . or perhaps anger management?"

29 AND COUNTING.

THE NANOVERSE.

Molecules loomed like small moons as Donna Troy and her new companions began their search for Ray Palmer. Encased in a transparent sphere of shimmering energy, courtesy of the Monitor's virtually unlimited technology, they shrank in size much as the Atom himself once did, discovering a whole new realm of existence at the subatomic level. Outside the sphere, electrons whizzed about spinning nuclei, looking like sparking comets. Atoms of various shapes and sizes collided with each other, sometimes linking to form larger molecules that resembled elaborate glowing constellations. Everything was in constant motion. Quantum particles blinked in and out of existence according to the capricious laws of probability. Donna thought she saw an asteroid-sized atom of oxygen suck two smaller hydrogen atoms into its orbit, forming a single molecule of water, but she couldn't be sure. Chemistry had never been her strong suit.

Is this what atoms and molecules really look like at this scale, she wondered, *or is my brain just processing all this bizarre sensory input into images I can sort of comprehend?* She suspected the latter; human eyes weren't built to see the world this way. *We've probably already shrunk beyond the wavelengths of visible light.*

"So where exactly are we supposed to be going again?" Jason Todd asked. He tapped his foot impatiently against the floor of the sphere, seemingly unimpressed by the mind-boggling scenery outside. "And how are we supposed to find the Atom in all this sci-fi craziness?"

Donna guessed that Jason was feeling out of his element. He was more used to beating up crooks in Gotham than embarking on microscopic odysseys. She, on the other hand, had already been from one end of the universe to another . . . and then some.

The Monitor spoke slowly, as though to a small child. "Before he disappeared, Ray Palmer often explored this so-called nanoverse. According to my research, he spent some time in one particular subatomic realm . . . to which we now travel."

"There's no guarantee we'll actually find the Atom there," Donna admitted. "The nanoverse is a big place, relatively speaking, but it's as good a place as any to start looking for him."

Jason shrugged. "If you say so," he said dubiously. A crimson mask once more concealed his features. "Anyway, don't look now, but it seems like we're getting somewhere."

Outside the sphere, molecules broke apart into atoms, which dissolved into swirls of pulsating quarks, gluons, bosons, and neutrinos. A single particle soon filled the horizon, growing larger and larger as the sphere and its passengers shrank to meet it. Oceans and continents covered the surface of what now appeared to be a full-sized planet. As the sphere came in for a landing amidst a vast, verdant jungle, Donna found it hard to grasp that this entire world was actually infinitesimal in size.

"Indeed," the Monitor confirmed. "We have reached our destination. Let us pray that it shall be the first and final stop on our journey."

"Yeah, right," Jason muttered. "We should be so lucky."

The golden sphere dissolved into the ether, leaving the trio standing in a sunny meadow surrounded by dense undergrowth. The tropical atmosphere was hot and muggy. Insects buzzed in the background. The torrid temperature came as a jolt after the autumnal chill of the cemetery back in San Francisco; Donna didn't envy Jason his heavy black leather gear. *He must be sweltering.* Glancing up she saw that the light and heat came from a glowing yellow orb high in the sky. *A solitary photon,* she speculated, *or some sort of radioactive particle?*

It took Donna a moment to realize how small they were compared to the scenery around them. Leafy ferns the size of pine trees towered over them. Grass blades as wide as broadswords stretched above their heads, hemming them in. A brightly colored bird flew by overhead; it looked like it was big enough to carry any one of them off in its talons. Donna hoped that it wasn't hunting for a snack.

Was there a reason that the Monitor had chosen to bring them into this world in such diminutive proportions? Frankly, Donna didn't like the idea of being Lilliputian-sized in an alien jungle. Who knew what kind of predators were lurking in this lush, primeval wilderness? Wouldn't it be safer if they were bigger than, say, field mice?

She turned to ask the Monitor for an explanation, but a sudden rustling in the greenery put them all on guard. "Looks like we've got company," Jason said. He drew a twelve-inch Bowie knife from his belt. "Wanna bet they're not friendly?"

"We don't know that," she rebuked him, but assumed a defensive posture just in case. She heard multiple life-forms moving in the bushes all around them. "Remember, no unnecessary violence!"

Jason smirked. "Don't tell me that," he quipped. "Tell *them.*"

A party of armed warriors burst through the high grass walls, surrounding them on all sides. Donna blinked in surprise. She wasn't quite sure what sort of beings she had expected to find on a subatomic particle, but the last thing she'd expected was . . . ape-men riding giant frogs?

But that was exactly what confronted them now. Shaggy primates, who vaguely resembled Earth's ancient Neanderthals, sat astride massive amphibians the size of hippopotamuses, holding on to the reins of their warty mounts. Crudely sewn animal skins were reinforced by breastplates and armbands carved from polished bone. The warriors brandished primitive spears, clubs, and shields. Deep-set eyes regarded the strangers with undisguised suspicion.

They're roughly the same size we are, Donna realized. *That must be why the Monitor shrank us down so far, so that we could more easily communicate with the natives.*

"Name yourself, outlanders!" one of the ape-men demanded. An intricate carved ivory helmet and voluminous fur cloak suggested that he was in command of the warriors. His sloping forehead and prognathous jaw reminded Donna of Gnarrk, a good-hearted caveman who had once fought beside the Teen Titans. The fangs of some deadly predator dangled on a cord around the chieftain's neck. "How dare you invade our kingdom?"

"Please, we come in peace!" Donna held up her empty hands as a gesture of goodwill. "We are seeking a friend of ours. You may know him as Ray Palmer, or perhaps the Atom."

"You will find no friends here!" the chieftain growled. "And we will not betray Ray Palmer to the likes of you!" He glared venomously at the Monitor. "I know a demon when I see one!"

The Monitor bristled at the charge. "I am Monitor, not a shadow-demon." He strode aggressively toward the mounted ruler. "If you know where the Atom may be found, you must tell us immediately."

"Hold your tongue, abomination." The chieftain goaded his frog forward to meet the Monitor. He beat his fist against his chest. "I am Winn-Dar, ruler of this domain, and I do not answer to the commands of outsiders!"

Poison sprayed from swollen glands above the huge amphibian's bulging eyes. The toxic discharge splattered harmlessly against the Monitor's personal force field, but the powerful alien frowned in annoyance. His right hand glowed ominously as he pointed at the frog.

"No!" Donna pleaded. She stepped between the Monitor and the indignant chieftain, anxious to keep the situation from escalating out of control. "Hear us out, I beg you. Give words a chance before bloodshed!"

Jason stepped past her. "Nice try, Donna, but there's only one language these missing links will understand." His carbon steel knife gleamed in the light of the micro-sun.

Winn-Dar spied the blade at once. "Attack!" he commanded his warriors, who lunged at the intruders from all sides. Furious whoops and war cries precluded any further discussion, and Donna reluctantly went on the defensive. A monstrous frog leapt toward her, seemingly intent on crushing her beneath its webbed feet, but she blocked its descent with one hand. Grabbing hold of the amphibian's clammy belly, she hurled it over her head into a throng of warriors behind her. The frog's startled rider let out a yelp as his steed crashed headfirst into his own kinsman, scattering them across the meadow.

Another frog-rider bounded at her from the left. "Die, she-devil!" the mounted hominid bellowed as he swung the jawbone of an unknown beast at Donna's head. Amazon training came to the fore as she easily parried the blow with her bracelet. The crude weapon shattered against the silver wristband. "Sorry," she said as she knocked him out of his saddle with a super-strong right cross. He was out like a light before he hit the ground. Riderless, the panicked frog jumped over Donna into the safety of the beckoning jungle.

A few yards away, another warrior charged at the Monitor from behind. *"Rrraahhhh!"* he roared as he raised his club to batter the stranger's brains in. But the Monitor casually teleported out of the way so that the warrior's club swung through empty air instead, leaving the baffled ape-man gaping in confusion.

"Can you conclude this bestial melee soon?" the Monitor asked as he reappeared a few feet away from where he had been standing before. His arms were clasped behind his back while he surveyed the battle with obvious boredom. "The longer we must search for Ray Palmer, the less likely we shall find him in time."

"Do not speak his name, foul creature!" Winn-Dar shouted. He shook his stone-tipped spear in the Monitor's direction. "If it was from you he fled, then let your hunt end here!"

Intent upon the inhuman Monitor, the chieftain was caught off guard when Jason sprang at him from the side, knocking him off his steed. They tumbled together onto the floor of the meadow, Winn-Dar's body cushioning Jason's fall. The ivory helmet tumbled from the Neanderthal's thick skull as Jason softened him up with a vicious punch to the jaw.

"Listen, jackass!" Jason knelt atop the fallen ape-man, his knee pressing down onto Winn-Dar's chest. He waved his knife in his opponent's face. "It's obvious Ray Palmer is a friend of yours. Great. Us too."

"Jason, wait!" Donna deflected an oncoming spear with her bracelet as she spotted the potentially tragic drama unfolding only a few yards away. Along with the combatants, she froze at the sight of the chieftain's extreme peril. The other warriors looked on uncertainly, anxious over the fate of their

leader. Donna wished she could assure them that Jason meant Winn-Dar no harm, but she wasn't sure that was the case. The former Robin didn't play by the old rules anymore.

To his credit, the defeated ruler refused to let the knife-wielding youth intimidate him. "You claim to be friends of Palmer?" He snorted derisively. "That would be easier to believe without your blade in my face!"

"You asked for it," Jason replied, "with the lousy welcome you gave us." He nodded at Donna and the Monitor. "Now, my friends here are reasonable people, but I'm not, and I'm tired of being jerked around." He poked the tip of the dagger into the chieftain's nostril. "So tell me where to find the Atom or your nose will bleed out the back of your skull!"

Is he bluffing? Donna wondered. *By the gods, I hope so!*

Winn-Dar stared cross-eyed at the knife. A trickle of blood ran from his nostril. The entire meadow seemed to hold its breath, waiting to see what happened next. Donna considered tackling Jason, but even at super-speed she wasn't certain she could stop the other Titan from killing his hostage if he really wanted to. Jason had pretty fast reflexes—and what seemed like a hair-trigger temper.

"Gods below," Winn-Dar exclaimed. "You really mean it!" He surprised Donna by laughing heartily. A smile transformed his Neanderthal features. "Hah! I did not think the world of humans produced such warriors!"

Jason backed off and helped the chieftain to his feet. "It produced Ray Palmer, didn't it?"

"That it did," Winn-Dar agreed. He gestured to his troops, who obediently lowered their weapons. "Although I fear your world has also done its best to crush his spirit."

Satisfied that the battle was over, Donna approached Jason and the chieftain. "This is true," she admitted, recalling the heartbreaking events that had afflicted the Atom in recent years. "He has seen much sorrow in our realm."

Winn-Dar nodded gravely. "He did not speak of it, but his woe was plain to see when he passed through here some time ago. In years past, he was a merry hero who once did my people a great service, but now he seems to have lost his way. We told him that only powerful magicks could undo the doom that had befallen them."

The Monitor joined the conference. "And where would one seek such magicks?"

"For that, you must consult the shaman." The chieftain turned to address his people. "Bring forth the Wise One!"

Waving blades of grass parted behind the warriors and a newcomer entered the meadow. A hooded cloak, dyed a brilliant shade of red, hid the shaman's features. Small and slight of build, the nameless mystic walked softly through the grass. Charms and amulets adorned her slender arms and neck. A necklace of cowrie shells rattled gently as she approached them. Winn-Dar and his warriors bowed their heads in respect.

Jason shook his head in disbelief. "You gotta be joking! We're not seriously planning to take our marching orders from some pint-sized witch doctor?"

"Quiet," Donna shushed him. "On Paradise Island, one learns to heed the counsel of the oracles." She bowed her own head to the hooded figure and pressed her palms together, forming a steeple beneath her chin. "We are honored by your presence."

"Hail, travelers," the shaman greeted them in a high-pitched, mellifluous voice. She drew back her hood, revealing the elfin features of a young girl who appeared no more than six years old. More evolved than her Neanderthal cohorts, her waifish face was fine-boned and delicate. Large golden eyes hinted at wisdom far beyond her apparent years. Straight red hair fell past her graceful shoulders. Arched eyebrows gave her a distinctly fey appearance. "I am K'Dessa, high priestess of this realm."

"You?" Jason laughed at the very idea. He knelt down in front of the little girl. "You're barely old enough to—"

K'Dessa didn't let him finish. "I was igniting suns when your people had fins, Jason Todd." Arms crossed boldly over her chest, the tiny shaman met Jason's startled gaze with total confidence. "Yes, I know who you are. I also know from whence you and your companions have come, and what you desire. Ancient prophecies foretold of three travelers who would become the 'Challengers of the Unknown.'" Her golden eyes gleamed with occult knowledge. "The Ray Palmer passed this way on his journey, but he has left the inner worlds behind. You must seek him amidst the myriad Earths of your own plane of existence."

Myriad Earths? It took Donna a moment to realize what K'Dessa meant. "The Multiverse?"

Unlike most mortals, Donna was well aware that there were at least fifty-two alternate versions of Earth, located in parallel universes separated by sturdy dimensional barriers. Had the Atom somehow learned how to slip past those barriers?

"Aye," K'Dessa confirmed. "Unable to find peace here, he left to find a new life on another Earth."

"Which Earth?" the Monitor demanded. "Which universe?"

K'Dessa shook her head. "That I cannot say. I know only that the spirits have spoken to me of a great disaster that only the Ray Palmer can avert. Find him you must, so allow me to send you on your way." She raised her hands above her head. An unearthly green glow radiated from her childish form. The cowrie shell necklace rattled a percussive melody. Unseen voices chanted from the ether, and the world of K'Dessa and her people began to shrink away before Donna's eyes. "Farewell, Challengers. And should you encounter the Ray Palmer in time, tell him that we are praying for him . . . and for all the worlds that be."

Donna grabbed on to Jason's hand as the shaman's spell whisked them away.

28 AND COUNTING.

METROPOLIS.

Located five hundred feet below the city, Project Cadmus was the world's foremost genetics facility. The top secret think tank, whose existence Jimmy had stumbled onto a few years back, struck him as his best shot at getting to the bottom of his mysterious new powers. Fortunately, the project's scientists seemed eager to oblige.

"We've been tracking your exploits as Mr. Action," Dr. Serling Roquette divulged as she escorted Jimmy through one of Cadmus's many underground corridors. The sixteen-year-old prodigy looked and dressed like any ordinary teenage mall rat, complete with flip-flops, denim shorts, and a faded black T-shirt advertising a punk rock band Jimmy had never heard of. Few people would ever guess that the slim young blonde was actually the project's head of genetics. "You come up with that costume yourself?"

Says the girl with the two-toned spiked hair, Jimmy thought. "That bad, huh?"

Serling shrugged. "I'm more curious as to why you took up crime fighting. What exactly makes that a natural response to incipient meta-human capability?"

"Maybe it's not for other people," Jimmy answered, "but I've been on the sidelines of the hero scene for years. 'Superman's pal,' you know?" He tried not to sound too ungrateful. "And it's been an honor, but still . . . a part of me feels left out and less than. Like I'm starving to death with my nose pressed up to the bakery window."

"Really?" Curious blue eyes peered at him through the lenses of her chunky white eyeglasses. "Because most costumed vigilantes have complicated, stressful lives."

"They also have a purpose," he explained, "and . . . a destiny, I guess. Things I always hoped would materialize for me someday." They walked past a series of experimental labs and menageries. Windows offered glimpses of various genetically engineered oddities, like a glow-in-the-dark chimpanzee and water-breathing rabbits. "I suppose I hoped that my new powers meant that I'd finally earn a place at the table with the people I admire most."

He neglected to mention his humiliating audition at Titans Tower. *What good are these wacky powers if I can't fight beside Earth's greatest heroes?*

Stainless steel doors parted with a *whoosh* as they arrived at a high-tech laboratory packed with futuristic hardware so advanced that Jimmy couldn't begin to guess its functions. Computers lined the walls. A flat steel bed was surrounded by robotic arms, also known as waldoes. Impressive-looking scanners and lenses were affixed to the ends of the arms. Dials and gauges were installed in the sides of the examination table. A posted notice read: WARNING. MUTAGENIC MATERIALS. HANDLE WITH CARE. A glowing green crystal, embedded in some sort of X-ray projector, looked suspiciously like kryptonite.

I hope Doogette Howser here knows what she's doing.

Unpleasant memories of Arkham surfaced as, at Serling's request, he stripped down to his boxer shorts. Blushing in embarrassment, he thought he heard the teenage scientist snicker, but maybe that was just his imagination. He lay down atop the cold metallic table while she attached electrodes to his chest and temples. She confiscated his signal-watch, then strapped his limbs to the table. "Just to keep you from squirming."

"What does this thing do again?" he asked nervously.

"You won't feel a thing," she assured him, tightening his bonds. "It's like a CAT scan, only more metaphysical."

She retreated to the safety of an enclosed control room at the south end of the laboratory. A thick sheet of transparent Plexiglas cut her off from Jimmy, leaving him alone in the sterile chamber. The apparatus around him started humming ominously. He tugged experimentally on his restraints. "How different?"

"You ever hear of biofeedback?" Her voice emerged from an intercom overhead. "This device measures your brain waves and cerebral activity. It then manufactures a three-dimensional, holographic composite of your subconscious mind for analysis." As she expounded learnedly on the sophisticated technology involved, it was easy to forget that she was still just a teenybopper. "Past studies, you see, suggest that the brain waves of meta-humans are significantly different from those of normal humans. . . ."

"I'll take your word for it," he interrupted. Suddenly, being an everyday mortal didn't sound so bad. He didn't care for the idea that there was something weird going on in his brain. *I like my gray matter just the way it is.*

"Just relax," she told him. "Let the Ambient Neural Ultra Spectrometer do its thing."

Talk about a mouthful, he thought. "Why don't you just use an acronym?"

"Think about it."

She flicked a switch, and automated sensors whirred around Jimmy's supine form, scanning him from a variety of directions. The humming of the machine seemed to penetrate his skull, so that his whole brain felt like it was full of static. His forehead started throbbing painfully. Brightly colored energies arced between the elevated scanners. The flashing lights hurt his eyes, forcing him to squeeze them shut. Swollen veins pulsed beneath the electrodes affixed to his temples. *Wait a sec,* he thought. *I thought she said this wasn't supposed to hurt!*

"Okay, we're up and running," Serling reported via the comm system. "Oh-to-the-crap!"

Her startled exclamation caused his eyes to snap open. His jaw dropped as he spied the source of her consternation.

A shimmering holographic wall had materialized above him, winding like a serpent just below the ceiling. An ineffable golden light radiated from the immense wall, while the armored figures of bizarre alien beings appeared to be melded to the dense stone or marble. Their empty eye sockets glowed with preternatural energy. Their immobile faces and bodies blended with the hard, unyielding substance of the barrier. Planetary spheres floated above and below the coils of the wall, which dwarfed the surrounding holographic worlds. An incredibly complex equation, couched in exotic, indecipherable symbols, snaked its way along the length of the wall.

"Come again?" Serling asked aloud. Whatever she had been expecting to find buried in Jimmy's unconscious mind, this clearly wasn't it. "Who Spielberged your synapses?"

"The Source," Jimmy whispered hoarsely. Somehow he knew instinctively that the awe-inspiring panoply represented something called the Source Wall, which divided the physical universe from a higher realm beyond. The Source was the ultimate mystery behind all of Creation, at least according to the New Gods. And the figures adorning the Wall were no mere sculptures; they were the Promethean giants, a race of ancient immortals who had sought to breach the barrier, only to become part of it for all eternity. It was said, although by whom Jimmy could not recall, that the soul of a New God returned to the Source upon the death of its corporeal shell.

Had Lightray's spirit already rejoined the Source? What about Sleez's?

An agonizing spasm prevented Jimmy from ruminating any further on the subject. Electricity crackled around his aching skull. An excruciating sound, like shattered glass scraping against bone, filled his ears. His mouth tasted like ash. Ozone tickled his nostrils. Prismatic auras obscured his vision. Nausea twisted his stomach in knots. His brain felt like it was going to explode. "I don't feel so good," he confessed.

"Jimmy!" Serling blurted. "Your head! It's growing!"

What? He spotted his reflection in the polished steel ceiling. The teenage genius wasn't joking; his brain was literally expanding beneath his scalp, blowing up like a balloon. Throbbing veins stood out upon his inflated cranium. A terrifying thought gripped him: What if his head really did explode? "Something's wrong!" he cried out. "Stop this!"

"I'm trying!" she shouted back. Lifting his oversized head from the table, he glimpsed her through the protective Plexiglas screen. She was frantically working the controls, but without any obvious success. "I can't shut it down! Your brain is telepathically attacking the spectrometer!"

The holographic Source Wall blinked out of existence. The static in Jimmy's brain diminished in volume and, for a moment, he thought the worst was over. "You're doing something!" he encouraged Serling. "I feel different. . . ."

Different, but not necessarily better. The pressure inside his skull gave way to a soggy feeling all over his body. Spikes protruded from his skin even as his body softened into a flabby, gelatinous mass. Ringed suckers opened up along his arms and fingers, so that he looked like some bizarre genetic hybrid of an octopus, a porcupine, and an jellyfish. Only his red hair, blue eyes, and freckles kept him slightly recognizable as James Bartholomew Olsen. Sticky electrodes slid off his slimy skin, only to get tangled in the quills. "Help!" he gurgled. "What's happening to me?"

"I don't know!" Serling answered. "You're overloading the sensors!"

He heard a definite note of panic in her voice. An overhead monitor erupted, emitting a shower of white-hot sparks onto Jimmy, who yelped in pain. Oozing free of their bonds, his elastic limbs flailed about wildly. An automated sensor arm crashed to the floor. A salvo of razor-sharp quills speared expensive electronic equipment. Sparks and smoke filled the laboratory, along with the smell of burning circuitry. A blaring alarm assaulted his eardrums. Crimson heat-rays shot from his eyes, leaving scorch marks on the walls and ceiling. A second later, icy blue freeze-rays cracked the Plexiglas screen between Jimmy and the control room. "RED ALERT!" a recorded voice announced over the loudspeaker. Blinking red lights flashed around the laboratory, bathing the chamber in an eerie bloodred radiance. "RED ALERT!"

"Sorry!" Jimmy said, flinching at the rampant destruction. He yanked the remaining electrodes off his skin and rolled clumsily off the table onto the floor. His arms and legs were stretched all out of proportion, but somehow he managed to stand upright. Concentrating with all his might, despite the emergency sirens and lights, he fought to keep his rubbery bones at least partially solid. "I can pay for this. . . ."

"Those sensors are three million apiece!" Serling informed him.

"Okay, I really *can't* pay for it. . . ." He looked around desperately for someplace where he couldn't cause any more damage. And not just because of the money; with his powers out of control like this, it was only a matter of time before he accidentally hurt or killed Serling. The Plexiglas screen between them looked like it was ready to shatter at any minute. *I gotta get out of here . . . pronto!*

His frantic gaze fastened on a circular drain built into the floor. A brilliant, if revolting, strategy popped into his overstimulated brain. Grimacing, he flung himself onto the drain and let his flesh and bones melt into a syrupy mess. The sickening smell of raw sewage wafted up from the pipes below. "This is gonna be gross. I just know it."

Leaving Project Cadmus behind, he slid down the drain.

27 AND COUNTING.

METROPOLIS.
EARTH-THREE.

The eldritch chanting of the spirits still echoed in Donna's ears as the newly christened Challengers of the Unknown suddenly found themselves standing on a rooftop overlooking a brightly lit modern city. Neon signs garishly adorned towering skyscrapers and casinos. Horns honked impatiently in the streets below. A blimp drifted by overhead, advertising an X-Treme Wrestling tournament. Although the sky was clear, the weather felt like fall— and much cooler than the microscopic jungle world they had just departed.

"We're back on Earth," she realized. "But which Earth?"

The Monitor consulted a display screen upon his right gauntlet. "The third," he informed them soberly. He glanced around at their surroundings. "This is their Metropolis."

Of course, Donna thought. Scanning the skyline, she spotted the Daily Planet Building to the south. Much like the other buildings in the vicinity, it seemed gaudier than the Metropolis she was familiar with, more like Vegas or Hub City than the Big Apricot. Lottery numbers flashed upon an illuminated ticker running along the equator of the spinning bronze globe atop the newspaper's corporate headquarters. Gazing down from the rooftop, she spied a proliferation of strip clubs, liquor stores, gun shops, and graffiti. The open display of vice reminded her of Jimmy Stewart's nightmarish glimpse of his hometown in *It's a Wonderful Life*—after all the good he'd done had disappeared. She scowled in disapproval. *Surely Ray Palmer wouldn't choose this ugly mirror world as his new home?*

"Hey, Donna." Jason gestured with his thumb at something behind them. "Check this out."

Donna realized belatedly that they had landed in front of an enormous billboard bearing an oversized photo of a glamorous, raven-haired woman wearing a ruby-studded tiara. A black leather choker adorned the model's throat above a generous display of cleavage. Crime Pays! proclaimed the huge block letters printed on the billboard. The jarring motto, as well as the cruelly seductive look on the woman's face, kept Donna from identifying the subject of the portrait right away. "By the gods," she gasped as she finally recognized her sister's classically beautiful features, "is that Diana?"

Vandals had defaced the billboard, spray-painting a bright red mustache and whiskers onto the woman's smirking face. A scrawled message, Slime Preys! provided a terse rebuttal to the sign's original message.

"I suppose you think that's funny?" an indignant female voice challenged them from above.

Spinning around, Donna looked up to see three costumed figures hovering in the air above them. The newcomers resembled distorted versions of Superman, Batman, and Wonder Woman. The latter was clearly the woman from the billboard, minus the painted-on facial hair. Hands on her hips, she glared down at the Challengers, clearly unamused by the mischief done to her portrait. In place of Wonder Woman's star-spangled uniform, she wore the tight leather gear of a professional dominatrix. A silver lasso dangled from her belt.

"Huh?" Jason blurted. "Is this the Justice League of this world?"

"Actually," the Monitor informed them calmly, "they're the exact opposite. Meet the Crime Society of America."

Crime Society? Donna thought. *That doesn't sound good. . . .*

The black-clad woman laughed harshly. "Did you hear that, Ultraman, Owlman? They think we care about 'justice.' " She sneered at the very notion. "Have you ever heard anything so absurd?"

"Of course not, Superwoman." Instead of a bright red S, Ultraman bore a scarlet U upon his chest. Otherwise, he was a dead ringer for Superman, aside from his cold eyes and surly expression. His red cape flapped in the breeze. His fists were clenched at his sides. "Who wants justice when revenge is so much more satisfying?"

"Like you know anything about satisfying your wife," Owlman taunted his teammate. Large round lenses protruded above the sharp beak of his cowl. A heavy-caliber pistol was holstered to the hip of his intimidating gray body armor. A wide-eyed owl-emblem was embossed upon his chest. Apparently unable to defy gravity on his own, the masked villain swooped through the air by means of artificial glider-wings. "I thought that was my department!"

Ultraman's face flushed with anger; the gibe had obviously hit a nerve. He unleashed a blast of heat vision at Owlman, who banked out of the way only heartbeats before being singed. "Watch your mouth," Superman's evil doppelganger fumed, "before I weld it shut!"

Owlman reached for his gun.

"Now, now, boys!" Superwoman flew between the two men, physically holding them apart. "You can fight over me later." She nodded at Donna and the others. "Right now I've got a score to settle with these three!"

"Wait!" Donna protested. "I think there's been a misunderstanding!" She held up empty hands. "We're just looking for our friend!"

"Well, you've found an enemy!" Satisfied that her jealous husband was no longer going to tear Owlman apart, Superwoman dived at Donna with phenomenal speed. Before Donna knew it, the other woman's fist was squeezing her throat. Sheer momentum carried them off the rooftop into the open air high above the pavement. "I don't know where you're from, Sparkles, but there's one thing you should know." Superwoman's blue eyes gleamed maliciously. "Around here, evil always triumphs over good!"

Meanwhile, Ultraman targeted the Monitor. "You look like an alien!" Grabbing on to the top of the billboard, he ripped it from its foundations, then hurled it down at the armored extraterrestrial. "I *hate* aliens!"

Undaunted by the villain's attack, the Monitor incinerated the falling billboard with a blast from his gauntlet. Superwoman's vandalized portrait went up in flames. "This altercation is getting us nowhere," the Monitor complained. "I shall continue our search in a less distracting environment."

He vanished in a shimmer of light, much to the aggravation of Ultraman, whose flying fists passed harmlessly through the empty space the alien had occupied only instants before. "Spoken like a true coward!"

I'll say, Jason thought, as he watched the Monitor abandon them. *Thanks for nothing, creep!*

It looked like Ultraman would be coming after Jason next, but the caped villain suddenly cocked his head to one side. "Hang on," he said irritably. "Sounds like my wife bit off more than she could chew." Alerted by his super-hearing, he cast a scornful glance at Jason before flying off after Donna and Superwoman. "This punk's all yours, Owlman."

"Fine with me," the other villain said. In the shadow of a looming water tower, Owlman touched down onto the rooftop in front of Jason. His collapsible glider-wings folded compactly beneath his arms. "You know, you kind of look like my sidekick, Talon," he told Jason. "I think I'm going to enjoy beating you to a pulp!"

"Please!" Jason replied sarcastically. "You're nothing but a second-rate Batman."

"No." The Darker Knight plucked a silver capsule from his Utility Belt and tossed it at Jason. "You are."

The capsule exploded against Jason's chest, releasing a cloud of thick yellow gas. Jason clamped his jaws shut, holding his breath, but it was no use. The caustic fumes invaded his nostrils and throat. Tears streamed from his burning eyes, and his lungs felt like they were on fire. The rooftop seemed to spin around him as an overpowering sense of dizziness turned his limbs to rubber. Nauseous, he dropped onto the sooty, tar-papered roof.

Owlman straddled his prone body. Grabbing Jason roughly by the collar, he rolled the helpless vigilante onto his back. A serrated razorang appeared in his hand. "Your intestines should make a nice Father's Day gift for Commissioner Wayne," he hooted. "I'll have to remember to include a card."

"I don't think so," Donna said. Her silver bracelets flashed in the moonlight as she seized Owlman by his cowl and flung him dozens of feet into the air. He let out a startled cry before crashing through a neon sign over a block away. Sparks and broken glass cascaded down onto the city streets.

Jason blinked at Donna through watery eyes. *Boy, am I glad to see you!*

She knelt beside him. "Jason! Are you okay?" Concern shone in her striking blue eyes. She leaned over him and, for a second, he thought (hoped?) that she might give him mouth-to-mouth resuscitation, but the moment passed and she simply helped him sit up instead. "Wow." He coughed, concealing his disappointment. His head began to clear as he took a couple of deep breaths of oxygen. "You really care."

"Gee, we're not interrupting anything, are we?"

Ultraman and Superwoman landed heavily on the rooftop. Jason saw that the female villain looked a little worse for wear. Blood dripped from a fat lip, while her own lasso was tightly lashed around her wrists. Ultraman smirked, seemingly enjoying his wife's humiliation, while he untied her. She glared furiously at Donna.

"I underestimated you before, slut, but I'm ready for you this time." Freed from her bonds, Superwoman cracked the lasso like a bullwhip. Sizzling red heat-rays shot from her eyes, startling Donna, who barely managed to deflect the blasts with her bracelet in time. "Your tricky Amazon moves won't save you much longer!"

Whoa, there! Jason thought, scrambling to his feet. A wave of dizziness rushed over him and he grabbed on to Donna's shoulder for support. *Where'd those eye-beams come from? Diana can't do that back on our Earth!*

"How 'bout we tear them apart like wishbones?" Ultraman suggested. Neither of the villains appeared terribly concerned about Owlman's fate. "Whichever of us ends up with the smaller halves has to submit to the other in our Fortress of Depravity."

Superwoman's eyes lit up. "Ooh, I like that idea. You're on!" She rubbed her hands together in wicked anticipation. "The girl first!"

"On three," Ultraman said. "One, two . . ."

Jason didn't like where this was going. *Somebody wake me up from this nightmare.*

"Three!"

The sadistic couple lunged toward the two Challengers, only to smack headfirst into a glowing carnelian force field that materialized from out of nowhere. Accompanied by his trademark transporter effect, the Monitor reappeared before Donna and Jason.

How about that? Jason thought. *He didn't ditch us after all.*

"I've scoured this Earth's resources," he reported calmly, as though a pair of bloodthirsty super-villains wasn't seconds away from playing tug-of-war with the two humans' flesh and bones. "Ray Palmer is not here, at least not the one we seek."

Jason wondered what kind of microscopic sicko passed for the Atom on this twisted planet. *Probably some sort of human virus or bacteria,* he guessed. *Or maybe the world's tiniest Peeping Tom.*

"Our continued presence here is unnecessary." The Monitor entered a new set of coordinates into his gauntlet. "We're leaving."

"Dammit!" Ultraman swore from the other side of the force field. His fists pounded uselessly against the barrier. "We haven't killed you yet!"

Frustrated by his failure, Superwoman lashed her husband with her lasso. "You're letting them get away!"

Sorry, freaks, Jason thought. *You're going to have to take out your disappointment on each other.*

The transporter carried the Challengers away.

26 AND COUNTING.

THE CARIBBEAN.

*"**Riahc,** esira!"*

The deck chair lifted off the stage, carrying a nervous-looking volunteer from the audience. White knuckles gripped the seat of the chair while the ten-year-old's sandaled feet dangled over ten feet above the boards. A packed audience gasped in appreciation, then let loose an enthusiastic round of applause. Performing in the onboard theater of a cruising luxury liner, Zatanna took a bow. A live band struck up a spirited rendition of "Witchy Woman."

Zee sure knows how to put on a show, Mary thought. Inconspicuously seated in a back row, she joined in the applause. The floor rolled gently beneath her. Since dropping in uninvited on the SS *Lemaris,* she'd learned a thing or three about cruise ships. One, it was a cinch to sneak aboard when you could fly. Two, on a boat full of tourists living out of their suitcases, almost anything passed as evening wear, even her slinky new costume. Three, they sometimes booked top talent for their passengers' entertainment.

Zatanna Zatara (her real name, believe it or not) was probably the world's most famous female magician. Her trademark top hat, tails, and fishnet stockings had been mimicked by countless imitators, but there remained only one Zatanna. *"Nruter ot roolf!"* she commanded the levitating chair, reciting the words of the incantation in reverse. The footlights lit up her sapphire eyes and glossy black hair. The chair touched down upon the stage, and the pint-sized volunteer wasted no time hopping off the seat. "Thanks for your help, Tommy," Zatanna said warmly. She treated the audience to a dazzling smile. "Let's give our brave volunteer a hand!"

Look at her, Mary thought, clapping along with the others. *Hiding in plain sight.* Probably only Mary knew that Zatanna's magic was no mere trickery; it was the genuine article. *Nobody here has any idea how powerful she really is.* When she wasn't performing onstage, Zatanna often used her mystical gifts to defend humanity from all manner of occult menaces. *I could learn a lot from Zee. . . .*

Back in Gotham, the Riddler had suggested that Mary needed a mentor. As much as she hated to admit it, he might have had a point. And who knew more about combining magic and heroism than Zatanna? The showbiz sorceress had even once been part of the Justice League.

"Aw, puh-leeze!" a heckler jeered from one row behind Mary. A vodka martini sloshed in his hand. Mary could smell the alcohol on his breath even from a couple of seats away. "We can all see you did it with wires!" He hollered loudly at the stage, slurring his words. "Nice try, darlin', but your talent's all in your legs!"

Who is this ass? Mary glared murderously at the drunk. Would anyone even miss him if he suddenly disappeared? Everyone would think that he'd just stumbled overboard; it probably happened all the time. She could just fly him up above the clouds, then "accidentally" let him go. . . . The delicious fantasy played out in her mind, tempting her, but she reluctantly dismissed it as beneath her. *He's not worth the effort.*

Besides, Zatanna dealt with the heckler far more amusingly. *"Emutsoc ekil anaid!"* she commanded, and the drunk's loud Hawaiian shirt and Bermuda shorts instantly transformed into an ill-fitting knockoff of Wonder Woman's star-spangled costume, complete with gilded bustier and tiara. The entire audience erupted into laughter. Cheers and applause followed the mortified drunk as he retreated clumsily from the theater. Mary approved wholeheartedly. *That's showing him, Zee,* she thought gleefully. *I knew you were my kind of magic-user!*

Eager to get some serious face time with Zatanna, Mary waited impatiently through several standing ovations before the glamorous magician disappeared in a puff of brightly colored smoke. Mary was just starting to ponder how best to make her way backstage when a hand gently dropped onto her shoulder and a lilting voice whispered in her ear.

"Hello, Mary," Zatanna said. "What brings you here?"

Mary twisted around in her seat to find Zatanna standing right behind her. *Whoa,* she thought. Wisps of polychromatic smoke wafted past Mary's nose. "You knew I was here?"

Zatanna nodded. "I sensed you from the stage. All that magic—and anger—was hard to miss." She eyed the younger heroine with concern. "You seem troubled, Mary."

Is it that obvious? Mary thought, embarrassed that Zatanna had seen right through her. *Does she know what I considered doing to that heckler?* "Um, to be honest, I was hoping we could talk."

"All right," Zatanna agreed readily. She gestured toward the exit. "Let's get some fresh air."

They strolled out onto the promenade deck outside. A warm tropical breeze rustled Mary's hair. Moonlight shimmered on the rippling surface of the Caribbean Sea. Gentle waves lapped at the ship's hull. Guardrails prevented anyone from falling overboard; life preservers waited just in case someone managed to do so anyway. The night air had a salty flavor. The beautiful evening lured dozens of other passengers out onto the deck. They ambled leisurely past Mary and Zatanna, paying little attention to the two women.

"I'm surprised your fans are leaving us alone," Mary commented. Zatanna was still decked out in her tux and tights after all, while Mary's costume could easily be mistaken for that of a magician's lovely assistant. "I figured we'd be swamped by ardent admirers and autograph seekers."

"I cast a low-level cloaking spell over us," Zatanna explained. "We're not exactly invisible per se, just flying below the radar." She leaned back against the guardrail. Constellations glittered in the sky above her. "So how can I help you, Mary?"

Mary didn't know Zatanna well, but she found herself opening up to the other woman without hesitation. Zee's friendly, down-to-earth manner made her easier to talk to than, say, Madame Xanadu, or even Billy. Mary filled Zatanna in on everything that had happened to her since waking up from her coma, including the extreme measures she had employed against the likes of Clayface and Pharyngula. Zee listened patiently to the entire story, neither interrupting nor judging her. After what had happened at the Rock of Eternity, Mary appreciated Zatanna taking the time to hear her side of the story.

"I see," Zatanna said, after Mary wrapped up her narrative. Her gorgeous face held a pensive expression. "What happened to Black Adam?"

"He just . . . left," Mary lamented. "So here I am, with all this magic and no instruction manual. I mean, it's not like I haven't had power before, but it's not quite the same. And there's so much of it. . . ."

"I know," Zatanna said with a worried tone. "I can feel it surging inside you, almost like—"

A sudden disturbance off the starboard bow interrupted her diagnosis. A muffled boom came from beneath the waves. Blazing yellow bolts of energy shot *upward* into the clear night sky. Only seventy yards away from the ship, the sea churned and foamed violently. Ten-foot waves rocked the *Lemaris*, sending passengers tumbling onto the deck. Frightened men, women, and children yelped in alarm, and grabbed on to the nearest rails or posts. A white-faced mother frantically wrestled her wailing children into life jackets. Other passengers fled the swaying deck for the uncertain safety of the ship's interior. It was a like a scene out of *Titanic*, but without Celine Dion's cloying song.

Holy crap! Mary thought, springing into action. Obviously her chat with Zatanna was going to have to wait. Taking to the air, she flew straight toward the fiery energy beams. "Hang on!" she shouted back at Zatanna, who remained aboard the tempest-tossed cruise ship, clinging to the rail. "I'm going for a closer look!"

"Be careful, Mary!" Zee called out urgently. "We don't know what forces are at work here!"

"Don't worry about me!" Mary snapped, experiencing a flash of irritation at Zatanna's needless coaching. Coruscating rays of light sizzled all around Mary as she zoomed defiantly into the midst of the barrage. Sea spray pelted her face. She tasted brine upon her lips. "I'm not exactly an amateur, you know. I can take care of mys—!"

A tremendous waterspout erupted from the sea below her. The geyser slammed into Mary with titanic force, knocking the wind out of her while simultaneously drenching her from head to toe. Coughing and sputtering, her eyes and nose filled with salt water, she almost didn't notice that the eruption had hurled a humanoid figure toward the vulnerable ocean liner.

"Mary!" Zatanna cried out in warning. "We've got company!"

I see him, I see him! Mary thought impatiently. Wiping a soggy lock of hair away from her eyes, she took a second to catch her breath before flying back toward the *Lemaris*. Meanwhile, the blurry figure was already arcing down toward a deck full of stunned passengers who seemed frozen in place by shock and surprise. *Move, you idiots!* Mary railed silently. Even pouring on the speed, she knew she couldn't get there in time. *You're going to get flattened!*

Fortunately, Zatanna was also on the scene. *"Enoyreve evom kcab!"* she commanded, and a wave of invisible force gently but firmly cleared the area directly in the path of the falling body. *"Dna yats kcab!"*

She got the bystanders out of the way with only seconds to spare. The mysterious figure crashed onto the deck, reducing a discarded deck chair to splinters. "Ohmigod!" a horrified tourist exclaimed. "What the heck is that?"

Not human, that was for sure. Although a torn blue and white wetsuit concealed much of the creature's burly form, scaly green skin covered his face and hands, while more scales showed through the ragged tears in his garment. Webbed hands and feet disclosed his aquatic nature. A spiked coral helmet, missing its face visor, protected his skull. Purple bile trickled from the corner of his mouth. Sharpened claws extended from his fingertips. Bulging muscles suggested that the formidable merman was no pushover. Still and silent, he sprawled lifelessly upon the soaked deck. Scorch marks blackened portions of his wetsuit.

Wait a second, Mary thought as she descended toward the supine figure. *I know who that is.* The wisdom of Zehuti, the ancient Egyptian god of learning, informed her that the collapsed merman was none other than Slig, an evil New God from Apokolips. He was the commander of the Deep Six, a strike force of water-breathing warriors that had invaded Earth's oceans on more than one occasion. Last she'd heard, they'd given Aquaman a hard time during the Infinite Crisis. *What's he doing here . . . and where's the rest of the Six?*

"Watch out, Mary," Zatanna cautioned her. Water dripped from her long black hair; the spray from the geyser had obviously splashed everyone on the deck. "He could be . . ."

"Dead?" Mary suggested. She didn't know whether to be disappointed or relieved that Slig looked like he was in no shape to put up a fight. *I wonder how my powers stack up against a New God these days?*

Zatanna shook her head. "Dangerous."

"DEATH!" Slig's eyes snapped open, revealing slitted red orbs. He scrambled to his feet, looking just as panic-stricken as the freaked-out vacationers. "Death comes for me! I must escape his wrath!" His open jaws revealed sharklike pointed teeth. "Gole . . . Jaffar . . . Kurin . . . all my Deep Six brothers, dead by his hand!"

Whose hand? Mary wondered. Who was scary enough to wipe out an entire pack of New Gods? Hovering above the deck, she put off tackling Slig in hopes of learning more. "Spill, fish boy! What're you babbling about?"

Ignoring her query, he slid across the wet deck with unexpected speed. Webbed fingers closed around the ankle of an unlucky tourist, who instantly underwent a startling metamorphosis. Gills formed along the poor guy's throat. Fins sprouted from his arms and legs. Scales spread across his skin. His Hawaiian shirt and Bermuda shorts were torn to shreds by the violent transformation. Within seconds, an ordinary senior citizen had changed into something resembling the Creature from the Black Lagoon. Piscine eyes stared agog at his mutated mitts.

"Worthless dry-skins!" Slig hissed. He charged into a dense clump of passengers, grabbing on to them one after another. Arms and legs turned into tentacles. Bony shells covered flailing bodies. Mortal men and women devolved into hybrid sharks, barracudas, eels, cephalopods, and crustaceans. "You shall be reborn as beasts of the sea, the better to mask my escape!"

Mary kicked herself for not stopping Slig earlier. "You slimy sea monkey!" She dived at the berserk sea-god, seizing his helmet with both hands. Her anger exploded in a flash of eldritch lightning that went off right in his face. "Stop touching people!"

He roared in agony. "Foul creature! What have you done to me!" The glare from the thunderbolt faded away, revealing scarred white eyes surrounded by scalded green flesh. Greasy yellow tears leaked from the smoking sockets. "I'm blinded!"

Serves you right, Mary thought. She struggled to hold on to her slippery foe, who thrashed wildly within her grasp, desperate to break free. Muscles conditioned to withstand the awesome pressures of the deep managed to hold their own against Mary's preternatural strength. Slig was at least seven feet tall, but Mary's ability to defy gravity gave her the height advantage. The spines on his helmet snapped off in her fingers. "Stop being such a crybaby!"

"Mary!" Zatanna shouted. She sounded appalled, but by what Mary wasn't sure. "Back down a notch until we find out what this is all about!"

He's turning people into sea monsters, Mary thought, surprised by Zee's disapproving tone. She got a fresh grip on Slig's helmet. Her fingers dug into the hardened coral, which cracked beneath the pressure. *Isn't that enough?*

She tried to get Slig in a headlock, but he twisted free before she could secure the hold. A taloned hand, questing blindly, grabbed on to the front of her dress and ripped it down the middle, exposing a lot more cleavage than before. *Hey, watch it!* she thought indignantly. *Who does he think I am? Power Girl?* The vicious claws didn't even scratch her skin, however.

"Foolish human!" His rank breath smelled like spoiled sushi. He raved deliriously. "You don't understand. The Killer is here!"

"What killer?" Sparks flew from her knuckles as she slammed her fist into his face. Cartilage crumpled loudly. He went flying backward into a steel bulkhead, shattering a solid glass porthole. Cold red blood streamed from his flattened snout. A strip of ragged black fabric still clung to one talon. Mary followed up with a devastating blow to his gut. "You're the one causing all the trouble!"

She was about to turn Slig into a fish fillet when Zatanna came running up behind her. "Mary, I said back down! What's *wrong* with you?"

"Me?" Mary couldn't believe that Zee was giving her grief at time like this. "You saw what he did." She glanced down at her suddenly low-cut costume. "Look at my dress!"

"Forget your wardrobe!" Zatanna scolded. She pointed at the shambolic mass of transformed humans charging toward them. They seemed compelled to defend Slig from any or all attacks. "There are innocent people here. We need to attend to them!"

Mary looked away from her battered opponent. By now, the promenade deck resembled some sort of bizarre aquatic freak show. Almost two dozen mutated monstrosities flopped and slithered toward Zatanna. Rent clothing was strewn about the deck. A limbless gray worm that resembled nothing so much as a gigantic sea cucumber wiggled across the textured metal floor, leaving a trail of mucus behind it. The translucent ichor glistened in the moonlight.

"Okay," Mary said. "That's disgusting."

Zatanna scowled. "No matter what happened to them, they're still innocent people, Mary! We have to help them without hurting them."

The monstrous worm rose up in front of Zatanna, seemingly intent on devouring the world-famous celebrity. A voracious maw, lined with hundreds of razor-sharp fangs, opened wide.

"Jeez, Zee, I haven't gone senile," Mary replied irritably. She had seen the passengers turn into monsters less than five minutes ago. Despite Zatanna's admonition to be gentle with the mutant horde, she flew between the giant worm and Zee, then delivered a magically charged right hook to the lunging creature. The blow didn't kill the beast, but it did stun it long enough to keep Zatanna from disappearing down its slimy gullet. "Just make with the magic!"

The sorceress didn't bother thanking Mary for the save. Instead she raised her hands and gestured dramatically at the worm. Her eyes glowed with mystical energy. *"Trever ot namuh mrof!"*

No puff of smoke accompanied the spell; presumably Zatanna saved such theatrics for her performances onstage. Without any fanfare, the huge wormlike creature morphed back into a trembling, middle-aged man whose unclad form could have benefitted from a few more hours at the gym. He blinked in confusion, as though trying to figure out how he had ended up naked and surrounded by sea monsters. "What the—?"

"You're safe now, sir." Zatanna wiped her forehead, as though reversing the transformation had been harder than it looked. She turned to face the rest of the mutated victims. "One down, only twenty more to go. . . ."

Mary flew above the deck, picking out her next target. *I'll bet I can knock them out faster than Zee can cure them.* She was zeroing in on a rampaging lobster-man when a brilliant flash off the bow seized her attention instead. "Zatanna! Heads up!"

A glowing figure, radiating a blinding white light, burst from the sea, momentarily turning night into day. Shielding her eyes with her hand, Mary tried to see who it was, but the incandescent glare was too intense; all she could make out was a vaguely masculine silhouette. Forced to look away, Mary saw that the stranger's explosive entrance had dragged up several other figures in its wake. Scaly bodies, bearing a distinct familial resemblance to Slig, drifted lifelessly to the surface of the foaming water. Gaping green holes in the center of their chests informed Mary in no uncertain terms that the rest of the Deep Six were now literally food for the fishes. No wonder Slig was scared out of his mind!

"That's it!" Zatanna exclaimed, staring aghast at the floating corpses of five New Gods, as well as at their painfully luminous executioner. "I'm contacting the Justice League. This is getting way too cosmic for the two of us!"

"No way!" Mary resented the implication that she couldn't handle this emergency on her own. What was the use of having all this power if she still had to call in the big guns when things got tough? "I'm not going to sit back and let other people do my job!"

Zatanna was taken aback by her reaction. *"Your* job?"

"No!" Slig blurted. "The Killer is here! I can feel it!" He dropped to his knees upon the deck. His blind eyes beseeched the radiant figure. "Slig shall be your humble servant! I will spit in the face of Darkseid if only you will give me my life!"

Cowardly slug! Mary thought scornfully. *A god should have more pride.*

"Look out!" Zatanna shouted as a beam of golden light shot from what might have been the eyes of the Deep Six's murderer. The golden ray passed right through Mary, producing only a slight tickling sensation, before taking a sharp downward turn toward the prostrate Slig. The beam struck the god directly in the chest—and a volcanic burst of energy exploded from inside him. His bloodcurdling scream was cut off abruptly as he toppled over onto his back. A steaming cavity, identical to the ones carved out of his comrades' breasts, left him as dead as the rest of the Deep Six. The smell of his burnt flesh filled the air. Mary had a sudden craving for seafood.

His homicidal mission completed, the assassin shot up into the sky at the speed of light. In a heartbeat, he had completely vanished from sight, leaving only his grisly handiwork behind. "Wow," Mary remarked. "I've seen some brutal things before, but . . ."

"A little help here?" Zatanna called out. Stalking across the deck, the transformed passengers seemed intent on avenging their master's death. The besieged magician gestured hastily. *"Egnahc! Egnahc kcab!"*

A handful of monsters reverted to human form, but many more creatures remained. Zatanna was backed up against the rail as she attempted to muster the strength for another spell. Perspiration gleamed upon her determined face. Her ivory brow furrowed in concentration. *"Nruter ot lamron!"*

This is taking too long, Mary thought impatiently, watching Zatanna's efforts from above. At this rate, they'd be at this all night. She swooped over the heads of the remaining sea devils, then paused in midair. Closing her eyes, she called upon the power of Isis. *It's only magic. How hard can it be?*

"What are you doing?" Zatanna asked in confusion.

You can do this, an encouraging voice whispered inside Mary's brain. *You have the power.*

"Fixing things faster," Mary declared confidently. Her eyes opened, revealing glowing orbs ablaze with mystical fire. Electricity crackled around her floating body, then zapped the milling creatures below. Nearly a dozen simultaneous lightning strikes instantly transformed scales, fins, and shells back into bare skin. All at once, the battle-scarred promenade deck went from being a mutant aquarium to an impromptu nudist colony. Mary figured that was an improvement, although some of the scrawny and/or flabby bodies on display almost made her think otherwise. Disoriented men and women tried awkwardly to cover themselves, much to Mary's amusement. *I'm betting this is one cruise they'll never forget!*

Zatanna spared the mortified passengers any further embarrassment. *"Steknalb rof lla!"* she pronounced, conjuring up a slew of blankets from the ether. Apparently, making fabric materialize took less effort than undoing Slig's original enchantment. The gray wool blankets descended like manna from heaven, draping themselves over the trembling tourists.

Mary didn't begrudge Zatanna her cleanup efforts. She was still too exhilarated by her own triumph to worry about anyone's modesty. Almost in passing, she noticed that her own garment had magically repaired itself. *See?* she thought smugly, more than a little pleased with herself. *Who needs the Justice League?*

"Wow!" she enthused out loud. "Did you see that, Zee?"

Zatanna nodded gravely. She regarded Mary with new eyes. "I didn't realize you had that kind of power."

"Eh, who cares?" Mary said with a shrug. She didn't want to show off *too* much. "Let's just be happy that we averted what could have been a major maritime disaster."

"I suppose," Zatanna murmured. Even though the nameless killer was long gone, and Slig's victims restored, she still sounded worried. The soaked magician gazed up at Mary as though she had never seen her before. "Mary, I'm concerned about you. . . ."

Me? Mary thought. *Whatever for?*

She felt terrific.

APOKOLIPS.

"Everything dies," Darkseid observed as he removed the figures of the Deep Six from his chessboard. Torches illuminated the spartan war room as he ruminated on the demise of the piscine warriors. "And like the Prometheans before them, so shall the New Gods pass into the Stygian depths of oblivion."

He contemplated the inanimate replica of Slig in his grip. The remainder of the figures he swept into a carved ivory box next to the board. "They are but pawns, sacrificed in a battle beyond their primitive conceptions of life and death." His crimson eyes glowed in anticipation of the cataclysm to come. "At the end of an age where time, space, and reality will bow before me, only Darkseid shall rise to wield universal power—and decide who lives and dies in the new Multiversal dynasty."

He crushed the figure in his fist, so that painted green powder rained down onto the chessboard. Random flecks settled onto the adjacent figures of Mary Marvel and Zatanna.

The game continued.

25 AND COUNTING.

GOTHAM CITY.
EARTH-15.

The neon jungle of Earth-Three gave way to an open plaza inside a peaceful city park. Metal benches and waste bins lined the paved square. Moonlight filtered through the bare branches of venerable oaks and elm trees, casting long shadows onto the paved pathways leading away from the plaza. Sleeping pigeons perched atop a marble statue of some forgotten Revolutionary War general, and a geyser of water rose from the center of a concrete fountain. The spray from the water felt cold against Donna's face.

"Another Earth," she realized. "Hopefully better than the last one."

Jason coughed. His voice was still scratchy from the gas he'd inhaled during their fight with the Crime Society. "So where the hell are we now?"

"Earth-15," the Monitor stated. "Gotham City."

Right, Donna thought. Now that she had a chance to get her bearings, she recognized the familiar skyline of Jason's hometown. Gloomy Gothic architecture mingled with modern high-rises. The corporate headquarters of Wayne Enterprises, all gleaming glass and steel, shone like a beacon in the dark. A clock tower informed her that it was five past midnight, which explained why the park appeared to be deserted. The Bat-Signal shone brightly over the tops of the skyscrapers. Apparently this Gotham also had a Dark Knight.

"Are you sure?" Jason asked skeptically. "It looks too . . . clean."

The Monitor dismissed his objections. "Not all versions of Gotham City are as filthy and crime-ridden as your own."

"Oh yeah?" Jason snapped. He angrily kicked over a trash can, spilling garbage onto the pavement. "Then why don't I just make myself feel more at home?"

Donna tried to calm him. "Jason, please—"

"No, Donna!" he interrupted her. "I'm getting sick and tired of this wild-goose chase!" He wheeled about to get into the Monitor's face. He poked the powerful alien in the chest. "You're a Monitor. Your people are supposed to see all and know all, but you can't even find one guy?"

To Donna's relief, the Monitor didn't simply obliterate Jason. "It is more complicated than you realize, human. Each Monitor is responsible for only one of the fifty-two universes, and it is forbidden for us to interfere outside our jurisdiction." He glanced around apprehensively, as though half expecting to face the judgment of his peers at any moment. "I watched over only your own world, Earth-One. This universe is under the purview of another Monitor. We should not be here."

"But can't you ask your fellow Monitor for assistance?" Donna inquired. "Surely he—or she—would know if Ray Palmer was here."

The Monitor shook his head. "That would not be wise. There has been . . . dissension . . . amongst our ranks over such issues. Each Monitor guards his own territory zealously, and I fear we do not always see eye to eye."

"But if you explained the importance of our mission," Donna pressed him, "made the other Monitors understand what was at stake . . . ?"

"And what would that be?" a gruff voice intruded from above. "And how does that involve my city?"

Donna looked up in surprise to see Batman—or at least, a Batman—rappelling down a length of shimmering golden rope. His scalloped black cape spread out behind him as he descended to the ground. His boots touched down lightly onto the floor of the plaza. The winged emblem on his chest matched the Bat-Signal shining overhead. He didn't look happy.

The Dark Knight wasn't alone either. Wonder Woman hovered in the sky above them, holding the other end of her Golden Lasso. Her star-spangled skirt, gilded breastplate, and jeweled tiara were almost identical to those Wonder Woman wore back on Earth-One. "Diana?" Donna said hesitantly before getting a closer look at the flying Amazon's face. Her jaw dropped as she recognized the face as the same one she saw in the mirror everyday.

Wait a second, she thought. *This world's Wonder Woman is . . . me?*

Batman glared suspiciously at the Challengers. "I don't know who—or what—you people are, but I'll tell you this: I don't like imposters."

The Monitor held up his hand. "Wait. Before there is any unneeded conflict between us, I can explain our presence here."

"Good," Wonder Woman said. She lassoed the Monitor with the golden lariat, binding his arms to his sides. "The Lasso of Hestia will ensure that you speak the truth."

The Monitor glanced disdainfully at his enchanted bonds. "Your primitive magicks are unnecessary. My companions and I are from a parallel version of your planet and have no intention of posing as anything other than what we are."

"An alternate Earth?" Batman scrutinized Donna and Jason. Something about him struck Donna as slightly off. His hostile tone sounded different from that of the Batman she knew, but also strangely familiar. "Do you truly expect us to believe you?

"Hey!" Jason blurted. "Your voice . . . !"

"Sounds like mine," Batman said, nodding grimly. "I already noticed that."

By the gods, Donna thought as the truth sank in. *That's not Bruce Wayne; that's another version of Jason!*

The Dark Knight confronted his startled doppelganger. "Still wearing a domino mask, eh? Guess you never made the leap from sidekick to team leader."

Jason bristled indignantly. "I don't need a string of snot-nosed Boy Wonders traipsing after me. I'm my own man now!"

"Then you only have one person to disappoint," Batman said.

Before the two men could go at it any further, a miniature figure suddenly appeared upon Batman's shoulder. Glowing atomic orbitals circled the tiny figure, who grew from one inch to doll-sized in a matter of seconds. Donna's heart leapt in excitement. *It's the Atom*, she thought. *We've found him!*

Her momentary jubilation evaporated, however, as she realized that this Atom was a *woman*. Springing from Batman's shoulder, the brightly costumed heroine landed on the ground before them. Her red and blue uniform matched the other Atom's, right down to the stylized atomic insignia on the forehead of her hood, but her long blonde ponytail and feminine figure made it abundantly clear that she was *not* Ray Palmer. The shimmering orbitals faded from view as she assumed normal human proportions. She seemed thrilled by the Monitor's revelation.

"I *knew* there was a multiverse!" she enthused. "I've been trying to prove its existence since I was five." She eagerly approached the bound Monitor. "How did you make it through the interdimensional barrier?"

"Never mind that," Batman said. "Why are you here?"

Donna stepped forward. "We're trying to find a friend. He's our Earth's version of the Atom."

"There's another me out there?" the female Atom asked. She sounded a few years younger than the rest of them. "Fascinating!"

Jason looked her over dubiously. "This chick is your Atom? What is she, twelve?"

"For your information," she replied, "I'm eighteen. Who the hell are you supposed to be, the smart-ass Robin?"

Wonder Woman alighted onto the pavement. She released the Monitor from the golden lariat. "Jessica Palmer *is* the Atom," she said in defense of her comrade. "She graduated from MIT at the age of eight."

"We don't know these people, Donna." Batman scowled at Wonder Woman. "Stop handing out personal information."

"Don't be paranoid, Jason," she rebuked him. "My lasso confirms that they're telling the truth."

Donna shook her head at the sight of their counterparts, whose debate had a familiar ring to it. *This is like looking into a fun-house mirror.*

"Even still," Batman insisted, "why are we helping these people? I'm not convinced they know what they're doing."

Jason swaggered over to look his other self in the eye. He clenched his fists. "You want to test that theory?"

"Don't have to," Batman said curtly. "I've already calculated it in my head. Of the three hundred possible attack sequences you might try, given the distance and environment, the outcome would be the same. You'd lose."

He turned his back on Jason, dismissing him. Jason's face flushed with anger. "You son of a bitch!" He lunged at Batman from behind.

But the Dark Knight was ready for him. "Attack from the rear . . . a sure sign of weakness." Spinning about with blinding speed, he flung out his cloak like a matador's cape, snaring Jason in its voluminous depths. The weighted tips of the cape smacked against Jason's body with brutal force. Stunned and tangled within the swirling folds, Jason couldn't stop Batman from expertly flipping him onto the pavement. The Dark Knight's boot pressed down on Jason's chest, pinning him to the ground. "Looks like I'm better at being you."

Donna and Wonder Woman exchanged disgusted glances. They pulled the men apart. "If you two macho jerks are done comparing jockstrap sizes," Donna scolded them, "maybe we can actually get down to the business of finding Ray Palmer?"

"He's not on our Earth," a confident voice assured her. A shadow fell over the nocturnal scenery as a soaring figure descended from the sky. A familiar red S was emblazoned on the newcomer's bright blue chest. A matching red cape fluttered in the breeze. Flowing blonde hair spread out behind her.

"Supergirl?" Donna blurted.

"Superwoman," Kara Zor-El corrected her. She landed lightly among them. Her costume echoed that of her celebrated cousin. She seemed older and more mature than the flighty teenage heroine Donna remembered from back home.

What is this? she wondered. *The world where all us apprentices took over the family businesses?* She was afraid to ask what had become of this Earth's versions of Clark, Bruce, and Diana.

"You didn't need to get involved in this," Batman groused. "We were handling it on our own."

"It's no problem," Superwoman said. She turned her piercing blue eyes on the Challengers. "I scanned the Earth from my Fortress in the Arctic. Your Atom is not here. I'm afraid this was a wasted trip."

"I wouldn't say that," Donna replied. She smiled at her own twin. "Being here is like looking into a crystal ball where all your dreams are realized." No wonder this Gotham looked cleaner and less dangerous than its equivalent on Earth-One. "It gives one hope."

The Monitor sighed wearily. "Sentimental musings aside, we have to go." He adjusted the controls on his gauntlet. "We have many more Earths to search."

Wonder Woman held up her hand. "Your quest can wait just a while longer." She took Donna by the hand. "Sister, may I have a word alone with you?"

Puzzled, Donna glanced at Jason and the Monitor, silently requesting their indulgence. *Who am I to ignore my better self?* She let Wonder Woman guide her down a tree-lined path until they were out of earshot of the others. "What's this all about?"

Wonder Woman gazed at her sympathetically. "Sister, I sense confusion within you, an uncertainty I myself once knew too well." Her familiar blue eyes seemed to probe the depths of Donna's soul. "When mighty Zeus learned his first wife, Metis, was pregnant, he consumed her lest the son she carried supplant him upon the throne of the gods. But swallowing Metis caused Zeus great suffering. To rid himself of the pain, he instructed Hephaestus to split open his head . . . and from that wound was born Athena, goddess of wisdom. Ultimately, Athena was the only one of Zeus's many offspring that he entrusted with his magic shield and the secret of his lightning bolts."

What's she getting at? Donna wondered. "I'm familiar with the story."

"My point," Wonder Woman answered, "is not to mold your life around what you believe others expect. If you are indeed destined to become the Wonder Woman of your world, then you will be."

"But you don't understand," Donna protested, revealing hidden doubts that she would have never dared divulge to anyone except, well, herself. "I have no real past of my own. I was magically created from a fragment of the real Diana's soul, when she was just a child. I sprang into existence from out of nowhere."

Wonder Woman smiled slyly. "Then you have much in common with Athena."

Oh. Donna had never really thought about it like that before. She wasn't sure quite how to respond. *I guess Athena did all right for herself, despite her unorthodox origins.*

"All right, ladies. Time's up." Jason barged into the discussion. He nodded back toward the plaza. "Mister Monitor is getting restless, and if I hear him mutter about the Great Disaster one more time, I'm going to kill him . . . and then we'll be stuck here for good."

Wonder Woman did not object to the interruption. "Indeed, I must not delay your quest any further. My thanks for your patience." She took Donna's hand again. "I hope my words will provide you with some comfort in the days to come."

"You've given me a lot to think about," Donna admitted. She gave her twin's hand a grateful squeeze. "Thank you."

They followed Jason back to the plaza, where the Monitor and this Earth's heroes awaited them. Now Barbie-sized, the female Atom teased Batman as she perched upon his shoulder once more. "Admit it, Jason. Doesn't it make you feel better to know that Bruce is still alive somewhere in another incarnation?"

"It makes no difference to me," he said tersely.

"Uh-huh." She placed her miniature palm beneath his chin. "Let's see, sudden intake of breath, slight increase in heart rate, and an *almost* imperceptible catch in the voice . . ." She chuckled in amusement. "Once a Boy Wonder, always a Boy Wonder, eh?"

Was it just Donna's imagination, or was Batman actually blushing?

"Can it, Tinkerbell," he growled.

The Monitor gestured for Donna and Jason to join him. "Are we quite ready to depart?" He keyed the coordinates of another Earth into his gauntlet. "I hope you will not feel obliged to indulge in such time-consuming social activities at every continuum we visit. The fate of worlds without end may depend—"

Before he could finish his familiar admonition, a blinding golden glow lit up the night. "Uh-oh," Jason muttered. "I don't like the looks of this."

Donna's eyes widened in surprise as a *second* Monitor emerged from the transporter beam. Ignoring the various heroes present, he regarded his kinsman with obvious disapproval. His voice was stern and unforgiving.

"Brother, this ends now."

24 AND COUNTING.

METROPOLIS.

A heavy manhole cover clanged against the asphalt as Jimmy climbed up out of the sewers. Exhausted by his escape from the underground laboratory, he found himself back in Suicide Slum again. He was sore and tired and smelled like an open latrine, but at least he was human once more. His freakish metamorphoses and runaway powers had receded once he'd gotten far enough away from Project Cadmus's probes and scanners. Mercifully, his brain no longer felt like it was threatening to burst his skull. He was just plain old Jimmy Olsen again, if only for the moment.

That's good enough for me, he thought. Right now he just wanted to get back to his apartment and take the world's longest shower. Swimming through sewage was not his idea of a good time. *I only hope I didn't wreck that lab too much before I slipped down the drain. Maybe I should write Serling an apology later on, once I'm feeling a little less disgusting.*

However, before he could go home and clean up, he needed to find something to wear. Rummaging through a Dumpster behind the neighborhood mission, he found a faded green T-shirt and a grimy pair of jeans. The clothes were a few sizes too big and weren't likely to land him on Metropolis's best-dressed list, but he figured they'd do in a pinch. The last thing he needed this afternoon was to get picked up for indecent exposure. He felt uncomfortably exposed without his signal-watch, which he had left behind at Cadmus, but he could always ask Superman for a spare the next time he saw him.

He wriggled into the T-shirt and was just pulling on the jeans when, abruptly, an ominous shadow fell over him, accompanied by a loud buzzing noise. "There you are!" a voice announced from above. "I have found you at last!"

Yikes! Jimmy thought. *What now?*

An insectoid figure swooped down from the sky. Three pairs of scaly white wings flared out behind her. An ovoid helmet and body armor, made of a glossy chitinous material, protected the intruder but failed to disguise her feminine curves. Twin antennae sprouted from small openings in her crimson helmet. Her hard white exoskeleton concealed whatever softness might lie beneath the armor. Polished opals adorned her boots, belt, and gauntlets, and amber lenses in her faceplate hid her eyes.

"Who?" Jimmy blurted. As far as he knew, he had never seen this alien apparition before. "That is, *what*?"

With one leg in, one leg out of his jeans, he stumbled backward and turned to flee. Gloved fingers grabbed on to his collar with surprising strength. Mighty wings flapped furiously above him, and his bare feet lost contact with the pavement. Holding on to Jimmy with just one hand, the female insectoid soared upward into the clear blue sky, rapidly leaving the squalid alley behind. Jimmy held on to the loose jeans tightly as he dangled helplessly above the city. Within seconds, he was hundreds of feet in the air.

"Do not resist, Earth-bug," his captor admonished him. Her voice had a buzzing quality, like a fly or a honeybee. Jimmy guessed that she wasn't from around here, and he didn't mean Metropolis.

"D-don't make me hurt you, lady!" he threatened, even though none of his oddball powers had kicked in. *Does that mean I'm not in serious danger yet?*

"Highly unlikely," she replied with what sounded like a trace of amusement. "Not to mention unnecessary. I merely wish to have words with you, away from any lurking shadows."

The city's streets and skyscrapers spread out beneath them like an incredibly detailed diorama. Years of being carried aloft by Superman had largely inured Jimmy to such heights, yet the stranger's precarious hold on his collar left him praying that she didn't have butterfingers. Would his new powers save him if he plummeted toward the ground? He was in no hurry to find out. "Who are you anyway?"

"Call me Forager," she declared over the steady humming of her wings, "for it is my sacred duty to seek out answers and bring home the truth."

Forager? Jimmy had once known another being by that name: a humanoid insect from New Genesis, home of the New Gods. His people, "the bugs," dwelt in vast colonies beneath the surface of the planet, far below the floating palaces of the New Gods, who largely regarded the humble bugs with disdain. Despite his lowly status, however, the original Forager had often fought beside Superman and the New Gods in order to defend his people from Darkseid's insidious schemes. According to Superman, he had died saving the cosmos a few years ago.

So who was this new Forager? Did she also hail from New Genesis? Obviously, she wasn't the same bug, returned to life. The first Forager had been male, while, judging from her shapely thorax, his replacement was clearly female. . . .

Flying swiftly through the sky, she carried Jimmy downtown toward the Daily Planet Building. A large bronze replica of the planet Earth rotated slowly atop the landmark structure. Jimmy let out a sigh of relief as Forager dropped him lightly onto the roof of the building. The familiar globe was a reassuring sight. Whatever happened next, at least he was back where he belonged. Chances were, Clark, Lois, and Perry were only a few stories below. Unless they were out on assignment, of course. He wished again that he had hung on to his signal-watch.

Forager alighted onto the roof, facing Jimmy. "I know the question that burns in your mind right now."

"You do?" Although tempted to bolt for the stairs, Jimmy decided to hear her out. The fact that his powers hadn't manifested yet suggested that the stranger meant him no harm. He chose to take that as an encouraging sign.

"Of course," she replied. Her wings folded in behind her. "In a city of millions, why did I single *you* out?"

"Actually, I'm mostly wondering if I can put my pants on."

She ignored the quip, even though he was only half joking. "I require your help, Jimmy Olsen."

"You know me?" he asked.

She nodded grimly while he finished dressing. The stomach-turning stench emanating from his person didn't seem to bother her; perhaps her olfactory senses worked differently? Or maybe her helmet just kept the smell out. "The New Gods are being hunted by an unknown assassin."

"Yeah, I'm sorta working that story." Forager *had* to be from New Genesis, he figured, if she was investigating the murders of Lightray and Sleez. "Anyone new bite the dust?"

"Barda of Apokolips," she stated.

Jimmy's heart sank. "Big Barda's dead?" Although raised on hellish Apokolips, the statuesque warrior woman had rebelled against Darkseid and forged a new life as a super heroine here on Earth, fighting alongside her husband, Mister Miracle. Jimmy couldn't imagine how devastated Scott Free must be right now; he and Barda had loved each other fiercely. "Aww, no! That's *awful!*"

"Far worse is the crux of the problem," Forager said coolly. Jimmy guessed that she hadn't known Barda personally. "Bad enough that their bodies are slain, but the souls of the murdered gods are lost. Could they have been spirited away by the assassin? Are they being held hostage even now, denied their rightful place beyond the Source Wall?"

Jimmy suddenly remembered the holographic wall that had materialized while he was being examined at Cadmus earlier, as well as the gaping holes in the chests of Lightray and Sleez. Had Barda's heart been missing as well? All these mysteries were connected somehow, he realized, but, just like the Joker had taunted him, he still couldn't see the big picture yet.

Maybe Forager held the missing pieces of the puzzle?

"Jimmy Olsen," she addressed him solemnly, "you have had more contact with the New Gods than any other Earth-bug. Furthermore, you have been present at the deaths of two of the victims. I humbly request that you join my search for the missing souls. It may be the single most important quest our worlds will ever know."

He had no idea how to respond to a plea like that. "I, um . . . I mean . . . I've kinda got a lot of my own stuff going these days. . . ."

"This is more important than the needs of any single being," she insisted, refusing to let him off the hook. "Whoever stole those souls is now in possession of a power the likes of which could destroy all of reality and bring about the creation of the Fifth World!"

Jimmy was aware that the mythology of New Genesis held that the birth of the New Gods had heralded the dawn of the Fourth World, although he had always been a little fuzzy on what exactly the previous three Worlds had been. "Oh man, you mean the end of the world. . . ."

Honestly, an impending cosmic crisis was way more than he had bargained for. At the moment, he was tired and filthy and wanted nothing so much as to go home and veg out for a while. Let the Justice League or the Teen Titans assist Forager on her quest. He just wanted the universe to leave him alone for a few hours. Was that too much to ask?

On the other hand, he recalled guiltily, hadn't he just told Serling Roquette that he was tired of only being Superman's sidekick, that he craved some grand destiny of his own? And hadn't he insisted to Robin that he was eager to use his enigmatic new abilities to help people? *Well, Olsen, here's the opportunity you were waiting for. Are you ready to put your money where your mouth is?*

"Okay, Forager," he agreed. "This is what I wanted to sign up for, so I'm in." He nodded decisively. "I'm your man."

Although maybe they could swing by his apartment first, for a quick shower, a change of clothes, and a snack? He hadn't eaten anything since breakfast. . . .

"Excellent." Her helmet concealed her expression, but he could tell she was pleased. All six wings vibrated enthusiastically. "Let's not waste any time."

Before he could suggest a detour, she pressed one of the translucent gemstones on her gauntlet. Apparently the studs were more than decorative; a deafening blast, like a sonic boom, only louder, preceded the appearance of a circular portal through time and space. A brilliant white light issued from the shimmering vortex, which hovered in the air before Jimmy, who immediately recognized it as a Boom Tube, a means of interstellar transport used exclusively by the New Gods and their allies. Advanced alien circuitry far beyond mortal comprehension lined the inner walls of the tube, which seemed to stretch endlessly toward some unknown destination elsewhere in the cosmos. Via Boom Tubes, even distant New Genesis and Apokolips could be reached in a matter of seconds.

"Wait a minute!" he protested. "You haven't even told me where we're going yet!"

But Forager was in too much of a rush to explain. Placing a palm against his back, she shoved him through the portal into the intense white light, then dived through after him. The incandescent gateway dilated shut behind her.

A second boom thundered atop the Daily Planet Building, causing pedestrians several stories below to gaze up at the cloudless sky in confusion. The portal blinked out of existence, leaving only fading echoes behind. Attracted by the staggered blasts, Lois Lane came charging up onto the roof, eager to uncover the source of the noise. "Hello?" she called out curiously. "Is anyone there?"

No one answered.

The roof was empty.

OUTSIDE GOTHAM CITY.

*"**Ekat** su emoh."*

Zatanna's magical incantation instantly transported her and Mary from the deck of the *Lemaris* to the front yard of a creepy Gothic mansion hidden away in the woods. Spiked turrets rose from the looming stone walls. Bat-winged gargoyles perched upon the battlements. Majestic columns and gabled arches adorned its brooding façade. Gray slate shingles seemed to swallow up the moonlight. A winding stairway, guarded by two stone griffins, led up to the imposing front entrance. No light escaped the mansion's shuttered windows. The somber edifice looked completely dark.

"Welcome to Shadowcrest," Zatanna said.

Mary took in the eerie scenery. With the cruise ship's tour cut short by Slig's attack, Zatanna had graciously offered to tutor Mary in the privacy of the magician's home. A chill in the air made it clear that they weren't in the tropics anymore. The Bat-Signal, shining in the distance, revealed that the woods were somewhere outside Gotham. "I'm confused," Mary said. "I thought you lived in San Francisco?"

"I do, most of the time." Zatanna led Mary up the stone stairway. A demonic face, complete with curved horns, was carved into the pediment above the front door. Mary thought it bore an uncomfortable resemblance to Pharyngula. "This is my father's estate, where I grew up." Mary recalled that Zee's dad, the Great Zatara, had also mixed showbiz with crime fighting. He had died saving the world several years ago. "I still use the place as a getaway when I need to relax."

A lamp flicked on overhead, illuminating the front porch. A booming voice startled Mary, who nearly jumped out of her boots. "WHO GOES THERE?"

"Hang on," Zatanna said. "I've gotta give the password." She faced the ponderous oak doors. " 'Hi, I've brought some literature. Can I share the Good Word with you?' "

Mary raised an eyebrow. *"That's* your password?"

"It is today." Zatanna winked mischievously. "There's a bit of voice recognition involved too."

In any event, the unlikely phrase did the trick. The heavy doors swung open with a rusty squeak. A butler, whose cadaverous features made Dr. Sivana look like the Big Red Cheese, greeted them. "Very good, madam. Welcome."

Holding aloft a lit candelabra, he led them into a spacious foyer, where Mary was surprised to find an entire crew of uniformed menservants, maids, and housekeepers standing at attention. Intricate tapestries and oil paintings hung upon polished wood-paneled walls. Spotless marble tiles added to the elegance of the stately entry hall. A sweeping staircase ascended majestically toward the upper reaches of Shadowcrest.

Mary was impressed. "You must be loaded to be able to maintain a staff like this at a place where you don't even spend much time."

"I do all right." Zatanna chuckled. She snapped her fingers and a crystal chandelier lit up the foyer. "But not *that* well. The truth is, these servants are just magical manifestations of the house. They're only around when I need them." She dismissed the servants with a wave of her hand. *"Ffats ekat a kaerb!"*

Mary's eyes widened as the entire retinue evaporated into thin air. "Pretty neat!" she enthused. "And they'll just come back whenever you summon them?"

"That's right," Zatanna said. "It's really pretty basic magic, Mary. The kind you'll be able to do when you're ready."

Sounds good to me, Mary thought, eager to explore her new abilities, although she wasn't quite sure what Zee meant about having to be "ready" first. After the way she had turned all those sea monsters back into the people aboard the cruise ship, Mary figured she was ready right now. *All I need is a little fine-tuning.*

Lamps and candles flared up along their way as Zatanna led Mary up the main stairway, then guided her guest through the sprawling mansion, which was packed with antique furniture, eye-catching artwork, and fascinating souvenirs. Framed vaudeville posters of Houdini, Zatara, Sargon the Sorcerer, Carter the Great, and other legendary stage magicians adorned the walls. Medieval suits of armor stood guard along a palatial corridor that seemed to go on for miles. Flickering shadows danced across the dark wooden wainscoting.

"Totally amazing." Mary complimented Zee on her home. "This place looked huge on the outside, but I swear it didn't look *this* big."

Zatanna grinned. "Yep, this house has lots of surprises." She gestured down the hall. "Next stop on the tour is the library. It's just down here."

"But what are all these other rooms?" Mary asked, consumed by curiosity. A closed door inscribed with ancient Egyptian hieroglyphics caught her eye. An open sarcophagus, propped up beside the door, held what appeared to be a genuine Egyptian mummy. Lengths of musty linen were wrapped around the mummy's stationary form. Its withered hands gripped a gleaming bronze scimitar. Papery brown skin peeked through the bandages over its face.

Given that her new powers derived from the bygone gods of the Nile, Mary was naturally intrigued. She reached for the doorknob. "You've only shown me a fraction of—"

"Mary, wait!" Zatanna called out in alarm.

The mummy's shriveled eyelids snapped open. Springing to life with surprising speed, he swung the scimitar between the door and Mary, driving her back. The blade missed her by inches, so close that she could feel the breeze generated by its passage. A voice as dry as the desert sands shouted at her in a dead language. His breath reeked of tanna leaves.

"*Yow!*" Mary exclaimed.

"Thanks, Hassan. It's all right," Zatanna said, calling the mummy off. He settled back into his sarcophagus. She took Mary by the elbow and gently escorted her away from the door in question. "You're not ready for some rooms yet, Mary."

"O-okay." Mary looked back over her shoulder at the Egyptian door and its undead guardian. Her racing heart, which had gone into over-drive when the sword-wielding mummy surprised her, slowly settled back down. Although embarrassed by the incident, she couldn't help wondering what exactly Zatanna was hiding behind those hieroglyphics—and why she wasn't willing to share that secret. *What else is she keeping from you?* a suspicious voice asked inside Mary. *Why does she keep insisting you're not ready?*

"As I was saying," Zatanna continued, "the library . . ."

A pair of double doors opened by themselves, admitting the two women into an astonishingly large private library. Packed bookcases, several feet taller than either Mary or Zatanna, lined the walls. Antique desks and plush chairs offered comfortable locales for reading and research. A spiral stair-case led up to a mezzanine. Candles ignited in the chandeliers overhead; it took Mary a moment to realize that the chandeliers were actually floating in the air, unsupported by any chains or hooks. A fireplace roared to life in one corner, casting a rosy glow on a nearby suit of armor. A stuffed dragon's head was mounted over the fireplace. An oval mirror, in a gilded filigreed frame, hung above a glass display case, and picture windows looked out over the moonlit estate below. Mary felt as though she had accidentally stumbled into Hogwarts.

"Wow," she whispered.

The abundant shelves were crammed with books, scrolls, clay tablets, and other documents. Mary was slightly overwhelmed by the sheer size of the collection. Wandering over to the nearest bookcase, she scanned the spines of various leather-bound grimoires, demonologies, memoirs, bestiar-ies, and other esoteric volumes. Her finger reverently traced the titles on their spines: *The Book of Fate, The Arion Chronicles, Chaos & Order, The Morpheus Prophecies, The Journals of Lady Johanna Constantine* . . .

"Some of these books look like they're centuries old," she said in an appropriately hushed tone. "I don't even recognize a few of these languages."

"That's because they're not *human* languages," Zatanna explained. "And most of those books go back a lot farther than hundreds of years. My family has been collecting them for a *looong* time."

Mary remembered hearing somewhere that Zee was supposedly descended from Leonardo da Vinci, as well as from a secretive race of sorcerers known as the *homo magi*. A framed photo of Zatanna's late mother, Sindella Zatara, occupied a place of honor upon the fireplace mantel. The beautiful blonde sorceress had perished while defending her daughter from her fellow wizards. An orphan herself, Mary sympathized with Zee's loss.

"You could say this is my Batcave," Zatanna said, showing her guest around the library. "I study here, brainstorm here, practice here."

A glass display case attracted Mary's attention. Inside the case was an impressive collection of mystical artifacts. Charms, crystals, amulets, orbs, rings, scarabs, masks, icons, dolls, fetishes, wands, and other talismans rested beneath a clear pane of glass, atop a sheet of black velvet. "Look at all of these," Mary burbled, gazing at the collection like a kid in a candy store. She hadn't seen a display like this since the Spectre had trashed the Rock of Eternity during his epic battle with Shazam. The wizard's own collection, accumulated over the course of millennia, had been hopelessly scattered by the ghost's insane rampage. Maybe some of those missing artifacts had ended up here?

"There's enough magical energy in that case alone," Zatanna said proudly, "to do pretty much anything you can imagine."

Mary could believe it. She felt the talismans' sorcerous potential calling out to her, even through the thick glass sheet. Just her proximity to such power gave her goose bumps. "It must be wonderful to have so much power at your command." She bet Zee had never been chased through the streets by a pack of ignorant skinheads. "Just wonderful . . ."

"It's also a big responsibility," Zatanna insisted. Walking over to a sagging bookshelf, she gathered an armload of dusty tomes and dropped them onto a waiting desk. "Here, these should get you started." She beckoned to

Mary. "We'll start with the basics, then work our way up to more challenging material."

Mary hesitated, unable to tear herself away from the case of mystically charged trinkets and tchotchkes. It was hard to get enthused about poring through piles of moldy old books when all these delectable toys were right at her fingertips, just waiting to be played with. It was a crime to let them just sit there, gathering dust. "Can't we test-drive some of these?"

"In time," Zatanna promised. "But only after you've mastered the fundamentals." She blew a layer of dust off a slender volume. "Handing you such talismans now would be like giving a loaded gun to a child."

Child? The magician's patronizing tone pushed all the wrong buttons. "I am not a child!" Mary snarled. Her temper combusted. How dare Zatanna treat her like some inexperienced kid? Had she forgotten who exactly had saved all those people on the *Lemaris*? "If you think these stupid books are so great, *you* read them!"

Lightning leapt from her fingertips, zapping the stacked volumes, which abruptly took flight. Flapping their covers noisily, the airborne books swarmed Zatanna like pigeons descending on bread crumbs. She anxiously batted them away with her hands.

"Skoob pots ginylf!"

The disenchanted tomes rained down onto the floor, but Mary had already found something better to do. Her fist smashed through the glass protecting Zatanna's trophies. Blue flames flashed momentarily as her innate magical strength overcame whatever protective wards Zatanna had placed over the display case. Her eager fingers closed around a particularly tempting prize: a crystal-studded Atlantean scepter that positively reeked of magic.

"Ooooh . . ." Mary gasped as an ecstatic rush of energy thrilled her senses. Her skin tingled all over. Her hairs stood up on end. "No wonder you wanted to keep this for yourself." Unable to contain the wand's intense preternatural force, she started throwing off sparks of raw magical energy. Phantom winds whipped her hair into a frenzy. "So much power . . ."

"Mary, no!" Zatanna shouted in alarm. "You can't cut loose like that in here. It's like tossing a match into a tinderbox!"

A stray spark animated the suit of armor, which started clanking across the floor. The mounted dragon's head roared and breathed fire, the bright orange flames singeing the spines of the nearest books.

The power of the scepter, joined to Mary's own gods-given might, intoxicated her. She raised the wand high above her head, glorying in the rapturous sensation. "I came to you for help, Zatanna," she accused the other woman. "I thought you were on my side. Why would you keep these things from me?"

She's jealous of you, an inner voice answered her. *Jealous of what you can become!*

Of course. That was the only explanation that made sense.

"That's enough!" Zatanna said crossly. She held out her hand. *"Retpecs emoc ot em!"*

An unseen force snatched the wand from Mary's hand. "Hey!" she protested as the precious talisman, and all its irresistible magic, returned to Zatanna. Mary felt as though she had been dashed with a bucket of cold water. *Talk about a buzzkill!*

She glared furiously at Zatanna. Lightning flashed in her eyes. "You shouldn't have done that."

But Zatanna didn't seem to care what Mary thought. "You know," she said, a severe expression on her face, "I thought that you might be some sort of sorcerous savant, but it turns out you're just a brat." She brandished the glowing scepter. "And you're about to get spanked!"

You wish, Mary thought spitefully. She lusted for the power she had just known. An insatiable hunger gnawed at her very core. She launched herself at Zatanna, determined to wrest the scepter from the other woman's treacherous clutches. For all she knew, Zee had stolen the wand from the wizard in the first place. "You give that back! It belongs to *me* now!"

"Cigam reirrab tcetorp em!"

When she had to, Zatanna could talk faster than a New Yorker on a caffeine high. A hastily erected bubble of pale blue energy shielded her from Mary's initial attack, but the enraged super heroine had only just begun to fight for what she considered rightfully hers. Her gloved fists pounded relentlessly against the infuriating force field. Magical shock waves knocked Zatanna to the floor inside her bubble. "Mary, stop!" she pleaded. "What's come over you?"

Maybe I've finally caught on to the truth, Mary thought venomously, *that you're no different from Billy or Madame Xanadu. You all want to keep me weak and helpless and docile.* Lightning flashed whenever her knuckles collided with Zatanna's protective shields. *Well, to hell with that!*

Her fists smashed into the floor as the bubble instantly blinked out of existence, taking Zatanna with it. For a moment, Mary thought that her opponent had retreated from the fight entirely, then she heard Zatanna reappear several feet behind her. The resourceful sorceress counterattacked by summoning a Middle Eastern–looking brass lamp from a bookshelf.

"Eineg eruces reh, tub od on mrah!"

Like something out of the *Arabian Nights,* a djinn steamed out of the lamp. Swirling purple vapors materialized into a muscular figure with dark indigo skin, pointed ears, and scorching red eyes. His jet-black hair was pulled back in a topknot, and a black goatee added to his Mephistophelian appearance, as did his arched black eyebrows. A golden hoop pierced his left ear, and gleaming copper wristbands girded his powerful arms. Tattooed arabesques covered his bare chest, which dissolved into smoke below the waist. He laughed heartily, relishing his freedom from the lamp.

Stealing tricks from Aladdin, are we? Mary thought. *I'm not impressed.*

The genie seized Mary from behind, pinning her arms to her sides. His tight embrace would have crushed any ordinary girl. He chuckled lecherously in her ear, his spicy breath smelling of sandalwood and cinnamon.

"Luferac!" Zatanna reminded the djinn. *"T'nod truh reh!"*

Mary snickered at the other woman's restraint. "Treating me with kid gloves? Big mistake, Zee." She slammed the back of her head into the genie's face. Cursing in ancient Arabic, he loosened his grip long enough for Mary to grab on to his wrists with both hands and yank them apart. Whirling around, she tore into the djinn without mercy. Mystic energy crackled around her as she ripped the genie into fragmented wisps of smoke; it felt like tearing apart a wad of flimsy cotton candy. The genie's agonized scream echoed throughout the library. "I'm playing for keeps!"

"Ali!" Zatanna gasped. The empty lamp dropped onto the floor.

Mary turned on Zatanna. "You really had me fooled, Zee! I thought we were friends. Why even bring me here, huh? To steal the power Black

Adam gave me?" Her voice rose in anger. "To put me into one of your trophy cases?"

She tackled Zatanna head-on, slamming Zee into the bookcase behind her. The sturdy shelves wobbled precariously, and an avalanche of weighty tomes crashed down on Zatanna, knocking her to the floor. Half-buried beneath her own library, the dazed magician struggled to climb out from beneath the disorderly heap of books. "Mary . . . please," she whispered groggily. "You have to stop this. . . ."

"Don't worry, Zee," Mary answered. Her boots levitated above the carpet as she gazed down at the battered sorceress. "It'll be over before you know it!" Then nothing would come between her and all the power Zatanna had selfishly hoarded away. *It's all so obvious now,* Mary realized. *She never actually intended to teach me anything. She wanted to keep all this magic to herself.* Mary's eyes literally glowed with malice. *She couldn't stand that I was becoming more powerful than her. . . .*

Mary decided to give Zatanna a taste of what she envied. Tapping into her anger, she flung a magical thunderbolt at her so-called mentor. The jolt wouldn't kill Zee, but it might make her wish that it had. In any event, she would be in no shape to stop Mary from sampling the rest of the library's many occult treasures.

But, to Mary's surprise, Zatanna wasn't quite down for the count yet. Throwing up her hands to shield herself, she spat out a hasty incantation.

"Yram, kool ta eht rorrim!"

As though possessed of a mind of its own, the gilt-framed mirror dived to its mistress's defense, sliding between Mary and her foe. The unleashed lightning bolt struck the silvered glass—and bounced back at Mary herself. Thunder boomed inside the trashed library as lightning crashed against the startled heroine, changing her back into ordinary Mary Batson!

Wha—?

The unexpected transformation disoriented Mary. Her murderous rage vanished with her powers. The impact of the reflected thunderbolt catapulted her backward toward the picture window.

Zatanna took immediate advantage of the situation. *"Swodniw nepo!"*

Glass panes swung open obediently, and Mary went hurtling through the cold air outside the mansion. Zatanna must have given the lightning a little extra *oomph,* since Mary went sailing over the spiked fence surrounding the estate, finally crashing to earth in the grassy clearing beyond. She hit the ground hard.

Groaning, she climbed to her feet. No longer invulnerable, she felt sore all over. Her plain old jacket and jeans failed to keep out the chill of the evening. Mary shook her head in confusion, trying to figure out just how things had gone so wrong so fast. She stared in dismay at her fists. *What was I doing?*

Anxious to apologize, she ran up to the wrought iron gate of Shadow-crest. No surprise, it refused to open for her. "Zatanna, please!" she called out, hoping the other woman could hear her. "Let me explain!"

"Mary Batson." To her surprise, the iron bars of the gate twisted themselves into a rough approximation of a mouth. A rusty voice issued from the gate. "For violation of basic etiquette and decorum, and for acting in a generally nasty, evil manner, you are hereby banished from Shadowcrest henceforth." A heavy layer of fog billowed up from the ground, concealing the mansion entirely. "Do not bother to attempt to find this place, as it shall remain hidden from you forevermore."

The spreading fog swallowed up the gates as well as Zatanna's lavish estate, which vanished into the mists like Brigadoon. Mary ran forward into the clammy dampness of the fog. "Wait!" she cried out desperately. "I didn't know what I was doing. This power . . . it's too much for me!"

She reached out for the gate, but her groping fingers encountered nothing but empty mist, which quickly wafted away, taking Shadowcrest with it. Mary found herself alone in the shadowy woods, seemingly miles away from the nearest habitation. An owl hooted in the skeletal tree branches overheard.

"Please, Zatanna! I need your help! Just give me a second chance . . . please!"

The owl hooted in response.

23 AND COUNTING.

METROPOLIS.

"Wait a sec," Holly protested. "I thought this was supposed to be some sort of self-esteem workshop."

"Yes," a dark-haired staff worker assured her as she fastened a polished bronze breastplate over Holly's chest. A second attendant slid a steel bracelet onto the confused fugitive's forearm. "We're simply applying your ceremonial garb."

Holly glanced down at herself. A skirt of studded leather straps hung below the molded bronze cuirass. Metal greaves protected her lower legs. Steel-toed leather boots encased her feet. "Seriously, you *do* know this is battle armor, right?"

"Nonsense," the brunette said. She held out a bronze headpiece bearing the sculpted visage of a snarling panther. "Now, let's get you into your Purification Helmet."

Holly eyed the feline totem molded upon the helmet. A nod to her short-lived stint as a substitute Catwoman, or just a coincidence? She was already uneasy about the fact that Harley Quinn knew all about Holly's dubious past; heck, she had nearly fled the shelter after Harley had dropped that bombshell on her in the spa, but the Joker's supposedly reformed former squeeze had insisted that Holly's secret was safe among her Athenian "sisters." Every woman at the shelter, Harley had argued, was running from something, but this place was all about second chances. In the end, Holly had decided to hang around a little longer, mostly because she had nowhere else to go.

Now she was starting to have second thoughts. *What sort of self-help exercise requires body armor?*

The dressers clamped the heavy helmet over Holly's head and checked the fastenings on her "ceremonial garb" one more time. They led her out of the private dressing room into a colonnaded hallway, where she found several similarly armored women gathered outside a pair of towering wooden doors. Judging from their body language and what Holly could see of their faces, the other women looked just as baffled as she was. Herded together, they looked like refugees from a *Xena* convention.

"What in the world . . . ?"

Holly joined the other women. The metal armor jangled every time one of them moved. Holly recognized one of the armored girls as Tricia, another newcomer to the shelter. She gripped a nasty-looking forked weapon.

"Um," Holly said, "I couldn't help but notice that you're holding a trident?"

Tricia appeared puzzled by that as well. She stared nervously at the weapon. "Y-yeah."

"Okay, just seeing if you knew that." Holly guessed that the trident hadn't been Trish's idea. The African-American teenage runaway acted as though she had never held anything like it before. Holly noticed that some of the other girls were armed with maces, flails, whips, nets, and swords.

Did Hawkman have a yard sale or something?

A trumpet sounded somewhere beyond the ponderous oaken doors, which swung open to admit the armored women. Holly hesitated upon the threshold, getting a bad feeling about this. She had never explored this part of the shelter, so she had no idea what lay ahead. Athena's subordinates prodded the apprehensive girls forward. "Where have I seen this before?" Holly murmured aloud. "Was it in a movie? I'm pretty sure it was in a movie. . . ."

Sure enough, the doorway led to an impressive re-creation of an ancient Roman coliseum, complete with a sawdust floor and high stone walls. A domed sunroof offered a tantalizing view of a clear blue sky. The heavy doors slammed shut behind Holly and the others, and she heard a massive bolt being slid into place on the other side of the doors. Visions of Russell Crowe fighting for his life flashed through her mind.

"Oh yeah. I hated that movie."

A self-esteem workshop, my ass!

"My glorious sisters!" a booming voice addressed them. "Welcome to your future!"

Holly looked up to see Athena herself presiding over the occasion from a balcony overlooking the floor of the arena. An honor guard of spear-wielding Amazons flanked Athena. A velvet banner bearing the image of a Gorgon's bleeding head hung below the balcony. Writhing serpents were embroidered along the fringes of the bunting. During her stay at the shelter, Holly had learned that these symbols had long been associated with the mythological Athena, who was the goddess of warfare as well as wisdom. According to the legends, it was Athena who had taught Perseus how to slay Medusa. Holly still hadn't decided if the woman above was the actual goddess or just a charismatic namesake like Maxie Zeus, a deranged Gotham ganglord who claimed to be the genuine King of the Gods. Selina had always said Maxie was a real loser.

Wonder what she'd think of this Athena?

Certainly, the esteemed founder of the women's shelter looked more like a goddess than ever. A goatskin breastplate, known as the Aegis, was draped over her spotless silk robes. All eyes turned toward her regal figure. Her exotically accented voice rang out over the arena.

"Each of you has endured hardships. You have been overlooked, forgotten, trampled upon. Today, you will free yourselves from your pasts, eradicate your insecurities, and purify your souls. Unleash your fury, my sisters, and become warriors!"

Holly couldn't believe her ears. "Are you kidding me?" Athena didn't seriously expect them to engage in some sort of gladiatorial bloodbath, did she? "These are runaway girls, not Spartans!"

Her protests fell on deaf ears. Belying her words, Tricia suddenly turned on Holly. A ferocious war cry escaped the girl's lips as she lunged at Holly with the trident. Hours of training in hand-to-hand combat came to Holly's rescue as she deftly evaded the lethal thrust. Momentum carried Tricia past her and Holly stuck out her leg to trip the other woman, who took a header into the sawdust. Holly moved quickly to disarm the girl, only to discover that Tricia hadn't been the only woman to respond to Athena's stirring oratory. Grunts, groans, and clanging metal echoed throughout the arena as Holly found herself smack in the middle of an all-out free-for-all involving over a dozen would-be gladiators. Studded maces dented helmets. Armored bodies slammed against each other. Heated voices hissed, swore, and howled in fury as the aggrieved women took out years of suppressed anger and frustration on their fellow refugees. Blood and broken teeth spilled onto the sawdust.

Just my luck, Holly thought, *I'm the only one without a weapon.* She mentally crucified her neglectful dressers. *Thanks a lot, gals.*

She didn't want to hurt anyone, but with the melee raging all around her, she had no choice but to fight back in self-defense. Battling figures hemmed her in on all sides. A wild-eyed gladiator swung a mace at her head, but Holly rolled beneath the blow, then jumped back up onto her feet just in time to see another woman jabbing a sword in her direction. Two more fighters grappling in front of her blocked Holly's escape, so she grabbed on to their shoulders and used them for leverage as she swung around to kick the overeager swordswoman in the gut. The blade flew from the woman's hands as she tumbled backward onto the sawdust, nearly getting trampled by the brawling women nearby. She scrambled desperately after her sword, only to get kicked in the ribs by another girl.

Holly's eyes lit up as she spied a leather bullwhip, Catwoman's weapon of choice, in the hands of a young Hispanic woman a few feet away. The girl flicked the whip ineptly, obviously having no idea how to use it. It was embarrassing to watch. *What a waste,* Holly thought.

"I'll take that, thanks!" She elbowed the girl in the chin and yanked the whip from her fingers. It felt reassuringly familiar. Holly couldn't work the whip the way Selina could, but she *had* picked up the basics over the years. She cracked the whip in warning, carving out a little breathing room in the midst of the violence. The sharp report of the whip cut through the tumult. Fearful "warriors" backed away from Holly.

That's better, she thought. Taking a moment to catch her breath, she saw that at least a third of the gladiators had already had the fight beaten out of them. Their moaning bodies were strewn about the floor of the arena. Thankfully, the majority of the brawlers possessed more enthusiasm than skill; they wielded the archaic weapons clumsily, exhausting themselves as well as their opponents. Holly guessed that most of them had never been in a real fight before, let alone pitted themselves against the worst that Gotham's underworld had to offer. *Selina could take out this whole bunch without even breaking a sweat. . . .*

With maybe one notable exception.

Holly spied another warrior cutting a swath through the inept gladiators. A bronze faceplate, fashioned in the semblance of the classical Greek mask of Comedy, concealed the woman's features, but there was no mistaking her fighting abilities. Twirling a blunt cudgel like a baton, she bludgeoned the daylights out of her adversaries while nimbly evading every blow or thrust directed at her. She practically danced through the frenzied melee, leaving a trail of battered gladiators behind. None of the other women could even lay a hand on her.

Uh-oh, Holly thought. *Better keep an eye out for Funny Face there.*

A pair of charging warriors distracted her from the mystery woman. Whooping like they were hyped up on Joker Juice, they clearly intended to tag team Holly with extreme prejudice. Safety in numbers proved no protection, however, as Holly snapped her stolen whip. The lash wrapped itself around the lead attacker's waist, yanking her off her feet and directly into the path of her comrade. The partners went down in a clatter of clanging armor. Angry obscenities assailed the ears of the gods.

Holly jerked the whip loose and glanced around to see who was next. Only a few feet away, two dueling gladiators had managed to get the chains of their maces hopelessly tangled together. Cursing loudly, they struggled to free their weapons while simultaneously kicking at each other's shins. Holly didn't know whether to laugh or shake her head in dismay.

This whole thing is insane, Holly thought. *What's so "purifying" about encouraging untrained, emotionally damaged girls to beat each other up?*

She considered trying to break up the fight in front of her, but before she could intervene, the female dynamo embodying Comedy leapt between the two women. Kicking out her legs in midair, she nailed both women with her steel-shod heels, then landed adroitly on her feet a few yards away from Holly, who couldn't help being impressed by the stranger's agility. The masked woman triumphantly spun the cudgel above her head before taking a bow. She faced Holly across the suddenly silent arena. Holly realized belatedly that they were the last two women standing.

Holly tightened her grip on the bullwhip. *Fine,* she thought. *If Funny Face isn't going to back down, then neither am I.* Perspiration dripped beneath her helmet and armor. Adrenaline coursed through her veins. To be honest, part of her was enjoying the workout; it had been a while since she'd kicked a little butt. *Athena wants a show? Okay, let's give her one.*

Holly imagined Athena's cool gray eyes gazing down on them, but couldn't risk sneaking a peek at the balcony to see how their supposed benefactress was reacting to the spectacle so far. Wounded gladiators crawled away to the fringes of the arena, getting safely out of the way. Discarded weapons littered the ground. The hot sun shone down through the glass dome overhead. Naturally, the coliseum was not air-conditioned. The stuffy atmosphere reeked of blood and sweat. Holly figured she didn't smell too fresh either.

She and Funny Face warily circled each other, taking each other's measure. Holly briefly wondered what the other woman's story was before pushing the thought aside. *Win first; ask questions later,* she reminded herself. *Remember what they say about curiosity and cats.*

The masked woman made the first move, swinging at Holly with the weighted end of the cudgel. Holly darted to the left, dodging the strike, and came up quickly behind Funny Face. Holding on to a length of whip with both hands, she wrapped it around the other woman's throat like a garrote. "Ha!" she gloated as Funny Face let out a strangled gasp. The club slipped from her opponent's grasp as her fingers clutched at the oiled rope around her neck. Holly grinned victoriously. It was just like Selina always said: When in doubt, fight dirty.

Of course, she also said, Never drop your guard. . . .

Funny Face jabbed her armored elbow into Holly's side hard enough to dent the metal cuirass. The pain loosened Holly's grip on the lash and the masked woman yanked the rope away from her throat. Springing forward onto her hands, she slammed the soles of her feet into Holly's lower jaw.

Blood sprayed from a busted lip as Holly reeled backward, letting go of the whip, even as her acrobatic enemy flipped back onto her feet. Panting hard, both women assumed defensive positions as they circled each other once more, this time unarmed. Holly's whip lay on the ground nearby, tantalizingly out of reach, along with the fallen club.

Damn, she's good. Holly wiped the blood from her lips. *Need to switch tactics and move this fight inside.* Her eyes narrowed as she looked for an opening. The molded steel armor felt like it weighed a thousand pounds. She pined for her black leather catsuit. . . .

"I have seen enough!" Athena announced from above.

That's it? Holly thought. *The fight's over?* Just to be sure, she waited until Funny Face lowered her guard before doing the same. The two combatants turned toward the balcony. Athena smiled down upon them.

"You are among the lucky ones," she declared, "who have passed this sacred test. You, along with a few select others, will be making the pilgrimage to Paradise Island to achieve full citizenship among the Amazons!"

Holly gasped. She'd heard of Paradise Island, of course. Everyone had. That was where Wonder Woman was from: a mystical realm, hidden somewhere in the Bermuda Triangle, inhabited only by a race of immortal woman warriors. Like the underwater city of Atlantis, or the Bottle City of Kandor, it was one of those legendary places you read about but never expected to visit in your lifetime. Was Athena serious about taking them there?

"Awesome!" Funny Face squealed in delight. She removed her helmet to reveal the beaming face of Harley Quinn. She grinned exuberantly at Holly. "We both made it!" She sounded like they had just won the grand prize on some bizarre TV reality show. "Are you excited? I'm excited! We're going to Paradise Island!"

Holly had to admit that it sounded like a dream come true.

CHUNG LING SOO SQUARE.
CHINA.

The bustling village marketplace, hidden away in rural Mongolia, made Zatanna's spooky mansion look like Main Street, USA. A packed dirt road led between rows of outdoor stalls hawking all manner of occult artifacts and curios. Paper lanterns glowed brightly in the middle of the afternoon, and wind chimes tinkled in the breeze. Graceful temples and pagodas loomed behind the wooden booths and stands. Silk banners advertised potions and love charms in Mandarin, while the shoppers patronizing the merchants were just as exotic-looking as the wares they were haggling over. A genuine Chinese dragon, complete with a shaggy red mane, prowled the market, but nobody seemed at all alarmed by the beast's presence. A stooped old woman walked a saber-toothed tiger on a leash, and a glamorous Asian sorceress in a cherry red kimono glided overhead on a cloud. A plant elemental, who could have been Swamp Thing's skinnier cousin, was composed entirely of twigs and vines, and a slinky fox-woman walked hand in hand with a samurai warrior.

What is *this place?* Mary thought. Her magic word had restored her powers. She strolled aimlessly through the bizarre bazaar, taking in the sights. *And what am I doing here?*

"You look lost," a boyish voice addressed her in English.

Grateful to hear her native tongue, she turned around to see a slight young boy, scarcely past puberty, approaching her. Strangely, he was dressed like a Pilgrim from a Thanksgiving Day pageant. His severe black clothing, white collar, leggings, and buckled shoes looked extremely out of place in the remote Chinese village. His pale blue skin looked as though it rarely felt the touch of the sun, and his dark black hair and pointed ears, which reminded her of Black Adam, put Mary on guard. A plump ginger-colored cat with a singularly evil-looking expression perched upon the boy's shoulder. Its slitted green eyes regarded Mary with palpable disdain.

"Maybe," she conceded.

"My name is Klarion," he volunteered, "and this is Teekl. We're from Limbo Town, home to the lost population of Roanoke. I'm a Witch Boy."

"Good for you," Mary said suspiciously. She remembered hearing about Roanoke in school; the first English colony in the Americas, its inhabitants had vanished mysteriously over five hundred years ago. *Guess that explains the Puritan getup,* she thought, *assuming he's telling the truth.* "I'm Mary Marvel."

Klarion gestured at the sprawling bazaar around them. His soft voice had retained his ancestors' British accent. "What are you in the market for, Mary Marvel?"

I wish I knew, she thought. "To be honest, I just kind of stumbled onto this place."

That was true enough; ever since getting kicked out of Shadowcrest, she had been flying around the world at random, trying to figure out what to do next. She felt bad about the way things had turned out with Zatanna, but that didn't change the fact that she still needed to get a handle on her new magical powers. Maybe the Fates had led her to this place for a reason?

"Chung Ling Soo Square is a very insular community," Klarion observed. He stroked his familiar's furry head, eliciting a purr in response. "I'm quite surprised no one has tried to kill you yet."

Maybe they know better than to mess with me, she thought. "I recognized the concealment spell from above, but you're the first person to speak to me." She reached out to pet the cat, but backed off when Teekl hissed in warning. Orange hair rose up along the feline's spine. *What a nasty pussycat!* "So far I've only been cursed at in Mandarin and gotten some real dirty looks." She shrugged her shoulders. "Nothing I can't handle."

Klarion nodded as they wandered through the market together. "Clearly you possess some ability in the art of magic; otherwise, you wouldn't have found this place."

A trio of ghostly giants, as huge as they were immaterial, stepped over their heads. Enormous bags of bones were slung over their mammoth shoulders. Nobody in the market gave them a second look. Mary watched them slowly fade from sight.

"Let's just say magic and I are old friends, but I'm in the market for some new tricks." She decided to lay her cards on the table. "Maybe I've come to the right place?"

Klarion considered her words. "The problem with magic freely given is that it is never valued as much as that which is gained at a price."

Was that why things didn't work with Zatanna? Mary wondered. Zee probably took her magic for granted; she couldn't possibly comprehend how hard it was for Mary to keep control of Black Adam's unexpected gift. "I guess that's what happened with the last person who tried to help me."

Klarion seemed to understand. "Some rare folks are born with magic in their blood. Altruistic types are happy to share their abilities, but every other magic user has to barter."

Like I bartered with Black Adam? she thought. *What did I lose when I gained his power?*

They paused in front of a wooden stall hawking jade amulets and bracelets. Charms and incantations were engraved upon the talismans. Laughing children chased a walking corpse through the street behind them as a white-haired wraith floated by.

"What could I possibly barter with anyway?" Mary asked. Intrigued by the magical jewelry on display in the booth, she stepped closer for a better look.

The Witch Boy chuckled slyly. "You'd be surprised what passes for currency around here."

Swirling strands of ectoplasm issued from his fingertips, trapping Mary inside a glowing sphere. The boulder-sized globe spun about madly. "Hey!" she cried out, tumbling head over heels inside the sphere. "What the hell are you doing?"

"Don't worry, Mary Marvel," Klarion said. "And cover your ears."

"What?" She tried to break free from the translucent sphere, but its constant spinning threw her off balance. Dizzy and disoriented, she bounced clumsily against its walls.

"Your ears!" Klarion called out helpfully. He demonstrated by sticking his fingers into his own ears. Teekl buried his head beneath his paws. "Like this!"

Firecrackers went off loudly. Pyrotechnic green flames blasted the sphere, hurling it into the air away from the booth. Inside the careening prison, Mary was buffeted and tossed about. The noise of the firecrackers drowned out her indignant yelps. Startled shoppers gazed at the spectacle in alarm.

"There, there, brave Teekl," Klarion cooed to the agitated feline, who clearly did not approve of the racket. "Everything's fine!"

An aged Chinese wizard, awash in a flowing emerald robe, dashed out from the endangered stall. Golden dragons were embroidered on his garments. His long white beard flapped in the wind.

"Self-defense!" he shouted to his worried neighbors. "She approached my stall uninvited. Her raw magic disturbed my spells!" Greedy eyes assessed Mary through the shimmering walls of her prison. "I demand compensation!"

"Compensation?" The bouncing globe finally came to a stop upon a stretch of cobblestoned pavement. Regaining her balance, Mary tore her way out of the ectoplasmic sphere, which came apart into shreds of formless vapor. "For nearly nuking me?"

Charging across the street, she grabbed on to the old man by his collar and yanked him off his feet. The snow-white strands of his beard frizzed out from his face as a powerful jolt of mystical lightning shocked him to his bones. His eyes rolled inward until only the whites were visible. A whimper escaped his lips. Smoke rose from his robes.

"I'll give you payback, you wretch!" Mary snarled.

Klarion tapped her on the shoulder. "Mary?"

She glanced back at him in annoyance. "Yes?"

"Pardon me for interrupting," the Witch Boy said, "but I believe he will trouble us no more."

Huh? Mary turned back toward her victim, who was now trembling helplessly in her grasp. A twinge of guilt pricked her conscience as she realized for the first time just how frail and frightened the old man looked. His bloodless face was as white as a ghost's. His creased skin was as thin as rice paper. Rheumy eyes pleaded for mercy. *Holy Moley,* she thought. *He's scared to death of me.*

She let go of his collar and the vanquished wizard dropped awkwardly onto the ground. Gathering his singed robes around him, he scurried away from her as swiftly as his ancient bones could carry him. So intense was his need to escape that he abandoned his wares without a backward glance, frantic prayers spilling from his mouth.

"Wait!" she blurted, anxious to make amends. "I'm sorry. . . . I didn't mean . . ."

"Forget him, Mary Marvel," Klarion urged her. "You have more important things to consider . . . such as how to thank me for saving your life."

That got her attention. Whirling around, she confronted the boy and his cat. "And how exactly did you do *that*?"

"By shielding you within that protective cocoon, of course," he said, as though that should have been self-evident. "I knew that your interest in those jade trinkets would provoke a hostile reaction."

"Uh-huh." Mary knew she was being hustled. "No way. I could have handled that geezer just fine on my own." Her hands rested confidently upon her hips. "I'm not letting you blackmail me."

Klarion clutched his chest, as though deeply hurt by her accusation. "You'll find only charity in my heart, Friend Mary, not malice. All I ask in return for my service is just the tiniest, barest, most insignificant fraction of your power."

"Is that so?" she asked. "And what's in it for me?"

"A simple trade," he assured her. "For the merest taste of your occult puissance, I'll help you master the forces that rage within you."

At least he's up-front about it, she thought. *Unlike Zatanna, who promised me everything, then threw me out the first time I screwed up.*

She gave his offer serious thought. Certainly, she still needed help controlling Black Adam's tainted magic; look at the way she had just blown her top at that old man a few minutes ago. Why not make this deal with Witch Boy here? She had so much magic in her now that she could afford to spare him a spark.

"All you need do is take my hand," he explained.

Okay, Mary thought. She reached out to him until their fingers were less than an inch apart. "Just a touch," she reminded him.

Klarion wanted more, however. To her surprise, his slender blue fingers stretched like rubber and wrapped themselves around her wrist and upper arm. Latching on to her like leeches, the sinuous digits refused to let her go. Mary felt a sharp stinging sensation. Static electricity crackled beneath the Witch Boy's hungry fingers.

Teekl hissed in excitement. The cat's green eyes glowed with demonic glee. Claws extended, he lunged at Mary.

"Yes, Teekl," Klarion promised the familiar. "You can have her once she's drained."

Dammit, Mary thought. *I should have known this was a trick!* Her temper flared as she knocked Klarion away from her with a vicious backhanded blow to his face. His ductile fingers came loose, tearing away bits of skin beneath her black gloves. Teekl sank his claws into her shoulder, but she yanked the snarling cat from her flesh and flung him after his duplicitous master. The fiendish feline let out a caterwauling screech as it tumbled through the air, finally landing on its feet on the other side of the market.

Mary's blood boiled. It seemed like everyone was out to backstab her these days. *Fine,* she thought. *I can give as well as I get.* Lightning crackled about her, setting nearby banners and paper lanterns aflame. "Okay, Witch Boy! You wanted a drink from the fire hose? You got it!"

But it seemed like the little sneak had had enough. "T-Teekl . . . ?" he murmured weakly as he lay sprawled upon the pavement. Fresh bruises added a touch of color to his pallid face. He looked about anxiously for his filthy pet, who slunk to his side. The cat's hackles raised as it glowered back at Mary.

Mary considered eliminating these two once and for all, just to send a message to all the other snakes and liars out there. She was sick and tired of people who thought they could outsmart her.

Yes, Mary, a familiar voice whispered in her brain. *Kill them if you like. They won't be missed.*

It took Mary a second to realize that the voice was not her own. "Who said that?"

The one you're searching for.

"Right," Mary said sarcastically. She'd heard that before. "Someone else out to take what's mine."

Oh, I'm more like you than anyone. Follow my voice and you'll see what I mean.

Mary launched herself into the air. If nothing else, she wanted to find out just who had the nerve to invade her thoughts this way. Her clenched fists tore through the sky. "This better not be another trick."

Trust me, Mary. You won't be disappointed.

She left Klarion to deal with the angry merchants below.

22 AND COUNTING.

GOTHAM CITY.
EARTH-15.

"This is a gross violation of your jurisdiction, brother," the second Monitor declared ominously. "Your intemperate actions, however well-meaning, jeopardize the integrity of the Multiverse."

Although he obviously belonged to the same alien race, Donna noticed subtle differences between this Monitor and the one who had recruited her and Jason. This Monitor was clean-shaven, for one thing, and instead of cornrows, his long black hair was knotted in the back. His futuristic armor looked equally formidable, though, and, like his kinsman, he towered a head or two above the ordinary-sized humanoids populating the park.

"Called it," Jason gloated. "Didn't I say this was serious bad news?"

"Shut up," Donna said. Now was no time to be distracted by juvenile banter. Between the two of them, the godlike Monitors outclassed them all in power. She didn't want to get caught in the middle of a fight between them.

"Nix Uotan!" their own Monitor addressed the newcomer. "You do not belong here either. What business have you interfering in my affairs?"

"You forced our hand, Solomon," the new Monitor said. "Your reckless travels have not escaped the notice of the rest of our number. The Monitor of this world originally wished to confront you on her own, but we persuaded her that a more unified response was desired. Therefore I have been dispatched by our assembly to present our ruling." He crossed his arms over his chest. "You will surrender yourself to my custody and be returned to the Nexus of Realities, there to stand trial for crimes against the Multiverse."

"Crimes?" The original Monitor, whose name was apparently Solomon, raised his voice in anger. "Everything I have done has been to save the Multiverse from a universal threat!"

"That's enough, both of you!" Batman strode forward decisively. He snatched a Batarang from his utility belt. "I don't know which of you aliens is in the right, but this is my city and my world and I want some say in what happens here." Superwoman, Wonder Woman, and the female Atom formed ranks behind him. "The Justice League is taking charge of this situation right now!"

Nix Uotan glanced at the heroes in annoyance. With a wave of his hand, he teleported them away from the scene. "You see," he accused Solomon, "you have already disturbed the native inhabitants of this Earth." He turned his scarlet eyes on Donna and Jason. "Moreover, you have violated Multiversal law by removing these humans from their own Earth and exposing them to realities they were never meant to encounter."

"No harm was done to Earth-One by extracting these two," Solomon insisted. "They are both anomalies who should have remained dead in the first place. They were expendable!"

"What the hell?" Jason blurted. "You chose us because we're supposed to be dead anyway?"

Donna was equally stunned by the Monitor's revelation. *It makes sense, though,* she realized in retrospect. *If we die on this quest, or never make it back home, then our Earth will simply go back to the way it was before Jason and I returned from our graves. We* are *expendable—at least from a cosmic point of view.*

Not that this made her feel any less used.

"There are larger issues at stake than the disposition of these two humans," Nix Uotan maintained. "You must surrender to the will of the majority and abandon this forbidden campaign."

"Never!" Solomon said defiantly. "The End Time that was foretold is fast approaching. Only Ray Palmer can avert the Great Disaster!"

Donna recalled that K'Dessa, the pint-sized oracle of the nanoverse, had said the same thing. *So Solomon's not the only entity subscribing to this theory.*

"You are mistaken," Nix Uotan insisted. "This Palmer being you seek is without significance. Trust me, brother, he lives a life of no consequence."

Solomon mulled the other Monitor's words, then shook his head. "That remains to be seen."

"You will not come willingly?"

"I shall not," Solomon declared.

Nix Uotan sighed. "Then you leave me no choice." He stretched out his hand toward the Challengers. His gauntlet hummed loudly as it powered up. Crackling pink energies erupted from his upraised palm.

An identical blast issued from Solomon's palm, blocking Uotan's attack. The rival volleys flared brightly as they crashed together between the two Monitors, casting a ruddy pink radiance over the deserted park. Startled pigeons abandoned their roosts and flapped wildly away. "Get back!" Solomon instructed Donna and Jason.

"Not on your life!" Jason charged forward to join the fight, until a sudden shock wave sent both him and Donna tumbling backward across the plaza. Donna winced as she slammed into a metal park bench. Jason splashed down into the fountain. "Then again . . ."

The dueling Monitors appeared evenly matched. They faced off against each other, grappling head-to-head as unleashed cosmic energy flashed and sparked all around them. Their faces were contorted from the strain of their combat. The glare was so bright that Donna could barely tell them apart.

"This is futile!" Uotan shouted over the thunderous clash of their battle. "Wherever you flee, we will find you. Give up this madness!"

"What of you?" Solomon challenged him. "Would you kill me to preserve your precious rules?"

"You cannot defy our sacred code with impunity!" Gaining a momentary advantage, Uotan got past Solomon's defenses. A glowing hand, trailing energy like a comet, smacked Solomon across the face. "We are brothers! We must act as one!"

Solomon staggered backward. "Then we are brothers no more!" He spit a mouthful of blood onto the pavement and raised his palms once more. His gauntlets still seemed to have plenty of juice in them. "Dogma has blinded you all to the peril we face!"

This could go on all night, Donna realized. Launching herself into the fray, she struck Uotan like a missile. Her fists slammed into the other Monitor's chest, knocking him off his feet. He fired back at her with an energy-blast, but she deflected the bursts with her Amazonian bracelets. "Enough, Solomon!" she shouted at her ally. "Aren't you the one who is always going on about wasting time in pointless battles?"

"This is not your fight, Donna Troy!" he protested.

Donna disagreed. She was still pissed off at the Monitor for callously judging her expendable, but that didn't mean he wasn't right about the importance of finding Ray Palmer. "One for all, all for one, Solomon. This is our quest too."

"Right," Jason chimed in. Still dripping from his splashdown in the fountain, he drew a Glock from beneath his leather jacket and opened fire on the other Monitor. "Count us in."

The bullets bounced off Nix Uotan's personal force field. "Pathetic," he said as he lumbered to his feet and took aim at the gun-wielding human. "And hopeless!"

"Jason!" Donna zoomed toward the Monitor's target, shoving Jason out of harm's way only seconds before Uotan's blast struck the Revolutionary War statue behind him. The marble effigy exploded into a cascade of dust and shards. Pulverized stone rained down on Donna as she shielded Jason with her body.

"Thanks, babe!" he smirked. "I didn't know you cared."

"Don't get any ideas," she told him.

Solomon took advantage of the distraction created by Jason to nail Uotan with a powerful blast of his own. The other Monitor slammed into the trunk of a sturdy oak, cracking it in two. The top of the tree crashed down on top of him, momentarily trapping him beneath its weight.

Donna helped Jason to his feet, lifting him as easily as she might a rag doll. She called out to Solomon. "Time to go?"

"Decidedly," he agreed. He activated the controls on his gauntlet and a shimmering, transparent sphere appeared behind them. A portal opened in the side of the globe and he herded them toward the opening. "Quickly— before my brother recovers."

"Yeah, yeah." Jason sprinted into the sphere with Donna right behind him. "We know the drill."

Solomon joined them inside the vessel. The portal closed automatically.

"Halt!" Nix Uotan commanded. He heaved the fallen timber to one side and fired at the sphere. "This is futile. You cannot escape us!"

The energy-blast jolted the sphere, throwing its passengers off balance, but the desperate Monitor was too late. Outside the glowing walls of the globe, Earth-15 shimmered and faded like a mirage. Within seconds, the sky- line of Gotham City vanished from sight.

Here we go again, Donna thought. She brushed the powdered stone from her star-flecked black leotard. *But to where?*

21 AND COUNTING.

APOKOLIPS.

Enormous Fire Pits, each hundreds of miles in diameter, belched flames into the sky above a sprawling megalopolis. Thick black smoke darkened the sky, making it impossible to tell whether it was day or night. Only the incarnadine glow of the pits lit up the forbidding alien landscape. A thunderous peal resounded over the roar of the fires as the Boom Tube deposited Jimmy and Forager into the midst of a vast industrial wasteland. Transported here straight from the roof of the Daily Planet Building, Jimmy choked on the acrid fumes as he hastily took stock of his new surroundings. The scorching heat of the Fire Pits gave him an instant tan.

"Oh no!" he exclaimed. "Please don't tell me this is—"

"Apokolips," Forager confirmed. "Home of dread Darkseid."

That's what I was afraid of, Jimmy thought. He had visited this hellhole of a planet before—and barely escaped with his life. Looking up, he spied an entire squadron of flying Parademons zooming toward them. The vicious soldiers were Darkseid's shock troops, used to enforce his despotic rule over Apokolips. Antigravity glider-wings extended from their metallic green and yellow armor. Clenched steel gauntlets gripped futuristic lances and rifles. "Here comes the welcome wagon."

Forager braced herself for the attack. "Less talk and more fight, Earth-bug!"

Acid sprayed from her gauntlets as the first wave of Parademons assailed them. She nimbly dodged the jabs and blasts of snarling soldiers, bouncing across the sooty terrain like a gymnastic grasshopper, her overlapping wings flaring out behind her.

"Wait!" Jimmy hollered at the hostile troopers. "I don't want to fight you!" His body, however, had other ideas; overriding his conscious will, his superpowers kicked in automatically, striking back at the Parademons. Elastic limbs lashed the soldiers like swinging maces. A volley of needle-sharp quills elicited cries of pain as they penetrated minute cracks in the creatures' armor. A thorny fist slammed into a brutish face, shattering a mouthful of jagged fangs. Blood and saliva sprayed from the soldier's jaws. "Stop attacking!" Jimmy pleaded desperately. "I can't control myself!"

Forager, on the other hand, seemed more than happy to tear into Darkseid's troops. "That's it!" she cheered him on, while enthusiastically slashing and kicking at their foes. A growling Parademon lunged at her from behind, but she deftly flipped him over her shoulder so that he collided with a phalanx of oncoming soldiers. "Scrag them limb from limb! They are but soulless extensions of the Dark Lord's evil!"

"No! This is wrong!" Jimmy insisted. As monstrous as they were, the Parademons were just defending their own turf. *We're the intruders here.* Against his will, his rebellious fingers netted entire handfuls of Parademons and flung them into the air. His pliable flesh absorbed the impact of the aliens' blasts and blows, rebounding back into place after every strike. A fresh salvo of porcupine quills exploded from his skin. "I'm not like you, Forager. I'm not a warrior!"

She turned her antennae toward him. "That's not what it looks like from here," she buzzed back at him with what sounded like admiration in her voice. Despite her formidable fighting skills, however, the sheer number of their foes was taking its toll on the courageous insect-woman. Her glossy carapace was scratched and scorched in places. Turquoise blood ran down her side from an ugly wound in her shoulder. One of her wings was frayed and shredded. She was breathing hard.

There seemed to be no end to the savage Parademons; they kept on coming, wave after wave. Jimmy wondered how much longer they could hold Darkseid's storm troopers at bay. His ragged shirt and jeans hung in tatters upon his distorted frame. Perspiration dripped into his eyes, stinging them. His rubbery flesh began to feel the strain of absorbing too many assaults. Bruises blossomed across his aching torso; each new attack jarred his bones. The butt end of a metal lance smacked into his chin and he yelped in pain. A laser beam zipped past his skull, singeing his scalp. He smelled his own hair burning. *What was Forager thinking, bringing us here? We don't stand a chance!*

The relentless crush of enemy soldiers abated suddenly. The massed Parademons withdrew to several yards away, granting Jimmy and Forager a momentary respite. Grateful for the break, he dared to hope that maybe the worst was over. His elongated arms retreated back toward their sockets even as he wondered what had brought about this inexplicable cease-fire. His eyes searched the smoggy skies overhead, half expecting to see Superman flying to the rescue. Who else could chase the bloodthirsty Parademons away?

The rumble of heavy machinery crushed his hopes. Turning toward the noise, he saw a gigantic energy-cannon being wheeled into place. *"Uh-oh."* Jimmy stared down the barrel of the enormous weapon. An ominous hum rapidly increased in volume as the cannon charged up, and he shared an anxious glance with Forager. "This can't be good. . . ."

No wonder the foot soldiers had cleared out!

A smirking Parademon fired the cannon, and Jimmy's world disappeared in a blast of scalding energy.

EPHESUS, TURKEY.

The Temple of Artemis had been one of the Seven Wonders of the Ancient World, famed throughout Western civilization, but that was millennia ago. Generations of conquest, vandalism, and neglect had all but obliterated the once-magnificent structure, so that nothing remained but crumbling marble ruins falling to pieces in the middle of a marshy field, about fifty miles south of the nearest city. Truncated columns tilted precariously at odd angles, or else lay across the ground like fallen logs. Weeds sprouted between uneven stone tiles. A sculpted female torso, lacking both arms and a head, looked more like the Venus de Milo than Artemis of the Hunt. Vines strangled the broken pillars and lintels. A crescent moon cast mournful shadows across the site.

Descending from above, Mary Marvel was unimpressed by the forlorn remains of the temple. Turkey was a long way from Gotham City. Scowling, she wondered if it had been worth the trip.

It is, Mary, a voice assured her. *We're going to be good friends, you and I.*

"Uh-huh," Mary said dubiously. She was still trying to get used to the idea that the mysterious voice inside her head wasn't actually her own. For the longest time, she had confused the voice with her own thoughts, but she had finally realized that there was a separate intelligence at work here, insinuating itself into her mind, calling to her from somewhere both far away and disturbingly close. Intent on getting to the bottom of the mystery, and perhaps teaching the invasive speaker a lesson, she had followed the voice across the Atlantic to this desolate locale. "Friends, sure, assuming I don't kill you first."

Ooh. The voice sounded more amused than intimidated by Mary's threat. *You mean that. I like that.*

Mary touched down onto the ground. She glanced around at the scattered debris. Time and the elements had eroded a nearby frieze until it was almost illegible. Doric columns lay upon their sides like fallen redwoods; only a handful of terra-cotta roof tiles remained. "Why this place?"

"Artemis is the goddess of the moon," the voice replied. It took Mary a second to realize that she could now hear the voice with her ears as well as her mind. "Her temple seemed like a fitting place for us to meet face-to-face at last." The feminine voice spoke with an American accent. "You don't know how long I've been looking forward to this moment. We have so much in common after all."

"What do you mean?" Mary said warily. Klarion's trickery had left her wary of the nameless speaker's intentions. She peered into the shadows cloaking the ruins, searching for the source of the invasive voice. "Who are you . . . really?"

"Just an ordinary girl, granted ancient, godlike power, betrayed by those closest to her." A low chuckle escaped the shadows. "Sound familiar?"

A little, Mary admitted. She walked beneath a decrepit stone archway into the remains of an open plaza. A shaft of moonlight fell like a spotlight onto an outré figure perched upon a weathered marble pedestal that had once served as the base of a towering stone column. Intricate purple designs were embroidered on the woman's tight black costume. Polished silver crescents clasped the front of the outfit together. A cloak of purple feathers fanned out behind her head and shoulders, then trailed down behind her like a train. Her purple boots dangled above the cracked and uneven pavement. The skintight outfit flattered her voluptuous figure.

The flamboyant getup, which made Mary's costume look positively austere in comparison, seemed better suited to a Mardi Gras celebration than a midnight rendevous in an historical ruin, but it was the woman's striking countenance that truly captured Mary's attention. Her bone white skin was partially eclipsed by a dark purple shadow that covered fully half of the woman's face. *Some sort of birthmark or tattoo,* Mary wondered, *or just a dramatic makeup job?* Spiky black hair crowned the woman's scalp, while gleaming violet eyes regarded Mary playfully. A sardonic grin lifted the corners of the stranger's plum-colored lips. Tapered ears and fangs gave her a distinctly vampiric appearance. Slender white fingers fondled a glittering black diamond about the size of a large fig. The translucent gem sparkled darkly in the moonlight.

Mary didn't recognize the stranger. "And you are . . . ?"

"My name used to be Jean, but now?" She rose sinuously from her seat upon the decapitated base. "You can call me . . . Eclipso."

Eclipso! Mary was familiar with a notorious super-villain by that name, a vengeful demon who derived his power from a cursed black gem, just like the one in this woman's possession. But that Eclipso had been a brutish-looking male, not a weirdly glamorous woman. *Maybe they're related somehow, like me and Billy?*

"You don't look like Eclipso," she accused the other woman.

"You're thinking of my fiendish predecessor." She held up the sparkling gemstone. "The mystic power of the black diamond has passed on to me."

Just like I inherited Black Adam's power, Mary thought. "Good for you. But what's that got to do with me?"

Eclipso seemed untroubled by Mary's suspicious tone. She smiled invitingly at the younger woman. "Do you know how much potential you have,

Mary?" She gestured at the murky ruins surrounding them. "Throughout history, other sorceresses have stood upon this sacred ground. Circe. Medea. Morgaine Le Fey. Each of them a woman of great strength, ability, and passion, much like yourself. Each of them misunderstood and, like you, betrayed by those they loved."

A pang stabbed Mary's heart as she recalled waking up alone in that hospital, and Billy's harsh reaction to her new powers. *And I don't even know where Freddy is anymore. They both forgot about me.*

Eclipso nodded knowingly. "Yes, Mary. I'm aware that your family has turned their backs on you, leaving you on your own to be preyed upon by so-called mentors."

"You mean Zatanna, Klarion, and Madame Xanadu," Mary realized. She frowned as she recalled how the magical trio had attempted to undermine her. *If they had their way, I'd still be weak and helpless.*

"None of them truly wanted to help you, Mary." Eclipso came closer to Mary, until they were only a few inches apart. The lady in purple stood at least a head taller than the younger heroine. A heavy perfume, redolent of rare black orchids, accompanied Eclipso. "They were jealous of your power and sought to keep you from surpassing them."

Mary eyed Eclipso guardedly. "And how are you any different?"

"You think I want your power?" Eclipso laughed out loud. "How cute. Trust me, as impressive as you are, your might is trivial next to mine."

Mary bristled. "Is that right? Then what do you want from me?"

"I thought I'd found a kindred spirit in you, Mary." She sighed regretfully. "But I can see now that you're not ready to trust again so soon, that you'd prefer to go it alone." Eclipso shrugged and retreated from the moonlight, fading into the shadows. "Fair enough, Mary Marvel. I leave you in peace."

"No, wait!" Mary panicked at the prospect of being abandoned once more; this was like getting banished from Shadowcrest all over again. *I never said I wanted her to go away. I was just being a little more cautious this time. What if Eclipso is just the person I need to understand these new powers of mine?* "Eclipso! Jean!"

A rough male voice shouted at her from behind. "You there!"

Mary spun around to find herself confronted by three armed guards in military uniforms. Their leader, an ugly gorilla with a greasy mustache, bellowed in Turkish, but the wisdom of Zehuti allowed her to comprehend his words.

"What are you doing here? This a protected landmark." He drew his pistol from its holster and waved it in her face. "You must go!"

"But I'm not hurting anything," she insisted in the guard's own tongue. "I'm not doing anything wrong." The soldiers' surly attitude got on her nerves; these jerks had chosen the worst possible moment to give her a hard time. "What's it to you if I choose to be here?"

"Shut your mouth!" the soldier barked, glaring spitefully at the young woman. "We've had enough of you rich Americans and your arrogance. You think our rules don't apply to you? Well, maybe you'll feel differently after a few nights in jail." He unhooked a set of handcuffs from his belt and tossed them over to one of his men, who snickered and made a rude remark about Mary's legs. "Place her under arrest!"

What? Mary couldn't believe the men's nerve. They had no idea whom they were dealing with here. The cuffs jangling in his grip, the leering soldier stepped forward to take Mary prisoner, but he didn't get far. Mary threw out her open palm and a blinding flash of lightning froze the men in their tracks. "There!" she retorted. "Try and arrest me *now!*"

The color drained from the guards' flesh and uniforms, turning chalky gray. The spontaneous burst of magic had done more than just bedazzle the hostile guards; they had literally been transformed into marble, like the strewn remains of the bygone temple. The petrified men stood like statues amidst the fallen columns and archways. Only their modern uniforms and weapons demonstrated that they hadn't been resting here for thousands of years.

Mary gulped. *Did I really do that?* She had acted without thinking, but maybe her reaction had been a little extreme? The men had been pigs and bullies, who probably deserved everything they got, but still . . .

"Hah!" Eclipso chuckled softly in her ear. Distracted by her confrontation with the obnoxious soldiers, Mary hadn't even heard the other woman glide up behind her. "They wanted to guard these ruins so badly, now they can do so forever." She hurled a bolt of purple energy at the men's leader, reducing his stone pistol to gravel. "Very nicely done."

"Y-you think so?" Mary asked uncertainly. She was relieved—and grateful—that Eclipso hadn't condemned her like Billy and Zatanna had. Perhaps Jean really *was* on her side?

"Of course," Eclipso assured her. She laid a comforting hand on Mary's shoulder. Her violet eyes probed Mary's face. "How did it feel?"

Mary contemplated the stationary figures of the transformed guards. The men's bellicose expressions were stamped forever onto their petrified faces. Aside from their badges and uniforms, were they really all that different from, say, those muggers who had terrorized her back in Gotham City? Mary wondered how many other innocent tourists the men had threatened and brutalized over the years. *I was just minding my own business,* she recalled resentfully, *but they were going to throw me into some filthy Turkish prison anyway. Real tough guys, picking on one helpless-looking girl . . .*

"Actually," she admitted, "it felt pretty good."

Eclipso smiled. "I'm glad to hear that, Mary. It means you're on the right path."

That was just what Mary wanted to hear. *Take that, Zatanna!*

"It's weird, though," she confessed. "I didn't even know I could do that."

"This is just the beginning," Eclipso promised. She lifted off from the rubble, ascending into the cool night sky. The waxing moon, shining brightly above them, matched the silver crescents upon her throat and bodice. "Come with me, Mary. Let me help you explore your new abilities . . . and guide you to your ultimate destiny."

Which is? Mary wondered anxiously. She hesitated amidst the ruins, unsure if she should accept the other woman's offer or not. The old Eclipso had been a villain to be sure, but then again, so had Black Adam. Maybe this new Eclipso was different . . . and truly understood what Mary was going through. *Just because I have Adam's powers, that doesn't make me evil too, so it would be unfair to judge Jean on the basis of the old Eclipso's crimes.*

Besides, nobody else seems to believe in me anymore. . . .

Mary launched herself into the air after Eclipso. "Wait for me!"

20 AND COUNTING.

THE BLEED.

Roiling clouds of radioactive vapor churned outside the Monitor's energy-sphere. Crimson lightning lit up the billowing mists. A bloodred radiance suffused the stormy atmosphere, which seemed to stretch on endlessly in all directions. Turbulence rocked the globe beneath the Challengers' feet, making it difficult to stand upright. Donna braced herself against the curved wall of the sphere to keep from falling. *Talk about a bumpy ride,* she thought. *This thing needs seat belts.*

"So where are we now?" Jason asked. He scowled at the daunting scenery outside. "We taking a detour through Hell or something?"

Donna had to admit this unnamed cosmos had a distinctly infernal appearance. If she didn't know better, she'd think they were traversing Tartarus itself. *Minus the three-headed dog, of course.*

"My people call this realm The Bleed," Solomon informed them. "It is the formless void between the fifty-two universes." Unlike Donna and Jason, he seemed to have no difficulty maintaining his balance. He tracked their progress on a holographic display screen. "The Bleed's chaotic energies render it all but impossible to monitor, which should hide us from my brethren for the time being."

Donna was grateful for the respite. "But they're definitely after us, aren't they?"

"Yes," Solomon admitted. "The other Monitors refuse to accept my interpretation of recent events. They deny all evidence of the catastrophe to come. We can expect them to oppose us at every turn."

"Took them long enough," Jason muttered. "I thought you guys were supposed to be on top of things."

"I must confess to a deception," Solomon explained. "I uploaded a fifty-two-minute delay into the central Nexus, keyed into my own presence. What they monitored regarding me . . ."

"Had already happened almost an hour earlier," Jason grasped. "Sweet!"

"The stratagem bought us time." Solomon adjusted the navigational controls. "But, alas, they have obviously become aware of the discrepancy."

Donna nodded soberly. "So from here on, wherever we go, they can find us."

"That's going to put a real crimp in our grand tour of the Multiverse," Jason observed. He reloaded his automatic pistol. "We're going to have to fight our way to Palmer."

"No," Solomon said. "That will not be necessary. My brother revealed more than he had intended." He gazed past the transparent walls of the sphere at the hellish red maelstrom before them. "I now know *exactly* where Ray Palmer is."

19 AND COUNTING.

THE BERMUDA TRIANGLE.

"My God . . ."

Holly stood upon the prow of the *Minerva* as Paradise Island came into view directly ahead of the private yacht. Grecian temples and palaces gracefully adorned the sloping hillsides of the densely wooded isle, which rose from the sparkling blue waters of the Caribbean like a mirage. Even from miles away, you could tell that the marble buildings were no crumbling ruins; they looked like they were in perfect condition. The pristine elegance of the forbidden isle could not have been more different from the squalid Gotham slums Holly was accustomed to.

"Gods," Athena corrected her. Along with Holly and the other Amazon wannabes, the supposed goddess gazed out at their destination from the deck of her ship. A crown of electrum rested upon her piled brown curls. "And, yes, it is beautiful. Themyscira, eternal home of the Amazons."

Themyscira was the actual name of what the media had dubbed "Paradise Island." Now that they were almost there, Holly was starting to believe that Athena was the real thing after all. Who else could guide them straight to this mythical location? Wonder Woman's homeland was supposed to be magically hidden from the rest of the world. As far as Holly knew, not even Selina had ever set foot there before.

"Jeepers creepers, will you get an eyeful of that." Harley Quinn stared dreamily at the island as she leaned so far out over the front rail that Holly was afraid she was going to tumble overboard. Despite herself, Holly was starting to warm to the endearingly daffy ex-super-villain. It was hard not to respond positively to the pigtailed blonde's infectiously cheery disposition. "Sure beats a padded cell in Arkham!"

"I'll bet," Holly replied. A warm tropical wind rustled her hair, which had regained its reddish hue now that her temporary dye job had faded away. Like the other initiates, she was clad in the Amazonian armor that Athena had insisted they wear from now on. That struck Holly as a tad excessive, especially on a Caribbean cruise, but maybe the warrior goddess just wanted them to get used to wearing the heavy armor. *What the heck,* she thought. *When in Themyscira . . .*

The yacht rolled beneath their sandaled feet. "I can't wait to get back on solid ground," she admitted. She had gotten over the worst of the seasickness on the first few days of the voyage from Metropolis, but the oscillating deck still made her a little queasy. "How much longer before we dock?"

"We dock soon," Athena informed her. Her silken robes fluttered in the breeze. She strolled away from the rail. "But the rest of you get off here."

"What?" Holly asked. She wasn't sure she heard Athena right. The island was still at least a mile away.

"Your training begins now." Athena raised her voice so that all could hear. "Into the water, my warriors-to-be!"

"Wait a minute!" Holly pointed at the azure waters ahead of the yacht. Scaly green fins cut through foam-flecked waves. Serpentine snouts, sporting dagger-sized fangs, occasionally broke the surface before diving beneath the waves once more. Scores of prehistoric sharks and sea serpents infested the churning sea. "What about them?"

"The children of Ketos Aithiopos, mother of all sea monsters. The ancient guardians of our shores." Crossing the deck, Athena extracted metal lances from a wooden bin. She handed the weapons out to the young women she had brought here. "Outswimming them is a worthy test for any aspiring Amazon."

"No way!" Holly refused a spear of her own. Silly her, she had thought that the bin contained life jackets or something. "Anyone who would jump into that is insane."

"Cowabunga!" Harley shouted as she enthusiastically hurdled over the railing. She hit the water below with an enormous splash.

Holly rolled her eyes. "I rest my case."

But Athena wasn't taking no for an answer. She pressed the spear upon Holly, who became acutely aware that, stuck on a boat hundreds of miles from modern civilization, she didn't have a whole lot of other options. Holly watched glumly as, one by one, and with varying degrees of apprehension and excitement, the other girls followed Harley overboard, like lemmings voluntarily racing toward their doom.

So much for a mutiny. Holly grudgingly snatched the spear from Athena's hand. *Guess somebody's got to look out for the other newbies.* She glanced back at Athena as she clambered over the rail. "Any last words of encouragement?" The goddess obviously had no intention of getting her own feet wet. "An all-powerful protection blessing would be nice."

Athena seemed amused by the younger woman's irreverence. She smiled slyly. "Aim for the eyes, child."

"Whatever." Holly took a deep breath and jumped feetfirst into the foaming water below. After the sunny warmth of the deck, the sudden chill of her immersion came as a jolt to the system. The bronze armor weighed upon her like an anchor, so she hastily stripped down to the thin white linen tunic underneath. The discarded metal gear sank to the bottom of the harbor, but that was the least of Holly's worries. The authentic Amazon uniform wasn't worth drowning for.

Athena can take it out of my allowance, she thought wryly. *Or get her uncle Poseidon to retrieve it for her.*

Shedding her sandals as well, she kicked up to the surface, her head breaking above the waves, where she found herself starring in an extremely unnecessary remake of *Jaws 3-D*. Splashing about in the ocean, the other initiates desperately tried to fend off the ravenous predators besieging them. The serpents' tails whipped the water into a bloody froth, while their voracious maws lunged repeatedly at the would-be Amazons. Holly spared a moment to look for Harley, but failed to locate the Joker's demented ex amidst the aquatic tumult. Salt water splashed against Holly's face and lips. She thanked God—or the gods—that Selina had insisted that she learn how to swim. . . .

Who the hell does Athena think I am? Aquagirl?

A reptilian head that made Killer Croc look like Kermit the Frog burst from the water only a few waves away. Holly gulped as she stared straight down the bright pink gullet of a monstrous sea serpent. Rows of ivory teeth waited to strip the flesh from her bones. Its fishy breath turned her stomach.

Paddling to stay afloat, she maneuvered the spear into position. *Aim for the eyes,* she recalled urgently, only to discover that the hideous creature didn't have any eyes, only glistening expanses of scales where its ocular organs should have been. Holly cursed profanely. For a goddess, Athena gave lousy combat advice.

She jabbed at the monster's snout, but the point of the spear failed to penetrate the serpent's scaly armor. *Crap!* She dived beneath the waves just as the creature snapped at the empty air her head had occupied only a heartbeat before. Its rough hide scraped against her bare legs, drawing blood, as she frantically swam away from the hungry beast. Holding on to her breath, not to mention the spear, she stroked underwater for as long as she could before surfacing once more. She *thought* she was heading toward the distant island, but in the chaos it was hard to be sure. Blinking the salty water from her eyes, she anxiously scanned the horizon.

An appalling sight greeted her. Only a few yards away, a monster-sized shark chomped down on the mangled body of a headless swimmer. Blood and gore exploded from the shark's jaws as the mutilated remains of the nameless runaway fed its bottomless appetite. Despite her own peril, Holly cursed Athena's lethal training methods and "survival of the fittest" ethos. Talk about cutthroat competition!

Cutthroat . . .

A crazy idea struck Holly. Spear in hand, she swam *toward* the murderous shark. *Forget the eyes,* she decided as she dove toward the creature's exposed underbelly. *Aim between the scales.* Kicking upward, she drove the spearhead into the shark's throat with all her strength. Gallons of cold blood spurted from the savage gash, rendering the surrounding waters incarnadine. Reversing course underwater, Holly abandoned the spear and put as much distance as possible between herself and the wounded shark before surfacing to inspect her handiwork. Just as she'd hoped, the other sea monsters had been attracted to the huge outpouring of blood, turning on the injured shark in a cannibalistic feeding frenzy. Sharks and serpents alike snapped greedily at each other, momentarily ignoring the insignificant female morsels bobbing in the sea all around them. The children of Ketos were too busy devouring their own. Snapping jaws and ear-piercing wails added to the din.

"Now!" Holly hollered at the other girls. "While they're distracted!"

She spotted the island to the south. The safety of dry land called out to her and, not looking back, she paddled toward Themyscira as fast as her weary limbs allowed. The swim seemed to take forever, and every muscle in her body ached by the time she finally staggered out of the sea onto the sandy shore of Paradise Island. Breathing hard, she spit a mouthful of brine onto the beach. Water streamed from her soggy hair. Her chiton was soaked clean through. The bloody scrapes on her legs stung like the devil. All in all, she felt more like a drowned rat than a former Catwoman.

But we made it, she thought. *That counts for something.*

Lifting her head, she was glad to see several other women dragging themselves onto the shore as well. Some of the stronger gals assisted their weaker sisters. Holly was too exhausted to do a proper head count, but she got the impression that most of her fellow initiates had come through the harrowing ordeal in one piece. She looked around for Harley, but the pigtailed lunatic was nowhere to be seen. A genuine pang of grief caught Holly by surprise.

Aw, hell, Holly thought. *Guess the little nut didn't make it.*

As much as she hated to admit it, she was going to miss . . .

"Hey!" a high-pitched voice squealed gleefully. "Who's up for sushi?" Holly spun around to see Harley come wading out of the surf, holding aloft the speared head of a giant shark. The beast's meaty tongue dangled out one side of its gaping jaws. "I'm buying!"

Holly smacked her hand against her brow. She didn't know whether she was happy that Harley was still alive or she wanted to toss the harebrained blonde back into the drink.

Maybe a little bit of both.

Yet her relief that Harley had survived was sullied by the knowledge that not all of the shelter's former denizens had escaped the island's flesh-eating guardians. Holly recalled the shark's anonymous victim and a fresh surge of anger caused her to clench her fists. Goddess or not, Athena had no right to subject vulnerable young women to such blood sports. *There's something rotten going on here,* Holly concluded, *and it's up to me to get to the bottom of this scam before somebody else gets killed.* A determined look came over her face as she straightened her shoulders and marched up the beach to begin her undercover mission on Paradise Island. *If Athena thinks she can turn me into an obedient little Amazon warrior, she's not as all-knowing as she thinks she is. She's in for a big surprise once I get the goods on her.*

After all, that was what Catwoman would do.

APOKOLIPS.

The Armagetto was both the home and prison of the "Lowlies," the planet's oppressed masses. Some of the slaves had been born here; others were hostages and prisoners of war from throughout the universe, brought to Apokolips to spend the rest of their wretched existences providing brute labor for Darkseid and his favorites. Cruel overslavers enforced their master's rule, brooking no disobedience—as Jimmy had painfully discovered.

Jimmy trudged through the sooty streets with the other slaves. Their horrific task? Carrying the limp corpses of dead Lowlies to the perpetually blazing Fire Pits, where the anonymous bodies were turned into fuel for the infernos. Knowing that most of the fatalities had dropped dead from pure exhaustion, Jimmy couldn't help wondering if he was destined for cremation as well. He glanced at the slaves working beside him. They pushed on mindlessly, having lost all hope long ago. Their lifeless eyes never lifted from the pavement.

I've got to get out of here, Jimmy thought, *before I end up like them.*

The hot air seared his lungs. His tattered clothing was soaked with sweat. His stomach growled hungrily; the Lowlies were fed barely enough to stay alive. Jimmy guessed that he had lost at least ten pounds during his captivity. He wearily hurled another cadaver into the fires, then circled back the way he had come. On Apokolips, there was never any danger of running out of fresh corpses. As ever, he kept his eyes peeled for any sign of Forager, but without success; he hadn't laid eyes on the missing insect-woman since awakening to this never-ending nightmare. He prayed that she was still alive, and not just because she was his only ticket home.

"Daydreaming again, little fire-hair?" The shocking sting of an electrified lash cracked against Jimmy's back, eliciting a gasp of pain from his parched lips. An armored overslaver barked at the prisoner, "I've warned you before not to let your attention waver!"

Tell me about it, Jimmy thought, his entire body still quivering from the blow. He was already way too familiar with the jolting effect of the overslaver's lash. He staggered forward, maintaining his place in the alien chain gang. *This will make a great exposé for the* Planet, *assuming I ever make it back to Earth.*

"Careful with that one, overslaver," Captain Vyle, the commander of the guards, admonished his subordinate. His polished jade armor was more elaborate than those of his fellows as he viewed the scene from atop a levitating platform. A sharklike fin crested his helmet. "The Dread One has commanded that he not be killed."

Come again? Jimmy thought. "Dread One? You can't mean—"

"Silence, worm!" Vyle, whose name matched his nature, descended toward Jimmy, brandishing his own lash. "That name is not to be uttered by the likes of you!"

Jimmy took that as a yes. *But why would Darkseid want to keep me alive?*

"I think this one misses his little bug companion," the first overslaver said mockingly.

Vyle chuckled at the bizarre notion of someone actually caring for another. "Perhaps, Sergeant Flaay, we can arrange to have it fed to him."

Their taunts enraged Jimmy. Risking further punishment, he shook his fist at the heartless guards. "What have you done with Forager?"

"I'd curb that tongue, scum." Vyle stepped off his platform onto the pavement. Reaching down, he grabbed Jimmy by the throat, lifting the scrawny reporter off the ground, Darth Vader–style. Up close and personal with the sadistic commander, Jimmy was shocked to discover that Vyle had an extra mouth where his left eye should have been. Rows of chomping fangs lined the empty socket. "You may be of interest to the Dread One, but that doesn't entitle you to answers."

Jimmy stared in horror at the slavering maw beneath Vyle's brow; the surreal image reminded him of a recurring nightmare he'd had as a child. Not wanting to let his captors know how creeped out he was, he tried to muster a show of resistance, just to prove that they hadn't completely broken his spirit yet. "I may not look like much," he warned them, "but I have abilities. Tremendous powers that I'm not afraid to use against you!"

"Hah!" Sergeant Flaay laughed. "See how it bristles!"

"Empty words." Vyle casually tossed Jimmy aside, so that he landed roughly upon the unyielding pavement. The other Lowlies backed away fearfully, lest they also incur the commander's wrath. "The Dread One knows all, including the fact that your so-called powers only manifest when your life is in jeopardy." He sneered with *both* of his mouths. "Fear not. The overslavers of Apokolips are well schooled in the delicate art of torture. You won't die by our hands, but you may long for death's release!"

Vyle's lash snared Jimmy's feet, yanking him backward so that his skull collided with the pavement. An excruciating jolt of electricity triggered violent convulsions. Jimmy bit down hard on his tongue. The briny taste of his own blood filled his mouth.

"A taste of things to come," Vyle promised. He withdrew the lash, leaving Jimmy stunned and gasping upon the ground. His ankles burned where the lash had wrapped around his bare flesh. Vyle strode back onto his glider before addressing Flaay. "Bring this slug to me when the others crawl back to their cages. I think he warrants special attention."

"Yes, sir, Captain Vyle!" The overslaver saluted the departing commander, then dragged Jimmy to his feet and shoved him back into the line of prisoners. "Gonna be a long day for you, maggot! Your suffering has only just begun." He cracked his whip above Jimmy's head. "Now, back to work!"

Jimmy flinched at the sharp report of the lash. The worst part was, Vyle was absolutely right. His weirdo powers offered no protection from the tortures in store.

Unless . . .

A crazy, near-suicidal idea occurred to him. It was a desperate move, but it seemed the only alternative to a painfully protracted life of ceaseless abuse and servitude. *I have to go for it now,* he resolved, *before I lose my nerve.*

Darting from his place in the plodding procession, he sprinted back toward the gaping Fire Pit. The heat from the flames felt like a blast furnace, but Jimmy squeezed his eyes shut and kept on running. "Halt, Earthman!" the startled overslaver shouted. He sounded panicked at the ghastly prospect of his charge dying in defiance of Darkseid's orders. His heavy footsteps pounded after Jimmy. "Have you taken leave of your senses?"

Maybe, Jimmy conceded, *but what other choice do I have?* The intense red glare of the Fire Pit penetrated his closed eyelids. The blistering heat tried to drive him back, but Jimmy gritted his teeth and hurled himself forward. *One way or another, I'm toast. . . .*

He flung himself into the burning pit.

18 AND COUNTING.

NEPAL.

Chitwan National Park was once the exclusive hunting grounds of the country's ruling class. But now the sprawling forests and grasslands, nestled in the foothills of the Himalayas, were a nature preserve encompassing nearly a thousand square kilometers. Monkeys chattered in the leafy branches of evergreen sal trees while Bengal tigers stalked through shoulder-high elephant grass. Birdsong competed with the shrill laughter of the monkeys.

Chitwan was also home to one of the world's last remaining populations of the endangered one-horned Indian rhinoceros. Flying through the air alongside Eclipso, Mary spied a small family of rhinos grazing peacefully in a grassy meadow near a muddy watering hole. The ungainly beasts looked vaguely prehistoric. Their wrinkled hides hung in folds upon their massive frames. The curved horns of the adults pointed upward at the clear blue sky.

Unfortunately, the tigers weren't the only predators prowling the brush. Armed poachers, equipped with automatic rifles, crept stealthily toward the unsuspecting rhinos, whose horns were valued on the black market due to their allegedly curative properties. The greedy poachers no doubt hoped to make a killing, in more ways than one.

Not if I have anything to say about it, Mary thought angrily. She and Eclipso kept the sun behind them, so that the fierce glare masked their approach from the gun-wielding hunters below. "Talk about slimeballs," Mary muttered. Didn't these creeps know that there were less than three thousand Indian rhinos left in the world?

"Go ahead, dear," Eclipso encouraged her. Jean raised her feathered cloak to shield her face from the sun; the daylight seemed to disagree with her. "Show these mortal swine the error of their ways."

With pleasure, Mary thought. She swooped down toward the poachers even as the men were drawing aim on their defenseless prey. Intent on their targets, they didn't even notice Mary flying above them—until bolts of mystic lightning shot from her fingertips.

The sizzling blasts did not incinerate the men; Mary was more creative than that. Instead she instantly shrank the poachers to the size of squirrels. Lost in the folds of their own oversized clothing, the miniaturized poachers had to scramble to avoid being crushed beneath their own rifles. Their squeaky cries were barely audible.

Serves you right, Mary gloated. *Not so tough without your big scary guns, are you?*

The freak lightning also startled the wildlife below. Flocks of frightened woodpeckers and hornbills launched themselves into the air, while agitated monkeys jabbered noisily. The alarmed rhinos, unaware of their close brush with death, fled in panic, stampeding straight toward the transformed hunters. Mary grinned at the hilarious sight of the tiny naked figures running like mad to avoid being trampled by the pounding hooves of their onetime prey. The discarded rifles were smashed to pieces by the rhinos, who proved that they could run surprisingly fast when motivated to do so. Faster than the little poachers' doll-sized legs?

Maybe.

Mary briefly considered rescuing the shrunken hunters from the rhinos' path. She didn't actually want them to get crushed to death. Did she?

"Brilliantly done, Mary," Eclipso congratulated her. "You're developing a flair for poetic justice. You turned the tables on those cowardly vermin quite effectively."

"Thanks!" Mary basked in her new friend's praise, forgetting all about the micro-poachers' plight. At least *somebody* appreciated what she was doing these days. Just this morning, in fact, Mary had defended thousands of acres of virgin rain forest from shortsighted loggers and developers. There were over a hundred new trees along the Amazon now, all with anguished human faces. "It feels so good, Jean. So liberating to cut loose with my powers like this."

They soared away from the park, leaving the shrunken poachers to their fate. "That's how it should always feel," Eclipso assured her. "A few more lessons from me, and you'll be ready."

"Ready for what?" Mary asked. This wasn't the first time Eclipso had alluded to some special destiny awaiting Mary.

Eclipso smiled coyly. "All in good time, dear."

PARADISE ISLAND.

Paradise Island was hardly living up to its name.

If the Athenian Women's Shelter had been like a luxury hotel, Themyscira was turning out to be more like boot camp. Or so Holly thought as she busted her butt to complete yet another agonizing obstacle course. Flames erupted along the edges of the track, adding to the sweltering heat of the noonday sun. Holly's chiton was soaked with sweat. Her bare feet pounded against the rough gravel track.

"Keep moving, all of you!" an Amazon drill sergeant berated them from atop a wooden guard tower. The looming towers and barbed wire fences enclosing the training grounds made their new home feel more like a prison than a refuge. Ugly steel barracks and mess halls contrasted sharply with the lovely palaces and temples Holly had glimpsed from offshore. She and the other new recruits had been on the isle for at least a week now, and she had yet to set foot in anything resembling Paradise. "Is that the best you can do, you useless sows? You're pathetic!"

"That's *Ms.* Pathetic to you," Holly muttered as she dropped to the ground and wriggled beneath rolls of coiled razor wire. The jagged gravel scraped her knees and elbows. The back of her tunic snagged on a metal barb, which dug into the skin underneath. Holly winced, but kept on crawling forward on her belly. She was starting to wish that she had never heard of Athena. . . .

"C'mon, red," Harley Quinn called back to her. Ahead of the pack, the pixieish blonde sprang back onto her feet on the other side of the razor wire. Typically, Harley was treating the hellish ordeal like a lark. Glancing back over her shoulder, she grinned encouragingly at Holly. "Compared to prowling around Gotham with Catwoman, this should be a sleepwalk!"

"Your lips to my feet," Holly replied, panting in exertion. At this point, she no longer flinched whenever Harley alluded to Holly's colorful past. Gotham City and the rest of what the Amazons referred to as "Man's World" seemed thousands of miles away. Her fugitive status wasn't even an issue anymore. As far as she knew, Themyscira had no extradition treaty with the United States. . . .

So how come it feels like I'm doing time anyway?

Just beyond the razor wire, a mountainous sand dune awaited them. Harley charged up the forty-five-degree slope with Holly right behind her, struggling to keep up. Rumor had it that Harley's former BFF, Poison Ivy, had enhanced Harley's athletic abilities with some sort of herbal concoction of her own devising. Watching Harley blithely scale the dune, Holly was inclined to believe it. Running uphill through the shifting sand proved incredibly exhausting; Holly's own legs felt like lead. She heard the rest of the girls gasping and wheezing behind her. "Oh man, this is murder!" a breathless voice exclaimed. "It's too much!"

Holly looked back to see Tricia feebly battling the hill. The young black woman was a distant third behind Holly and Harley. The remainder of the initiates hadn't even cleared the razor wire yet, let alone made it to the dune. Stalled halfway up the slope, her whole body sagging, Tricia looked like she was on the verge of giving up.

Not a good idea, Holly thought. Their Amazon hosts frowned on failure; Tricia would be lucky to get fed tonight if she didn't complete the course. "You can do it, Trish!" Holly shouted. "Use your momentum!"

"Easier said than done!" Tricia grunted. Still, she took a deep breath, reached down deep, and came up with a fresh burst of speed that carried her another few yards up the slope. For a moment, Holly thought that Tricia might catch up with her, but then the other woman's feet slid out from under her and she went tumbling down the hill, churning up a huge cloud of sand as she lost all the ground she had made before finally coming to rest at the very base of the hill, where she collided with Marta, a refugee from Blüdhaven's gang scene, who had just made it past the razor wire. The two women collapsed into a tangle of sweaty limbs. "Dammit!" Holly cursed in sympathy.

"On your feet!" A female warrior, in full armor, showed the fallen women no mercy. She prodded them with the blunt end of her lance. "An Amazon never surrenders!"

Holly paused at the crest of the hill, tempted to lend Tricia and Marta a hand. Her hesitation did not go over well with the drill sergeant in the tower. "Keep moving!" the Amazon barked. "What are you waiting for, an engraved invitation from Olympus?"

"But . . ." Holly gestured at the floundering women below. What about teamwork and sisterhood?

"Every woman for herself!" the sergeant bellowed. She pointed to the dense woods beyond the sand dune. Holly saw Harley waiting for her at the bottom of the hill. "Into the brush, you two! Go! Go! GO!"

Holly got the message. Reluctantly abandoning Tricia and Marta, she scrambled down the opposite side of the dune to join Harley at the edge of the forest. Together they plunged into the thick underbrush. Inhospitable branches and leaves scratched against Holly, adding to the numerous small nicks and abrasions stinging her sun-baked hide. Gnarled roots threatened to trip her. Sunlight filtered down through the leafy canopy overhead. Drenched in sweat, she pined for the comfy hot tubs and saunas back at the women's shelter. At her new digs in the initiates' spartan barracks, ice-cold showers were the only amenities. "For this, I kicked ass in the arena?" she griped aloud. "Remind me to flunk next time."

Harley merrily led the way. She whistled a Disney tune as she plowed through the verdant foliage; if there was actually a trail through the brush, Holly couldn't see it. Tall pines and laurel trees blocked her view. Thorny bushes grabbed at her tunic. Small animals scurried through the brush. "C'mon, admit it," Harley teased her. "This is exhilarating!"

"You think?" Holly said dubiously. A displaced tree branch came whipping back toward her face and she ducked beneath it just in time. She tried to remember what sort of venomous reptiles had infested ancient Greece. Wasn't Orpheus's bride killed by a nasty snake?

"Sure!" Harley chirped. Annoyingly, she wasn't even breathing hard. "This is us, Holly . . . doing what we want, instead of being defined by someone else."

Holly wasn't so sure. Sometimes she suspected that Harley had merely transferred her blind devotion to the Joker to Athena instead. She sure seemed to have bought into the Amazon party line. *Once a follower, always a follower.*

But am I really all that different?

"Ooh! Check this out!" Harley enthused as they reached the perimeter of the training grounds, as marked by a chain-link fence topped by coiled razor wire. A narrow path ran along the base of the fence. Holly guessed that it circled back to the beginning of the obstacle course. She expected Harley to turn onto the path, but the blonde surprised her by running full-bore toward the fence.

"Harley?" Holly slowed to a trot, completely bewildered as to what her nutty new acquaintance was up to now. "Where . . . ?"

"Adventure beckons!" Springing into the air, Harley caught hold of an overhanging laurel branch and used it to flip herself over the top of the fence, clearing the razor wire by a matter of inches. She touched down lightly onto the ground on the other side of the fence. "Hah! They call that a wall? Back at Arkham, that wouldn't even stop Tweedledum and Tweedledee!"

Holly stared at Harley through the chain-link fence. "You're going AWOL?"

"I'm living life on my terms!" Harley exulted. She beckoned for Holly to follow her. "For the first time ever!"

I'm not sure this is such a good idea, Holly thought. Athena and her lieutenants had declared the rest of the island off-limits to the newcomers. Then again, maybe it was worth the risk to find out just what, if anything, Athena might be hiding beyond the fence? *And far be it from me to discourage Harley from showing a little independent thought. . . .*

Sighing in resignation, Holly launched herself at the same branch Harley had employed only moments before. Hours of gymnastics practice back in Gotham paid off as she successfully duplicated her cohort's acrobatic feat, nailing the landing just like a cat. Harley applauded loudly, obviously delighted that Holly had chosen to accompany her, and took off into terra incognita. Holly tagged along after her, hoping that she hadn't made a dreadful mistake. She wondered how long it would take the Amazons to figure out that she and Harley had strayed from the path, and what exactly the penalty was for desertion.

What's the Amazon equivalent of a firing squad?

Past the fence, the terrain rose steeply toward a range of rocky hills. The uphill climb was a challenge after the arduous obstacle course, but Holly took comfort in the fact that they would be heading downhill on the way back. Perhaps the altitude would afford them a good view of the rest of the island? The prospect kept Holly trudging upward, even though her throat was parched and she would have killed for a bottle of cold water. She kept her eyes peeled for any fresh streams or springs. Her stomach grumbled.

"Look!" Harley pointed excitedly at a shadowy cleft at the base of a granite cliff face. Darkness swallowed up the sunlight just beyond the lip of the opening. "A cave! Just like you-know-who's!"

Holly knew whom Harley was referring to. Selina had been known to visit the Batcave on occasion, although Holly had never personally wangled an invite from the Dark Knight. She doubted, though, that the nameless cave ahead held anything half as impressive as Batman's secret headquarters. "So?"

Harley insisted on seeing for herself. "Let's explore!"

"You're kidding, right?"

Harley smartly saluted the cave opening. "Junior Spelunker Harleen Quinzel, present and accounted for!"

"Not kidding," Holly realized glumly. She tried in vain to sound a note of reason. "Just for the record, this is an incredibly bad idea. Two unarmed women entering a pitch-black cave." She shook her head at the fact that they were actually contemplating such a foolhardy move. "That *always* goes well in the movies."

"See," Harley replied. "So there's no worries." She marched briskly into the darkness. "C'mon."

Clearly, Harley had never seen *The Descent*. "Sarcasm's completely lost on you, isn't it?" Holly asked as she bowed to the inevitable and followed Harley into the cave. *Probably full of bat guano or bears,* she thought crankily. She strained her eyes to see into the gloom. All she could make out at first was a dimly lit grotto that appeared to extend deep into the hillside. The sudden shade chilled her sweaty flesh. Goose bumps broke out across her skin.

Harley seemed disappointed by Holly's lack of enthusiasm. "What kind of a sidekick are you, red?"

Sidekick? Holly thought indignantly. *When did I become your sidekick?* She let her eyes adjust to the murky interior of the cave. Stalactites jutted down from the ceiling like dragon's teeth, and Holly had to duck to avoid bumping her head into one of the calcite fangs. Sleeping bats rustled overhead. She heard water dripping deeper within the cavern and debated whether it was worth looking for in the dark. Naturally, neither of them was equipped to go caving. They didn't even have a matchbook between them, let alone a flashlight.

She dimly glimpsed Harley's outline ahead of her. "You do realize we can't go back now. We've been gone too long. They've got to know we're missing by now."

Harley shrugged. "You worry too much. We're on a magic island, Holly! Maybe we'll find a flying carpet, or a lamp with one of those genie things inside!"

"Wrong culture," Holly pointed out, treading carefully over the uneven floor. "Try a winged horse, or Pandora's box, or . . ." Her voice trailed off as she heard herself playing along with Harley's magical treasure hunt fantasy. "I can't believe I'm having this conversation with you!"

Harley gave no indication that she was listening to Holly. "Yowza!" she exclaimed. "Get a load of this!"

Indirect sunlight, invading the cavern from outdoors, exposed a sizable cache of Amazonian gear. Swords, spears, shields, battle-axes, scrolls, a bedroll, armor, a quiver of arrows, a bow, and amphorae of various shapes and sizes were stacked haphazardly against the rugged wall of the cavern. Peering at the supplies, Holly saw at once these were no long-forgotten artifacts. Everything looked new and in excellent condition. The blades and arrowheads were freshly sharpened and free of rust. No dust had settled on the various pots and vases.

Harley reached the obvious conclusion. "Somebody's living here!"

"Indeed." A lurking figure lunged from the stygian depths of the cave. Striking with exceptional strength and speed, their attacker sent Holly flying across the grotto with a single blow, while simultaneously knocking Harley off her feet with a sweep of her arm. Armor jangled loudly. An unsheathed sword flashed in the dim lighting.

"Holy—!" Harley gasped as she hit the ground hard. "Did somebody get the license number of that Batmobile?"

"Harley, focus!" Holly snatched a sword from the piled gear and jumped to her feet. She tossed a spear to Harley, who wasn't too dazed to snag it from the air. The two runaways took up defensive postures, raising their weapons against . . . who?

Their foe stepped into the light, revealing a striking, raven-haired woman clad in ornate golden armor and sandals. A cloak of imperial purple was clasped to her shoulders by a pair of intricately detailed gold brooches. An eagle motif was emblazoned upon the woman's gleaming breastplate. A silver girdle circled her waist. A golden tiara, studded with rubies and sapphires, crowned her regal brow. Although she appeared older than either Holly or Harley, perhaps in her early fifties, her face had a timeless beauty that looked vaguely familiar. Nor had her age diminished her obvious fitness and vitality. Holly got the distinct impression that this woman could wipe up the floor with both of them without even trying.

"Hades beckons, false Amazons!" she denounced them angrily. Her own sword stood poised for combat. "Soon you will know it all too well!"

False Amazons?

"Whoa! Time-out!" Holly protested. "We're not with those Amazon chicks out there."

"Yeah!" Harley confirmed. "We kinda quit their stupid club!"

The fury in the older woman's eyes was replaced by a more thoughtful expression. She eyed Holly and Harley warily. The tip of her sword dipped slightly. She nodded toward the cave entrance—and the training grounds beyond. "*Those* are not Amazons."

"Yeah, we're tumbling to that," Holly said. She had been suspicious of this whole setup since day one. What kind of mythical sisterhood increased its ranks by putting homeless young women through hell? That hardly sounded like the kind of culture that would produce someone like Wonder Woman.

"My own people have departed the mortal realm," the armored stranger declared. "I alone remain in penance for past sins. I know not where these imposters hail from, but they are *not* of the sisterhood."

Okay, Holly thought. *Now we're getting somewhere.* This woman sounded like she might be able to help them get some answers as to what was really going on here. She cautiously lowered her sword. "We cool?"

The woman returned her blade to its scabbard. "Were you lying, I would know. Were you lying, you would be dead."

Holly gulped. "Good to know."

"What makes you so sure those Amazons are bogus?" Harley asked.

The formidable stranger addressed them solemnly. "I am Hippolyta, Queen of Amazons. I know my own kin."

Of course! Holly realized why the woman's face seemed so familiar. *She's Wonder Woman's mother.* Now that she knew what to look for, Holly could see the family resemblance. She thought she remembered reading that Hippolyta had died a few years back, but apparently the reports of the Amazon queen's death had been somewhat exaggerated.

But what's she doing hiding out in a cave on her own island?

"So even this Athena is bogus?" she asked.

"Athena?" Hippolyta's voice dripped with scorn. "She still calls herself Athena?"

"Duh!" Harley answered. "Where you been, living in a cave?" She glanced around. "Oh. Right."

Hippolyta disregarded Harley's babbling. "Athena," she repeated darkly. "There is irony in that."

Holly didn't get it. "How so?"

A cold smile played upon Hippolyta's lips. "She has taken the name of the goddess of wisdom." Her hand rested on the pommel of her sword. "None who dares trespass against me can truly be called wise."

Holly was suddenly very glad to be on Hippolyta's good side. The Queen of the Amazons was obviously no one you wanted to mess around with.

"Hey!" Harley blurted. "If that's not really Athena, then who've I been busting my hump for?"

Good question, Holly thought.

Hippolyta held up her hand abruptly. "Quiet!" She swiftly retrieved the bow from her armory and plucked an arrow from the quiver. She spun to face the mouth of the cave, where an enormous black dog suddenly filled the entrance. Drool spilled from its massive snout as it sniffed at the ground. A spiked collar girded its thick neck. A low snarl reached Holly's ears.

Crap! Holly recognized the beast as one of the savage warhounds Athena's lieutenants used to patrol their encampment. On occasion, the guard dogs had even been employed to "motivate" the initiates to run faster during training. Holly had vivid memories of the fierce canines nipping at her heels while heartless women warriors yelled at her to pick up the pace. No doubt the phony Amazons had set the dogs to track her and Harley down.

And people wonder why I'm more of a cat person!

Picking up their scent, the warhound bounded into the cave. Rubbery black lips peeled back, baring the beast's yellow fangs. It charged at them like Ace the Bat-Hound's meaner brother.

Hippolyta let loose her arrow, which thwacked into the dog's snout, narrowly missing its eye. The warhound growled in anger and kept on coming. Leaping at Hippolyta, it clamped its jaws around the bow and wrenched it from her grip.

"Bad doggie!" Harley scolded. "Bad! Bad!"

The warhound snapped the bow in two and spit the pieces onto the floor of the cave. It whirled around to attack Hippolyta once more. Holly didn't think she could get to the dog before it tore the queen's throat out, so she hurled her sword like a throwing knife. The blade sank into the beast's shoulders, eliciting a furious yelp from the enraged hound. Forgetting Hippolyta for the moment, it turned on Holly, who found herself unarmed against the bloodthirsty canine.

"Oh, come on!" she complained to no one in particular. "How is this fair?"

But before the beast could lunge at her, Hippolyta snatched the spear from Harley's grasp and vaulted across the cavern. Gravity added to the force of her thrust as she drove the point of the spear deep into the warhound's skull while alighting upon the ground. The monstrous dog convulsed once before dropping lifelessly at the queen's feet. She nodded in satisfaction as she wrested the spear from the dead hound's corpse.

"This breed has proven difficult to slay," she observed calmly. Canine blood spattered her face and armor.

"Not your first?" Holly guessed, grateful to be alive.

A look of weariness came over the queen's noble features. "There have been others," she conceded. She nudged the bloody carcass. "This one was set on your trail. There will be more."

"There's a piece of good news," Holly said drily, not that she hadn't figured the same. *Wouldn't you know it? I'm a fugitive again.*

Harley dropped to her knees beside the vicious brute that had nearly killed them. Her eyes were moist as she stroked the dead dog's fur. "Poor puppy . . ."

Hippolyta regarded Harley with puzzlement. "Is that one well?" she asked Holly. "She shows no outward sign of combat trauma, and yet . . ."

"Let's not go there," Holly recommended. They had more urgent problems to deal with than Harley's questionable sanity. "They've got a small army of those warhounds back at the camp. If they're all after us . . . ?" She didn't need to complete the thought. "Don't suppose you have a boat handy?"

Hippolyta shook her head. "You wouldn't be the first to try to escape. It never ends happily."

Holly remembered the sea monsters prowling just beyond shore. "I'll bet." She glanced around the cave, which didn't really seem large enough to hide all three of them on a permanent basis. "Any other ideas?"

The Amazon queen pondered the matter. "Perhaps, if you are glib enough, there is a way you can return without fear of execution . . . and be of some use to me."

"I'm listening," Holly said.

Hippolyta indicated the carcass on the floor. "Were you to return with this kill, and a thrilling tale of initiative taken . . ." She peered into Holly's eyes to ensure that the younger woman took her meaning. "The pretender and her acolytes tend to look favorably on blood sports. And I could make use of eyes that see from within her ranks."

She wants us to be her spies, Holly realized. *Undercover Amazons.*

Harley contemplated the massive corpse. "I dunno. Looks awful heavy."

"You won't need the entire carcass," Hippolyta assured them.

She raised her sword high. . . .

17 AND COUNTING.

APOKOLIPS.

Night, or what passed for night in the smoldering Armagetto, had fallen by the time a bizarre-looking figure furtively crawled out of the blazing Fire Pit. Dark green scales, each as thick as a tortoise's shell, covered Jimmy's body, shielding him from the all-consuming flames, just as they had for hours now while he hid within the pit. Gouts of bright orange flame escaped his lips every time he exhaled. Intricate designs, like circuit diagrams, were etched into his fireproof shell.

How 'bout that? Jimmy thought. *Looks like my crazy plan worked after all.* Just as he'd hoped, his unpredictable powers had activated in time to spare him from total incineration. Granted, he hadn't expected to transform into some sort of fire-breathing turtle-man, but he wasn't about to complain. Better a reptile than a pile of ashes.

Peering out through the smoke and flames, he scanned the ugly industrial complex beyond the pit. The overslavers and their wretched charges seemed to have retired for the evening, or perhaps they had simply moved on to feed another pit. In any event, the coast was clear. Jimmy took advantage of their absence to scuttle away from the smoky inferno behind him. Crouching low, and clinging to the shadows, he located a ventilation shaft leading into one of the megalopolis's many weapons factories. His scaly hands pried open the hatch and he crawled inside the shaft. A low ceiling forced him to stoop uncomfortably as he made his way down the horizontal vent. His fiery exhalations lit his way through the darkness. He fretted about setting off some sort of sprinkler system, but then again, that assumed that Darkseid actually cared about the safety of his slave labor.

Okay, first things first, he thought, as he paused to consider his next move. *How do I get off this crummy planet before Darkseid's goons find out that I'm still alive?* The key was finding Forager. *She brought me here. She can darn well get me home, if only I can find her.*

Maybe this way? He started moving forward again, driven by an inexplicable certainty that he was heading in the right direction. He couldn't explain how he knew this, but he felt strangely confident that Forager was up ahead somewhere. Another facet of his puzzling new abilities, or just wishful thinking on his part? The circuitry inscribed upon his shell began to emit a faint golden glow, which steadily increased in intensity the farther he proceeded. Jimmy chose to take that as a good sign.

He crept stealthily through an intricate maze of vents, service tunnels, and other conduits. The rumble of heavy machinery reverberated ceaselessly in the background. Periodic gusts of hot air and exhaust made him grateful for his impervious exoskeleton. Occasionally he heard footsteps in the corridors outside the tunnels. Jimmy froze and held his breath until the unseen guards or servants passed. Alien rodents, twice the size of Terran rats, hissed angrily at the fire-breathing intruder before scurrying in retreat. Greasy lubricants and industrial waste dripped onto his head and shoulders, streaking his shell. The cramped passageways smelled like gasoline and brimstone.

Jimmy recalled his nauseating trek through Project Cadmus's sewers. *How come I keep ending up as a tunnel rat?*

The booming machinery gradually receded into the distance. The glowing circuitry grew ever brighter. Jimmy sensed that he had progressed from the factories into Darkseid's gloomy palace. But where was Forager? An itch at the back of his brain guided him to a vertical shaft that led to a rusty metal grate many yards above Jimmy's head. A trickle of turquoise liquid dripped down the ladder before him.

Forager's blood?

Jimmy climbed the ladder. The bars of the grate were slick with the alien fluid. Jimmy lifted it just enough to peek out into the chamber above. *Please,* he prayed. *No Parademons or overslavers, please . . .*

"Forager!"

His insectile traveling companion was shackled to a canted metal rack, like a butterfly mounted for display. Although scratched and blackened in places, her chitinous armor appeared more or less intact, suggesting that she hadn't been tortured too severely yet, but fresh blood continued to seep from a wound in her shoulder. Jimmy remembered her being zapped by a Parademon's laser-rifle during their initial battle with Darkseid's strike force. He could hear her panting raggedly beneath her helmet. All six wings were retracted.

To his relief, she appeared to be alone in the dismal torture chamber, which was crowded with elaborate metal apparatus whose sadistic functions Jimmy didn't want to think too hard about. Being careful not to let the metal grate clang loudly onto the floor, he shoved it aside and hurried over to the upright rack. Forager's helmet concealed her expression. Jimmy couldn't tell if she was conscious or not.

"Hang on!" he said. "Let me get you out of there!"

He started to gently remove Forager's helmet. "Thank God you're still alive. . . ."

And, he discovered to his surprise, *strangely gorgeous.*

Glossy purple filaments, resembling human hair, swept across the top of her head. The elegant planes of her face had a lustrous vermilion sheen. Multifaceted compound eyes sparkled like polished yellow crystals. There was only the slightest hint of a nose, but her lilac-colored lips were plump and inviting. Slender antennae rose from her flowing purple locks.

Her alien beauty threw Jimmy off balance. *Cool your hormones,* he scolded himself. *She's a human-sized bug for crying out loud!*

He rapidly undid the clasps binding her wrists and ankles. Weakened by her ordeal, she slumped forward. He reached out to catch her. "It's okay," he assured her. "I've got you."

"O-Olsen?" she said weakly, sounding dazed and disoriented. Her antennae tilted toward him.

"That's right." He propped her up as she tottered upon shaky legs. Their close contact made it hard to concentrate on the business at hand. A honeyed fragrance tantalized his senses. "It's me, your pal Jimmy."

"Olsen!" Without warning, she lunged at him, knocking him backward onto the floor. Straddling him, she seized his throat with both hands and began squeezing the life out of him. Adrenaline, or the insect equivalent, boosted her strength, so that she suddenly seemed as fierce as ever. Jimmy's eyes bugged from his sockets. He gasped for breath. "Kill you! Must kill you!" she chanted, as though brainwashed. "Jimmy Olsen must die!"

"Forager, stop!" he wheezed. Her powerful hands clamped down on his windpipe; unable to breathe fire, the best he could manage was a few faint sparks. "What are you doing?"

He tried to shake her off, but her grip was like a vise. "Kill you . . . kill," she repeated over and over, while buzzing like an angry wasp. "Must kill you!"

Jimmy's arms went elastic, wrapping around her from behind and pulling her off him. He sucked in the fetid air as her fingers came away from his throat. His scaly limbs encircled Forager like the coils of a boa constrictor, binding her arms to her sides, yet she continued to writhe violently within his grasp as he scrambled to his feet. It took all his strength just to hold on to her.

He had no idea what had come over her. *Why's she so mad at me? It wasn't my idea to star her in a sci-fi version of* Hostel. "Stop it, Forager. You've got to snap out of this!"

At first, he didn't seem to be getting through to her. Then, to his surprise, the circuitry embedded in his scales emitted a brilliant flash that lit up the entire chamber. Even stranger, the light show was accompanied by a series of electronic *pings* that seemed to be coming from inside his very skull. *What in the world?* Jimmy thought. *Now what?*

The dazzling flash had an immediate effect on Forager. She stopped fighting back against Jimmy's pliable arms and shook her head in confusion. Her antennae twitched back and forth before turning again toward Jimmy. He saw his own reflection multiplied in her compound eyes. "Jimmy?" she said uncertainly, as though truly seeing him for the first time.

"Maybe," he replied. With his scaly skin, elongated arms, glowing circuits, and beeping skull, he barely recognized himself. "I'm not so sure anymore."

She scrutinized his transformed appearance with obvious fascination. Her gaze traced the complicated pattern of the circuitry etched upon his body. She listened carefully to the last few *pings* before they faded away. "Was that . . . ?" She sounded like she could barely believe what she was thinking. "Where did you get a Mother Box?"

The question startled Jimmy. A Mother Box, he knew, was a kind of living computer often employed by the New Gods. Among other things, they could be used to summon Boom Tubes of the sort that had transported him and Forager to Apokolips in the first place. *But what does that have to do with what's happening to me?*

"I don't have a Mother Box," he insisted. He wondered if Forager's own ability to produce a Boom Tube had been disabled by her captors. *Probably*, he figured. *They wouldn't want her teleporting out of here.*

"But . . ." she protested.

Come to think of it, Jimmy thought, *Mother Boxes* ping *just like I did*. He shrugged his shoulders, not ready to cope with yet another mystery. "I know." Frustration soured his voice. "Just chalk up another one for Jimmy Olsen, boy freak." He released his hold on Forager. "I'm just glad *whatever* happened calmed you down."

"Forgive me, my Earth-bug," she said sheepishly. "The only way I could deal with the pain they were inflicting on me was to go into a waking trance." She winced as her fingers delicately explored the bleeding wound in her shoulder. "I was simply protecting myself on instinct."

He thought that over. "And your instinct was to kill me? Nice."

"Yes," she admitted. "I . . . I have no excuse."

"Whereas I have no use for excuses," a third voice interrupted.

Jimmy and Forager spun around to see a smirking, middle-aged woman enter the dungeon. Her gaunt, haggard face reminded Jimmy of Margaret Hamilton in *The Wizard of Oz*, only without all the green greasepaint and warts. A ruffled green velvet gown, with a high collar, gave her a faintly medieval look. A matching cape was clipped to her heavily padded shoulders. Lacquered black hair met in a widow's peak atop her high forehead, as well as rising in hornlike peaks above her temples. A cruel smile evoked generations of mercilessly strict schoolteachers and librarians.

"Bernadeth!" Forager buzzed angrily.

Oh great, Jimmy thought. *I remember her now.* Bernadeth was one of the Female Furies, an elite corps of warrior women and assassins devoted to Darkseid himself. Plus, as if that wasn't scary enough, she was also the sister of Desaad, and said to be just as vicious as her sadistic brother.

"Better you had killed this mortal," she informed Forager, "than let him live to sample my charms." She drew a two-foot-long blade from a sheath at her side. The double-edged weapon glowed radioactively.

Jimmy stepped in front of Forager, shielding her with his body. *"Sheesh!"* he exclaimed. "Where does Darkseid dig up these nightmares!"

"Watch out, Jimmy!" Forager grabbed on to his arm from behind, as though afraid he might do something foolish—like maybe take on the sword-wielding hag unarmed. "Beware her *fahren-knife*! It burns her victims from the inside out!"

Judging from the quaver in her throaty vibrato, she was speaking from personal experience. Jimmy's blood boiled at the thought of Bernadeth torturing Forager in this very chamber. "You'll never touch her again, you skank!"

He mentally winced at his own tough-guy dialogue. *"Skank"? Yup, you're really going to make a top-notch reporter someday, Olsen. . . .*

"How deplorably touching," Bernadeth said with a sneer. "If futile."

Raising her glowing blade, she sauntered toward her targets. Forager tugged frantically on Jimmy's arm, urging him to flee, but he gently disengaged himself from her grip. "Stay back, Forager." Porcupine quills shoved their way up through his skin. Fire sprayed from his lips. "I think I can handle this."

Bernadeth swung the fahren-knife at Jimmy, only to get a face full of needle-sharp spines before her irradiated blade could connect with his head. More quills speared her velvet gown. *"Yeeeagh!"* she shrieked as the freakish attack caught her by surprise. Her body convulsed in agony . . . or was it ecstasy?

"Pain . . . delicious pain!" she moaned in rapture. A twisted smile spread across her face as she paused to savor the experience. Her pale, cadaverous features flushed with excitement. Fervid green eyes coveted Jimmy. "Come to me, pain-bringer. It has been too long since Bernadeth took a consort." A crooked finger beckoned to the flabbergasted porcupine-boy. "And make it exquisite!"

Jimmy's quills wilted. "Umm . . . pass?"

"No more delectable torment for Bernadeth?" She sighed in disappointment, then raised her glowing blade once more. "Then all the more agony for you!"

She charged at him with unexpected speed. The fahren-knife came swinging at his skull. Jimmy strained to launch another volley of quills, but, before he could even *try* to defend himself a second time, parallel beams of crimson energy zoomed through the doorway, striking Bernadeth's sword hand. She screamed again, this time less eagerly, as the lethal weapon went flying from her grip. She dropped to the floor, clutching her seared hand. Smoke rose from the scorched velvet glove. The nauseating stench of burning flesh and fabric added to the fetid odor of the torture chamber.

"Wretched meat-thing!" she snarled at Jimmy. No trace of perverse affection remained in her furious eyes. "The master looks favorably upon you!" She turned her attention to the empty doorway through which the twin heat-rays had come. "Bernadeth did not know, Lord Darkseid! Forgive me!"

Jimmy belatedly recognized the parallel rays as Darkseid's dreaded Omega Beams. They were like Superman's heat vision, he knew, only a hundred times more deadly.

Forager gazed at him in confusion. "The Dark Lord is protecting you?"

So it seems, Jimmy thought. *But I'll be darned if I know why.*

"Now would be a good time to make ourselves scarce," he decided. "You got another Boom Tube ready to go?"

Forager shook her head. "They confiscated my transport controls."

I was afraid of that, he thought. *Just our luck.*

They retreated back the way he'd come, rapidly descending the ladder into the byzantine maze of tunnels below. Jimmy led the way, turning this way and that, anxious to put as much distance as possible between themselves and the grisly dungeon. Not until Bernadeth's frantic pleas had completely faded into the distance did he slow down and attempt to get his bearings. He glanced around the leaky, slime-encrusted conduits, looking for some sort of familiar landmark. This *was* the route he'd taken before, wasn't it?

Forager kept close to his side. "Where now, Jimmy?"

"I don't know," he admitted. Translation: He was completely lost. *How do I find my way out of here?*

PING! His head started chiming like an impatient cell phone. Forager stared at him agog. "Jimmy! Your eyes!" Luminous circuit diagrams, like the ones on his scales earlier, shimmered across his field of vision. "I know that pattern!"

"Pattern?" The circuitry danced before Jimmy's vision like floaters.

"Mother Box," she said in awe. "And more: I see the Source in your eyes."

Jimmy gulped. "Maybe I'm turning into a New God."

"No." She eyed him thoughtfully. "Something else. Something . . . unique."

He wasn't sure he liked the sound of that. "Is that the real reason you tracked me down?"

"Yes," she confessed.

"So . . . I'm just prey to you?" He was surprised at just how hurt—and disappointed—he felt. "Something you can capture and exploit?"

She came nearer to him, so that they were only a few inches apart. He inhaled her perfume with every breath. "You were. Yes."

He pinned his hopes on her use of the past tense. "And now?"

She placed her hand gently upon his chest. His protective quills receded from her touch, leaving flushed pink flesh behind. He swallowed hard, dousing the last embers of his fire-breath, as she pressed herself against him. His body sensed instinctively that there was no danger here, at least not of the physical variety. His arms circled her waist, pulling her closer. Their lips met and he tasted the sweetness of her nectar. She buzzed fervently. Her antennae caressed his brow.

Jimmy hoped he knew what he was getting himself into.

Bernadeth crouched upon the sticky, bloodstained floor of the torture chamber, wherein she had spent so many blissful hours. She heard the redheaded Terran and his subhuman handmaiden flee the fortress, but made no effort to recapture them. Her throbbing hand testified that there were agendas at play here beyond her ken, and she had no desire to inadvertently incur Darkseid's wrath once more. Mere physical punishment was one thing, and even had its virtues under the right circumstances, but demotion and/ or summary execution were altogether different matters. Bernadeth had fought and schemed and betrayed to gain her current ranking in the Female Furies. The last thing she wanted was to lose all that because of one innocent mistake.

I'm not to blame, she thought indignantly. *Nobody told me that miserable worm was under Darkseid's protection!*

Footsteps sounded in the corridor outside and she flinched in anticipation of her lord's extreme displeasure. "I was deceived," she called out nervously. "The cunning mortal tricked Bernadeth." She kneeled before the doorway. "Please forgive this unworthy one. . . ."

A brilliant glow entered the dungeon as a luminous figure appeared in the doorway. "Forgiveness is no longer an option," a stern voice declared. A crackling nimbus of energy emanated from the figure's extended right hand.

"You?" Bernadeth squinted into the glare. Her eyes widened in surprise. She groped for her fallen blade, only to find it worryingly beyond her reach. "You're not . . ."

"The Fourth World is coming to an end. I am the harbinger." He stepped into the dungeon, illuminating every dank corner of the chamber with his preternatural radiance. "Your time has come . . . and, unfortunately for you, there is no pain in death."

Bernadeth's black heart exploded into flames as cosmic vengeance consumed her.

16 AND COUNTING.

PARADISE ISLAND.

"This? This is the reason you deserted your training?"

Athena stared down at the severed haunch of the giant warhound, which rested at the foot of her throne. Armored guards flanked the throne, while additional Amazons stood watch over Holly and Harley as they faced Athena's judgment. Holly couldn't help noticing how much grander and more opulent the beautiful temple was compared to the miserable barracks she and the other newbies had been stowed in. Marble friezes, depicting the founding of Themyscira, ran along the tops of the walls. Towering caryatids, sculpted in the likenesses of great Amazon heroines of the past, supported the high ceiling. An exquisite Persian carpet surrounded the throne. Incense perfumed the air.

Rank has its privileges, Holly thought, *and something here is* really *rank.*

She did her best to conceal her resentment as she defended herself before the scowling goddess and her armed attendants. "If we'd deserted, we wouldn't have come back."

"Yeah," Harley said. "We just figured, since we've all been busting our behinds, maybe some fresh meat would help keep morale up."

Holly shrugged. "The big dog was all we could find." Canine blood smeared their soiled chitons, which had definitely seen better days. Hauling the grisly trophy back though the woods and underbrush had been a chore and a half. "Not exactly prime barbecue material, but beggars can't be choosers."

"You slew the hound yourself?" Athena asked skeptically. She leaned forward to inspect their prize. "With what weapons? How did you fillet the meat from its bones?"

Outnumbered and unarmed, Holly tried not to look too worried. "We found a stash of old weapons in the hills."

"There was all kinds of rusty old Amazon junk," Harley attested. "No cute shoes in my size, though."

Athena pondered their words for an endless interval. *Is she buying this?* Holly fretted. A trickle of sweat ran down the back of her neck. Even with Harley at her side, there was no way they could defend themselves against Athena's elite honor guard. She prayed that Hippolyta had not overestimated her ability to put one over on Athena and her warriors. *Otherwise, we might be doggie chow.*

The counterfeit goddess rose from her throne. Her regal face held an inscrutable expression. She approached the two accused deserters.

"I shall expect you to show us this weapons cache later," Athena declared. "For now, your prowess speaks volumes." She laid approving hands upon their shoulders, bestowing her dubious blessing upon them. "There is a place in my elite for those who show such initiative." Her grip tightened, digging painfully into their flesh. Her gray eyes flashed a none-too-subtle warning. "Do not, however, let it happen again."

She released her grip and Holly let out a sigh of relief. *Ohmigod,* she thought, *we're actually getting away with it. We're not dead!*

Harley nodded a little too eagerly. "Okeydoke!"

"I think what she means is," Holly explained, "we live to serve."

At least until we find out who you really are, lady, and what your game is.

APOKOLIPS.

"I don't understand," Mary said. "What are we doing here?"

A moment ago, they had been on Earth. Then Eclipso had used the mystic power of the black diamond to transport them across the universe to possibly the most evil place in the cosmos. Mary had never been to Apokolips before, but she knew of its dread reputation. The wizard Shazam had often spoken ominously of the hellish planet and its infamous overlord. The New Gods were supposed to be just as formidable as the old ones from which the Marvels drew their powers . . . if not more so.

"Don't worry, dear," Eclipso said soothingly. She guided Mary down a torchlit corridor. Dense stone walls gave the alien fortress a forbidding atmosphere that made Zatanna's spooky mansion seem like Disneyland by comparison. Muffled screams escaped dungeons several levels below. An open window offered a glimpse of a smoky black sky. The crimson glow of the Fire Pits penetrated the corridor, so that the somber walls seemed splashed with blood. "I wouldn't have brought us here if I didn't think it was time."

Time for what? Mary wondered apprehensively. *Surely Jean doesn't think that I'm ready to take on Darkseid himself?* Her nerves faltered at the prospect. *I've learned a lot lately, and I'm stronger than I've ever been, but Darkseid has defied the entire Justice League.*

She took a deep breath of the palace's hot, oppressive air. Her costume clung stickily to her skin. Apparently, Darkseid wasn't big on air-conditioning.

"This way." Eclipso led Mary into an imposing stone chamber. Tiny figurines were positioned atop a chessboard. At first, Mary thought she and Eclipso were alone in the room, then she spotted an imposing figure standing upon an adjacent balcony, his massive arms clasped behind his back as he surveyed the stygian landscape outside the fortress. Either unaware of or unconcerned by the two women's arrival, he remained as still and silent as a statue. "My lord?" Eclipso addressed him.

The figure slowly turned around. Mary gasped out loud as she found herself face-to-face with the undisputed master of Apokolips. Darkseid's granite features reminded her of the petrified Sins at the Rock of Eternity, but were even more intimidating. His red eyes blazed like the Fire Pits outside. His deep voice rumbled from his chest. "Eclipso. What brings you here?"

Eclipso proudly presented Mary to Darkseid. "For your approval, Dark Lord, a powerful supplicant, newly versed in the ways of vengeance." She curtsied gracefully. "May she serve you well."

Huh? Mary thought, trying to keep up. Suddenly, everything was happening too fast. *We're not here to fight Darkseid? Jean wants me to join him instead?*

Eclipso gave Mary a discreet shove from behind, so that the confused heroine stumbled toward Darkseid. The sinister New God towered above Mary as he inspected her. "I—I'm not sure why I'm here," she stammered. "Jean said I was ready. . . ."

Despite her obvious uncertainty, she seemed to meet with Darkseid's approval. He held out his left hand. "Come to me, child. Know true darkness." A merciless smile sent a chill down Mary's spine. "I have many minions, but I can use a sorceress of your ability. I sense great potential in you."

"As did I," Eclipso said, quick to take credit for Mary's conversion. "She shall be a tremendous asset to our cause."

"Not so fast!" Mary blurted. Now that she'd had a chance to get over her initial shock, she realized that Eclipso had been working for Darkseid all along. Glancing more closely at the chessboard, she spied a six-inch replica of herself among the deployed figurines, which also included miniatures of Eclipso, Zatanna, Black Adam, Klarion, and even her brother. Anger overcame trepidation as she finally grasped just how deliberately she had been played. "I don't care who you are," she snapped at both Darkseid and Eclipso. With a sweep of her arm, she dashed the figurines from the table. "Gods or demons, you can't use human beings like toys!"

Darkseid frowned. "Your education is incomplete. The first lesson of power is that all beings are subject to the whims of their betters, even you!"

His eyes flashed balefully, and a pair of deadly Omega Beams converged on Mary, who blocked the attack with a shimmering force field. "Nice trick," she snarked, "but I saw it coming from a mile away." She stood her ground against Darkseid, even as Eclipso furtively signaled her to back down. Lightning crackled around Mary's upraised fists. "You want magic?"

Eclipso's bisected face went pale. "Mary, no!"

But Mary wasn't listening to the other woman, not anymore. "Try this!" she exclaimed as she flung a sizzling thunderbolt at Darkseid.

The blast, which shattered the stone tiles beneath Darkseid's boots, was powerful enough to blow apart an army of killer robots, but provoked only a grimace from the fearsome lord of Apokolips. "You have spirit, child," he conceded with what sounded like a hint of admiration, "but you are no match for me."

He stomped heavily upon the floor, triggering a seismic tremor that knocked Mary off her feet. Cowering behind him, Eclipso grabbed on to the game table to keep from falling. The scattered figurines bounced atop the quivering floor. Darkseid stalked toward Mary, crushing her miniature replica beneath his heavy tread. Springing into the air, Mary hoped that wasn't some kind of omen.

Maybe I'm pushing my luck here, she thought. As furious as she was at the villains for manipulating her, she wasn't sure she could take on both Darkseid and Eclipso simultaneously, and on their own ground no less. Perhaps a prudent retreat was in order?

"I'm out of here!" she announced defiantly. Fists first, she launched herself toward the ceiling, smashing her way out of the dismal war room. Rubble rained down behind her as she punched her way through level after level of the alien fortress. Darkseid's booming voice rang out behind her.

"She is your charge, Eclipso! Return her to me!"

Over my dead body, Mary thought.

15 AND COUNTING.

Earth was a *looong* way from Apokolips. Despite having the speed of Horus at her command, Mary felt like she had been flying through space forever before she finally glimpsed a tiny blue globe in the distance. The wisdom of the gods guided her toward home, while their divine endurance shielded her from the vacuum. Isis's magic had allowed her to traverse the dimensional boundaries separating Apokolips from the rest of the cosmos.

But even magic had its limits. Exhausted by her headlong flight across the universe, Mary paused for a breather in the asteroid belt between Mars and Jupiter. It felt good to set foot on solid ground again. Craters and ridges distinguished the rocky surface of the asteroid, whose gravity was barely noticeable. She gazed longingly at the Earth, roughly three hundred million miles away. Home, sweet home.

A flash of purple light intruded on her reverie. She scowled as Eclipso materialized upon the asteroid, only a few feet away from her former protégée. *Damn,* Mary thought. *I should have known that witch would catch up with me eventually.*

"There you are!" Eclipso declared. Despite the lack of an atmosphere, she had no trouble breathing or speaking, which Mary chalked up to Eclipso's own magic. The two-faced demoness threw up her hands in exasperation. "Oh, Mary, what were you thinking? Why did you run away like that?"

"Because you sold me out!" Mary angrily turned her back on Eclipso. "You fed me all this bull about how we were so much alike, how you wanted to help me. Then you gave me to Darkseid as an . . . an offering!"

Eclipso came around to look Mary in the face. She leaned casually against a granite tor. "You misunderstand my intent. I *presented* you to Darkseid to be anointed in the ways of darkness."

"Are you crazy?" Mary asked indignantly. "What made you think I wanted to get mixed up with that kind of evil?"

"All a matter of perception, Mary." She held the black diamond up to her eye like a monocle, peering at Mary through its translucent depths. "Haven't you been called *evil* at times? Think of Madame Xanadu, Zatanna, even your own brother. Haven't they all turned you away?"

"That's true," Mary conceded. Uncertainty flickered across her face. Maybe Jean had a point? "They didn't even give me a second chance."

Eclipso nodded slyly. "Think, child. You have the power to topple gods. Draw close to the Dark Lord, use your power to seduce him, vie for concubine . . . and when the time is right, when he is falsely confident of his dominion over you, *then* we strike him down!" She sauntered over to Mary and insinuated her arm around the younger woman's shoulders. She whispered into Mary's ear, "Do you see now? I wasn't offering you to Darkseid; I was offering all of Apokolips to you!"

Her mentor's depraved proposal was like a splash of cold water against Mary's face. The startled heroine couldn't believe what she was hearing. "A concubine? A whore?" She shoved Eclipso away from her. "Is that all I am to you? A means to an end?"

"No . . . wait!" Eclipso stammered, grasping that she had said the wrong thing. "That's not what I meant. . . !"

Mary wasn't hearing any more of it. She kicked herself for giving Eclipso even a chance to weasel her way back into her confidence again. "Forget it!" She snatched the black diamond from Eclipso's fingers and placed it before her eye just like she'd seen Eclipso do. "I can see the truth now, and you have nothing to do with it!"

A beam of violet energy shot from the gemstone, blasting Eclipso off the asteroid. The stunned villainess flew clear of the rock's meager gravity. She somersaulted backward through space. Luck alone kept her from crashing into one of the neighboring asteroids.

"Holy Moley!" Mary exclaimed. Despite herself, she was impressed by the gem's power. "I guess diamonds really are a girl's best friend."

Not yet defeated, Eclipso swiftly recovered from the attack. Halting her uncontrolled tumble through the asteroid field, she righted herself with respect to Mary. Her bisected face glared murderously at her onetime dupe, all pretense of friendship abandoned. "That's mine!" she snarled. Her outstretched fingers opened and closed convulsively, hungry for the stolen gem. "Give it back!"

Mary couldn't resist gloating a bit. She took off from the asteroid and flew toward Eclipso. She held up the glittering black diamond, flaunting it before her foe. "You know what they say," she taunted her erstwhile mentor. " 'Possession is nine-tenths of the law.' "

"No!" Eclipso shrieked, sounding positively crazed by her lust for the gem. She lunged at Mary with her fingers extended like claws. Her amethyst eyes were wild. "You can't have it! It's mine . . . MINE!"

She slammed into Mary, her momentum propelling them both into a nearby asteroid. Mary grunted with pain as they crashed into the rugged surface of the rock. Pulverized chunks of ice and stone forever escaped the asteroid. The impact jarred Mary, knocking the diamond from her grip, while her stunned body cushioned Eclipso's own collision with the rock. The frantic she-demon pounced eagerly on the gem. "Yes!"

"How . . . ?" A puzzled Mary rose from the center of a freshly carved crater. She had thought that Eclipso would be powerless without her precious jewelry. "How did you manage that?"

"Foolish child!" Eclipso fondled her accursed prize. "The black diamond and I are bonded. We are one." She floated off the asteroid so that she could sneer down at Mary. "How dare you attempt to come between us! We are Eclipso! We are one!"

A violet beam drove Mary face-first into the granite floor of the crater. The blow hurt like hell, but she found the strength to climb back onto her feet. Eclipso's maniacal fixation on the diamond reminded Mary of a certain ring-obsessed fictional character. "That all you got, 'Gollum'?" she challenged Eclipso, spitting out a mouthful of powdered silica. She hurled herself at the hovering woman like a missile. " 'Cause it's *my* turn now."

"I think not," Eclipso said. A second bolt of mystical energy halted Mary's charge, flinging her backward through space. Mary clenched her teeth, holding back a scream, as the searing blast scalded her skin. Eclipso cackled like the witch she was. "Ungrateful whelp! We offered you the darkness—and look how you repay us!" She soared toward Mary, her feathered cloak spread out behind her like the wings of a raptor. "Very well, then. I'll have your power for my own, long before I intended to seize it!"

Her scheming words reignited Mary's anger at being manipulated. "You lying witch!" she exploded. "You're just like all the others! All you ever wanted was my power!" She rocketed to meet Eclipso's assault head-on. Lightning crackled in her eyes and fists. "Want my power, huh? Have a taste on me!"

She struck the deceitful villainess like a comet. A golden thunderbolt shredded Eclipso's lavender aura, blasting both women clear of the asteroid field. Locked in combat, grappling for control of the black diamond, they careened through space at superhuman speed. They barely noticed Mars's ruddy brilliance as they barreled past the Red Planet toward Earth. Mary's fist was locked around Eclipso's throat, while the enraged demoness clawed at Mary's face with long purple nails. A hastily conjured force field blocked Mary's right cross. Eclipso held tightly on to her unholy gem. "Die, Mary Marvel!" she hissed. "And in death, surrender the power I crave!"

Face-to-face with Eclipso's naked malice and lust for power, Mary shuddered in recognition. *Is that what I looked like when I ransacked Zatanna's library . . . just to increase my own magical might? When I terrorized mortal criminals in the name of vengeance?*

It wasn't a pretty picture.

I thought I was strong enough to contain Black Adam's darkness, but really it's been controlling me, making me dance like a puppet at the ends of Eclipso's strings.

But not anymore.

She tore her gaze away from Eclipso's fiendish countenance. Ahead of them, Earth shone in space with a serene blue radiance that could not have been more different from the infernal glow of the black diamond. "You almost had me, Jean," she confessed. "I was almost just like you, corrupted beyond redemption, but now I've seen enough of the darkness to know that's not me."

"Brainless girl!" Eclipso mocked her. "Rejecting the only one who cared enough to show you how your power was truly meant to be used. Poor lost child! No friends, no family, no one to call your own." Hate contorted her elegant features. Spittle sprayed from her lips. "And no one to blame but yourself!"

They entered Earth's atmosphere, plunging toward the Atlantic Ocean like dueling meteors. The scorching heat of reentry tested Mary's invulnerability; her skin felt like it was on fire. Eclipso's feathered cloak erupted into flame, so that they left a blazing trail behind them as they descended into a clear blue sky. A cooling wind mercifully replaced the unbearable heat. The sea rushed up to meet them. Out of the corner of her eye, Mary thought she spotted a solitary island floating atop the surging waves below.

"It's over, Eclipso!" Mary felt more like herself than she had in weeks. Her mind raced back over everything that had transpired since she had naïvely accepted Black Adam's poisoned gift. "This power you crave has brought me nothing but misery. I don't want it anymore."

"No!" Eclipso wailed over the wind whistling past their ears. "Don't waste it! Give it to me!"

"Take it!" Mary shouted. She wrapped her arms around Eclipso to keep her adversary from escaping. The magic word erupted from her lips. "SHAZAM!"

A titanic thunderbolt struck both women. Eclipso convulsed in agony as the magical lightning charred her flesh, while Mary Marvel instantly transformed back into an ordinary teenage girl. A deafening boom drowned out Eclipso's screams. Unable to hold on to the flailing demon, Mary Batson let go of Eclipso. Gravity seized her and Mary quickly lost sight of the other woman as they plummeted helplessly toward the waiting sea.

She hit the water seconds later.

14 AND COUNTING.

PARADISE ISLAND.

Mary awoke upon a sandy shore. Waves lapped against her shoulders as she lay sprawled upon the shore, half in, half out of the ocean. Sand caked her face and hair. Clingy strands of wet seaweed were draped across her body. Her ragged T-shirt and jeans were soaked clean through, while her socks and sneakers had gone missing entirely. Her mouth tasted like brine. She felt sore and bruised all over. The hot sun beat down on her.

It was official. She wasn't Mary Marvel anymore.

Coughing violently, she retched cold salt water onto the beach. She struggled to lift her aching head from the sand. "Eclipso?" Her bleary eyes glanced from side to side, but found no trace of the treacherous witch. *What happened to her? To both of us?* Mary searched her foggy memory. The last thing she remembered was plunging into the sea after she gave up her powers. *Guess I survived the fall,* she deduced. *Barely.*

It seemed a miracle that she hadn't drowned before washing ashore . . . where exactly? She dimly recalled spotting an island earlier. Was that where she had ended up?

She dragged herself farther onto shore, out of the water. The effort exhausted her, proving beyond the shadow of a doubt that she was just plain old Mary Batson again. *It's gone,* she realized. *I don't feel Black Adam's power, his darkness, anymore.*

I'm free.

Water streamed from her drenched auburn hair onto her face. Mary wiped the hair and water away from her eyes. Climbing onto her knees, she crawled forward toward an uncertain future. Seabirds cawed somewhere overhead. A salty breeze chilled her trembling frame. Mary wondered if she had been marooned upon some nameless isle, or if maybe there was a beach resort just beyond the shore?

Metal clanked ominously only a few feet in front of her. A musky animal smell invaded her nostrils. A large wet nose sniffed her damp hair. A low growl froze her in her tracks.

Uh-oh, she thought. *Welcome to the jungle. . . .*

Swallowing hard, she lifted her eyes from the ground—and found herself face-to-face with some sort of monstrous hound that looked like a cross between a mastiff and a pit bull. All it needed was two more heads to be the spitting image of Cerberus, the mythical three-headed dog that guarded the gates of Hades. Slobber dripped from the hound's intimidating underbite. Massive forepaws were planted in the sand only a few inches away from her. Bloodshot red eyes seemed to regard her as a prospective chew toy. A spiked collar was clamped around the giant canine's bull-sized neck. Tracking the dog's leash with her eyes, Mary saw that the beast was not alone.

A pair of fearsome women warriors glared at Mary from behind their oversized watchdog. Polished bronze armor, of distinctly Grecian design, encased their trim, athletic bodies. Crested Corinthian helmets concealed their features. Their burnished helmets, breastplates, studded leather skirts, and greaves gleamed in the bright afternoon sun. Sheathed swords rested against their hips. Disk-shaped shields were strapped to their forearms.

Amazons. Mary identified the women at once. *Wonder Woman's sisters-in-arms.*

Suddenly, she had a pretty good idea where she was.

"Identify yourself!" commanded the Amazon holding on to the great hound's chain. The growling dog strained at its leash, eager to devour the intruder. "State your business!"

The second Amazon brandished a long metal spear. "You are trespassing on Paradise Island!"

Yeah, I kind of figured that out, Mary thought. The Amazons' tone was less than welcoming. *Maybe giving up my powers wasn't such a good idea. . . .*

APOKOLIPS.

"What is this place?" Jimmy asked.

After escaping from the torture chamber, Forager had led him to a secret lair deep within the bowels of the Armagetto. Hissing steam pipes and power cables crisscrossed the stark concrete walls and ceiling. Powerful engines thrummed in the background. Vermin scuttled through the dank tunnels beyond the cramped subbasement. The spartan furnishings consisted of a crude cot, a pair of rusty metal stools, and a portable stove. A hanging lantern provided just enough light to see by. An open footlocker held batteries, ammunition, and other supplies. Forager's bloodstained armor lay in a heap upon the floor.

"A hidden outpost for spying on Darkseid," she called out a from an adjacent shower stall. The spatter of cascading water muffled her voice somewhat. A grimy plastic curtain shielded her from his view. "I've used it as my base of operations on previous espionage missions here."

"I get it," Jimmy said. "Sort of your own private safe house." He changed into a suit of khaki coveralls he found hanging in a closet. "You've planned for everything, haven't you?" Taking a seat upon one of the stools, he heard the water shut off behind the curtain. "You know, I can't help thinking that maybe I'm slowing you down. If I'm keeping you from finding the lost souls of the New Gods . . ."

His voice trailed off as, amidst clouds of billowing steam, Forager emerged nude from the shower. Jimmy tried not to gape, but found it impossible to look away from her alien beauty. Without her chitinous carapace, the svelte insect-woman looked surprisingly human. Her lustrous pink skin was invitingly sleek and unblemished. True, her supple legs ended in three-toed claws, but Jimmy wasn't exactly staring at her feet. His freckled face blushed crimson.

"Ah," she buzzed, "the filth of Darkseid's squalid dungeons is off me at last." She seemed not at all self-conscious about her nudity. Plucking a well-worn towel from a peg, she began to dry herself off. "And please cease apologizing, Jimmy. If you were a hindrance, I would not have brought you to Apokolips in the first place."

Jimmy swallowed hard, distracted by the lovely vision before him. "O-okay."

"I must tell you something," she continued. "When you pressed your mandibles to mine—"

He recalled the sweet taste of her nectar upon his lips. "We call that a 'kiss.'"

"Yes, when you kissed me," she clarified, "I finally realized why you possess such astounding powers."

Jimmy jumped to his feet. "You did?"

She strolled across the basement, revealing a row of dorsal scales running down the graceful contours of her back. Jimmy realized belatedly that her wings had been artificial and merely part of the body armor she had worn before. "At that moment, I sensed within you the power of the gods."

"Whoa, there!" he protested. "I'm no god."

Her glittering compound eyes looked into his. Her slender antennae tilted toward him. "I said *gods*, Jimmy. Plural. You are, I believe, a soul-catcher."

A what? he thought.

PARADISE ISLAND.

"**Disaster,**" the Queen of the Amazons said gravely. "Do you know where that word comes from? Comets. Falling stars. Ill omens from above." Hippolyta gazed upon Mary, who nervously endured the queen's scrutiny. The youthful castaway shivered in the chilly gloom of the cave. "Now you turn up on our shores, claiming that you fell from the sky like Icarus."

Mary didn't understand what was happening. She'd expected the female sentries to escort her to the Amazons' walled city elsewhere on the island, so she was confused to find herself in a murky cavern instead. A jagged stalactite hung above her head like the Sword of Damocles. The spear-wielding sentries ensured her cooperation. Mary's damp clothes smelled like sea salt. She hugged herself to keep warm. *At least they left the dog tied up outside.*

"Tell me, Mary Batson," Hippolyta continued. "Did you try to fly too high?"

"Y-you know me?" Mary stammered.

The queen nodded. "Our paths have crossed before," she reminded Mary, "when divine power still coursed through you." Mary recalled fighting alongside Hippolyta during a big alien invasion a few years back, along with pretty much every other meta-human and magic-user on the planet. She was surprised that the Amazon queen recognized her out of costume.

There was no mistaking Wonder Woman's legendary mother, though. Her resemblance to Diana was striking. They had the same lustrous black hair, statuesque proportions, and piercing blue eyes. Now those eyes inspected Mary warily.

"I sense that blessing has been rescinded," Hippolyta stated. "So . . . how did you come to merit the gods' scorn?"

Mary blushed and stared sheepishly at the floor. "Jeez, where do I start?" she began. "When I was Mary Marvel, I had a family and a purpose. I felt . . . special. But then the power of Shazam was taken away, and I felt so empty and useless and lost." The guard on her right, the one with the incongruous Gotham City accent, nodded sympathetically. "I would've sold my soul to be a hero again . . . and I guess I did."

She spared them the messy details.

" 'Those whom the gods would destroy . . .' " Hippolyta mused, quoting Euripides. Mary's explanation seemed to satisfy the older woman; the queen's voice and expression softened. "But it seems you've purged that evil from your body and spirit. I sense within you nothing worse than regret."

Mary was grateful for Hippolyta's leniency, even if she wasn't entirely sure she deserved it. *I've got a lot to atone for,* she thought. But that didn't explain why they were meeting in this spooky cave. "Then why bring me down here like a prisoner?"

"Can't be too careful on this rock nowadays," the guard from Gotham explained. Orange bangs peeked out from beneath the brow of her Corinthian helmet. "There's a fake Athena out there, training phony Amazons."

"Yeah," her squeaky-voiced comrade confirmed. "It's like cheerleading camp, only run by Bin Laden."

Mary blinked in surprise. A fake Athena? Bogus Amazons? It was a lot to take in all at once. *Now what have I got myself mixed up in,* she fretted, *and without any powers to boot?*

"We're going to bring them down," the first guard declared, "but we need all the help we can get." Her streetwise blue eyes looked into Mary's. "You in?"

13 AND COUNTING.

Tears stream down Jean Loring's face. She writhes helplessly within the constricting bonds of the heavy canvas straitjacket. Her short black hair is matted and in disarray. Beefy guards haul her toward a waiting cell in Arkham Asylum as she peers frantically back over her shoulder at the man she loves.

"Ray! Don't let them take me!" Crazed blue eyes plead for mercy. Saliva sprays from her lips. "Don't do this to me! RAY!"

Ray Palmer looks on helplessly as the guards drag his ex-wife away. In happier days, he had often rescued her from all manner of perils, but this time she was beyond saving. Jean had condemned them both to this terrible moment when, unhinged by madness, she had murdered one of their best friends as part of an insane scheme to revive their marriage. Now he can do nothing but watch her join the other dangerous lunatics in Arkham, possibly for the rest of her natural life.

He has never felt so small.

Her desperate shrieks echo in his ears. "Help me! Ray! RAY!"

"Ray?"

Jean gently nudged his shoulder as she woke him from his nightmare. He sat up abruptly in their bed, his body drenched in sweat. Disoriented, it took him a second to remember where he was. . . .

IVY TOWN.
EARTH-51.

"Another bad dream?" Jean asked. Standing beside the bed, she gazed down at him in concern. A purple turtleneck sweater flattered her figure. Her stylishly coifed black hair curled over her shoulders. Silver crescent earrings sparkled in the dim lighting. "You poor thing. Perhaps you should see someone about these recurring nightmares. Maybe that nice Dr. Quinzel at the clinic?"

"After the holidays," he promised, although he privately doubted that therapy was the answer. How could he explain to a psychiatrist—or to Jean—that these "nightmares" were actually painful memories from another life . . . on another Earth? *I just have to put the past behind me,* he thought. *Somehow.*

Jean glanced at the atomic clock on the dresser, next to their wedding photo. "Anyway, nap time's over. You need to get up and get dressed. Our friends will be here soon."

Right, Ray remembered. *The Christmas party.* Rising from the bed, he paused to peer out the window at the peaceful suburban neighborhood outside. Snow carpeted their neighbors' roofs and front yards, although the sidewalks and driveways had already been shoveled clean. Christmas lights decorated every house in the cul-de-sac. Genuine snowmen shared the lawns with plastic reindeer, elves, and Wise Men. A life-sized replica of Superman, wearing a Santa hat, posed in the large inflatable snow globe occupying the Morrows' front yard. The kids across the street played fetch with their rambunctious Irish setter, the one that kept harassing the cat next door. Smoke rose from brick chimneys. A glorious winter sunset confirmed it was almost evening.

Gazing out at the tranquil holiday scene, he could *almost* forget that ghastly trip to Arkham. He turned toward Jean, seeing only the beautiful woman he had fallen in love with in the first place, not the mentally disturbed murderer he had left behind two years ago. His throat tightened with emotion. He discreetly wiped a tear from his eye. *I've been given a second chance here,* he reminded himself. *Another shot at happiness for both of us.* He shook his head, trying to clear any lingering vestiges of the nightmare from his mind. *I can't let it go to waste.*

Jean stood in the doorway, watching him. "I'll be down in a few minutes," he assured her. "Just give me a chance to straighten up."

"All right. But don't be long." She shot him a teasing smile before exiting the bedroom. "You know how punctual Barry and Iris are these days."

A hot shower and a change of clothes helped him put his memories of Earth-One behind him, at least for the time being, so that he felt more at home by the time their guests arrived. Ralph and Sue Dibny settled onto the couch beside Iris Allen, while Iris's husband, Barry, helped himself to a second plate of homemade Christmas cookies. Bright orange flames danced in the fireplace, making the living room warm and cozy. Brightly colored packages were piled high beneath the Christmas tree. Instead of the usual star, the handblown glass ornament atop the tree, a gift from his colleagues at the university, took the form of an atomic symbol. Matching "His" and "Hers" stockings hung from the mantel. Strings of popcorn hung upon the branches of the tree. Bing Crosby crooned softly from the stereo.

"Hey, Barry!" Ralph's arm stretched across the room to tap the Fastest Man Alive on the shoulder. His wavy red hair matched his garish holiday sweater. "Have you and Iris thought about joining the four of us for New Year's?"

Barry Allen grinned at his friend and former teammate. His blond crewcut was hardly hip, but seemed to suit him. "We'd be delighted, but if I have to sit through another 'Elongated Man Mystery' game, I'll be out the door faster than a photon."

"Heh!" Ralph's rubbery nose wiggled. "Understood."

Ray chuckled, enjoying the casual chatter and camaraderie, as he poured himself a mug of eggnog. He tried not to think about the fact that, back on that other Earth, Barry and Sue were both dead, Barry having perished during the original Crisis several years ago, while Sue had been savagely murdered by none other than Jean herself. . . .

But not this Jean, he reminded himself. *Not here.*

"Oh! Check this out," Jean said, nodding at the TV set in the corner. Plucking the remote from the coffee table, she clicked off the Mute command. "It's Diana."

The television, which had been tuned to coverage of tonight's Christmas celebration in Washington, D.C., flashed up a picture of Wonder Woman in full Amazon regalia. "Even Queen Diana of Paradise Island," Lois Lane-Kent reported, "is here to wish us all a very happy holiday."

"Would you look at Diana?" Sue sighed. She put down a piece of fudge, apparently having second thoughts about the fattening treat, even though the petite brunette hardly looked like she needed to diet. "I swear that woman never ages."

The broadcast cut to a shot of Superman descending from the sky above D.C., bearing a truckload of Christmas presents with bright red ribbons. His legendary S-shield was inscribed on every oversized crate.

"There's Clark," Barry said. "Still delivering food and toys to the under-privileged like a red and blue St. Nick. Good for him."

Ray smiled at the TV. "I love it when he dons the old duds. Even if it's only just once a year."

On this world, the Justice League of America had disbanded after successfully ridding the world of every major meta-human menace. There were no more super heroes anymore, nor any need for them.

"You ever miss the old days, guys?" Ralph asked the other men. "I still keep my stretchy uniform hanging in the closet. Just for old times' sake."

"Just hanging?" his wife teased him good-naturedly. "Fess up, honey. I know you put it on sometimes when you think nobody is looking."

He smooched her on the cheek. "Only because I know how it turns you on."

"Oh, Ralph!" Sue elbowed him playfully, her attractive face turning an embarrassed shade of red. "Behave!"

Barry sat down beside Iris. "Seriously, I don't mind not being the Flash anymore. The League did what it set out to do. We suited up to make the world a better place, spent five exciting years taking down all the bad guys, and . . . *presto!* Mission accomplished."

"Sounds good to me," Iris agreed. She wore her light brown hair in a fashionable bob. Her green cocktail dress was the color of mistletoe. "At least you're never late for dinner or anniversaries anymore." She shook her head at the memory. "Back when you were running around the world, fighting Captain Cold or whoever, you were always late for everything!"

Everyone laughed at the irony of the Flash, of all people, never being on time. Ray took another sip of eggnog.

"You're right, Barry," he said thoughtfully. "It's a good thing the League called it quits when we did, at the top of our game." He savored the happy ending they had all found on this best of all possible worlds. "Who knows? We could have ended up dead or . . ."

Insane, he thought, averting his eyes from Jean.

"Oh, Ray." She came up behind him and wrapped her arm around his waist. "I hate to impose, but the fire seems to be dying down."

He glanced at the hearth, where the crackling logs did appear to be on their last legs. "Say no more, darling." He reluctantly disengaged himself from her embrace. "I'm on it."

Throwing on a jacket, he ventured out into the backyard in search of more firewood. The crisp December weather felt invigorating after the toasty living room. His breath frosted before his lips. The smoky aroma of dozens of active chimneys added a piquant touch to the air. He took a moment to bask in the peace and quiet.

Now, this is living. A relaxing evening at home with lifelong friends, a loving wife, and a warm fire. He retrieved an armload of logs from a stack by the back porch. *A few more nights like this and those nightmares don't stand a—*

Then he glimpsed a trio of figures lurking in the shadows just beyond the white picket fence enclosing the backyard. Moonlight reflected off the snow, offering him a murky view of the strangers. One of them was obviously not human. . . .

Despair gripped his heart. The firewood tumbled from his arms. "Oh no."

He felt numb all over. Unable to face the reckoning upon him, he staggered back indoors and locked the door behind him. His jacket was too warm for inside, but he barely noticed the heat. He wandered back to the living room in a daze. *This can't be happening,* he thought. *It isn't fair. . . .*

"Er, Ray," Barry commented from the couch. "You kinda forgot the firewood."

Jean picked up on his distress immediately. "Ray? What is it?" A worried expression came over her face. "You look like it was fifty below out there."

Oh God, how was he ever going to explain this to her? "I . . . Jean, I'm so sorry. . . ."

"Sorry?" She rushed to his side. Her warm hand grasped his arm. "I don't understand. You're shaking like a leaf. . . ."

He stared into her confused, compassionate eyes. There was no trace of homicidal mania in those captivating blue orbs, only love and concern. His heart broke all over again. "I'm sorry," he repeated. "I deluded myself into thinking that I could avoid this, that the past would never catch up with us."

"What past?" She was trembling too now, as though his fear and dismay were contagious. A few feet away, their guests rose anxiously to their feet. Jean's grip tightened on his arm. "Ray, you're scaring me!"

A column of sparking energy manifested in the foyer leading to the living room. Startled gasps greeted the sudden arrival of the ominous trio Ray had just glimpsed outside. Apparently they had wanted to scout out the scene before making their presence known. Ray recognized Jason Todd and Donna Troy from Earth-One, although he could have sworn they were supposed to be dead. *Some sort of time-travel paradox,* he wondered, *or did their apparent "deaths" prove to be only temporary?* Lord knew they wouldn't be the first costumed heroes or villains to come back from what had seemed to be a violent demise. *Everyone thought I was dead once. . . .*

There was no mistaking their hulking alien companion either. Ray knew a Monitor when he saw one.

"Ray Palmer!" Donna gave him a friendly smile. She held out her hand as she stepped into the living room. Her sparkling black leotard and silver wristbands looked out of place on this peaceful world, where everyone else had hung up their capes years ago. "You're a hard man to find, you know that?"

"Donna Troy?" Sue Dibny blinked in confusion. Ray couldn't blame her; as far as his friends were concerned, the former Wonder Girl had left Earth to join the Green Lantern Corps back in 2001. She was probably the last person they expected to drop by uninvited.

Barry zipped over to Ray's side. The breeze whipped up by his speed rustled the branches on the Christmas tree. Ornaments tinkled like wind chimes. "What's going on, buddy?"

Ray buried his face in his hands. *It's over,* he realized. *I can't pretend any-*

more. The truth was coming out, whether he liked it or not. "I—I'm not this world's Ray Palmer."

"What?" Jean looked utterly baffled. "Sweetie, what are you saying? That doesn't make any sense."

If only that were true! "My nightmares," he confessed. "They're all real." He groped for some way to soften the blow, but it all came spilling out of him. "Where I come from, you're . . . different. You don't act like you."

"But I'm *me*," she protested. "I always act like me. . . ."

Ray sank into his favorite easy chair. He stared dolefully at the floor, unable to meet her eyes. "No, Jean. You're capable of murder." He choked back a sob. "On my world, you murdered Sue Dibny."

"Murder Sue?" Ralph exclaimed. He wrapped a protective arm around his wife. "Jean would never—"

"But *my* Jean did!" His estranged ex-wife had embarked on a premeditated campaign of terror against the loved ones of the Justice League, even faking an attack on herself, in order to lure Ray back to her side. "She did, and I . . . I was devastated. I did the only thing I could think to do. I ran away, disappearing into subatomic space. I thought that maybe if I became small enough, I could escape the pain."

Outside Arkham Asylum, on that horrible day, he had activated the size and mass controls built into his belt buckle, which employed a fragment of a white dwarf star to render him infinitesimal in size. A blue cowl and simple red and blue uniform transformed the grieving physicist into the Atom. . . .

"For a while, I was without direction, hopeless, but then I met a young mystic who filled me in on the true nature of the Multiverse."

"K'Dessa," Donna guessed correctly.

Ray nodded. "She spoke of fifty-two completely different Earths, each of them unique, yet still similar in some ways to my own. So I made it my business to learn how to slip between the universes on a quantum level and started searching for a place that might be able to bring me some peace of mind. But most of what I found was even worse than the world I came from. . . ."

He shuddered at the memory of some of the bizarre Earths he had encountered in his travels. A world of Gothic horrors where Batman was a vampire who preyed upon the blood of the wicked. A world where the Soviet Union won the Cold War, thanks to a patriotic Russian version of Superman. Worlds of Crime Societies and Extremists, where unstoppable super-villains robbed and murdered at will. A postapocalyptic Earth, devastated by a nuclear war. A world where the Nazis won World War II . . .

"I'd almost given up," he admitted, "when I found this world. So much like mine, yet blissfully untainted by many of the tragedies that had darkened my own Earth. I couldn't resisting seeking myself out, hoping that, perhaps, the sight of another Ray Palmer, living out a more idyllic existence, would somehow bring me comfort. But things didn't turn out the way I planned. . . ."

His memory flashed back to that fateful day two years ago.

Only two inches high, the Atom spies on his twin as the other Ray tinkers with complicated scientific apparatus in the basement of his comfortable home in Ivy Town. As nearly as he can tell, this world's Ray had also discovered the existence of the Multiverse and is even now preparing to test a portal designed to access alternate realities. Hiding upon a cluttered tool shelf, the Atom holds his breath as Ray-51 activates the device.

But the eager scientist had obviously miscalculated. The portal explodes in a burst of cosmic energy that instantly incinerates its inventor. Aghast, the Atom watches himself *die!*

The notion of taking the other Ray's place does not occur to the stunned hero immediately, but, once he overcomes his initial shock at his counterpart's abrupt demise, the idea steadily takes over his mind. After all, the Justice League is busy waging its final battles against the forces of evil. Perhaps this Earth still needed an Atom?

What really convinces him, however, is the note he finds scribbled on the other Ray's calendar: BLIND DATE WITH JEAN L. DINNER. 7:30.

"He wasn't really your Ray yet," he explained to Jean, who stared at him in bewilderment. He lifted his gaze from the floor. "I wasn't deceiving you, not really. It was like I had a second chance to make things perfect between us. We could be happy again, for good this time. . . ."

His voice trailed off as she turned away from him, unable to cope. Confused sobs racked her slender body. *Does she believe me,* he agonized, *or does she think I've lost my mind?* He reached out for her tentatively. "Jean? I'm still the man you fell in love with. . . ."

"What the hell?" Ralph's nose wiggled indignantly. "I've had enough of this bull!" Fists clenched, he glared at Donna and her companions. "I don't know what sort of game you're playing here, but . . . !"

"I'm so sorry," Donna replied, a guilty expression on her face. She appeared genuinely troubled by the turmoil she had caused. "But I'm afraid it's all true."

Barry scratched his head. "Parallel Earths, separated by some sort of vibrational barriers?" The scientist in him sounded intrigued by the theory. "I suppose it's possible. . . ."

"It is more than possible, Barry Allen," the Monitor stated firmly. Jean and the guests shrank away instinctively from the imposing armored figure. "Everything spoken of tonight is reality. And Ray Palmer is the very reason we are here."

"I don't understand," Ray said. "How did you find me?"

"One of my brethren inadvertently revealed your location," the Monitor explained, "when he tried to convince me that you were 'living a life of no consequence.' Nix Uotan could not have known that for a fact unless you were dwelling in the very universe he was charged to monitor." A scowl rendered the Monitor's saturnine countenance even more forbidding. "Clearly, he had a personal stake in obstructing our quest."

Ray had no idea who "Nix Uotan" was, but that hardly mattered now. "I don't understand. Why did you have to track me down anyway?" Moist eyes implored the intruders. His voice cracked. "Why couldn't you people just leave me alone?"

"The Multiverse has need of you, Ray Palmer." The Monitor strode across the living room toward the seated hero. He pointed a gloved finger at Ray. "You are destined to play a crucial role in events to come."

Ray refused to accept this. "But that's ridiculous! Why me?"

Jason Todd shrugged. "Don't ask me, dude. I'm just along for the ride."

His crimson mask failed to conceal his cocky attitude, which Ray remembered from Jason's days as Robin. "Jason?" Barry asked, belatedly recognizing the masked youth. He looked like he'd seen a ghost, and no wonder; on this world, it was the Joker's brutal murder of Jason Todd that had ultimately inspired the Justice League to put away all the super-villains once and for all. A memorial to the martyred sidekick occupied a prime location in Gotham City's ritzy Wayne Plaza. People still laid flowers in front of the statue on the anniversary of Robin's death. "This is incredible!"

"I'm sorry," Donna apologized again. "But the Monitor knows what he's talking about. We've come a long way to find you, Ray."

But I didn't want to be found! Ray had always liked Donna Troy, but right now she and her unwanted cohorts seemed like harbingers of doom, pronouncing a death sentence on everything he had managed to build for himself on this wonderful new world. "I wish you hadn't."

"Your personal desires are irrelevant," the Monitor declared. "You must come with us at once—or risk universal catastrophe!"

"No!" Ray lurched from his chair. "There are other heroes out there, fifty-two worlds' worth! Find someone else for your goddamn crusade! I'm not going anywhere!"

Donna tried to intervene. "I know this must come as a shock, Ray, but we wouldn't be here if we didn't think it was important." She laid a gentle hand on his shoulder. "K'Dessa herself spoke of a prophecy. . . ."

"I don't care!" He swatted her hand away. "I have a new life here, a new chance at happiness. I'm not giving that up!"

His friends came to his defense. Barry twisted a ring upon his finger and a hypercompressed red suit sprang from a hidden compartment in the ring. The lanky forensic scientist donned the uniform in a split second. Metallic yellow lightning bolts accented the skintight red costume. "If you want Ray, you'll have to go through the Flash!"

A look of profound annoyance darkened the Monitor's face. Without warning, he fired a blast of energy from his gauntlet. Burning plasma instantly consumed the Flash, reducing him to a charred skeleton before the very eyes of his wife and friends. The blackened bones clattered onto the carpet. "Barry Allen," the Monitor said coldly, "this time you die before the Crisis can take root."

"B-Barry?" Iris Allen let out a heartrending scream. "BARRY!"

Oh my God! Ray thought. The Flash had just been murdered in the blink of an eye. *He didn't even see it coming!*

"Stop it, Solomon!" Donna sounded equally horrified by the slaughter. She tackled the Monitor from behind, locking him in a bear hug. "Have you gone insane?"

"Do not deter me, Donna Troy!" There was a blinding flash as his personal force field expanded to break the heroine's hold, flinging her backward into the Christmas tree. The plus-sized Douglas fir crashed down onto the couch. Glass and crystal ornaments shattered noisily. Jason Todd scrambled to check on Donna, while Ralph and Sue hustled Iris away from the fight. Meanwhile, the Monitor calmly ignored the tumult. "If Ray Palmer refuses to abandon his counterfeit existence on this planet, then perhaps we must strip away its trappings!"

His volcanic red eyes zeroed in on Jean.

No! Ray thought. He leapt between the deadly alien and his wife. *Not her!*

Rebounding from Solomon's counterattack, Donna charged at the Monitor. Broken glass and pine branches crunched beneath her silver boots. Solomon turned to face her. His right gauntlet glowed in warning. "I would have thought *you* would be more reasonable, Donna," he said in a disappointed tone. "Surely you appreciate what is at stake here!"

"Reason with this!" Donna snarled. Her super-strong fist collided with the Monitor's jaw. He stumbled backward, bumping into the coffee table. The pitcher of eggnog toppled over, spilling its foaming contents over the table. Donna pressed her attack against the murderous alien. A second blow slammed into Solomon's gut, denting his armor. "You didn't have to kill anyone! We could have talked to him!"

Ray saw an opportunity to get Jean to safety. "Ralph! Sue!" he yelled at his friends, who still looked shell-shocked by Barry's fiery death. "Take care of Iris! Get the hell away from here!" He grabbed Jean by the arm and tugged her away from the demolished living room. "Hurry, Jean! Please!"

"What?" Traumatized blue eyes stared back over her shoulder at the furious conflict destroying their home. Solomon hurled Donna through a plate glass window. A freezing gust of wind invaded the house. Snow blew onto the carpet. Jason Todd snatched a broken plate from the floor and hurled it like a Batarang at the Monitor's face. Unable to process it all, Jean hesitated in the hallway beyond the living room. "Where are you taking me?"

"Away!" He pulled harder on Jean's arm as he hurried her toward the steps leading down to the basement. Part of him hated abandoning the others, but saving Jean had to be his first priority. *I'm the reason she's in danger,* he thought guiltily. *I can't fail her now. Not again!*

They reached the bottom of the stairs. Fluorescent lights lit up the cluttered cellar where this world's own Ray Palmer had died. Lab equipment occupied wooden shelves and workbenches. Insulated pipes and cables snaked across the ceiling. An oil furnace rumbled in the background. The hot water boiler gurgled in the corner. Fresh tile concealed the scorch marks left behind by the explosion two years ago. Ray prayed that history was not about to repeat itself.

He fiddled with the controls on his belt buckle. He had to calibrate this carefully to avoid trapping them between worlds. "Trust me," he begged Jean. "We have to escape this reality!"

"Escape? This reality?!" Her voice skirted the edge of hysteria; this was obviously too much for her to take in all at once. She tore herself away from his grasp, her tearful blue eyes staring at him like she didn't know who he was anymore, not that she ever really had. "Ray, listen to yourself! Don't you realize how crazy this sounds?"

No crazier than a fanatical alien crashing our Christmas party and killing Barry, he thought. He stepped forward and gently took her in his arms. *If only I had more time to prepare for this . . . !* "It won't happen again, Jean. I promise."

She still didn't understand. "What won't happen? What do you mea—"

"Palmer!" An entire section of the ceiling disintegrated and the Monitor descended through the gap. He hovered above the floor of the basement, glowering down at the cornered humans like the Angel of Death. "This is journey's end, Ray Palmer. You have nowhere left to run!"

That's what you think, Ray thought. He frantically adjusted the controls on his belt, but the minute he let go of Jean, she bolted in panic away from the Monitor. "Wait, Jean! Come back!" His mouth went dry with fear. His heart pounded against his rib cage. "You won't shrink with me if I'm not holding you!"

The Monitor turned his attention to Jean. "Is this insignificant female the reason you refuse to accompany us?" he asked Ray. Without waiting for an answer, he aimed his gauntlet at Jean, who was now cowering behind the bulky iron furnace. "Very well. In a moment, nothing more will bind you to this world."

"Leave her alone, you monster!" He launched himself at Solomon, but the powerful being effortlessly knocked Ray aside. He crashed into boxes of unpacked lab equipment, piled high against a wall. An avalanche of heavy cardboard boxes tumbled onto him. Dazed, his head ringing, he shouted for help. "Donna! Jason! Somebody!"

As though in answer to his desperate cries, a shimmering column of light materialized between Solomon and his helpless target. Ray's eyes widened in surprise as *another* Monitor emerged from the flickering transporter beam. Unlike Solomon, this alien was clean-shaven and wore his long black hair tied up in the back. He looked mad as hell.

"Hold, brother!" the newcomer commanded. "This woman is under my protection. You have inflicted enough damage on my world."

Solomon reacted angrily to the other Monitor's interference. "Stay out of this, Nix Uotan! You cannot hide Ray Palmer from me any longer!"

"What transpires on this Earth is none of your concern," Uotan replied. "I was under no obligation to divulge the Atom's whereabouts to you." He glanced at the bruised figure beneath the boxes. His inhuman red eyes held a hint of sympathy. "If I chose to grant him refuge on my world, that was my prerogative."

Solomon clenched his fists. "But I have found him nonetheless!" Throwing out one arm, he blasted a hole in one wall. Plaster and masonry flew apart, exposing a charred patch of frozen earth beyond the walls of the basement. The explosion alarmed Jean, who let out a frightened shriek. The Monitor let the impact of his demonstration sink in before speaking again. "Surrender Ray Palmer to me now or I will reduce this placid Earth of yours to a wasteland!"

"Not so fast, pal!" A Bowie knife bounced off the back of Solomon's skull. Jason Todd dropped down through the gap in the ceiling, followed immediately by Donna Troy. A split lip and bruised forehead testified to the severity of her clash with the berserk Monitor, but she looked ready for more. Jason drew an automatic pistol and took aim at Solomon's head. "I'm supposed to be the trigger-happy one around here, remember?"

"Do not try my patience further!" Solomon barked at his traveling companions. "This is now between my onetime brother and me." He advanced aggressively toward the other Monitor. "Well, Nix Uotan? Shall we resume our duel?"

"Gladly!" the other Monitor said. He extended a glowing palm before him. "You must pay for transgressing upon my domain!"

Crawling out from beneath the heap of boxes, Ray hastily assessed the situation. The Monitors faced off against each other, each powerful enough to reduce the entire neighborhood to rubble, if not all of Ivy Town, while Donna and Jason stood poised to join the conflict as well. Ray could only imagine the devastation in store, with Jean trapped at ground zero. *This is all my fault,* he realized. Barry's gruesome death tore at his conscience. *There's only one thing left to do. . . .*

"Wait!" he shouted at Solomon. "I'll go with you—if you'll leave this world alone!"

His offer caught the ruthless Monitor's attention. He cocked his head in Ray's direction. "You consent to join our crusade? You will fulfill your destiny?"

"Yes, you murderous bastard! Yes!" Ray clambered to his feet. He pleaded hoarsely with the looming alien. "Take me back to my own Earth. Throw me into another cosmic Crisis. Just leave Jean and the rest of this world alone!"

Solomon nodded gravely. "These terms are acceptable to me." He turned back toward the other Monitor. "So, Nix Uotan, are you still prepared to fight me for this mortal's sake?"

"Perhaps that will not be necessary." Lowering his guard, the second alien gazed sadly at Ray. Something about him made him seem more humane than his merciless kinsman. "My apologies, Ray Palmer. In light of your past sufferings, I was willing to overlook your presence here, even going so far as to conceal your location from my fellow Monitors, but my true duty is to this universe and its native inhabitants. I fear it is time you depart this realm . . . for all time."

Ray felt his heart die a second time. Yet he stood up straight, stoically facing his fate. "I understand," he said. "I don't belong here. I never really did."

"Ray! What are you saying?" Overcoming her fear, Jean stumbled out from behind the furnace. Her eyes were red from crying. Mascara streaked her cheeks. Soot smeared her purple sweater. "You can't go with these . . . creatures! You belong here . . . with me!"

"I'm sorry, Jean." He resisted the urge to go to her, knowing that if he held her in his arms again, he would never be able to let her go. "There's no other way." He smelled Barry's scorched bones smoking upstairs and prayed that Iris and the others had gotten away safely. He wouldn't be able to live with himself if anyone else got hurt because of his deception. "I'll never forget the time we had together." He started to choke up, but somehow managed to get the words out. "You gave me back something I thought I'd lost forever."

And now I've got to throw it all away again.

"Ray, no!" She started toward him, but the kinder, gentler Monitor grabbed on to her shoulders, restraining her. She struggled to get free, but could not break loose from the alien's powerful grip. "Let go of me!" she wailed. "I want to go with him!"

"That cannot be allowed," Uotan said sorrowfully. "The immutable laws of the Multiverse have already been violated enough. You must remain on this Earth, where you belong, while these others must return to their own universe at once."

"NO!" Jean shrieked. She writhed in the Monitor's iron grasp, like a madwoman caught in a straitjacket. Loose black hair fell across her face. Crazed blue eyes implored Ray. Saliva sprayed from her lips. "Don't do this to me, Ray! Don't leave me! RAY!"

Ray felt like he was trapped in a never-ending nightmare. He couldn't stand another minute of this. "All right," he told Solomon bitterly. "You win. Let's go." Why drag this torture out a second longer? He could only pray that he hadn't just condemned another Jean to madness, that she would somehow recover from this ordeal in time. "Take me back to Earth-One."

"About time," Jason muttered. He retrieved his knife from the floor. "The sooner I get back to Gotham—*my* Gotham—the better."

"You are mistaken," Solomon informed them. He pressed a stud upon his gauntlet and a shimmering golden sphere surrounded Ray, Donna, Jason, and himself. "We are returning to our own universe, but not to Earth. Ray Palmer's destiny awaits elsewhere."

"What?" Donna blurted. Fists raised, she eyed the Monitor warily. "Where are we going now?"

A cryptic smiled appeared on Solomon's face as he revealed their true destination.

"Apokolips."

12 AND COUNTING.

PARADISE ISLAND.

The banquet hall in Athena's palace was the site of a lavish feast. Long wooden tables were piled high with savory sturgeon, bread, cheese, figs, pomegranates, and honeyed wine. After subsisting on little more than gruel for weeks, the Amazonian initiates eagerly dug into the generous spread. Silver goblets and cutlery clinked as the fit young women chattered brightly amongst themselves, often with their mouths full. An elevated dais, garlanded with fresh flowers, looked down upon the festivities. Moonlight poured into the chamber from a marble archway behind the raised platform. Flutes and lyres contributed to the merriment. A roaring fire kept the winter chill outside. Drooling warhounds prowled the floor, searching for scraps, or else gnawed on bones before the hearth. The delicious aroma of the feast wafted through the air.

Not that Mary was in any position to enjoy the repast. Disguised as a lowly scullery maid, wearing nothing but a coarse burlap smock, she shuffled from table to table, refilling the other women's goblets from a heavy clay amphora. Her mouth watered, and her stomach grumbled, at the sight and smell of the tempting delicacies. Still, at least nobody seemed to be paying any attention to her. . . .

"Watch what you're doing, Cinderella!" Harley Quinn exclaimed as Mary slopped some wine over the edge of Harley's goblet. The blonde was seated next to Holly Robinson at one of the benches facing the tables. Harley grabbed on to Mary's hair and yanked her head down onto the table. "Relax," Harley whispered under her breath. "I'm just reinforcing your cover, pretending to punish the clumsy slave girl."

Mary's cheek was flat against the grainy tabletop. "Hating you right now," she whispered back. She held on tightly to both the amphora and her temper. Her jaws clenched as she forced herself to count to ten. *Mission or no mission, Harley's lucky I don't have my powers anymore.*

"Bad slave!" Harley scolded, to the amusement of the other girls at the table. She let go of Mary's hair and roughly shoved her away from the table. "No more spilling the wine or I'll bop you on the nose with a rolled-up newspaper!"

The derisive laughter of the Amazon wannabes scalded Mary's ears as she stumbled over to the next table, laboring beneath the weight of the wine-filled vessel. That infiltrating the palace as an anonymous servant had all been part of Queen Hippolyta's plan did little to ease her humiliation. *Talk about pride coming before the fall,* she thought. Getting made fun of by the Joker's psycho ex was proof positive of just how far she'd sunk since accepting Black Adam's toxic gift. *Although I suppose it's nothing more than I deserve. . . .*

She still wasn't sure how much of her recent misbehavior could be attributed to Eclipso's influence, Black Adam's darkness, or her own human failings. *Probably some combination thereof,* she guessed, *but that doesn't really let me off the hook. I'm still accountable for my own actions . . . and for letting other people lead me astray.*

The jeers and laughter died away, and an expectant hush fell over the banquet hall, as Athena herself, in full regalia, entered through the archway. The false goddess strode to the front of the dais. Her voice rang out over the assembly.

"After weeks of training, I know in my heart that the proud women in this room would rather drown in their own blood than yield an inch to their oppressors. Time and time again, each of you has proven her valor to me and to each other. Athena salutes you and embraces you all as sisters. Here you have been schooled in the noble art of combat. Here you have been given the skills to survive. And one day soon you will pick up your swords and thrust them into the hearts of our enemies." Her voice soared as she held out her arms in benediction. "You fight like warriors. You bear the scars of warriors. You eye the world around you as you would an adversary. Soon you shall be . . . Female Furies!"

Cheers erupted from the feasting women. They raised their goblets to toast the glorious future Athena had just laid out before them. But something about Athena's stirring oration didn't sit right with Mary.

Female Furies? Mary felt certain that she had heard that term before, but she couldn't immediately remember where. Times like this she wished she could still rely on the wisdom of the gods, as opposed to her own fallible mortal memory. *Not that that vaunted wisdom stopped me from losing my way in the end . . .*

Athena snapped her fingers, summoning four young women via the archway behind her. Each of the quartet sported handcrafted armor of unique design. A crested helmet concealed the features of one initiate, whose six-foot frame was encased in lacquered black plate metal. Fearsome tattoos marked the face of a dark-skinned woman whose satiny, two-piece outfit had an exotic South Asian look; jewel-studded blades jutted from her knees, elbows, and collar. A miniature skull, chiseled from a glittering emerald, was lodged in her navel. Bladed Indian weapons known as *katars* rested upon her hips. Beside her stood a pale, deceptively slight-looking woman boasting a shaved skull and skintight blue leather. Artificial wings, and silver chain mail, gave the fourth and final woman the intimidating aspect of an avenging angel or Thanagarian. The women spread out behind Athena, standing stiffly at attention. Their faces bore looks of grim determination and/or unquestioning obedience.

Mary heard Holly gasp in surprise. "Tricia?" the Gotham girl murmured. Holly stared wide-eyed at the black girl on Athena's right, the one with all the lethal ornamentation. *Guess there's some history there.*

"Today," Athena proclaimed, "these four of your sisters will show you the path . . . as our first full Amazonian Furies!"

Mary wondered why Holly and Harley hadn't rated such status yet. Could it be that Athena still had doubts regarding their loyalty? *That doesn't bode well. . . .*

The other initiates greeted their comrades' elevation with enthusiasm. "FURIES!" they chanted, pounding their goblets upon the tabletop. Holly and Harley joined in the raucous chorus, the better to blend in with the rest. If anything, Harley whooped it up more than anybody else. She bounced up and down upon her bench. "FURIES! FURIES!"

Athena silenced the cheers with a gesture. "Heed my words, my sisters. The days ahead will sorely test our resolve. Brutish warriors from Man's World will attempt to crush our spirit. Every nation will be arrayed against us. But take heart! They cannot conquer women such as we. Our strength and fury will drive them into the ground until rivers of blood flow—"

"That's enough!" Mary hurled the amphora to the floor, where it shattered loudly upon the marble tiles. She just couldn't take any more of this, watching all these gullible young women fall for Athena's lies. "Are you people crazy? She's trying to seduce you with flowery rhetoric about the glories of war and vengeance. I've heard this kind of talk from Eclipso—and this so-called goddess is manipulating you the same way!"

One table over, Holly buried her face in her hands. "Oh no, she is *not* doing this. . . !"

"She isn't?" Harley gulped down the last of her wine. "Sure sounds like it to me!"

Athena was unfazed by Mary's accusations. "Oh dear, it seems we have a disgruntled servant among our ranks." She turned to the newly anointed acolytes behind her. "Furies, kill her!"

"With pleasure!" The one named Tricia launched herself from the dais. She plucked her *katars* from her hips. Defenseless, Mary braced herself for the Fury's attack. Her back was up against a colossal stone caryatid. She realized she didn't stand a chance.

I don't regret a word, though.

"You're not killing anyone, Trish!" Holly sprang from her seat, intercepting Tricia in midleap. Her fist collided with the other woman's jaw.

Harley executed a backward flip off her bench, landing directly in front of Mary. "Keep behind me, big mouth!"

The tall Fury in the ebony armor charged at Harley and Mary. "We have traitors among us!" she snarled. "Kill all three of them!"

"Wait!" Mary pleaded, even as Harley defended her from the armored stranger. The blonde parried the Fury's blows with her Amazon bracelets. Mary shouted over the din of battle, "This is stupid! Athena is just using you!"

Landing atop one of the banquet tables, Tricia recovered from Holly's punch. She glared murderously at the impertinent redhead as she massaged her bruised jaw. "You *dare* attack me! One of Athena's Elect?" She slashed at Holly with her *katars*. The blades sliced the air as Holly dodged the strikes as nimbly as a cat. Cups and plates clattered to the floor as the two women dueled upon the cluttered tabletop. Food and drink spilled over into the other Amazons' laps. Tricia's tattooed face turned a livid shade of purple. "I'll gut you and feed the pieces to my dogs!"

Less than ten paces away, Harley flipped the black knight directly into the path of the pale, bald-headed Fury, who found herself knocked off her feet by her own comrade. Confusion reigned as the tangled Furies bowled over several of the jostling spectators as well. Harley laughed uproariously at the slapstick spectacle, and Mary had to admit that the irritating flake knew how to fight. "Come on, ladies!" Harley called out to the scattered initiates, who seemed torn between fleeing the violence and competing with each other for the best view. They crowded around the combatants, adding to the chaos. Harley wagged a finger at her audience. "What happened to the whole 'Sisterhood of Paradise Island' vibe we had going here?"

The same thing that happened with my best friend and soul mate, Eclipso, Mary thought bitterly. *It was all just a scam to take advantage of vulnerable young women . . . and turn them into killers.*

"Is that the best you've got, Tricia?" Holly ducked beneath the Fury's *katars* and delivered a solid uppercut to her chin. Tricia toppled backward onto the tabletop, landing flat on her back amidst squashed cheese and figs. "Don't you get special training points for brownnosing Athena?"

The winged Fury flapped angrily above them, looking for an opening. Holly grabbed a silver platter from the table and hurled it like a discus at the second-rate Hawkgirl impersonator. The spinning tray clipped the soaring Fury in the skull, throwing her off course, and she crashed headfirst into a nearby column. "Thank you for flying Air Paradise!" Holly quipped. "Happy landings!"

Up on the dais, the goddess finally lost her composure. "Why is this taking so long?" she screeched. "Kill them, my Furies! Kill them now!"

A new voice interrupted Athena's tirade. "If anyone dies today, pretender, it shall be you!"

Hippolyta marched through the archway onto the platform. An unsheathed sword occupied her right hand. A gleaming shield, embossed with the emblem of a magnificent eagle, rested upon her strong left arm. Her purple cape rustled behind her.

"You!" Athena blurted. Her startled face betrayed her shock. "*You* can't be here!"

"I've been away too long!" Hippolyta advanced on Athena. Her sword flashed in the moonlight. "This island is not your personal training ground! The gods bestowed it upon us as a place of peace and harmony!"

"Awesome! It's the queen!" Harley pumped her fist in the air. "Kick her phony-baloney ass, your majesty!"

Hippolyta swung her sword at Athena, forcing the false goddess to retreat to the very edge of the dais. "Peace and harmony are for weaklings!" Athena sneered. Bright orange bolts of energy blasted from her fingertips. "You should have stayed away, Hippolyta! You no longer rule here!"

"That's where you're mistaken." Hippolyta jumped above the destructive blasts, which reduced a portion of the dais to splinters instead. Smoke rose from the charred timbers. "Show them who you really are! Reveal the true face of the deceiver!"

Her blade slashed past Athena's defenses. The sword's point sliced across the goddess's porcelain features, drawing a crimson line upon her cheek. Athena squealed in pain. "My face!" she cried out—as a carefully crafted illusion shattered.

Athena's regal façade blurred and wavered, like an out-of-focus television signal, before blinking out entirely. The elegant, silk-draped goddess vanished, replaced by a stocky figure very different in appearance. Where Athena had been, there now stood a craggy-faced harridan whose matronly frame was corseted into studded leather armor. A mane of thick white hair framed her scowling face. Cruelty and contempt were etched upon her deeply furrowed countenance. Icy blue eyes peered out from beneath bristling black eyebrows. Scaly green chain mail protected her stout legs. A dark red cloak with a raised collar was clasped to her shoulders. Glowing energy-gauntlets hummed upon her wrists. Mary recognized the hideous crone at once.

Holy Moley! It's Granny Goodness!

The name, bestowed upon the evil New God by Darkseid himself, was one of the Dark Lord's crueler jests. Granny Goodness was infamous for the hellish orphanages she administered upon Apokolips, whose sole purpose was to mold the lost children of Armagetto into bloodthirsty minions of Darkseid. Mary's heart sank as she suddenly remembered why the term "Female Furies" had sounded so familiar. The Female Furies of Apokolips were Granny's prize students, the cream of her sadistic crop. Now, it seemed, she'd expanded her vile franchise to Paradise Island.

Did Eclipso know about this? Mary worried, disturbed to discover that she had not yet escaped Darkseid's malign ambitions. *Were she and Granny working together, or were they competing for the Dark Lord's approval?*

"Evil child!" Granny croaked hoarsely. Reddened fingers came away from her injured cheek. "You actually hurt your Granny!"

"You're no kin of mine!" Hippolyta shot back. "And that wound is but a precursor to the punishment that awaits you!" Her shield deflected another blast from Granny's gauntlets. "Alone against you, I knew I might not prevail, but with good, strong women at my side, you falter like the coward you are!"

"No! Damn you!" Immortal blood dripped down Granny's face as she hastily depressed a button upon her gauntlet. A thunderclap shook the palace as a swirling vortex opened up in the air above the dais. Fearing Hippolyta's wrath, Granny darted into the vortex with surprising speed. She disappeared into the shimmering Boom Tube.

"Witness!" Hippolyta commanded all present. She raised her sword in victory. "Defeated, she flees with her tail between her legs!"

Mary breathed a sigh of relief. Had the evil infesting Themyscira been routed so easily? Abandoned by their goddess, and stunned by the revelation of her true appearance, the Female Furies looked floored by Granny's retreat. Their arms drooped slackly at their sides. Tricia's *katars* slipped from her fingers as she stared numbly at the vortex that had swallowed her divine leader. Like the other Furies, she didn't seem to have any more fight in her.

It's over, Mary thought.

Or maybe not.

"Hey!" Harley protested. Bounding onto a table, she ran the length of the table toward the lingering Boom Tube. "That ugly broad scammed us all! We can't let her get away!"

She dived into the vortex after Granny.

Mary and Holly exchanged disbelieving looks. "She didn't . . . " Holly muttered.

"Yeah, she did." Mary took a deep breath as the Boom Tube began to fade from sight. Within moments, the portal would be gone for good, along with Harley Quinn. Mary glanced at Holly. "You wanna . . . ?"

Holly ran toward the Boom Tube even as she shook her head in dismay. "I swear I'm going to kill her one of these days!"

"Not if I get her first!" Mary insisted. She sprinted after Holly, quickly catching up with her. Side by side, they raced for the portal, which was closing up right before their eyes. *Infuriating or not,* Mary thought, *Harley did save my life just now.*

Holly seemed startled to find Mary accompanying her. She looked dubiously at the unarmed girl. "Are you kidding, Mary? What are *you* going to do?"

The Boom Tube loomed before them, filling up Mary's vision. She glimpsed a shimmering corridor, lined with bizarre, unearthly circuitry. Coruscating energies hummed and crackled. Her skin tingled. The scent of ozone invaded her nostrils. Nightmarish memories of Apokolips sent a chill down her spine.

"I'll figure it out later," she said.

They threw themselves into the unknown.

The vortex closed behind them with a resounding *boom.*

11 AND COUNTING.

APOKOLIPS.

Despair burned freely from the planet's core, fouling the atmosphere. The entire world moaned, a sound that chilled the soul with its dull emptiness and infernal malevolence. Walls a thousand feet high enclosed a sprawling megalopolis that burst upward like a pestilent boil as charnel winds extinguished the pallid stars from view. On the horizon, towering techno-temples rested on the half-calcified bones of a billion failed genetic experiments, thrusting upward into the smoky black sky, while across this revolting graveyard of the universe, the muffled, maddening, and monotonous whine of blasphemous wails rose from inconceivable subterranean torture chambers. Gigantic Fire Pits belched enormous gouts of flame.

Donna gazed out over the hellish cityscape. The hot air scorched her lungs. "On my list of the worst possible places to be, this is number one."

Along with Ray Palmer, the Challengers stood atop the roof of a concrete workhouse in the filthy Armagetto. Donna recognized the dismal setting from past battles against Darkseid and his minions. Turning away from the ugly spectacle, she confronted the Monitor. "Why exactly are we on Apokolips?"

She kept her guard up. Ever since Solomon's brutal execution of that alternate version of Barry Allen, she didn't trust the Monitor one bit. *He may very well have the safety of the entire universe in mind,* she thought, *but he's made it all too clear that he's willing to sacrifice any one of us to achieve his aims.*

So did that make him a dangerous ally—or a mortal enemy?

"Yeah. What's the scoop?" Jason demanded. He methodically polished his knife while keeping a wary eye on their surroundings. So far their arrival had gone unnoticed, but that wasn't likely to remain the case. "Why this detour to Darkseid's backyard?"

"That is no concern of yours," Solomon said brusquely. His armored hand was clasped firmly onto the Atom's shoulder, lest his latest recruit attempt to elude them once more. Ray's winter jacket was soiled and torn from the battle back on Earth-51. His red-rimmed eyes held a haunted expression. "Suffice it to say that I have business on this accursed globe—as does Ray Palmer."

"Me?" Ray blurted. "Are you out of your mind? I don't want anything to do with this place!"

Donna wondered if he was having second thoughts about joining their bizarre expedition. *Not that I blame him,* she conceded. *I'm starting to question whether this was such a good idea myself. Prophecy or no prophecy.*

"Hold it together, Palmer," Jason said irritably. He glared at Solomon. "I'm sure our red-eyed buddy has a good reason for bringing us here. At least he'd *better* have."

"As I said," the Monitor replied, "that is my own affair." To Donna's surprise, a column of light suddenly cut off Solomon and Ray from her and Jason. Solomon consulted a display screen on his gauntlet. "Come, Ray Palmer. We can tarry here no longer."

"Hey!" Jason shouted. He lunged at the glowing figures, but they had already grown too immaterial to grab on to. Donna watched in dismay as the Monitor and Ray began to fade from view. Jason kicked the rooftop in frustration. "What about us?"

"You have served your purpose for now," Solomon declared, even as his sepulchral voice diminished in volume. "Our paths part here."

On Apokolips?

"Wait!" Donna called out, but it was already too late. The Monitor had vanished, taking the Atom with him. She and Jason were on their own, and stranded on the most dangerous planet in the Multiverse.

With no way home.

APOKOLIPS.

"It was foolish to follow me!" Granny Goodness cackled. She stood upon the bleachers of a vast assembly hall within the forbidding confines of her infamous orphanage. Ugly gray masonry, barren of any ornamentation, testified to the soul-destroying bleakness of Granny's infamous institution. "I cannot believe that I thought you mortal trulls had the potential to join my Female Furies." The genuine articles were perched on the wide cement tiers behind Granny, while a squadron of armed Parademons fanned out before her. "Now my true Furies will rip you to pieces! Kill them, girls!" she exhorted her lethal favorites. "Do it for Granny!"

"Are you kidding?" Harley jeered back. She and Holly and Mary crouched behind dense concrete columns, which provided them momentary shelter from the sizzling blasts of the Parademons' energy-rifles. The unleashed firepower chipped away at the pillars. Bursts of orange energy burned through the barriers, narrowly missing the three women. Harley shouted over the din, "I don't know the meaning of the word *fear*!"

"Harley," Holly quipped, her back pressed up against a column, "you don't know the meaning of *most* words."

Mary rolled her eyes. "I hate to interrupt your oh-so-funny banter, but is there a plan we should be following?"

I can't believe I'm back on Apokolips again, she thought. *And without my powers this time.* Unlike her armored companions, Mary had only a tattered smock to protect her from their enemies and the elements. The interior of the orphanage was cold and drafty, the better to toughen Granny's unfortunate charges. The chilly cement floor leeched the heat from Mary's bare feet. Smoky fumes rose from mounted torches. The stale air reeked of old sweat and fear. Mary shivered uncontrollably. *What was I thinking, jumping through that Boom Tube after Harley?*

Paradise Island was light-years away now. Mary briefly wondered what had become of Hippolyta, who had stayed behind to restore order to Themyscira. No doubt she had her hands full dealing with an island full of confused Amazon wannabes. Mary figured they couldn't count on the Amazon queen coming to their rescue. Hippolyta had no way to get to Apokolips even if she wanted to.

We're on our own, Mary realized. *And up against an entire planet of evil gods.*

"Plan?" Holly shrugged. "Don't look at me. I didn't book this trip."

Granny continued to rail at them from behind the massed Parademons. Mary didn't have the nerve to peer around the corner of the pillar, but she could readily imagine the crone's livid face. "If you've come to free the gods, you're going to fail miserably!"

Free the gods? Mary exchanged a startled glance with Holly. "Did she just say . . . ?"

"Ha!" Harley gloated. Her face lit up with glee. "I knew this was a good idea." She gave her accomplices an unmistakable I-told-you-so look. "Say something mean to me now!"

"Very well," an amused voice replied from behind the Earthwomen. A flexible steel band whipped out and wrapped itself tightly around the lower half of Harley's face, gagging her. A muffled gasp barely escaped the wide silver ribbon. "I'm going to tear your head off and feed it to my plasmid eels!"

Spinning around, Mary saw three Female Furies charging at them from behind, having obviously circled around them via the orphanage's labyrinthine passageways. She recognized them as the elite of Granny's hand-trained warriors. Although she had never fought them before, she knew of their vicious reputation. *They gave Supergirl a rough time a while back.*

"The name is Lashina," the leader of the Furies declared as she yanked Harley off her feet, "for obvious reasons." Chrome-colored strips accented a dark blue bodysuit that fit tightly over her athletic figure. A sleek black ponytail whipped about behind her head. A horizontal metal band divided her face in two, protecting her nose. Cruel blue eyes gleamed above the steel noseguard. Contempt dripped from her ruby lips. "Allow me to introduce your friends to Stompa."

The latter was a veritable behemoth of a woman, the size of Solomon Grundy or Gorilla Grodd. A double-breasted brown leather uniform encased her hefty frame. A skull and crossbones was imprinted on the brow of her hard plastic helmet, which made her look like the world's largest roller derby contestant. Tinted brown goggles concealed her eyes, but not the outrage in her voice. "Which one of you skinny bitches hurt our Granny?" she demanded as she stamped her heavy antimatter boots upon the floor.

An earthquake shook the assembly, knocking Mary off her feet. A deep crack snaked across the quivering cement floor. Dust rained down from the rafters. Mary heard Holly crash to the ground as well. The other girl swore.

A third Fury sprang toward Mary. "I'm Mad Harriet!" She laughed maniacally. Her crazed grin and wild green mane immediately reminded Mary of the Joker, if the Joker were an alien madwoman with jaundiced yellow skin, chartreuse hair, and bulging green eyes. A metallic breastplate shielded her torso, while a lime-colored loincloth flapped between her legs. Her fur-trimmed boots matched her green hair. Shining steel gauntlets were equipped with razor-sharp claws. "And you made my Granny upset!"

"Granny is god!" Stompa picked up the refrain. "We worship our Granny!"

Holly scrambled to her feet, but Stompa lowered the boom again. Another earth tremor rocked the corridor, sending pulverized stone into the air. A loud rumbling noise drowned out Mary's gasps. Sprawled backward upon the bucking floor, she was tossed about helplessly, which saved her life, ironically enough. The jarring vibrations threw off Mad Harriet's attack, so that the lunatic's claws missed Mary by a hair. The gleaming razors slashed the empty air only inches away from Mary's face.

Talk about a close shave!

"Wow," Holly said sarcastically, leaping toward Stompa. Unlike Mary, the former Catwoman used the earthquake to nimbly propel herself toward the hulking Fury. A steel-toed Amazon boot kicked Stompa in the teeth, causing the gargantuan woman to reel backward. She teetered precariously atop her bulky legs. "You must scare the crap out of cockroaches. . . ."

Holy Moley! Mary thought, impressed and encouraged by her ally's fighting skills. Out of the corner of her eye, she spotted Harley grappling with Lashina. Spinning like a dervish, Harley had somehow managed to unwind the lash about her head. "Hold still, curse you!" Lashina hissed as Harley ducked and dodged the Fury's whistling namesakes. "Stop jumping about like an accursed bug!"

"I got a better idea," Harley said brightly. She snatched up a piece of fallen rubble and flung it at Lashina's head. The rocky fragment smashed against the woman's noseguard, pelting her eyes and mouth with flying pieces of stone. "Hold *this* with your face!"

Was that enough to defeat Lashina? Mary had no time to find out as Mad Harriet came at her again. "Slice and dice! Dice and slice!" Still shaken by the tremors, Mary backed away fearfully on all fours, but the insane Fury was too fast for her. She pounced on Mary, pinning her to the ground. A cold metal gauntlet closed around Mary's throat. Sharpened claws pricked her flesh, barely breaking the skin. Harriet's leering face was mere inches away from Mary's. Spittle sprayed her cheeks. The Fury's hot breath smelled like sour milk. "Choppy choppy, little girl!"

Only heartbeats away from being turned into heroine salad, Mary played dirty. Harriet squealed in pain as Mary bit off the tip of the Fury's long, pointy nose.

Ugh! Mary spit the nauseating morsel onto the floor even as Harriet leapt away from her, clutching her mutilated nose. Blood sprayed through her clawed fingertips. "You bad toy, you!" she howled, no longer grinning like a loon. Deranged eyes spun in their sockets. "I'll kill you! Kill! KILL!"

Mary wasn't going to stick around to give Harriet a chance to get even. Rolling over onto her hands and knees, she hastily stumbled to her feet. She looked anxiously for her companions, but saw that the girls from Gotham were still caught up in their own life-or-death battles. Holly was sitting piggyback astride Stompa's brawny shoulders, her arms locked around the Fury's throat. *"Ungh!"* she grunted as she fought to topple the larger woman. "Why won't you fall?"

"Release her!" Four surly Parademons arrived to reinforce the Furies. They aimed their rifles at Holly.

"Okay!" Holly flipped Stompa over so that the huge Fury slammed head over heels into the gun-wielding guards, who scattered like bowling pins. "She's all yours!" The assembly hall shook as Stompa hit the ground with tremendous force. Holly somersaulted onto the floor, springing up just in time to see Lashina deliver a vicious blow to Harley with her trademark metal whip. The flashing silver ribbon smacked Harley across the face, knocking her onto her butt. "Oh no," Holly gasped.

"How pathetic!" Lashina towered over Harley, who, struggling up onto her knees, wiped the blood from her split lip. Lashina's whip spun like a propeller blade as the pissed-off warrior woman prepared to deliver the coup de grâce. "You were supposed to be a Fury?" Lashina snorted in derision. "You're not worthy of—"

"Shut up!" Holly leapt to her friend's defense. Her heel collided with Lashina's jaw.

Good one, Mary thought as she raced away from Mad Harriet, who chased her down an adjacent corridor. "My face! My beautiful face!" the injured Fury shrieked. She bounded after Mary like a bloodthirsty hyena.

"Do they not have mirrors on Apokolips?" Mary wondered aloud. Mad Harriet had been no beauty even before Mary gave her an impromptu nose job. Mary's feet pounded against the cold stone floor as she ran for her life. Glancing back over her shoulder, she saw the vengeful Fury gaining on her. Bloody claws reached out for the defenseless young woman. "I am *so* missing my powers right now!"

"Miserable meat bag!" A trio of Parademons appeared before Mary, blocking her path. They hefted their rifles at the sight of the fleeing girl. "Gun it down!"

"Oh, you've got to be kidding!" Mary exclaimed. Thinking fast, she hurled herself facedown onto the floor, so that the soldiers' guns targeted Mad Harriet instead. The startled madwoman skidded to a halt as she suddenly found herself facing an Apokoliptian firing squad. Muzzles flared.

"Wait!" she hollered, but not soon enough. A merciless hail of energy beams shredded Mad Harriet's flesh, reducing her to a gory wreck on the hallway floor. Whimpered moans informed Mary that Harriet was still clinging to life. Was it even possible to kill a New God?

The scorching gunfire was over in a second as the trigger-happy Parademons realized their error. "Uh, that was ill-advised," one of them gulped. He sheepishly lowered his weapon, all but forgetting about Mary as he contemplated the enormity of what they had just done. "Granny's going to eviscerate us, isn't she?"

A finger tapped his shoulder from behind. "If I were you, I wouldn't worry about Granny," Holly advised as she and Harley ambushed the distracted Parademons. Mary climbed back to her feet as the other two women made short work of the guards and confiscated their rifles. The unconscious soldiers soon lay in a heap upon the floor. "We need to get out of here ASAP!"

Harley winked at Mary. "Nice moves for a serving wench."

"Ha-ha," Mary replied. She wished Harley would drop the slave-girl jokes; still, she couldn't complain. Compared to Mad Harriet, Harley seemed positively sane.

The pigtailed blonde lobbed the spare rifle over to Mary. "Just like a camera," Harley promised. "Point and shoot . . . preferably in the direction of evil."

"Forget it." Mary tossed the weapon aside. She had already come too close to the dark side, under Eclipso's insidious tutelage, to compromise her values once more. "No guns. And I'm not killing anyone either."

I may not be Mary Marvel anymore, she vowed, *but I'm not going to take after Black Adam again. No matter what.*

Harley stared at her like *she* was the crazy one. "You believe this kid?"

Holly shrugged. "Let her do it her way."

Thanks, Mary thought, glad that the redhead didn't try to talk her out of her decision. She opened her mouth to say as much, only to be distracted by a peculiar buzzing at the back of her mind, almost like a chorus of whispered voices straining to be heard. Now that the fighting had died down for a second, she could almost make out what they were saying.

Come, Mary Batson. Deliver us from evil. . . .

"What . . . ?" Mary whispered under her breath.

Her companions failed to notice her bemused state. They had other things on their minds. Harley slung her rifle over her shoulder. "Okay, let's go put Granny in a retirement home."

Holly nodded grimly and started off down the corridor.

"Guys?" Mary called out to them. "There's . . . Well, I don't want to say 'voices,' but I'm hearing what sounds like . . ."

"Voices?" Holly supplied.

Harley frowned. "What voices? I can't hear anything." She eyed Mary skeptically. "Does somebody need her daily dose of thorazine?"

Mary recalled that Harley had been a psychiatrist at Arkham Asylum before becoming one of the inmates. "The gods," she insisted, knowing just how crazy that sounded. "I hear the voices of the gods."

It was true. This wasn't like before, when Eclipso had insinuated her voice into Mary's thoughts. Mary recognized the voices of the gods from the good old days, when they had freely bestowed their wisdom and power upon her. Before everything went wrong.

"The gods?" Holly shrugged again. At this point, the streetwise Gotham girl seemed inclined to take just about anything in stride, no matter how far-fetched. "This should be interesting."

APOKOLIPS.

Darkseid contemplated the figurines upon the chessboard. Discarded pieces, including Eclipso and Mad Harriet, rested in a box alongside the board. Silence hung over the gloomy war room until a sudden flash of light heralded the return of his opponent. He raised his smoldering gaze from the game to greet the Monitor as he transported into the chamber.

"Welcome back, Solomon." Darkseid gestured at the board before him. "Shall we resume our game?" He spied a red and blue figure in the Monitor's right hand. "Ah, I see you have recovered your missing pawn."

"No thanks to you," Solomon replied sourly. "Or my fainthearted brethren." He placed a miniature replica of the Atom upon the board, not far from the figures representing Jason Todd and Donna Troy. "But I am prepared now to pit my strategy against yours—for the sake of the universe."

Darkseid nodded. "The endgame is upon us, Monitor." He moved the Jimmy Olsen figure across the board. "Despite your added pawn, you will note that I have placed you in the Lucena position." He smiled craftily. "Check."

Solomon appeared unalarmed by his opponent's move. His fingers lifted "Mary Batson" from the board and placed her closer in proximity to Granny Goodness. "While the Innocent is still in play, I am not yet defeated."

A transparent play, Darkseid thought, *and one I had already anticipated.* He laughed out loud at the Monitor's audacity. "Good to see that you still have some fight in you, Solomon. It will be interesting to see how your gambit plays out."

10 AND COUNTING.

APOKOLIPS.

"Could you have picked a more heavily guarded place?" Holly complained.

A half dozen moaning Parademons were sprawled upon the steps leading up to an enormous steel door. Scorch marks blackened their helmets and uniforms. Smoke rose from their twitching bodies. Rifles in hand, Holly and Harley kept their eyes and guns focused on vanquished guards, just in case any of them were playing possum.

Harley nudged one of the unconscious guards with her foot. "Yeah, seriously, Mary, what's up?"

"I swear, the gods are here!" She ran barefoot up the steps to the imposing gray door. Iron rivets studded the face of the door, which was large enough to admit an elephant provided you knew the secret password. "I can hear them calling to me. Just behind this door!" She shoved against the barrier with her meager mortal strength, but the ponderous door wouldn't budge. "But how can we open it?"

"No problem." Harley cranked her rifle up to full power. "Step aside, short stack!"

The muzzle of the weapon flared brightly. Mary dived out of the way.

Energy crackled loudly as a bright orange beam blew open the door. Mary threw up her arm to protect her eyes from the flash, but as the glare faded, a stronger, even more intense light emanated from whatever lay beyond the ruptured door. She stepped uncertainly into the effulgent glow. The pure white light bathed her wide-eyed face.

"Wow."

She squinted into the light. The dazzling illumination was almost too bright to look at directly, but she could vaguely make out a multitude of humanoid figures suspended in some kind of high-tech alien vault. Arcane symbols, pulsing with mystic energy, were engraved upon the crystalline walls. A pair of mammoth braziers flanked the vault, spewing flames toward the ceiling. The very air seemed charged with static electricity. The light seemed to come from the figures themselves, while the vault appeared to stretch on for miles. The figures hung in midair, held in place by blinking strands of circuitry and raw energy. They looked like fireflies caught in a futuristic web. Agonized voices echoed inside her brain.

Help us, Mary Batson. Free us from these hellish bonds.

Holly and Harley entered the vault behind Mary. "That's them?" Holly asked in a hushed voice. "The gods?"

Mary nodded. "The entire pantheon."

"I don't suppose they have any all-knowing advice on how to pick the lock?" Harley asked, showing no more reverence in the presence of genuine deities than she ever did. " 'Cause I left my cosmic keys in my other armor." She raised her rifle and took aim at a flashing piece of apparatus at the center of the matrix. "Aw, what the heck? Let's just blow the thing up. . . ."

"Hey!" Holly reached out and lowered the barrel of the rifle. "Enough with the guns already!"

"What?" Harley protested. "It worked before! I was all *zzzakkkk*! And the door went all—"

"Harley!" The redhead's voice took on a warning edge.

Her companions' bickering barely registered on Mary's consciousness. She murmured softly as the trapped gods called out to her from their unholy captivity. "Really? But I'm not . . . I mean, I don't have that power anymore. . . . All right, if you say so . . ."

"Please tell me you're talking to them and not to yourself," Holly said. She looked like she was having second thoughts about this whole escapade. Mary couldn't blame her; they were a long way from the East End of Gotham. Holly was definitely out of her element.

"Don't worry," Mary said. "I know what to do, but you might want to move back in case this actually works." Without further explanation, she knelt before the glowing matrix and bowed her head in respect. She took a deep breath. Despite the gods' urging, she wasn't absolutely convinced that this wasn't a waste of time. She whispered tentatively. "Er . . . Shazam?"

Thunder boomed in the alien vault. Lightning struck from the heavens.

And Mary Marvel was reborn.

Not the dark Mary Marvel, born of Black Adam's tainted magic and Eclipso's seductive wiles, but the bright and shiny Mary Marvel of old. The World's Mightiest Maid rose triumphantly from her knees. Her grimy smock had been transformed into a pristine white dress that wasn't nearly as tight as the slinky black sheath had been. A *gray* thunderbolt was emblazoned on her chest, perhaps as a reminder of her brief flirtation with darkness. A short white cape with golden trim framed her trim figure. A golden sash belted her waist. Golden boots and wristbands completed the outfit.

"Great," Harley cracked. "I don't think I'll be able to smack her around anymore."

Mary felt the untainted power of the gods coursing through her. Her throat tightened. A single tear traced its way down her cheek. "Thank you," she whispered.

No longer confined within the vault, the gods and goddesses of ancient Greece appeared before the awestruck women. Their luminous figures towered above Mary and the others, transcending the confines of the spacious chamber. All-powerful Zeus, King of the Gods, stood in the forefront of the pantheon, while the other Olympians spread out behind him. Athena—the *real* Athena—reigned at her father's right hand. A magnificent crested helmet graced her head. Her sacred Aegis shone as brightly as the Golden Fleece. An owl, the eternal symbol of wisdom, perched upon her strong right arm. Her cool gray eyes regarded the women before her.

"The faith of your kind has been the gods' ever-present joy," the goddess said warmly. "Now our imprisonment has come to an end, and vengeance will be wrought upon the head of our captors."

"Whoa!" Holly exclaimed. "She is so much more impressive than that phony."

Harley backed away nervously. "I hope this was a good idea."

"I came as quickly as I could," Mary said. Staring at the gods in all their glory, she couldn't help wondering how Darkseid and Granny Goodness had managed to capture them in the first place. Were the New Gods truly that powerful? Mary felt out of her league. "I still find favor in your eyes? I thought you had forsaken me."

Athena spoke for the gods. "You were tested, child, not abandoned. Your trials were perilous and, for a time, you strayed from the light, but having freed us, we grant you absolution."

"Now, hold on one minute!" Harley objected. "We totally helped! And there was plenty of peril on our end." She stepped up beside Mary. "I mean, we fought, like, a gajillion ugly-faced monsters and whatnot!"

Holly looked utterly mortified and appalled. "Harley, shut it! Don't piss off the gods!"

Two more goddesses came forward from the pantheon. "The feisty one, known as Harley Quinn, amuses Thalia," said a redheaded, curly-haired deity whose sly face bore an impish smile. Her pink cheeks were flushed with merriment. She clutched the Mask of Comedy against her bosom. "And these mortals have not yet completed their trials."

Diana, goddess of the hunt, agreed. Bangs of light brown hair hung above silver eyes that gleamed like moonlight. A quiver of arrows was slung over her shoulder. Anger colored her voice. "The foul New God who imprisoned us yet prospers."

"Though you have fared well thus far," Thalia declared, "no mortal flesh can stand against a New God and survive." She glanced at Zeus, who gravely nodded his approval. "So shall we grant you power to combat our enemies and see them punished for their transgression!"

Rays of divine magic shot from the goddesses' eyes at Harley and Holly respectively. Twin nimbuses of golden light enveloped both women, briefly hiding them from Mary's view. She stared in wonder at the unexpected miracle taking place before her eyes. *Okay,* this *I didn't see coming.*

The light withdrew back into Thalia's sparkling green eyes. "Harley Quinn, I grant you a small portion of the cunning of Thalia, muse of comedy!"

"Ohmi . . . gods!" Harley burbled in delight. Transformed by the muse's gift, she now wore a comic variation on the Amazon armor that bore a distinct resemblance to her old super-villain costume. Her bright yellow pigtails poked through the dome of a bright red helmet with two large eye holes. Intricate engravings on her banded steel collar depicted slapstick scenes from ancient Greek farces. Her breastplate and leather skirt gleamed as though brand-new. The toes of her boots curved upward in a pixie-ish fashion. Her stolen rifle had been replaced by a ridiculously oversized mallet, so that she looked like a cross between a female gladiator and a clown.

That sounds about right, Mary thought.

"And I, Diana," the other goddess proclaimed, "grant Holly Robinson a portion of my strength and skill as a huntress!"

The redheaded runaway had also been transformed. A lightweight tunic of the finest white doeskin showed off her lithe figure. A quiver of silver arrows rested against her back. A polished wooden bow now occupied her hand. But more than just her attire and arms had changed; Holly herself had undergone a subtle metamorphosis. Slitted yellow eyes, tapered ears, and sharpened fangs gave her an unmistakably feline appearance. No longer just a sidekick or surrogate, Holly was now truly a catwoman.

"Uh . . . thanks?" she said uncertainly.

APOKOLIPS.

A blazing yellow bolt of lightning tore apart the turbid red sky, momentarily lighting up the wretched city below. Thunder reverberated across the Armagetto.

"Whoa!" Jason exclaimed. "That's not regular lightning!"

It most certainly is not, Donna thought. She and Jason watched the fireworks from the roof of the workhouse. The intense glare left spots dancing in her vision, but that wasn't all; Donna had dwelt too long among the

Amazons, as well as the Titans of Myth, not to recognize the power of the gods at work. She had seen lightning like this before.

"Shazam," she whispered.

Jason's eyes widened behind his mask. "You think . . . ?"

"Yep," Donna said. For the first time since the Monitor abandoned them, hope surged inside her. "I do."

Jason scratched his head. "But what would Captain Marvel be doing on Apokolips?"

Raising her hand to shield her eyes from the stormy sky above, Donna squinted at a forbidding stone edifice several blocks away. As nearly as she could tell, the mystical thunderbolt had struck one of Granny Goodness's notorious orphanages. Smoke and flames rose from the damaged building. A sign of the gods' displeasure?

"Let's find out," Donna said. Lifting Jason into her arms, she soared off the roof of the workhouse toward the site of the disaster.

Here's hoping lightning doesn't strike twice.

Granny Goodness fled her orphanage. An honor guard of Parademons accompanied the distressed crone as she scurried through the squalid alleys of the Armagetto. "This is a travesty!" she fumed aloud, aghast at the sheer ignominy of her retreat. "I can't believe those miserable vermin actually freed the gods!"

"Hurry, Granny!" the commander of the guard urged her. His goggled eyes nervously swept the vicinity. "We must get you to a safe location. Ahead lies Darkseid's keep, and no force in the universe, not even the Terran gods, can penetrate its defens—AWK!"

A silver arrow pierced his shoulder, cutting off his pleas. Granny looked up in dismay as Mary Marvel and her allies descended from the rooftop of an adjacent techno-temple. "Who you calling 'vermin,' you ugly old goat?" Holly jeered as she drew another arrow from her quiver. The three women fell upon the startled Parademons like the champions they were. Energy-blasts exploded uselessly against Mary's chest as her fist struck with the strength of Hippolyta herself. Harley swung her clown-sized mallet with devastating effect. Arrows flew from Holly's bow with superhuman speed and accuracy. *Holy Moley,* Mary thought. *She could give Green Arrow a run for his money!*

"Hey, Granny!" Harley hollered. "Why don't you act your age and die?"

The girls' startling transformations did not escape Granny's notice. "The gods . . . they gave you . . ."

"Superpowers!" Harley crowed. She walloped another Parademon with her mallet. "Pretty neat, huh?"

Granny abandoned her guards. "Sacrifice your lives for Granny!" she exhorted as she fled as fast as her aged legs could carry her. Rallying to the cause, the remaining guards formed a line to defend Granny's retreat. They aimed their rifles at the female invaders.

"Fire!" the highest-ranking lieutenant commanded. "For Granny!"

An arrow struck him in the forehead and he toppled lifelessly onto the pavement. His sudden demise shattered the resolve of the surviving Parademons, who broke ranks and fled frantically into the nearest murky alleys. Their dead and wounded comrades were left to the tender mercies of their foes.

"Holly!" Mary cried out in protest. "I said no killing!" She had been counting on Holly to keep Harley's homicidal tendencies in check, but it seemed that the redheaded catwoman had acquired some of the ruthlessness of Diana the Huntress along with her new weapons and abilities. *This could be a problem,* she thought.

Holly shrugged. "Get over it, kid. We're at war."

"Umm, guys," Harley interrupted. She peered down the grungy avenue before them. Clouds of noxious smog obscured the view. "The disease-ridden toilet-licker has run off."

"No problem." Holly sniffed the polluted air. "I've got her scent."

Harley made a face. *"Eww!"*

A low growl escaped Holly's lips as she sprinted down the alley after Granny. Harley hurried after her on foot, while Mary soared above the grimy pavement. "But seriously now," Harley asked, "you can really smell the old bag's trail?"

"Yes," Holly snarled, "and, actually, she *does* smell like a disease-ridden toilet-licker."

Mary found that way too much information. "Do I want to know how you know what that smells like?"

"I used to be a junkie," Holly admitted casually. "In another life." Her slitted eyes narrowed as she spotted her prey. "And there's our heifer, hoofing for that big building up there."

Darkseid's somber fortress loomed ahead of them. Mary suppressed a shudder as she recalled her previous visit to the Dark Lord's inner sanctum. Had that been only a few weeks ago? She flew faster, anxious to catch up with Granny before the evil old woman gained the safety of the stronghold. New powers or not, Mary was in no hurry to take on Darkseid himself again.

To be honest, she wasn't entirely sure what to do with Granny if and when they ran her to ground; it wasn't as if they could exactly turn her over to the local authorities. *Maybe we can just teach her a lesson before forcing her to send us back home?* She hoped, for the other girls' sake, if not for Granny's, that she could stop Holly and Harley from killing Granny in the name of the gods. *I can't let them get carried away with their new powers the way I was.*

But before the women could intercept Granny, a blinding light suddenly manifested in the desperate harridan's path. The intensity of the glare was such that Mary was forced to avert her eyes, but not before glimpsing the silhouette of a masculine figure at the center of the light. For a second, Mary thought that maybe Zeus himself had decided to personally punish Granny for her sins, but she sensed nothing familiar about the presence before her.

"Umm, who is that guy?" Harley asked. She and the other girls halted in their tracks, daunted by this unexpected new development. They backed away instinctively.

"I don't know," Holly said, "but I hope he's on our side."

Me too, Mary thought.

"You . . . ?" Granny blurted. Judging by the quaver in her voice, she recognized the newcomer. She threw up her gnarled hands in defense.

The unearthly voice that issued from the incandescent figure was not one that Mary had ever heard before. "Granny Goodness, your orphanage is in ruins; your world is on the brink of becoming something entirely new. The Fourth World ends and with it comes the extinction of the New Gods!"

A searing bolt of golden energy engulfed Granny, incinerating her instantly. Squinting into the glare with watery eyes, Mary caught a fleeting glimpse of the crone's charred skeleton before Granny's remains disinte- grated into ashes. Suddenly, stopping Mary's companions from killing the old woman was no longer an issue.

Granny Goodness was no more.

His work done, the luminous figure launched himself into the lurid red sky above, swiftly disappearing from sight. Mary didn't even think about flying after him.

Holy Moley! she thought. *What was that all about?*

The three girls stared speechlessly at the smoldering embers. "Wow!" Harley said finally. "It's like when the big fish eats the little fish and then a bigger fish eats the big fish. I know, 'cause I used to feed goldfish to Mister J's piranhas."

Holly sighed wearily. "Shut and up and stay away from that fire."

"I have powers now," Harley pouted, "so be nice!"

Mary's eyes gazed up at the heavens, where no trace of the killer's glow- ing trail remained. "Who was that?"

"Who cares?" Holly lowered her bow. "He saved us the trouble of offing Granny ourselves."

"That's great and all," Mary said. "But wasn't Granny our ticket home?"

Silence ensued as the truth sank in. Granted, Mary figured she could probably fly all the way back to Earth if she had to, like she had after defy- ing Eclipso. But, despite their sometimes annoying personalities, she wasn't about to leave the other two girls stranded on Apokolips. *Besides,* she thought, *last time, I had the magic of both Black Adam and Isis to speed me home. This time I wouldn't be able to rely on any powers other than my own.*

Harley could only manage to take their dilemma seriously for a moment or two. "Not to worry; we've got powers, remember? We can find another way." Turning away from Darkseid's fortress, she blithely took off down a random alley. "C'mon."

The humor in the situation was not lost on Mary. She exchanged a wry look with Holly. "We're back to following her again?"

Holly shrugged. "The good news is she tends to fall into—"

They rounded a corner and skidded to a halt, almost bumping into

Harley, who was staring goggle-eyed up at the sky, where an attractive brunette in a sparkly black leotard hovered above the alley. Her bare arms cradled a young man wearing a black leather jacket. A crimson domino mask concealed the youth's identity.

"Mary Marvel?" Donna Troy gasped in surprise.

9 AND COUNTING.

APOKOLIPS.

Darkseid removed Granny Goodness from the chessboard.

"The clock is counting down to its final moments," he declared. "Our game draws near its end, as does reality as we know it."

Solomon glowered at Darkseid from the other side of the board. "The death of the Fourth World does not concern you?"

"Unlike you, Monitor, my vision extends beyond the fifty-two realities." Darkseid repositioned Jimmy Olsen upon the board. "All things must end, true, but they will do so on my terms." He stepped back to take a look at the larger picture. "Take consolation in the fact that you never stood a chance against me."

"Your arrogance betrays you," Solomon accused. He reached for the Atom. "I still have pieces in play."

Ouch! the Atom thought as the Monitor's giant fingers squeezed his ribs. He clenched his teeth to keep from crying out as Solomon moved him across the board. The doll-sized hero tried not to move a muscle; the last thing he wanted was for Darkseid to realize that he wasn't just a playing piece but the genuine article. *All the better to spy on you, you monster.*

He still hadn't forgiven Solomon for murdering Barry Allen, but, where

Darkseid was concerned, it wasn't hard to figure out who the greater of the two evils was here. If the fearsome master of Apokolips had some nefarious new master plan in the works, the Atom wanted to know all about it.

Good thing I kept a miniaturized version of my costume in my belt buckle!

"You fool," Darkseid mocked the Monitor, seemingly oblivious to the deception going on right beneath his granite nose. "Don't you see? I have controlled both sides of the board from the beginning. What does it matter to me if the Fourth World ends in flame and fire? As long as the Fifth World is born in my own image!"

The Fifth World? The Atom resisted an urge to gulp. His tiny heart was pounding so hard he couldn't believe Darkseid couldn't hear it. *Darkseid wants to reshape all of reality?*

"We shall see, God of Deceit." Solomon plucked the Atom from the board and activated his transporter beam. A cascade of flickering quantum particles cast a veil between the Atom and the cavernous war room. "This game is not yet over."

Darkseid made no effort to prevent his opponent's departure. "Very well, Monitor. Make your final move." A glow appeared in his hand and he placed a figure of Solomon himself upon the board. "The end is finally upon us, and, as was inevitable, Darkseid shall triumph over all!"

The New God's merciless laughter rang in the Atom's ears as the Monitor teleported him away.

APOKOLIPS.

"**Donna** Troy?" Mary gasped.

Of all the beings she had expected to encounter in the fetid alleyways of the Armagetto, Wonder Woman's foster sister was nowhere on the list. Mary had fought beside Donna and the other Teen Titans before, and knew she could trust her, but what in heaven's name was Donna doing on Apokolips?

And who was that masked youth she was carrying?

"Okay," he cracked, "this isn't quite what I was expecting."

Tell me about it, Mary thought.

"Let's skip the pleasantries," Holly said. She lowered her bow, apparently recognizing the world-famous Titan as well. *"Please* tell me you have a Boom Tube!"

Harley waved at their fellow Earthlings. "Hi there!" She sounded positively starstruck by Donna's unexpected appearance. "Can I tell you how much I've always loved that outfit? The sparklies are *sooo* cool! Are they actual stars?"

Donna looked nonplussed by Harley's reaction. She descended to the pavement and put down her male companion. "Mary, who exactly are these people you're with?"

A hasty round of introductions followed as the two teams compared notes. Mary was surprised to learn that Jason Todd was alive again, but had to admit that he hardly looked like a corpse. More discouraging was the discovery that Donna and Jason were just as stranded on Apokolips as Holly and Harley were. *No way can I fly this entire gang back home,* Mary realized, *not even with my new powers.*

"Women's shelter and we fought each other," Harley babbled at Donna, telling the perplexed heroine more than she ever wanted to know about the other women's various misadventures, "and then we took this boat ride and fought these sea serpent things, and *then* we hit Paradise Island and we were Amazons, only Athena wasn't really Athena; she was this old bag who was, like, totally evil. . . ."

Holly cut to the chase. "So we're stuck here? Still?"

"Join the club!"

A new voice entered the discussion. Mary looked up in surprise to see . . . *Jimmy Olsen?*

At first she thought the towheaded reporter had been captured by a Parademon, but then she realized that the armored figure carrying Jimmy down from the sky looked slightly different from Darkseid's loyal shock troops. Filmy wings and twin antennae gave the flying woman a distinctly insectoid appearance. Her segmented armor was made of a glossy, shell-like material, as opposed to steel. A helmet concealed her features, so Mary couldn't tell if she was human or not. But she definitely seemed to be on Jimmy's side.

"Watch your step, my Olsenbug," the stranger buzzed as she carefully lowered him to the pavement. Her own boots touched down lightly beside him. Overlapping wings folded into the back of her thorax. "Do you know these humans?"

"You bet!" Jimmy said. A soiled set of coveralls, of the sort worn by many of Darkseid's slave laborers, suggested that he had been on Apokolips for a while. "Some of them, at least." He introduced his new girlfriend. "Forager, meet Mary Marvel and Donna Troy." He grinned at Mary. "Let me guess, that was your thunderbolt that ripped the roof off Granny's place?"

"Guilty as charged," she admitted, hoping that was all she would have to confess to. *Has he heard anything about my recent excesses back on Earth? Has Donna?* She took stock of the motley collection of characters assembled in the alley: *Superman's buddy, Catwoman's protégée, the Joker's ex, the original Wonder Girl, the second Robin, some sort of alien bug-lady, and me.*

"Holy Moley!" she exclaimed. "It's like a sidekicks convention . . . on Apokolips, no less!"

Donna arched an eyebrow. "That's one way to look at it, I guess."

"Watch who you're calling a sidekick," Jason grumbled.

Holly's hackles rose. "Never mind all that!" Feline claws extended from her fingertips. "How the hell are we getting out of here?" She fixed her slitted eyes on Jimmy. "Can't you whistle up a ride from Superman?"

"Sorry," Jimmy said, instinctively backing away from the agitated cat-woman. "I lost my signal-watch a while back."

"Terrific," Holly growled. "Just great." Her whiskers twitched irritably. "You'd think the gods would've offered us a ticket home along with the new duds and powers."

"The gods have larger matters to attend to," a booming voice rang out from above. A flash of shimmering energy caught Mary's eye, drawing her attention to a rusty fire escape overlooking the alley. A large alien figure materialized upon the metal landing, which creaked beneath his weight. Mary recognized the bearded entity from the original Crisis.

"Holy Moley! It's the Monitor!"

Donna and Jason immediately tensed for battle. "On your toes, people!" Jason warned. To Mary's surprise, he drew an automatic pistol from beneath his leather jacket. "Trust me, you don't want to turn your back on this creep!"

"Huh?" Holly blurted. Following Jason's lead, she fitted a silver arrow to her bow and took aim at the Monitor. Harley hefted her clown-sized mallet. "What the hell is a Monitor?"

Donna didn't bother to explain. She raised her silver bracelets defensively. "If you're here to spill any more blood, Solomon, we're ready for you!"

Blood, Mary thought? *Whose blood is Donna talking about?* She gave Donna a puzzled look. *I thought the Monitor was a good guy.*

"Spare me your hostile posturings," he said impatiently. "You humans think violence solves everything."

"You're the one who went berserk on Earth-51," Donna accused him, "then abandoned Jason and me here!"

"Your recriminations no longer bear any relevance," Solomon insisted. He gazed down on the misplaced mortals as though judging them from on high. His foreboding tone and expression raised goose bumps on Mary's skin. "Darkseid's insidious plans near fruition and drastic action is required if we are to prevent him from conquering all."

A tiny figure, unnoticed by Mary before, stirred upon the Monitor's shoulder. The inch-high human sprang from his perch, increasing in size with every second. By the time the brightly costumed hero landed nimbly on the ground among them, Mary realized that the Monitor's miniature passenger was none other than the Atom.

"He's telling the truth!" he confirmed. Glowing atomic orbitals whirled around him as he rapidly assumed his normal stature. "The entire universe is in terrible danger!"

A look of relief came over Donna's face. "Ray! You have no idea how glad I am to see that you're still okay." She rushed to see him. "But where did Solomon take you? What did you learn?"

"You may trade tales of your exploits later," the Monitor interrupted. "For now, there is nothing more to be accomplished here. It is time to return you to Earth for the final chapter of this cosmic drama."

"Thank God!" Holly exclaimed. "I have no idea who you are or what you're talking about, but, boy, am I ready to get off this stinking planet!"

"Are you sure?" Harley asked. "We haven't really seen all the sights yet. . . ."

Holly kicked the other girl in the shins.

"Wait a second," Jimmy protested. "I'm not going anywhere." His freckled face took on a more serious expression. "Forager and I came here for a reason. I'm not going anywhere until I find out what's happening to me— even if that means confronting Darkseid himself."

Donna stared at him in shock. "Confront Darkseid? You can't be serious!" She was obviously horrified by the very idea. "That's suicide, Jimmy!"

"No one is asking you to join me, Donna." His mind seemed made up. "I have to do this."

"But, Jimmy," Donna persisted, "you . . . against Darkseid? That's madness. You can't face him alone!"

"He shall not be alone!" Forager stood beside Jimmy defiantly. "Go your own way if you must. *We* have a war to finish and a god to kill!"

Mary was impressed by the insect-woman's loyalty, but couldn't help thinking that Donna had a point. "Think about what you're doing, Jimmy."

"You haven't been around," he replied. "You don't know what I've been through." His arms were crossed over his chest. "Darkseid is the answer. . . . I know it."

"You are correct, James Olsen," Solomon declared. "But Darkseid is not the only one who knows what part you play in his plans." Lifting off from the fire escape, he floated down to the floor of the alley to join the humans, who backed away apprehensively. Jason and Holly kept the dour alien in their sights. Forager shielded Jimmy with her body. "I too have the answers you are searching for."

Donna stepped forward to confront the Monitor. There was obviously bad blood between them. "Talk fast, Solomon."

"I have no reason to do otherwise." He pointed at Jimmy. "Olsen is the reservoir, the one place in the Multiverse, where Darkseid knew he could store certain . . . energies."

"The souls of the New Gods," Jimmy guessed. "*Darkseid* put them in me?"

The Monitor nodded. "He allowed them to be hidden inside you . . . until a time of his choosing when he will reclaim the souls for his own purposes."

"And my powers?" Jimmy asked.

"A precaution," Solomon explained, "to preserve your existence until Darkseid has need of you. Activated only when your life is in immediate jeopardy."

Jimmy ran his hand through his hair, overwhelmed by everything the Monitor was telling him. "Okay. I guess that makes sense—in a freaky sort of way. But why *me*?"

The Monitor frowned irritably. "Think, dolt! You are Superman's best friend. What better guarantee of protection against random dangers or the interference of other celestial entities? No doubt Darkseid took perverse amusement in the fact that Superman himself would be the unwitting guardian of his most precious pawn."

Jimmy's face paled as the truth sank in. "Because he knew Superman wouldn't let anything happen to me?"

"Indeed," the Monitor confirmed. "And when the New Gods are dead, and all their power resides in a single vessel, then Darkseid shall confiscate the power—and leave you lifeless!"

That sounds like Darkseid, all right, Mary thought. She took a certain comfort from finding out that she and the would-be Amazons on Paradise Island weren't the only ones who had been manipulated by Darkseid and his duplicitous minions lately. Apokolips's scheming ruler seemed to have a lot of irons in the fire these days. *All part of one vast master plan?*

She looked at Jimmy. "So, you still want to take on Darkseid, tough guy?"

"Confronting him is no longer an option," Solomon declared. "He is too close to his goal." He glowered at Jimmy. "If you try, I will personally destroy you to deprive Darkseid of the power contained within your pathetic mortal frame."

"You mean you'll try!" Jason snapped. He tried to rally the other heroes. "All right, folks. We've got the info we wanted. Let's off this backstabbing son of a bitch!"

"Okay!" Harley said cheerfully. She ran toward the Monitor, swinging her mallet. "Dibs on his skull!"

Donna yanked the hammer from Harley's grip. "Everybody, back off!" She appealed to reason. "I don't like Solomon any more than the rest of you, but we need to think this through!"

"Since when, Wonder Clone?" Harley grappled with Donna, like a kid groping for a favorite toy. "Gimme back my mallet!"

"You shortsighted apes!" the Monitor railed in exasperation. "The Fourth

World is dying and Olsen is Darkseid's key to survival, to total domination." He shook his fist at Jimmy. "I cannot allow him to have you!"

Jimmy gulped. "Now, hold on a second. . . ."

"Gimme! Gimme!" Harley squealed.

The Monitor lost his temper completely. "Damnable humans! Extinction looms and still you bicker endlessly! Exactly like my fellow Monitors, who dither while the Multiverse trembles on the brink of annihilation. Do you not see? Inaction is death!" His gauntlets flared brightly and golden spheres formed around Mary and the others. "You deserve extinction, in my view, but you shall have one last chance to avoid that fate." He shouted at the fearsome citadel towering in the distance. "Darkseid, bear witness to my final move!"

"Wait!" Mary shouted. "What are you doing?"

"Ooh!" Harley momentarily forgot about her purloined hammer. "Pretty lights!"

The humans disappeared from sight.

8 AND COUNTING.

METROPOLIS.
EARTH-ONE.

"Ohmigosh!" Jimmy blurted. "We're home!"

He and his new companions suddenly found themselves atop the Daily Planet Building, right back where he and Forager had started out weeks ago. They scrambled to keep their footing atop the huge, slowly spinning bronze globe. Forager grabbed on to Jimmy's hand to keep him from slipping on the inclined surface beneath their feet. A magnificent view of Metropolis was spread out before them beneath a clear blue sky. A crisp winter breeze rustled Jimmy's hair. Compared to the fetid alleys and smoggy miasma of Apokolips, the sunlit city looked like heaven on Earth.

"That all-knowing bastard!" Jason Todd cursed the Monitor. "Who does that guy think he is, just zapping us around the Multiverse like this?" He braced himself against the back of the huge steel I in the *Daily Planet* logo girding the globe. "I'm sick of this crap!"

Jimmy barely knew Jason, but he had already figured out that the embittered vigilante had a real chip on his shoulder. Still, he wasn't sure he disagreed with Jason on this point. "I don't understand," Jimmy said. "Why explain what's happened to me, what I've become, only to dump us right back at the beginning?"

"Lesson I've learned in this show," Donna advised him. "Never trust a Monitor."

"Or a goddess!" Harley griped. She looked back and forth between herself and Holly in dismay. Her jester's helmet had disappeared, along with her monster-sized hammer. Both women were now clad in armored breastplates and leather skirts straight out of ancient Greece, so that they looked like extras from some cheesy female gladiator movie. "Those sneaky Olympians took our powers back!"

"Looks like it," Holly agreed. No longer feline in appearance, she was now just a tough-looking redhead with a thick Gotham accent. She balanced nimbly atop the rotating globe. "Guess the gods figure they got what they wanted."

Harley scowled. "Drag. That giganto hammer they gave me made me look totally cool."

"It was a mallet," Holly corrected her. "And it made you look like a melon-squashing comedian."

Harley shrugged her shoulders like she didn't think that was such a bad thing. "You say tomato; I say giganto. . . ."

Mary Marvel ignored the other girls' banter. She looked worriedly at the Atom, who was gazing dolefully out at the familiar skyline before them. His troubled expression was obvious even through his blue cowl. He didn't seem all that happy to be home. "Ray . . . are you gonna be okay?"

"How about I get back to you on that?" he replied.

Jason seemed unconcerned with the Atom's state of mind. "So, is that it? Is this stupid wild-goose chase over yet?" He peeled his domino mask from his face. "We can start getting back to our lives now, right?"

"Um, hello?" Jimmy tapped his own chest. "Did we all forget the Darkseid bait dangling inside me?"

"Holy Moley!" Mary exclaimed. "That's right." She pouted, sounding almost as fed up as Jason. Although he didn't know the details, Jimmy got the impression that this adventure had been unusually hard on her. "Is this nightmare ever going to end?"

"Gods, I hope so," Donna said.

The Atom shook himself out of his dolor. "Okay, if we're going to do something about Jimmy, standing around on top of the Daily Planet all day won't be much help. I say we take him straight to the Justice League." He looked over the motley crew of sidekicks and hangers-on. "No offense to anyone here, but, from what I heard on Apokolips, we're in the big leagues now."

"None taken," Donna assured him. "Sounds like a plan to me." She turned toward Holly and Harley. "If you girls want to opt out of this, no one will fault you."

"Thanks," Holly replied. "To be honest, I'm not sure how much help we'd be now that the gods have revoked our powers. This whole thing is getting way too cosmic for me." She grabbed Harley by the hand and led her toward a maintenance hatch hidden behind the P in Planet. "C'mon, Harley. We're outta here."

Jimmy was kind of glad to see them go. He hadn't forgotten, although Harley apparently had, that the pigtailed blonde had once stalked him back during her loopy super-villain days. *I'll bet she doesn't want to get anywhere near Batman and rest of the Justice League.*

"Tootle-loo, kiddies!" Harley waved good-bye as she and Holly disappeared down the hatch. "Don't forget to write!"

Good riddance, Jimmy thought.

"You know," Mary said, somewhat sheepishly, "I hope you don't think I'm deserting you too, but I desperately need to know what happened after I left Paradise Island." She lifted off the roof and floated upward into the sky. "Plus, I really want to check in with my family."

It dawned on Jimmy that nobody had seen Captain Marvel or Captain Marvel Jr. since that big fight with Black Adam several months ago. He wondered what had become of them. "Yeah, of course," he called out to Mary. "Don't sweat it."

"Thanks, Jimmy!" Mary said. "Catch up with you later!"

She zipped away, quickly disappearing from sight. *Funny,* he mused, *I thought Paradise Island was the other direction.*

In any event, he hoped she found what she was looking for.

FAWCETT CITY.

Mary Batson, she scolded herself. *You are such a liar.*

The rent on the small apartment had been paid forward for at least a year. Billy's doing, no doubt. Mary pulled on a clean sweater as she headed to the fridge and helped herself to a can of soda. A hot bubble bath had helped put the stench of Apokolips behind her. A pop album played softly on her stereo.

Paradise Island. Yeah, right. The way she figured it, Hippolyta surely had everything under control on Themyscira now that Granny Goodness was dead meat. She didn't need Mary's help to straighten out a bunch of confused, powerless Amazon wannabes. *But I couldn't exactly tell Jimmy and the rest that I just needed a break from everyone else's problems.*

A twinge of guilt pricked her conscience. *Is this some leftover Eclipso or something?* she fretted. *Am I being selfish?*

"Nah," she assured herself. As far as she was concerned, she had paid her dues, and atoned for her dip into the dark side, by freeing the gods, helping to liberate Paradise Island, and getting Holly and Harley back to Earth alive. Let the Justice League deal with Darkseid from now on. "I just need a little 'me time' to relax and recharge my batteries."

"Is that what you call it?" an impossibly deep voice said in amusement.

Mary recognized the voice at once. The can of soda slipped from her fingertips, falling unnoticed onto the kitchen floor, as she turned in shock toward the open doorway behind her. Beyond the threshold, a startling sight greeted her eyes.

Darkseid was sitting in her living room, reclining comfortably in the comfy faux-leather easy chair she had picked up at Goodwill a few years back. The TV remote was sitting on the coffee table in front of him, as though he had just settled in to watch something on cable. The sheer incongruity of the image left her flabbergasted.

"Hello, Mary," he said calmly. "You didn't think I had forgotten about you, did you?"

Overcoming her shock, she reacted quickly. "Shazam!"

Thunder boomed and a mystic lightning bolt smashed through the window. Arms akimbo, Mary Marvel faced her unwelcome visitor defiantly. Smoke rose from the scorched carpet at her feet.

"In my home? How dare you?"

Her dramatic transformation did not rattle him one bit. "Darkseid dares all."

"What are you doing here?" she demanded.

"A simple matter, really." He leaned forward. "In your final battle with Eclipso, you left a little something behind."

He held out his hand, and Mary braced herself for an attack, but then she spied the tiny black sphere, no larger than a pearl, gripped between his thick fingers. A pulsating dark radiance emanated from the sphere, which appeared to be composed entirely of roiling black energy. The presence of the sphere made Mary's skin tingle. She felt drawn to it.

"W-what's that?" she gulped. Her clenched fists dropped limply to her sides.

"I believe you know very well what this is," Darkseid said. "It's your power."

"No . . . I have my power." Tearing her gaze away from the glowing pearl, she turned her back on Darkseid. She crossed her arms over her chest. A quaver in her voice undermined the determination she tried so hard to project. "The gods gave it back to me!"

"They gave you a degree of power," he conceded, "but not what you possessed when last we met. You are *diminished*. The gods no longer fully trust you. They have lost their faith in you." He chuckled mercilessly. "You know I'm right. You can feel it, can't you?"

A mirror on the opposite wall offered Mary a glimpse of her reflection. The dark gray thunderbolt on her chest, no longer shining brightly golden as before, seemed to confirm the gods' altered opinion of her, that she was now tainted in their eyes. *Who's to say they won't withdraw their power from me again?* she worried. *Like they did with Holly and Harley?*

She could feel the power of the black pearl tugging at her. Her heart pounded at the thought of claiming that power once more. Her face flushed with both shame and excitement.

"No! I don't care!" She glared back at Darkseid over her shoulder, while carefully averting her gaze from the alluring poison in his hand. "That little ball of evil is . . . well, it's evil! And that's not me!"

"So you say, Mary." He rose from the chair. The floorboards creaked beneath his heavy tread as he came up behind her, still holding out the miniature sphere. "But let me ask: When you held this power, did you *feel* evil?"

Not exactly, she thought. *Maybe a little reckless sometimes, but was that really so bad?* She couldn't resist sneaking a peek at the pearl, then discovered that she couldn't look away. Slowly, almost against her will, she turned around to face Darkseid. The tempting sphere hovered above his outstretched palm, only a few inches away from her face. All she had to was reach out and take it. . . .

"Remember, Mary," Darkseid urged her. "Remember how you really felt."

A tear leaked down Mary's cheek. She couldn't deny the yearning deep within her. "I felt . . . strong," she admitted hoarsely, her voice barely more than a whisper. "I felt stronger and more confident than I ever had before."

Or since.

Darkseid smiled in approval. "You see, evil is a mere abstraction. A matter of perception." He stepped forward, bringing the tantalizing sphere even closer. "Do you hear it, Mary? How it sings to you? Calls to you? Take it. Be complete. Be strong once more."

Mary's hand reached tentatively for his gift, even as she wrestled painfully with her conscience. She remembered how the gods had cruelly "tested" her before, how the Monitor had effortlessly transported her across the cosmos without even asking her permission. Would he have been able to do that if she had still possessed the power Darkseid now offered her? Even with her original powers restored, it seemed that she remained at the mercy of powerful entities who treated her like a pawn in their cosmic games. A sob tore itself from her throat as she faced the awful truth.

I'm still just as helpless as before. . . .

Her fingers hesitated above the shimmering sphere. Her heart ached for the strength and confidence it promised her. She had never wanted anything so much in her life, not even all those enticing magical talismans back at Zatanna's mansion weeks ago. *I'm so sorry,* she thought. *I can't help myself. . . .*

Swallowing hard, she stretched her fingers toward the pearl, only to have Darkseid withdraw it slightly. She experienced a moment of panic as he closed his fingers around the sphere, hiding it from her sight. *No,* she thought frantically. *Don't take it away!*

"All I require is one tiny favor," he insisted.

Mary didn't care anymore. *I resisted Eclipso in the end,* she rationalized. *I can turn the tables on Darkseid too, when the time is right.*

But first she *had* to have her power back.

"All right," she consented. "Whatever you say."

He opened his hand and Mary eagerly seized her prize.

Yes!

Thunder boomed once more. Lightning flashed.

Black clouds gathered over the city.

PARADISE ISLAND.

Hippolyta, adorned in all her queenly raiment, watched from atop a rocky outcropping in the harbor as her new subjects labored to remove the last remnants of Granny Goodness's harsh regime from Themyscira's sacred shores. Teams of eager young women, singing merrily as they worked, tore down the false goddess's ugly barracks, watchtowers, and barbed wire fences while their sisters helped restore the island's marble temples and palaces. Waves lapped gently against the slick stone pedestal beneath her sandals. Seabirds circled overhead beneath Apollo's heavenly chariot. The fresh air held an invigorating salty tang.

The work goes well, she thought. After driving the pretender from her realm, she had been pleased to discover that the homeless young women left behind were more confused than corrupted. Although they were not true Amazons, they had readily embraced the ideals and values of the Sisterhood once Hippolyta had shown them the truth. Even Granny's favored ones, her newly christened "Female Furies," had seen the light after the pretender's true nature was exposed. Indeed, there had proved to be much dissatisfaction with Granny's brutal discipline hiding within the hearts of her misguided followers. None mourned her departure.

Hippolyta was not certain how many of the girls would ultimately choose to remain on Themyscira, but for now she was happy to offer them sanctuary. As far as she was concerned, they were her responsibility now.

Let it be as the gods will. . . .

A cloud passed before the sun, casting an unexpected shadow over the hopeful scene. Thunder rumbled in the distance and a sudden chill fell over her soul. Deep in her heart, she sensed the gods' displeasure—and the seduction of a heroine. Her sorrowful eyes turned toward the distant horizon.

"Oh, Mary," she whispered sadly. "What have you done?"

7 AND COUNTING.

WASHINGTON, D.C.

The Hall of Justice occupied the grassy Mall in the middle of the nation's capital, not far from the Smithsonian and the Lincoln Memorial. A gleaming steel and glass structure, flanked by twin rectangular towers, the world-famous headquarters of the Justice League of America, Earth's premier super-hero team, was an impressive sight that drew visitors from all over the world. An angular piece of modern art, evoking Superman's crystalline fortress in the Arctic, rose from the center of the pellucid reflecting pool in front of the Hall. Three-story-high bas-reliefs of Justice herself, complete with blindfold and scales, embossed the bronze façades of the twin towers, while the central building, whose shape resembled a rising sun, arched gracefully before the horizon, like a shining steel rainbow promising hope for the future. Throngs of tourists were lined up in front of the main entrance of the Hall, which, besides being the JLA's official meeting place, also served as a museum showcasing the League's myriad trophies and accomplishments.

The design of the elegant building, Donna knew, had been a collaboration between Wonder Woman and the JLA's resident architect, John Stewart, aka Green Lantern. As she and her allies descended toward the Hall, she couldn't help admiring her foster sister's work. *Let's hope that Diana and the rest of the League are in attendance today,* she thought, *and not defending an alien planet on the other side of the galaxy.*

"Here we are," the Atom muttered. Only two inches tall, he held on to her raven locks as he perched upon her shoulder. "Oh boy."

She couldn't miss the apprehension in his voice. "Something the matter, Ray?"

"Just a little nervous about seeing the rest of the League again," he admitted. Before disappearing two years ago, the Atom had been a longtime member of the team. "I just vanished before, never told them I was leaving or . . . Well, there's a lot I need to explain."

I'm sure nobody blames you, Donna thought. After everything Ray Palmer had endured, thanks to his lunatic ex, she felt confident that his former teammates would understand and sympathize with his desire to seek a new life elsewhere. *I've felt the same way at times.*

She opened her mouth to say as much, but Jason spoke up first. "Yeah, I get that and feel for ya, but you're going to have to be angsty some other time." Jason was cradled in Donna's arms as they flew toward the Hall. His domino mask was once more affixed to his face. A few yards away, Forager transported Jimmy through the air. "Darkseid, man. Remember?"

"I know," the Atom said solemnly. They touched down on the Mall, before a mob of gaping tourists, who hurried to snap photos of the newly arrived heroes with their cell phones and portable cameras. "Okay . . . let's yank the Band-Aid off and get this over with already."

"Oh, it's over all right!"

Without warning, thunder boomed and a sizzling lightning bolt struck the ground at the Challengers' feet. The jolt knocked Donna off her feet, causing her to lose her grip on Jason, who swore loudly as he tumbled onto the shattered pavement. The Atom was flung from her shoulder. Jimmy Olsen yelped a few feet away, while Forager buzzed in alarm.

What in Hera's name? Dazed, Donna scrambled to her feet. The sudden glare of the thunderbolt left blue spots dancing before her vision. Her ears rang with the echo of the deafening thunderclap, which had seemingly burst from a clear blue sky. A chill fell over her as dark clouds abruptly obscured the sun. Frightened tourists fled in panic. Donna looked up in amazement at the source of the disturbance. "You?!"

Mary Marvel hovered in the air above the reflecting pool, but the teenage heroine looked very different than she had only hours ago. Her traditional white and gold uniform had been replaced by a slinky black number that struck Donna as better suited to a villainous femme fatale than the virginal young sidekick she remembered. Her long brown hair blew wildly in the wind. A cruel smirk transformed her formerly girlish features. Lightning slashed through the suddenly stormy sky above her.

Donna blinked in disbelief, almost at a loss for words. "But . . . ?"

"But nothing!" Mary said arrogantly. "Mary Marvel's back in black . . . and better than ever!"

"I don't understand," Donna protested. What could have happened to Mary in the short time they had been apart? "You've faced evil before and won. Why this? Why now?"

Mary flew toward her. "You're right. I was tempted by evil, not too long ago, but that was all Eclipso's influence. *She* was evil, not this power. The power's what I make of it!" Her malevolent glee belied her words. "I'm not evil, Donna. I'm driven!"

She fired another lightning bolt, but this time Donna dodged the blast. An unlucky patch of lawn was seared to a crisp.

"Oh, honey." Donna raised her Amazonian bracelets defensively. "Listen to yourself! Can't you tell that you're making a terrible mistake?"

"I haven't done anything wrong!" Mary insisted. "I've just taken back what's mine. This power belongs to me. Darkseid understands that. And all he wants in return is"—she pointed her finger at Jimmy—"him!"

Darkseid? Donna thought. Her heart sank at the realization that the evil New God had somehow seduced Mary Marvel over to his side. *I should have realized he was behind this.*

"Me?" Jimmy flinched as Mary targeted him. "Aw, come on!"

Forager stepped in front of Jimmy. "You will not hurt the Olsenbug! You will not even touch him!" Her wings vibrated indignantly. She shook an armored fist at Mary. "You shall have to kill me first!"

"Not a problem!" Mary slammed feetfirst into the pavement, only inches away from the fierce insect-woman. The impact shattered the concrete and sent both Forager and Jimmy flying backward across the plaza. Chunks of pulverized cement exploded across the open area like shrapnel. Heavy frag-

ments splashed down into the reflecting pool. Tepid water sprayed everywhere. Clouds of gritty dust billowed upward.

Donna realized that there was no reasoning with Mary. "Jason!" she
called out as she reluctantly rushed to battle. "We can't let her get Jimmy!"

"Yeah!" Gun in hand, he charged after her across the wreckage. "I'm
on it!"

Forager was way ahead of them, though. Already recovered from
Mary's initial assault, she lunged at their former ally. "Do not underestimate me!" The two women traded blows amidst the debris, while Jimmy
looked on in dismay. "I've faced a thousand Parademons, and yet I live to
fight on!"

Mary was unimpressed. She blocked Forager's punch with her left
arm, then delivered a titanic right cross that propelled Forager straight into
the nearby Washington Monument. The insect-woman's chitinous armor
smacked loudly against the towering marble obelisk. "In case you haven't
noticed, bugsy," Mary gloated, "you're way out of your league!"

Donna feared Mary was not exaggerating, at least where Forager was
concerned. *Mary never used to be able to fling lightning from her fingertips,* she
thought. *What other new powers has Darkseid endowed her with?*

"I don't want to hurt you, Mary!" Donna shouted as she slammed her
own super-strong fist into Mary's jaw, staggering the out-of-control heroine.
Distracted by her victory over Forager, Mary hadn't even seen the blow coming. "But we can't let you have Jimmy!"

A few yards away, Jason took up a defensive position in front of Jimmy.
Brandishing his Glock semiautomatic, he tried to get a clean shot at Mary.
"Get the lead out, Olsen!" he barked. "Power up already!"

"I can't!" Jimmy cried out. "It only works when my life's in danger . . . and
I don't think she means to kill me!" He watched helplessly as an angry Mary
grappled with Donna high above the trashed plaza. Fury contorted Mary's
face. Grabbing on to Donna's throat, she savagely attempted to throttle the
other heroine with her gloved hands. Jimmy gulped at Mary's crazed expression. "Not sure she feels the same way about you guys, though . . ."

"Let go of her!" Jason yelled. Gunfire blared as he emptied the Glock
at the back of Mary's head. The bullets bounced harmlessly off her glossy
scalp, but the distraction allowed Donna to break free of the other woman's

stranglehold. Twisting from Mary's grip, she retreated to catch her breath. Ugly bruises mottled her smooth neck.

"Please, Mary!" Her fingers gently massaged her injured throat. "Let us help you!"

"I don't need your help!" Mary snarled, outraged by the mere suggestion. Shrugging off the blistering fusillade of bullets, she dived at Jason, even as the trigger-happy vigilante slammed a fresh cartridge into his gun. "I'm sick of you, my brother, Zatanna, Klarion, and all your condescending attitudes!" She was only seconds away from smashing into Jason like a missile in a miniskirt. "Well, look who's helpless now!"

Right before she hit him, however, the jagged iron sculpture from the center of the reflecting pool came plowing into her from the side. The massive projectile knocked her off course, sparing Jason by a matter of inches, and rammed her into the base of the Hall's western tower. Iron crashed against the reinforced bronze plating, crushing Mary between them. The clang of crumpled metal rang out across the Mall.

Donna heaved a sigh of relief. Standing atop the sculpture's star-shaped pedestal, she lowered her arms, grateful that she had managed to hurl the one-ton piece of artwork at Mary in time. "Well, I suppose that bought us a few seconds."

"Thanks!" Jason hollered. He glanced irritably at the Hall of Justice. Metal barricades had descended over the exterior glass windows, to protect both the building and any visitors trapped inside, but there was no sign of any reinforcements coming to their aid. "Hey, Donna, how is it we're having a knock-down, drag-out right on the JLA's doorstep and they're nowhere to be found?"

"Guess they're busy elsewhere," Donna said. She wondered if maybe Mary—or Darkseid—was using some sort of arcane magic or super-science to block any alarm signals coming from the headquarters. Thankfully, any innocent bystanders had already fled the Mall, although Donna heard the sirens of emergency vehicles converging on the scene. A news helicopter arrived to capture the breaking story from above. Donna guessed that neither the police nor the media were likely to intimidate Mary. "I think we're on our own."

Jason spat in disgust. "Typical." Holding on tightly to his gun, he hurried to Jimmy's side. "Screw the League, then! I'm grabbing Olsen and getting him as far away from her as I can."

Good idea, Donna thought. She doubted that one big chunk of metal would be enough to put Mary Marvel down for the count, especially now that Darkseid had supersized her powers somehow. "Speaking of MIA, where'd the Atom run off to?" She quickly scanned the debris-strewn battleground, but failed to spot the miniature hero. Was he lying unconscious somewhere, too tiny to be seen readily, or had his nerve failed him in the end? The Ray Palmer of old, the stalwart member of the Justice League, would have never deserted his allies like this, and yet . . . was it possible that the tragic events of recent years had broken his spirit more than any of them had realized? "I hope he didn't desert us," she murmured.

She didn't want to think so, but then again, she had never expected Mary Marvel to go bad either. . . .

The screams of twisted metal seized her attention. Electricity crackled over the surface of the mangled iron sculpture as Mary brusquely tossed Donna's improvised missile aside. She rose from the battered base of the tower, brushed off her skirt, and ascended into the sky above the plaza. Her hair was a trifle mussed, but otherwise she looked alarmingly unscathed. Pissed-off blue eyes glared down at Donna and the others.

"Enough's enough!" she said testily. "I have a promise to keep, and I intend to keep it."

"A promise to Darkseid?" Donna challenged her. "A promise that could cost Jimmy his life?"

Mary shrugged off Donna's accusations. "Heru!" she called out, imploring the ancient Egyptian deity better known to the West as Horus. "Lend me your speed!"

Donna glanced anxiously at Jimmy. Jason was tugging on the towheaded reporter's arm, trying to hustle him away from the Mall, but Jimmy appeared understandably reluctant to abandon Forager, who was sprawled upon the chipped pavement surrounding the Washington Monument. "Here," Jimmy urged the groggy insect-woman as he crouched beside her, assisting her to a sitting position. "Let me help you."

"Come on!" Jason said impatiently. "Get a move on!"

But not even Donna was fast enough to stop Mary Marvel. Moving so swiftly that she was nothing more than a satiny black blur, she whooshed down from the sky and snatched Jimmy away from his guardians before Donna or anyone else could even catch a breath. She zoomed away at lightning speed, leaving the thunderstruck Challengers behind. Within a heartbeat, both Mary and her captive were completely out of sight.

"Nooo!" Forager shrieked. She reached out desperately, but Jimmy was long gone.

Jason kicked the pavement. "Dammit!"

Donna shared their frustration. Flying over to join her remaining companions, she vented aloud. "I don't believe this! After everything we've been through, just to lose him to Darkseid like this . . . !"

"No." Forager climbed to her feet. Her armor was cracked and scuffed, but her resolve was apparently still intact. Twin antennae quivered passionately. "I shall track the Olsenbug," she vowed, shaking her fist at the heavens. "And I will find where that black-hearted witch and Darkseid have taken him . . . even if it leads us to the very end of Creation!"

Donna was impressed by her courage and determination, which would have done an Amazon proud.

"All right," Donna said. "But first we need some serious backup."

6 AND COUNTING.

OUTSIDE METROPOLIS.

"Olsen," Darkseid greeted him. "How nice to see you again."

Jimmy was backed up against the wall of a rocky gorge somewhere in the Blue Mountains northwest of Metropolis. Darkseid gazed down at Jimmy from a ledge overlooking the narrow ravine, while Mary Marvel stood by on a lower ridge. She didn't look at all guilty about delivering the frightened reporter into Darkseid's clutches.

I don't understand, Jimmy thought. *She wasn't like this on Apokolips!*

"Darkseid," Jimmy replied, trying hard not to tremble. "I—I'm not afraid of you."

His show of defiance provoked a laugh from the arch-villain. "Ha! I admit you've been a source of great amusement to me these past months, James Olsen, but now the time has come to take back that which I have given you: the souls of the New Gods." He extended his hand, which glowed ominously. "Don't worry. It *will* be very painful."

Jimmy could just imagine. Vivid memories of Lightray's and Sleez's butchered corpses, with smoking holes in their chests, flashed before his mind's eye. But he wasn't about to beg for mercy. If this was truly the end, he was going down fighting—just like Superman would.

"Yeah? Good luck with that," he challenged Darkseid. "Or did you forget that I've got powers now too?"

He threw out his arms, and pictured a volley of razor-sharp quills piercing Darkseid's stony gray flesh. He visualized his legs stretching like taffy, carrying him up and away from the lonely ravine. He tried to call upon the astounding speed he had tapped into once upon a time in Metropolis. Heck, he was even willing to dissolve into jelly again.

But nothing happened.

"Indeed, you have great power," Darkseid conceded, "so long as I permit it."

Twin beams shot from his eyes, blasting apart the rugged terrain beneath Jimmy's feet. Reeling backward, Jimmy threw up his hands to protect his eyes as granite splinters pelted his face. His butt landed hard on the uneven floor of the gorge.

"Give it up, red," Mary advised him. She sounded like she thought she had his best interests at heart. "Why drag this out when you don't stand a hell of a chance?"

"I'm disappointed to hear such language coming from you, Mary," a familiar voice scolded her. Hope flared brightly in Jimmy's heart as he spotted Superman flying down from the sky, faster than a speeding bullet. The Man of Steel's powerful right fist collided with Darkseid's chin, sending the startled villain flying from his rocky perch, while Mary Marvel nearly jumped out of her high black boots in surprise. Superman cast a disapproving glance in her direction. "You could really use a better role model!"

Forager came bounding into the gorge after Superman. "Olsenbug!" Her eyes and antennae anxiously searched his face for injuries as she hugged him so hard his ribs hurt. Her armored helmet failed to conceal her relief at finding him again. Fluttery wings retracted into her back.

"Superman!" Jimmy exclaimed. "Boy, am I glad to see you! But how . . . ?"

"Donna contacted me via the Hall of Justice," he explained. "Darkseid blocked my telescopic vision somehow, but, thanks to Forager, we were able to track you down." Landing in the gorge between Jimmy and Darkseid, who was even now rising ponderously back onto his feet, Superman stood ready to do battle with the sinister New God. "The rest of you should back away and find someplace safe." The bright red S on his chest contrasted sharply with the sinister darkness of Darkseid's and Mary's attire. His scarlet cape rustled in the cold mountain breeze. "This is about to get ugly."

Less than fifty yards away, amidst a pile of fresh rubble, Darkseid faced his foe. "Kryptonian," he snarled. "Do you mean to confront me alone?" He sneered mockingly. "I'm a touch insulted. I'd have expected the entire Justice League to rain down upon me at once."

"They're tied up right now with a living tsunami on the planet Rann," Superman said. "But there's no need to wait for them. This is between you and me. You had the New Gods murdered, didn't you? And now you're going after Jimmy." Superman didn't often lose his temper, but Jimmy could tell from his tone that the hero was genuinely angry. "The way I see it, it's past time for me to put you down for good."

"You're mistaken, Kryptonian," Darkseid answered. "The end of the New Gods is the Source's doing, not my own, but I alone shall survive to rule over the Fifth World to come, and nothing you can do shall stop me!"

His Omega Beams struck the ground, triggering a massive earthquake that caused the wall of the gorge to crumble. An avalanche of shattered stone came roaring down the side of the mountain. "Jimmy!" Superman shouted, momentarily looking away from Darkseid. He looked torn between rescuing Jimmy and guarding him from Darkseid and Mary. "Your defensive powers?"

Jimmy tried to stretch to safety, but to no avail; his fragile limbs remained stubbornly inelastic. "Darkseid turned them off! I can't. . . !"

"Fear not!" Forager threw herself atop Jimmy, shielding him with her armored form. Heavy boulders bounced off her back and shoulders. "I will get the Olsenbug to safety!"

"Aww, that's sweet," Mary Marvel jeered sarcastically. Heedless of the falling debris, she launched herself at Jimmy and Forager, even as Superman struck back against her malevolent master. "But who's gonna save you?"

The ground shook as Superman waded forward against the full force of Darkseid's fearsome Omega Beams until he was right up in the villain's face. The searing radiation hurt almost as much as kryptonite, but Superman kept on coming. "If that's your best shot, Darkseid, you might as well give up right now."

"Oh, you needn't concern yourself with that." Darkseid blocked Superman's strong right fist with his beefy arm. Seizing the hero's shoulders, he shoved Superman down onto his back. "I only wished to bring you close enough to—"

Superman's eyes flashed crimson. A brilliant burst of heat vision struck the villain's face, blinding him. "Close enough to what?" Springing to his feet, Superman grabbed on to Darkseid's craggy face with his bare hand and flung him halfway across the ravine. The capsized New God crashed upside down into a granite cliff face. A landslide buried Darkseid beneath a heap of rubble. Seismic meters all over the state jumped in alarm.

I have to admit that felt good, Superman thought. He had foiled Darkseid's nefarious schemes, and battled his vicious minions, numerous times over the years, but Darkseid himself had usually refrained from getting his own hands dirty, preferring to manipulate events rather than engage in hand-to-hand combat with "lesser" beings. Too many of their past encounters had ended in frustrating stalemates, with Darkseid grudgingly returning to Apokolips to plot anew. *Not this time,* Superman resolved. *It's about time we finally went to head-to-head. If Darkseid wants Jimmy, he's going to have to take me on personally.*

An explosion of cosmic energy blew apart the mountain of debris on top of Darkseid. The cataclysmic shock wave hurled Superman into the air, rocketing him into the side of the mountain. Stunned by the force of the blast, he rolled downhill into the battle-scarred ravine, where Darkseid waited at the center of a newly carved crater. Fury had replaced hauteur upon the villain's features as he glowered wrathfully at the Man of Steel. Incarnadine energy crackled around his clenched fists. "You dare lay hands on mighty Darkseid?" he roared. "YOU DARE?!"

"Yeah, I do dare." Shaking off the effects of the explosion, Superman flew at Darkseid. His tattered red cape flapped behind him. His knuckles pounded into Darkseid's face. Black blood sprayed from the villain's lips as his head was knocked to one side. "Guess I'm just not a big fan of murderous tyrants!"

With no thought for his own safety, Superman hammered away at his foe.

Less than ten yards away, Forager sprang as nimbly as a grasshopper, deftly evading Mary Marvel's angry fists, while Jimmy Olsen looked on desperately, wishing there was something he could do to help. "Keep still, dammit!" Mary cursed in frustration. Her swinging fist took a chunk out of a large gray boulder, but missed Forager completely. Mary looked like a frustrated exterminator chasing after an annoying cockroach. All she needed was a giant flyswatter.

"Never!" Forager replied. She used Mary's own shoulder as a brace to flip over the frustrated ex-heroine while delivering a savage kick to Mary's rear as she landed nimbly behind the other female. "Only when the last breath of life leaves me will I—"

"Fair enough!" Mary interrupted. Running out of patience, she unleashed a blast of bright blue electricity that jolted Forager like the world's biggest bug-zapper. The insect-woman convulsed in shock before dropping limply to the ground. Her body twitched spasmodically amidst the dust and rocks.

"Wow." Mary grinned at her victim. Her electrified hair settled back down over her shoulders. The azure sparks surrounding her svelte form slowly flickered away. "What an annoying pest!"

Jimmy stared in horror at Forager's collapsed body. She was moving, at least, which meant she was still alive, but just how badly had Mary hurt her? Worse than Bernadeth back on Apokolips?

He couldn't believe that it was really Mary Marvel who had done this. *She's Captain Marvel's sister for Pete's sake!* he thought. *It's like Supergirl going bad!*

"You've become a monster!" he accused her.

"Oh, whatever, Jimbo." Turning her back on Forager, she strode calmly toward Jimmy. "It's not like *I'm* going to kill you." There was no trace of mercy in her eyes or voice. "Just hang tight until Darkseid finishes up with your pal, so *he* can kill you. Cool?"

Jimmy backed away fearfully.

"Not cool!" Donna Troy declared as she leapt down into the gorge. Her boots slammed into Mary's back, smacking her facedown into the ground. Looking up in relief, Jimmy saw Jason Todd standing on the ridge above him. Jimmy guessed that Donna had flown him here. "Sorry not to get here sooner," she apologized. "But you try keeping up with Superman!"

Mary threw Donna off her and clambered to her feet. She shook the grit from her hair as she faced off against Jimmy and his latest defenders. Her irate face was caked with powdered stone, but wasn't even bruised. "You should've stayed out of this, Donna!"

"No way, Mary." Donna raised her fists as she got between Mary and Jimmy. Jason scrambled down the side of ridge to join them. "This is it. We tried to talk sense into you, but you wouldn't listen."

"Yeah, you've got this coming, bitch!" Jason added.

Mary snickered. "You think you and the Boy Wonder there can take me down?" She wiped off her face and clapped the dust from her hands. "Okay, prove it!"

She charged at them with murder in her eyes.

Another punch got past Darkseid's defenses. Superman smiled grimly as the vainglorious New God went flying into a mountaintop several miles away. Solid granite shattered like glass, sending thunderous echoes through the wooded valley below. Superman's super-hearing detected a stampede of panicked wildlife racing madly away from the hillside. *Good*, he thought. *There's no need for any innocent animals to get hurt by this conflict.*

Darkseid slid down the side of the peak before rising to face Superman again. Despite the hero's best efforts, his foe seemed as arrogantly confident as ever. "That's it," Superman taunted him as he flew at Darkseid. "Get up. Keep fighting." The wind whooshed past his ears as he aimed his bare fists at the villain's skull. "I'm not ready to call it quits yet either!"

"I won't deny I've found your moralistic petulance amusing," Darkseid replied, his arms crossed boldly across his barrel chest. "But, frankly, this sort of rank barbarism is beneath me. I grow weary of it." He yawned theatrically. "Time to put your interference to an end."

Twin Omega Beams shot from his eyes. Soaring toward Darkseid, Superman braced himself for the agonizing touch of the death rays, but, at the last minute, the parallel beams suddenly executed a sharp turn, veering around Superman and heading back toward . . . Jimmy!

Jimmy gently eased Forager's helmet off as he knelt beside her. To his relief, he found her breathing steadily. Her multifaceted eyes fixed on his as she gradually regained consciousness. A trickle of turquoise blood escaped her lips. He placed his hand against her neck and tried to take her pulse. It seemed a bit rapid, but how was he supposed to know what was normal for her? She wasn't exactly human after all. . . .

I don't care, he thought. *She's the only good thing that's happened to me since this whole mess began.*

The blare of gunfire, as well as angry grunts and curses, rang out behind him. Despite his concern for Forager, he couldn't resist glancing back over his shoulder at the heated battle going on only a few yards away, as Donna and Jason fought furiously to keep Mary away from him. Unfortunately, even though they outnumbered her two to one, they seemed to be losing ground at the moment; whatever Darkseid had done to Mary had obviously amped up her powers to a frightening degree. Jason fired round after round of ammo into the indestructible super-vixen, while Mary grabbed on to Donna's throat and yanked her off her feet, just like Captain Vyle had done to Jimmy in the slave pits of the Armagetto. He winced in sympathy. "Jeez. They don't have a prayer, do they?"

"Jimmy?"

"Forager!" He temporarily forgot the fight as he turned back to his alien sweetheart. "You're awake!" Placing one arm beneath her, he tenderly lifted her head from the ground. He felt a nasty bump beneath her silky purple hair. "Great, 'cause we gotta—"

"Jimmy!" she exclaimed. Her golden eyes looked past him at something above them. "Coming for you . . . !"

His head pivoted in time to see Darkseid's Omega Beams zipping toward him. Hoping to lure them away from Forager, he jumped to his feet and ran away from the sizzling scarlet rays as fast as he could. He zigzagged madly across the uneven terrain, trying to shake the beams, but they copied his every turn. "Yikes!" he shouted. "They're following me!"

Forager tried to get up, but, lacking the strength, collapsed weakly back onto the ground. "Forgive me, my Olsenbug! There is no escape for you!"

A jagged stone cliff blocked his path. He frantically tried to scramble up the side of the ridge, but the loose gravel kept sliding out from beneath his feet. He fell, scraping his knee on a sharp-edged boulder. Blood soaked through the knee of his grimy coverall. "Ouch," he yelped, but the pain was nothing compared to the excruciating agony that transfixed his body as the Omega Beams struck him from behind.

"No!" Forager cried out in despair. "JIMMY!"

He expected the souls of the New Gods to explode from his chest, leaving a smoking corpse behind, and yet, to his surprise, the intense pain was over in an instant. Jimmy stared down at himself in confusion, wondering why on Earth he was still alive. His skin tingled all over.

"Huh?"

A Boom Tube heralded the return of Darkseid, who teleported back into the gorge, only a few paces away from Jimmy. A moment later, Superman came flying back onto the scene. He looked equally baffled by Jimmy's survival. His X-ray vision checked his friend out from head to toe.

"What have you done to him?" Superman demanded.

"Nothing, really," Darkseid said smugly. "I've merely unlocked the fail-safe I installed in him when I made him into my cosmic vessel." He waved his hand at Jimmy, and a queasy feeling came over the perplexed reporter. "Say good-bye to your super friend, Olsen!"

Jimmy's joints locked up. His pink skin took on a bright emerald hue, and a luminous green aura suddenly enveloped his body.

No! he thought. *What are you doing to me now?*

Superman gasped out loud and crashed to the earth, as though he had suddenly lost the ability to defy gravity. A sickly green pallor came over his face. Bulging veins protruded from beneath his skin as he writhed in torment on the rocky floor of the gorge.

Ohmigod! Jimmy realized. *I've turned into kryptonite!*

Superman tried to crawl away, but Darkseid casually zapped him in the

back with his searing eye-beams. "Oh no, Kryptonian. You aren't going anywhere." He turned to smirk at Jimmy. "And neither are you, Olsen."

His emerald brow furrowed in concentration, Jimmy strained to reverse
the transformation, but without any success. Waves of killing radiation
spilled from his body, making Superman weaker and weaker. He tried to
get away from his friend, only to find himself frozen in place. An anguished
grunt escaped his lips, but otherwise he couldn't move a muscle.

"It's useless to struggle," Darkseid informed him. "I control you now."
His arms clasped behind his back, he strolled over to where Superman lay
dying. "Besides, don't you want to be at your dear friend's side as he breathes
his final breath?"

This is a nightmare, Jimmy thought. Paralyzed, he could do nothing but
stand by while Darkseid used him to execute the greatest hero on Earth.
Jimmy didn't want to die, but, at the moment, he would have gladly traded
his own life, not to mention all his newfound superpowers, just for a chance
to save his best friend. *Please, don't let this happen!*

Darkseid savored Jimmy's misery. "There is nothing you can do, Olsen.
Darkseid pilots you now and the controls are embedded deep within your
very core. . . ."

5 AND COUNTING.

JIMMY'S BRAIN.

The cerebellum, the "little brain," was tucked away in the hindbrain, below the much larger cerebrum. Synapses sparked between clusters of neurons linked by branching dendrites and axons. Fatty layers of myelin protected the neural fibers, while pulsing veins and capillaries throbbed with every heartbeat. An eerie green radiance lit up a convoluted maze of grooves and folds leading through the cerebellum's twin hemispheres. Overlapping lobes quivered like jelly. Dripping neurotransmitters smelled like brine. The temperature inside the brain was hot and feverish.

"Ow," the Atom moaned, slowly stirring to consciousness. He found himself sprawled atop a bed of damp, sticky glial cells, where he must have collapsed when zapped by a sudden burst of intense brain activity. His own microscopic nerves still felt fried from the jolt. *Would it have killed whoever rewired this brain to properly insulate it,* he thought crankily, *so that minuscule people like me don't get electrocuted when it fires up?*

He had taken refuge inside Jimmy's brain during Mary Marvel's sneak attack outside the Hall of Justice, hoping to get to the bottom of Jimmy's on-again, off-again powers. Exploring carefully, he had made his way through the cerebral cortex down to the hindbrain before being knocked out cold by . . . what?

Something happened to Jimmy; that's for sure.

Lifting himself from the gooey brain matter, the Atom took a moment to get his bearings. Jimmy was obviously still alive, although his blood was pumping at an alarming rate. He could hear the posterior inferior cerebellar artery beating loudly deep beneath his feet, like a subway car shaking the pavement above. The synapses were still firing like they were supposed to, creating a strobe effect inside the brain's muggy interior, but how come everything was so . . . green?

Contrary to popular wisdom, the "gray matter" of a living brain was usually flushed red with blood. Ordinarily, hiking through the brain on foot was like spelunking through caves of spongy red jello, but now everything around him was suffused with a strangely familiar emerald effulgence that seemed to emanate from every cell and fiber of Jimmy's brain. Looking around in confusion, it took the Atom a second to recognize the distinctive green tint.

It's kryptonite, he realized in shock. *Jimmy's radiating kryptonite?*

The Atom didn't know how that was possible, but he guessed that Superman was somewhere nearby—and in serious trouble. *All the more reason for me to figure out what Darkseid's done to Jimmy's brain and shut it down, pronto!*

The bouncy glia beneath his boots felt like a children's moonwalk ride as he investigated a network of metallic filaments intertwined with Jimmy's own ganglia. The Atom had been tracing the path of the artificial-looking circuitry right before he had been shocked unconscious. Crystalline flecks glinted amidst the filaments, which were intricately wedded to the pulsing brain matter. Ray was a physicist, not a neurosurgeon, but he had shut down enough evil telepaths' brains to know his way around, and this bizarre biological circuitry was like nothing he had ever seen before.

It's like H. R. Giger meets RadioShack, he thought. *How in the world am I supposed to get a handle on this?*

The cerebellum played a crucial part in controlling the human body's senses and motor controls, so he knew he had to be careful what he did here. One mistake could render Jimmy blind or paralyzed or worse. Yet he knew he had to do something about the alien apparatus infiltrating Jimmy's brain. Beneath the toxic glow of the kryptonite, he cautiously reached for an array of blinking crystals that looked like they might be a transformer of some sort.

Maybe if he cut the current . . . ?

ZZAKT! He yanked back his hand as emerald sparks stung his fingertips. "Okay, so much for that plan," he muttered. Getting electrocuted again wasn't going to help Jimmy any, let alone save the universe from Darkseid's malignant designs. The Atom paced back and forth before the baffling technology. Even though he had no idea what was going on outside Jimmy's skull, he couldn't help sensing that time was running out. He remembered Darkseid gloating over his master plan back in his fortress on Apokolips. Who knew how much longer they had before the arch-villain turned the entire Multiverse into a living hell?

Think, Palmer! He concentrated with all his might on the insidious improvements to Jimmy's "green matter." Gritting his teeth, he scrutinized every nanometer of the corrupted neurons, looking for some clue as to how to disable the arcane circuitry without killing or crippling Jimmy. He would have killed for an instruction book written in any earthly language. *You're supposed to be a genius, so figure this out!*

"Are you enjoying your last moments, Kryptonian?" Darkseid gloated. "I know I am, although I admit my attention's been usurped by young Mary." He turned away from Jimmy and Superman to admire Mary's lopsided battle against Donna and Jason. "Look at her fight. Such power. Such vigor. Such *anger!*" He chuckled in approval. "When the Fifth World dawns, I just might let her live."

Her opponents, on the other hand, were unlikely to last that long. Running out of ammo, Jason holstered his gun and tackled Mary head-on. A twelve-inch knife appeared in his hands and he jabbed it straight at the golden thunderbolt emblazoned on her chest. Darkseid admired his ruthlessness, but not his lack of common sense. The tip of the blade shattered against Mary's insignia, leaving him defenseless before her superior speed and strength. A backhanded slap dropped him like a sack of potatoes. He landed flat on his back amidst the rubble and didn't get back up again. Blood seeped out from beneath his skull, staining the floor of the gorge.

"Jason!" Donna cried out. She flew at Mary with her fists stretched out before her. Sunlight flashed off her silver belt and bracelets. Her outraged face no longer held the slightest bit of sympathy for the other woman. "I swear by the gods, Mary. . . !"

Mary laughed at Donna's approach. "You want your boyfriend so badly?" She grabbed Jason by one ankle and swung him like a club at the oncoming heroine. Jason's head smacked against Donna's face, knocking her out of the sky. She crashed to the ground at Mary's feet, providing an easy target for Mary, who clobbered her over and over with Jason's limp body. She looked like she was playing a grotesquely brutal game of Whac-A-Mole, using the former Robin as her hammer. Donna tried to fight back, but every time she lifted her battered face from the debris, Mary pounded her back down into the dirt . . . until Donna finally stopped moving. Only her labored breathing revealed that the super-powerful Amazon still possessed a spark of life.

"Heh." Mary casually tossed Jason aside as she stood triumphantly over Donna's prone body. "How about that? Looks like I'm the last girl standing!"

Indeed, Darkseid thought. It seems Eclipso was right to see potential in you. A pity she did not live to see her efforts bear such delicious fruit . . .

The unnatural green light flooded the inner corridors of Jimmy's brain, serving as a constant reminder that something was terribly wrong. The Atom realized that there was no time to conduct an exhaustive analysis of the artificial implants infesting the cerebellum. I can't stall any longer, he realized. I have to do something.

His eyes zeroed in on the blinking array before him. At a loss, he wondered how his fellow League members would handle a situation like this. I know what Hawkman would do, he thought. The avian avenger, who was probably Ray's closest friend in the League, had a fondness for medieval weapons like maces and battle-axes. What did Carter say once? His teammate's words of wisdom came back to him:

"When in doubt, break things."

The Atom took a deep breath, then grabbed on to the crystalline array with all his strength. Hostile electrical impulses shot up his arms, numbing him, but he didn't let go. The alien gizmo resisted his efforts to wrench it free, but, using the white-star technology embedded in his costume, he increased his strength disproportionately to his size. Sparks flew from the infected synapses as the entire array came free at last. Jumping backward from the unleashed energy, he let the crystalline lattice slip from his stinging fingers.

The kryptonite glow flickered all around him, then went out entirely. The emerald brain matter took on a more natural reddish hue. Only the strobe-like glare of flashing synapses allowed him to see his way around the murky cortical folds. Bright arterial blood pulsed warmly beneath his feet. He could only pray that meant Jimmy wasn't brain-dead yet.

I did it! he exulted. *I think. . . .*

His triumph was short-lived, however, as a loud scuttling noise suddenly echoed through the winding convolutions, growing louder by the second as the source of the uproar grew ever nearer. To his alarm, a horde of silvery alien insects came rushing toward him. Vaguely resembling beetles, they clattered over and under each other in their eagerness to tear the Atom apart. Although the size of fleas, they looked as large as king crabs to the tiny Atom. Their scaly shells bore the same alien circuit patterns as the array he had just dislodged. Angry pincers snapped at him.

"Uh-oh," he blurted. What were these things? Apokoliptian antibodies?

His only consolation as they swarmed over him, biting and clawing at his flesh, was the realization that he must have done something right to stimulate this kind of attack.

He could only hope that it wasn't too little, too late.

"Aack!" Jimmy gasped.

He felt a sudden shock at the back of his skull, then realized that he could move again. The bright green glow of the kryptonite evaporated, and he stared down at his hands in wonder, watching his flesh turn pink again. *Thank goodness!* He had no idea what had broken Darkseid's spell, but he couldn't have been happier. He glanced anxiously at Superman and was relieved to see the Man of Steel recovering as well. The greenish pallor retreated from Superman's complexion as Earth's yellow sun restored his strength. His swollen veins constricted. *Yes!* Jimmy rejoiced. *It's a miracle!*

Darkseid was taken aback by this unexpected turn of events. "This can't be!" he objected. "You're mine to control!"

Oh yeah? Jimmy thought. *We'll see about that.* He sensed instinctively that something had changed fundamentally inside his brain, freeing him from all of Darkseid's fiendish constraints. He could feel the stolen power of the New Gods surging through him, merging with the unique abilities Darkseid himself had endowed him with. He was in command of the power now, not the other way around. Now he just needed to take it to the max—and buy Superman the time he needed to recover fully.

Jimmy clenched his fists and concentrated. A hoarse grunt erupted from his throat as yet another freakish transformation racked his body. The soiled coverall came apart at the seams as his size and mass increased at an exponential rate. Thick, olive green scales spread across his exposed skin. Webbing formed between his fingers and toes. Bony claws sprouted from his nails. Darkseid, Superman, and the entire gorge seemed to shrink beneath his gaze as his head ascended toward the clouds.

"Holy Moley!" Mary exclaimed. She craned her head back to take in the entire mind-boggling sight. "Now, that's freaking sweet!"

Jimmy Olsen, helpless cub reporter, was gone. Towering in his place was a colossal turtle-man standing over fifty feet tall. Bulging reptilian eyes sported beady black pupils. Overlapping layers of horny scutes, each the size of parking spaces, armored his mammoth body. Only his flame red hair and freckles rendered him recognizable as he loomed above the startled villains like a prehistoric behemoth.

"You want the power inside me, Darkseid?" Jimmy reached for the smaller-looking New God with his giant claws. "Come and get it!"

4 AND COUNTING.

OUTSIDE METROPOLIS.

The suburban community of Bakerline was usually a quiet place, comfortably removed from the fast-paced hubbub of the city. Strip malls, supermarkets, and fast-food restaurants served miles of peaceful residential neighborhoods, where the biggest news was generally a bake sale at one of the local churches, or maybe a hotly contested high school football rivalry.

But none of that mattered today as the innocent suburb was laid waste by a titanic battle between two enormous, inhuman figures. Jimmy Olsen, now a gigantic turtle-man, grappled furiously with Darkseid, who had grown to equally Brobdingnagian proportions to confront his former pawn. Banks and hardware stores were smashed to smithereens as the wrestling giants lurched against them. Broken glass and masonry rained down into the streets. Flames erupted from collapsed homes and buildings. Gushers sprayed from fractured hydrants and water lines. Sirens blared above the thunderous din of the battle as ambulances, police cars, and fire trucks raced through the endangered community, trying futilely to cope with the devastation left in the giants' wake. Abandoned vehicles blocked traffic. Screaming men, women, and children ran frantically through the streets like extras in a Japanese monster movie.

"You will most certainly suffer for this, Olsen!" Darkseid bellowed. His stentorian voice reverberated for miles in every direction. Their epic struggle had carried them all the way from the Blue Mountains to Bakerline, leaving a trail of utter destruction behind them. Now over fifty feet tall, the evil New God towered over the hapless business district in their path. He butted his armored skull into Jimmy's jaw.

"Not if I've got anything to say about it!" Jimmy swiped his reptilian claws across Darkseid's chest, gouging the villain's indigo armor and driving him backward into the redbrick façade of a three-story department store. The unlucky establishment caved in beneath Darkseid's tremendous mass. Parked cars were squashed beneath the villain's boots. Jimmy's webbed feet crushed an empty SUV.

Darkseid lashed back at Jimmy, who landed hard on the mini-mall across the street, flattening the entire complex. "I don't know how my control over you was pried from my grasp," Darkseid ranted, "but no matter. I will still kill you, and the very essence of the New Gods will flow from your corpse into me!" His crimson eyes blazed like hellfire. "The Fifth World will be mine to shape as I will!"

"Over my dead body!" Jimmy blurted. "All fifty feet of it!"

"I don't get it," Jason griped. "How the heck did Darkseid get so freakin' big?"

Superman dropped him, Donna, and Forager off on the roof of a deserted apartment building before flying away to join the relief efforts. Thankfully, the entire JLA had teleported back from Rann in time to assist in the evacuation. From their elevated vantage point, Donna watched as the League did what they could to cope with the emergency. The Flash hurried panicked civilians to safety at lightning speed. Green Lantern used his power ring to scoop up entire crowds in spheres of glowing emerald energy. Wonder Woman rescued stranded bystanders from rooftops with her Golden Lasso. Hawkgirl carried out her own airborne rescues. The Batwing made a rare daytime appearance, spraying burning buildings with fire-retardant foam.

Superman rescued injured men and women from mountains of collapsed debris. Green Arrow and Black Canary, freshly returned from their honeymoon, defended storefronts from looters. His trick arrows and her sonic cry sent the troublemakers packing.

"He's Darkseid," Donna replied simply. Her face and bones still ached from the vicious pounding she had received from Mary Marvel. A bandage was wrapped around Jason's injured skull, while Forager's arm was in a splint. Superman had wanted to take all three of them straight to the hospital, but they had insisted on seeing this earth-shattering drama through to the end. There would be time enough to tend to their sprains and concussions later—assuming the world was still around tomorrow.

"Indeed," Forager confirmed. "The dark one's powers are beyond imagining. I still fear for my Olsenbug's safety."

I don't blame you, Donna thought. *But at least we don't have to deal with Mary at the moment.* The traitorous ex-heroine had bailed on Darkseid right after Jimmy decided to emulate Godzilla. Donna scowled angrily as she recalled how the other woman had betrayed the Challengers and left them for dead. *I've got a score to settle with that bitch, but not today. . . .*

She suspected Jason and Forager felt the same.

First, someone had to stop Darkseid from conquering all of reality. And, from the looks of things, that all depended on . . . Jimmy Olsen?

"Perish, Olsen!" Darkseid roared. "And provide me with that which I alone deserve!"

Their gargantuan strife had torn a destructive swath through Bakerline all the way to the banks of Hob's River. A powerhouse blow sent Jimmy reeling into the large suspension bridge connecting the suburbs to the city. Iron supports and trestles splashed down into the churning water. Jimmy's webbed feet found purchase on the silty floor of the river. The cold water invigorated his huge reptilian frame. He grabbed on to the bridge, wresting it from its moorings, and swung it like a club at Darkseid. Steel girders and concrete smashed against the New God's dark blue helmet. The clamorous impact rattled windows all across Metropolis.

"What you deserve, huh? Well, mister, you've got it!"

* * *

Tinier than ever, compared to Jimmy's colossal new proportions, the Atom scurried stealthily through the quivering canyons of the oversized brain. The silvery antibodies, which had also grown in proportion to Jimmy's cerebellum, now looked as large as crocodiles. They scuttled about aggressively, clacking their pincers together, but, without even shrinking on his own, the Atom had become too insignificant to attract their notice.

Thank heaven for small favors, he thought. *No pun intended.*

His blue and red costume was sliced and shredded from the antibodies' assault. Countless minor scratches and lacerations stung like hell, but, taking a quick physical inventory, he appeared to have escaped serious injury. Jimmy had undergone his inexplicable growth spurt just in time.

A violent tremor shook the cerebellum, knocking the Atom off his feet. A ledge of spongy gray matter cushioned his fall, yet the seismic disturbances continued to toss the Atom from side to side. The Atom felt like he was stuck inside the San Andreas Fault during a major earthquake. Climbing back onto his feet, he stumbled awkwardly over the shuddering cerebral jelly. "Jeez, Olsen," he griped. "What the hell is going on out there?"

He was tempted to exit the brain through the nearest convenient orifice. Unfortunately, he still had work to do inside Jimmy's violated cranium. Although he seemed to have turned off the kryptonite effect, and somehow transformed Jimmy into a giant, by disabling that one biomechanical implant, still more alien circuitry extended deeper into the innocent reporter's hindbrain. Like a prospector tracing a vein of glittering ore through a sweltering underground mine, he followed the flickering circuitry down the cerebellum into the brain stem, along the path of the posterior inferior cerebral artery, until he glimpsed a brilliant golden glow up ahead.

That better not be just an overactive synapse, he thought as he squeezed through a slimy cortical fold to get a closer look. The light was so bright that he had to shield his eyes with his hand. Blinking into the glare, he stared in wonder at the source of the dazzling illumination. *Paydirt,* he realized at once. *That is definitely not a synapse.*

Embedded in the throbbing fissures of the medulla oblongata was a crystalline disk boasting intricate patterns of glowing circuitry. Alien symbols, of unknown meaning and origin, were etched into the surface of the crystal. The arcane characters vibrated before the Atom's eyes as though imbued with literally supernatural power. Raw energy emanated from the disk, enough to make his hair stand on end.

"Oh my God," he intoned. Ray Palmer was not a religious man, especially given everything he had endured over the past few years, but a sense of genuine awe flooded over him as he beheld the futuristic artifact before him. He knew in his bones that he had discovered the hidden repository in which Darkseid had trapped the souls of the New Gods.

And was it just his imagination, or could he actually hear their voices whispering at the back of his mind, calling out to him in unison?

Free us, Ray Palmer. Return our souls to the Source.

The tide of battle was turning against Jimmy.

In the heart of Suicide Slum, not far from where Jimmy had witnessed Sleez's death, Darkseid seized the giant turtle-man's throat. Scarlet energy flared from Darkseid's gauntlet, delivering a volcanic shock to his foe. Smoke rose from Jimmy's singed red hair. His scales cracked and blistered. He let out a high-pitched yowl that sounded like a tyrannosaurus in its death throes. His clawed hands slashed wildly at Darkseid's wrist, but could not break the New God's death grip upon his throat. Darkness encroached on Jimmy's vision as he started to black out.

"All this destruction, all this struggle," Darkseid mocked him, "and all you've managed to overcome is my patience." He levitated from the trampled cityscape surrounding them until they were floating in the air high above Metropolis. An unnatural vortex, composed of turbulent black clouds, formed overhead as though the atmosphere itself was reacting to the cataclysmic forces unleashed today. Violent winds filled the air with debris. Heat lightning flashed over the city. The rivers girding Metropolis were whipped into froth.

It's over, Jimmy realized. His arms dropped to his sides as the last of his strength deserted him. He hung helplessly in Darkseid's grasp, his webbed feet dangling above the demolished slum, while praying that somehow Superman and the Justice League would succeed where he had failed. Darkseid's just too powerful. *I can't beat a god. . . .*

"Now," Darkseid proclaimed for the all the universe to hear, "for the Fifth World to be mine, Jimmy Olsen must die!"

"Or not," a much smaller voice disagreed.

The Atom leapt from Jimmy's ear, rapidly gaining size and mass as he did so. At the same moment, Jimmy suddenly shrank back to his own normal proportions. His scaly hide melted away so that he was no longer a turtle-man, but simply plain old Jimmy Olsen once more. "What?" Darkseid gasped as the tiny mortal slipped between his fingers.

Jimmy plummeted toward the ground. A cold wind rushed past his face, reviving him just in time to see the broken pavement rushing up to meet him. Closing his eyes, he braced himself for the final, fatal impact. *Just my luck*, he thought. *I escape Darkseid just to get splattered all over what's left of Suicide Slum!*

"Don't worry, Jimmy. I've got you." With only seconds to spare, Superman swooped to the rescue. He grabbed on to Jimmy and swiftly flew him away from Darkseid. Opening his eyes, Jimmy saw the rest of the Justice League hovering at the fringe of the battle, waiting for the right moment to intervene. Donna and Forager waved at him from a glowing emerald platform generated by Green Lantern's power ring. Standing between the two women, Jason Todd nodded sullenly in his direction. He was relieved to see that they all were still alive.

Especially Forager.

"You're safe now," Superman promised. "Thanks to the Atom."

Shimmering atomic orbitals surrounded the Atom as he let the swirling winds carry him onto the top of one of the few dilapidated buildings left standing in this urban war zone. He touched down on the tar-papered roof of the tenement. The luminous rings around him faded as he assumed his normal human height. His right hand held on tightly to a palm-sized glowing disk.

This is it, Ray Palmer realized. *This is why the Monitor sent Donna and Jason chasing all through the Multiverse to find me. This is my moment.*

An ordinary man or hero might have been intimidated by the fact that Darkseid was now the size of a skyscraper, but the Atom was used to facing foes many times larger than himself. "Hey, stoneface!" He held the glowing crystal disk up so that the giant villain couldn't miss it. Waves of neo-divine energy emanated from the captured artifact. "I've got your little soul battery! Straight from Olsen's medulla!"

Darkseid's crimson eyes widened in alarm. For the first time in recorded memory, fear showed upon the tyrant's face. "What? It cannot be!"

"You want it?" the Atom taunted him. "Well, tough!"

Without hesitation, he crushed the soul-catcher in his fist.

3 AND COUNTING.

METROPOLIS.

"NOOO!" Darkseid shouted.

A pillar of cosmic fire escaped the Atom's palm, blasting into the sky like a sparkling golden geyser. Darkseid grasped desperately at his prize, but the released energy shot past his clutches as it rocketed beyond Earth's atmosphere into the uncharted depths of outer space. Free at last, the souls of the murdered New Gods sought communion with the Source.

Darkseid's fury knew no bounds. "Ray Palmer!" The turbulent storm clouds dispersed as the lord of Apokolips shrank back to a mere eight feet tall. Confronting the impertinent mortal atop the roof of a squalid human domicile, he sensed the manipulative hand of the Monitor behind this unfathomable reversal. "You've dabbled in these affairs for the last time. I may not have brought you back to this world, but I shall most gladly remove you from the game!"

He stalked toward the Atom, who backed up to the very edge of a precipitous drop. Darkseid's armored fingers flexed murderously. Death by Omega Beams was too merciful a punishment; Darkseid intended to crush the Monitor's despicable pawn with his own hands. Glowing orbitals enveloped the

Atom as he attempted to shrink to safety, but Darkseid would not be deterred by so pathetic a stratagem. *You will pay for your effrontery,* the villain vowed, *even if I have to destroy the entire nanoverse!*

But before he could wreak his vengeance, the unmistakable detonation of a Boom Tube thundered directly overhead. A luminous passageway opened up in the sky above Metropolis.

"Who?" Darkseid blurted. By his count, the rest of the New Gods were dead. Before traveling to Earth for the penultimate stage of his grand endeavor, he had seen both Apokolips and New Genesis reduced to celestial ghost towns, devoid of all life. Even Desaad's endless scheming had availed him naught in the end; the torturer had been executed in his own dungeon. Darkseid alone had survived the final culling. There could be no one left to traverse the cosmos in this manner except—the realization struck the villain like the crack of doom—he who slew the New Gods in the first place.

A radiant figure emerged from the Boom Tube, which swiftly dissipated behind him. Looking up, Darkseid beheld a humanoid male clad in formfitting armor of burnished cobalt and bronze. His athletic build was less stocky than Darkseid's. A tinted visor concealed the newcomer's eyes. His square jaw had a determined set.

"Greetings, brother," the Infinity Man said. "We meet again—for the final time."

Once, the being before him had been known as Drax, Darkseid's older brother and heir to the bloody throne of Apokolips. An idealist, Drax had dared to dream of a lasting peace with the gods of New Genesis, until his brother shrewdly betrayed him and seized his power for his own. For years, Darkseid had believed Drax dead, consumed by a cosmic conflagration that Darkseid himself had engineered, but in time he had learned that his brother had instead been thrown beyond the Fourth World into the realm of the Infinite, a transcendent dimension where the ordinary laws of time and space did not apply. Reborn as the Infinity Man, he had provided a check to Darkseid's most grandiose ambitions, all in the name of the Source.

The time has come, Darkseid realized. He had long suspected that his accursed brother was the true agent of the New Gods' destruction. All thought of the Atom fled his mind as he prepared himself, physically and mentally, for his inevitable confrontation with the God-Slayer. A conflict born countless millennia ago, when he first usurped his brother's destiny, would finally be resolved this day. *One way or another.*

"Well met, brother." Hatred burned in his blazing red eyes. "I hope you do not expect me to submit willingly to extinction?"

The Infinity Man landed on the rooftop opposite Darkseid. "Stay your Omega Beams, Uxas!" he said, addressing his brother by his birth name. Darkseid had taken on his more fearsome sobriquet, one fraught with meaning in the prophecies of the New Gods, upon stealing his brother's birthright. "Reconsider, Uxas. The moment is cast. Our time is done. But how you meet it will determine the fate of your spirit. Think beyond your overweening ambition and anger. Surrender to the will of the Source."

"Pretty words," Darkseid retorted, "from one whose hands drip with the blood of the New Gods!"

The Infinity Man did not deny the accusation. "I am but the agent of the Source. The Fourth World has been judged and found wanting. Eons of endless strife between New Genesis and Apokolips have left the Multiverse no better for the constant warfare." His voice rang with near-religious fervor. "A new and different tomorrow comes this way!"

"I'm not so easily put to pasture," Darkseid declared. His brother's sanctimonious platitudes did not impress him. If anything, they only strengthened his resolve to outwit destiny and turn this epochal upheaval to his advantage. "The Fifth World shall indeed come to pass, but it shall be mine!"

Wasting no further time on meaningless debate, he gave his brother a taste of his Omega Beams. The scarlet rays ricocheted off the Infinity Man's impervious armor, lighting up the skies like a deadly fireworks display. Discharged energy crackled loudly. Ozone filled the air.

"This changes nothing, Uxas!" He returned Darkseid's attack with his own show of force. Golden Infinity Beams shot from his visor, striking Darkseid at close range. Coruscating waves of lethal energy shot forth in every direction as the rival gods contended with all their might. The blinding glare and ear-shattering clamor of their clash could be seen and heard as far away as Gotham City. "At long last, your treachery is at an end!"

* * *

The *Infinity Man?*

Superman was shocked by the identity of the New Gods' murderer. He had fought beside the Infinity Man before, usually against Darkseid and his minions, and had always considered the extradimensional warrior one of the good guys. It was hard to believe that he was truly responsible for the deaths of Lightray and the others.

Although Rao knows he's powerful enough to take out his fellow gods. . . .

Racing through the sky, Superman led the Justice League toward the destructive conflict tearing his city apart. Batman's jet-powered Batwing sliced through the air, while Green Lantern, Wonder Woman, and Hawk-girl soared under their own power. The Flash zipped through the devastated streets below. The Atom crouched upon Superman's shoulder, holding on tightly to the collar of the Man of Steel's cape. Donna Troy had volunteered to join the fight, despite her injuries, but Superman had convinced her and Jason to stay behind and guard Jimmy and Forager, both of whom were pretty roughed up by their recent tussles.

"Hey, Clark," Green Lantern said as they approached ground zero. An emerald aura, generated by his own willpower, surrounded his airborne form. His power ring shone brightly upon his fist. "Whose side exactly are we on here?"

Good question, Superman thought. Ordinarily, his first instinct would be to target Darkseid, but right now he just wanted to break the gods' fight up before it destroyed all of Metropolis. "We can sort out the good from the bad later," he informed the rest of the team. "Let's just shut this family squabble down ASAP!"

"Sounds good to me," Batman said grimly from the cockpit of the Batwing.

"Agreed," Wonder Woman assented. They'd had their differences in the past, but today they were all on the same page. "Earth is no place for sibling rivalry of this magnitude."

I couldn't have put it better myself, Superman thought.

"Stop this!" he hollered at Darkseid and the Infinity Man as the heroes converged on the bloodthirsty immortals. He fired a blast of heat vision to get their attention. Batman unleashed a batwinged missile that exploded between the two gods, temporarily driving them apart. Wonder Woman spun her Golden Lasso. Green Lantern willed glowing emerald chains around Darkseid, binding the villain's arms to his sides. Hawkgirl swung at Darkseid's head with a spiked mace.

The Infinity Man glanced at the JLA in annoyance. "Heroes of Earth, leave us be!" Wonder Woman snagged him with her lasso, but he effortlessly passed through its shimmering links. "This fight is mine and mine alone. Depart immediately and you will be spared!"

"Not a chance!" Superman flew between the Infinity Man and Darkseid. "This is my city—and my planet—and I'm not going to see it wrecked by your private vendetta!"

"Spare us your territorial indignation!" Darkseid growled. Exerting his godly strength, he broke free of Green Lantern's restraints, which evaporated into a spray of chartreuse sparks. The psychic feedback provoked an anguished groan from the emerald hero, who tumbled backward clutching his skull. Hawkgirl's mace shattered against the arch-villain's helmet. He swatted her aside. "Soon all worlds shall belong to Darkseid!"

The Infinity Man's visor glowed purple and an irresistible surge of antigravity catapulted Superman away from the New Gods, back toward Wonder Woman and the others. Drax threw out his hands, and the heroes suddenly found themselves trapped inside a floating geodesic sphere, composed of transparent orange energy. "Forgive me, Kryptonian," the Infinity Man said, "but you and your allies cannot be allowed to interfere with my sacred duty. Thus I must cut short your misguided heroics by encasing you within a prison of solidified light."

"What?" Superman exclaimed. He pounded against the shining barrier with his fist, but its adamantine walls refused to budge. His fellow heroes joined their efforts to his. Wonder Woman removed her tiara and attempted to slice through the unyielding light with its razor-sharp edges. Regaining his concentration, Green Lantern drilled at the wall with a jackhammer composed of emerald light. Hawkgirl beat her feathery wings against the cramped confines of their cage. The Batwing fired lasers at its edges.

Yet not even their combined resources could make a dent in the sphere.

* * *

"Cease your futile resistance, Uxas!" the Infinity Man exhorted Darkseid as they resumed their contest. Unable to withstand the tremendous forces at play, the flimsy tenement building disintegrated beneath their feet. Crushed stone and mortar rained down on the blasted ghetto below, leaving the dueling gods suspended hundreds of feet above a smoking wasteland. "Would you destroy this hapless world merely to preserve your own existence?"

"My name is Darkseid!" Locking his fists together above his head, he brought them crashing down against the crest of his brother's helmet. The blow staggered but did not drop his formidable adversary, and Darkseid followed up the attack by firing a burst of red-hot plasma at his opponent's face. "And I will lay waste to all creation before I surrender to the likes of you!"

"So be it," the Infinity Man proclaimed. His tinted visor cracked by Darkseid's latest assault, he retaliated by delivering a solid jab to his brother's gut. "But surely you have not forgotten the prophecy?" He recited an infamous augury dictated by the Source itself at the very dawn of the Fourth World. " 'Brother shall meet Brother in the bloodred light of the Fire Pits, and there they shall decide the War.' " Golden light seared Darkseid's flesh. "That day is upon us, brother!"

A sudden tornado hurled them apart. The whirlwind whipped against Darkseid's face, spinning him through the air. Glancing down in surprise, he saw the Flash, overlooked before, running in circles directly beneath them. The Fastest Man Alive seemed determined to blow them out to sea, far from the teeming mortal metropolis.

"Enough!" the Infinity Man shouted impatiently over the howling winds. He waved his hand at the Flash and the irritating speedster was instantly teleported inside the same unbreakable orb that contained his trapped compatriots. "These valiant mortals shall not keep me from my task!"

Darkseid took advantage of his brother's distraction to blast him in the back with the full force of his Omega Beams. "Insufferable fool! I write my own destiny." The sneak attack stunned the other immortal, and Darkseid savagely kicked his brother toward the ground dozens of stories below. "Today shall belong to Darkseid!"

Engulfed in bright, luciferous flames, the Infinity Man crashed into the heart of the city.

Superman and his fellow heroes watched the appalling spectacle from within the floating sphere. He prayed that they had managed to evacuate the city in time. He strained his super-hearing in search of innocent bystanders, but all he heard were the frightened cries and whimpers of terrified civilians many miles away from ground zero. His X-ray vision scoured the ruins of the collapsed buildings. Thankfully, there appeared to be no casualties trapped beneath the rubble.

"I don't care what the Infinity Man said," the Flash said beside him. Wally West carried on the legacy of his uncle, Barry Allen. He tried to vibrate his atoms through the shimmering barrier, only to bounce back into Superman. He zipped about the sphere in frustration. "We've got to do something here!"

Superman knew how he felt, but he also understood that matters had escalated beyond even the League's control. The best they could do at the moment was make sure that ordinary men and women survived this literal apocalypse as best they could. "This is brother versus brother now, Wally. This is between gods."

A steaming crater, over a mile in diameter, now occupied the center of the slum. The blackened ruins resembled the wreckage of Granny Goodness's orphanage back on Apokolips. Darkseid felt quite at home as he descended into the depths of the crater. His imperial armor was charred and dented. Painful scars and burns defaced his stone gray flesh, but he paid his physical discomfort no heed. He would endure any ordeal, any torment, in his quest for ultimate power.

He found his brother's smoldering form sprawled at the bottom of the pit. The Infinity Man's once-gleaming armor lay in pieces amidst the blazing embers. The heat and impact of the warrior's descent had glazed the cracked floor of the crater. Drax's helmet had come loose, exposing his battered visage for the first time in ages. Darkseid barely recognized his brother's face. Blood dripped from an ugly gash across his brow. Teeth were cracked and missing. Cuts, scrapes, and blisters formed a mosaic of suffering across his muscular body. More blood pooled beneath him.

"So much for the will of the Source," Darkseid gloated. Placing his boot atop Drax's skull, he ground his brother's face into the broken glass. "I should have made sure you were dead the first time we clashed, but I shall not make that mistake again. Your genocidal campaign is over. Now it is your turn to die."

The Infinity Man stirred beneath his tread. "Never," he grunted through cracked and swollen lips. An unexpected burst of antigravity hurled Darkseid away from his brother, who leapt ferociously from the ashes. Without giving the startled villain a chance to recover, Drax pounced upon the other god. Fists imbued with preternatural might pounded away at Darkseid's face and torso. "You cannot defeat me, brother! Ours is a battle of wills, and mine is untainted and true. I am evolution's champion, the harbinger of the Fifth World, while you have ever walked the dark path of Anti-Life!"

Darkseid was caught off guard by his brother's renewed ferocity, but he quickly recovered from his surprise. *I should have known he wouldn't fall so easily,* he chastised himself. Accelerated healing and superhuman endurance were among the Infinity Man's gifts. *But even without the souls of the departed New Gods at my disposal, Darkseid too is a force to be reckoned with!*

Marshaling his strength, he threw Drax off him and lunged at his brother. The shock wave from their collision toppled nearby buildings. Mangled cars and trucks bounced into the air before crashing back down onto sundered blacktop. Snapped steel girders jutted from the ground like twisted pieces of abstract art. Smoke and dust blanketed the sky. Flames erupted from the ruins. The entire neighborhood looked as though it had been blasted back into the Stone Age.

"Heh!" Darkseid chuckled. Locked in combat, their contorted faces only inches apart, they fought hand-to-hand, neither combatant giving an inch. Spittle sprayed from Darkseid's lips. He spit a mouthful of black blood onto the battlefield. "I don't see your vaunted Fire Pits, brother, so what good is your talk of prophecy now?"

Blood streamed down Drax's face from his wounded forehead. Sweat dripped from his straining limbs. "I shall fulfill my mission, Uxas, even if I must die to do it! Our deaths will mark the birth of a new age!"

Darkseid laughed at his brother's fanatical ravings. "That's the spirit! A pity you did not fight for your throne half so fiercely." Sensing victory at hand, he was willing to be magnanimous. "These are the words of one worthy to be called my brother!"

"And yet we are nothing alike!"

The Infinity Man broke free of Darkseid's hold and rammed his fist straight into his brother's chest. The weathered breastplate yielded to his might and his arm plunged elbow-deep into the arch-villain's rib cage. Darkseid roared in agony as the God-Slayer yanked back his arm. "What was it you said?" Drax asked. "No Fire Pits?" Gouts of bloodred flame erupted from the gaping cavity in Darkseid's chest. A foul black organ was clutched in the Infinity Man's grip. "Your hellish heart is Fire Pit enough to fulfill the prophecy!"

"N-no. . . !" Darkseid dropped to his knees. He clutched at his wounded chest. The awesome power of the Omega Force, which had rendered him invincible throughout his reign, gushed out between his fingers despite his frantic efforts to contain it. Spidery fissures spread across his face and limbs. Lifeless gray skin began to flake away, flaying him alive. Raw, red muscles melted from his bones. An aura of crackling crimson plasma ate away at his very being. "Not me . . . it was never meant to be me. . . !"

"Ever so arrogant, Darkseid, right to the bitter end." The Infinity Man gazed implacably down at the once-dreaded master of Apokolips. The unleashed energies gushing from the villain's chest built toward an inexorable chain reaction that would ultimately consume them both. Resigned to his fate, Drax made no attempt to escape the inferno to come. "Farewell, my brother."

A fireball the size of Krakatoa exploded around them.

2 AND COUNTING.

METROPOLIS.

Green Lantern did his best to contain the shock wave within an enormous emerald force field. But even still, several city blocks were leveled by the volcanic demise of the New Gods. The Infinity Man's energy-sphere vanished with him, freeing the JLA to cope with the collateral damage. Superman scanned the ruins for any trace of either Darkseid or his adversary, but reported not even microscopic fragments of their remains. Batman, Green Arrow, Black Canary, and the rest of the team fanned out to assess the extent of the disaster and render whatever aid they could. A pounding rain poured down from the sky, as though the heavens themselves wept over the extinction of a pantheon. The torrential downpour helped to extinguish the multiple fires ignited by the gods' final battle. Miles of yellow police tape were strung up around the perimeter of the blast site.

The observation deck of the Daily Planet Building, which had miraculously survived the city's latest brush with destruction, offered Donna and the other Challengers an elevated view of the battle's aftermath. She and Jason and the Atom watched as Superman put out a burning homeless shelter with his super-breath, while the Flash constructed temporary housing at the speed of light. Wonder Woman transported emergency supplies in her invisible jet. In the street below, Jimmy helped Forager into an ambulance. A heavy fire blanket was draped over Jimmy's naked shoulders.

"Wow." Donna contemplated the cataclysmic events they had just borne witness to. "Darkseid defeated at last . . . I never thought I'd live to see the day." She glanced up at the stormy sky. Were cool alien eyes viewing this very scene from afar? "I wonder if this is what the Monitor intended all along?"

"Maybe," the Atom said. "We may never know."

"Screw that!" Jason snapped. "Screw you all in fact!" He stomped away from the guardrail, turning his back on Donna and Ray. A noticeable limp hinted at the extent of his injuries. Ripping away his mask, he revealed a pair of swollen black eyes. Bruises and a busted lip attested to the brutal beating he had received from Mary Marvel back in the mountains. His tattered leather jacket was stained with his own blood. "I'm through with all this cosmic anomaly garbage. All I want now is to get far away from the rest of you!"

Although she sympathized with his frustration, Donna was still hurt and offended by his attitude. "Oh, real nice, Jason!" she accused him. "You know, you're not the only one who's been used and betrayed here." Her head still throbbed where Mary had hammered her into the ground. "After everything we've gone through together, I would have hoped for more from you. Haven't you learned anything through all this?"

"Yeah," he spat in disgust. "I've learned the saving-the-universe racket is for suckers." Favoring his sprained ankle, he hobbled toward the elevator. "Have a nice life, losers!"

Speechless, Donna and the Atom watched Jason exit in a huff. Ray shook his head in disapproval. He gave Donna a bewildered look, as though he couldn't believe Jason's appalling behavior. "That bitter young man used to be Robin?"

"And a Teen Titan," Donna added sadly.

She wondered what she had ever seen in him.

1 AND COUNTING.

METROPOLIS.

Jimmy had played the scenario out in his head a thousand times. He was at the Pulitzer Prize ceremony, accepting the award for his acclaimed journalistic account of everything that had transpired over the past several weeks. But when he looked into the audience, he saw fifty-two Supermen, fifty-two Batmen, even fifty-two Beast Boys for God's sake. Fifty-two variations of a nearly infinite number of heroes and villains looking back at him. And that was when he realized that there was no way he could write the story. Who would believe it?

"It figures," he said as he stared gloomily at the floor of his apartment. He sat backward upon a rickety kitchen chair, his arms and chin resting on its back. A half-empty glass of orange juice dangled precariously in his grip. "The biggest story of my career and it can never be told."

"Yes. Well, life's full of disappointments," Forager buzzed unsympathetically, while she rummaged in the refrigerator behind him. A two-piece Lycra jogging outfit revealed that her alien metabolism had already healed the wounds she'd received from Mary Marvel. Her antennae twitched irritably. "Did I tell you that I'm still furious over missing out on the final battle with Darkseid?"

Only eight times today, Jimmy thought. He had apologized repeatedly for having to leave her behind when he went Godzilla on Darkseid's butt, but it didn't seem to have done any good. Forager's ego had been smarting ever since.

"Hey, O.B." She sorted through the leftovers in the fridge. "Is this Chinese food still good?"

Jimmy repressed a sigh. *You know a relationship is headed for the Dumpster,* he mused, *when your cute extraterrestrial girlfriend shortens her pet name for you from "Olsenbug" to just "O.B."* He rotated his chair to face her. "Try some. If nothing moves in your mouth, then yes."

The quip failed to elicit a smile, let alone a chuckle, from the stir-crazy insect-woman. Being cooped up in Jimmy's apartment during her convalescence had left her notably short-tempered. Jimmy was starting to wonder if they had anything in common at all now that they were no longer united in a common quest—and he was just an ordinary cub reporter again.

His extraordinary powers were gone. Ever since the Atom had extracted the soul-catcher from his brain, and liberated the trapped spirits of the New Gods, he hadn't displayed a single unusual ability. *Just as well,* he thought. *They never brought me anything but trouble.*

Forager sniffed a cardboard container of three-day-old chow mein, then lobbed it into the trash. She closed the refrigerator with unnecessary force before turning to face Jimmy. Her slender arms were crossed over her chest. Her inhuman features bore a serious expression.

"Seriously, James, we have to talk."

Ouch, Jimmy thought. *The phrase that every guy loves to hear.*

IVY TOWN.

Ray Palmer's living room was uncomfortably similar to the one he had left behind on Earth-51. No surprise there; Jean had helped pick out the furnishings in both universes. The only difference was that this house hadn't been trashed by a berserk Monitor.

Yet.

Home again, Ray thought morosely. He slumped on the couch in front of the silent TV. A stack of unopened mail was piled on the coffee table. The furnace churned noisily downstairs. The fireplace was cold and empty. A heartbreaking operatic aria played softly on the stereo. The soprano's tragic lamentations fit his mood.

To their credit, the Justice League had done a good job of looking after Ray's house during his long absence. A paid housekeeper had kept everything spick-and-span. Yet of all the bizarre places he had visited in the last two years, none felt more desolate than this lonely suburban home, which was way too big for one solitary super hero, even when, as now, he was his normal height. He couldn't help wondering how that other Jean was coping fifty dimensions away, in a reality he would never see again.

He hoped she was happy.

"So now what?" he wondered aloud. The League had been supportive, giving him time to acclimate before reporting back to duty, but was that really what he wanted to do with the rest of his life? His career as the Atom had cost him the woman he loved—twice. Was that even a life he wanted to live again?

The doorbell rang, interrupting his moody ruminations. *Who on Earth?* Ray wondered. He wasn't expecting anyone.

He was tempted to ignore the bell and pretend he wasn't home, but curiosity prevailed. Dragging himself off the couch, he went to the door. He opened it tentatively, half expecting to find a Jehovah's Witness or a youngster selling Girl Scout Cookies. Instead he discovered a tall brunette woman wearing casual attire.

"Donna?"

"I knew it," she said cryptically. Without asking for an invitation, she stepped inside the house. Her piercing blue eyes probed his own. "You too, huh?"

Ray closed the door behind her and followed her into the living room, where she shucked off her leather jacket and made herself at home upon the couch. He sat down on the arm of the easy chair across from her. "Me too, what?"

"That antsy, unfulfilled look in your eyes," she explained. "I know that look from my own mirror."

Her confident assessment unnerved Ray, who tried to shrug it off. "It's only natural we should feel at loose ends. We've been through a lot."

"And?" she prompted him.

No answer came. Ray squirmed awkwardly on the arm of the chair. *What else is there to say?*

"Yeah, I know," Donna said. He had to remind himself that, unlike the Martian Manhunter, she couldn't actually read his mind. "It bugs the hell out of me too."

GOTHAM CITY.

The Bat-Signal shone above the city like a second moon. Jason Todd stood upon the rooftop of an abandoned warehouse down by the waterfront. Honking horns and police sirens filtered up from the grimy streets below. It was another busy night in Gotham.

He sneered at the bat-winged emblem in the sky. Once, when he was young and naïve, the Signal had promised adventure and excitement. Now it only reminded him of his lost innocence—and a life that had been abruptly taken from him.

"Still fighting the good fight, eh, Bruce?"

Part of him had never forgiven Batman for not avenging his "death" by killing the Joker, let alone for moving on with his life and training a new Robin. *To hell with it,* he thought. *That's water under the bridge now. No more masks and capes for me.*

He'd seen firsthand just how insane that life could get. . . .

A muffled whimper reminded him that he still had business to take care of tonight. Turning his back on the Bat-Signal, he strode over to where a helpless figure, his arms and legs tightly bound with duct tape, struggled uselessly upon the floor of the roof. Gang tattoos marked the man's shaved skull. Perspiration glistened upon the faded ink. Bloodshot eyes were wide with fear. More duct tape was stretched across the prisoner's mouth. Blood dripped from a broken nose.

"They say knowledge is power," Jason said with a smirk. "As a made man in the underworld, I'm sure you know that."

The gang member mumbled something unintelligible. Judging from the man's panicked expression, Jason figured he was about ready to squeal. Rumor had it the Penguin was running guns in this neighborhood, and Jason really wanted to get a lead on the operation before Batman did. *If nothing else,* he thought, *I can use the ammo.*

He drew a switchblade from his black leather jacket and flicked it open. "So lay some knowledge on me, smart guy."

Forget that Multiverse crap, Jason thought. *This where is I belong. In the streets and alleys where I can make a difference—my way.*

Too bad Donna couldn't see that.

IVY TOWN.

"Ray, you were there," Donna reminded him. "You saw what almost happened." She showed no sign of budging from his couch anytime soon. "Godlike beings playing games with the cosmos, with every living soul their pawn." Her pensive eyes searched his face. "Doesn't that trouble you?"

He looked away, avoiding her gaze. "I try not to think about it."

"Really?" she asked. "And how's that working out for you? Because I know it's keeping me up nights."

Ray felt a headache coming on. He squeezed the bridge of his nose. "What do you want, Donna?"

She got up from the couch. "An answer."

"Okay," he grumped. "And the question?"

She fixed him squarely in her sights. "Who monitors the Monitors?"

Huh? It took him a second to realize what she was getting at. "Oh no! Absolutely not!" Throwing up his hands to ward off the very idea, he spun around and started to walk out of the room. He shook his head in denial. "Are you insane?"

Surely, she couldn't be serious!

THE KAHNDAQI DESERT.

Moonlight reflected off an arid wasteland that stretched for miles in every direction. Towering sand dunes shifted slowly beneath the relentless push of a cold desert breeze. The skeleton of a dead camel lay half buried in a gully, the remains stripped to the bone by windblown grit. A brawny figure, clad in a black silk uniform, contemplated the forbidding landscape surrounding him. A golden thunderbolt adorned his chest.

"Of all the kingdoms and empires that have come from the desert," Black Adam mused aloud, "none have ever been able to match its stark majesty and cruel beauty." He tipped his head to the sky. "Wouldn't you agree, Mary?"

Guess those pointed ears of his heard me coming, she thought as she descended from the sky behind him. Her boots touched down upon the lifeless sands. "Ancient history isn't really my thing, but as far as 'cruel beauty' goes, I'm with you all the way."

She wasn't surprised to find him here; this was his ancestral homeland after all. Nor was she startled to find that he had apparently regained his own powers, even after surrendering a portion of them to her months ago. Kind of like Billy kept his powers after sharing them with Freddy. Frankly, she was glad that she wasn't the only Black Marvel in the world. There was at least one other person on Earth who understood what it was like to wield this power. *Now that Darkseid's gone for good, I'm a free agent. And I can team up with whomever I like.*

He grudgingly turned to face her. His saturnine features were hardly welcoming. "Indeed?"

"Sure," Mary said. "You should have seen me stomping gods and super heroes. You were right all along. The Justice League and the others, they're no threat to beings like us. We can make our own rules."

She didn't expect Black Adam to greet her like a long-lost sister, but she figured he'd be impressed by how well she'd followed in his footsteps. *Who knows?* she thought. *Adam and I have both lost our families, so maybe we can form a new Black Marvel Family?*

But instead his voice dripped with contempt. "Spoiled, willful child. I have always done what I must, while you simply do what you want."

"Want?" Mary felt like she'd been slapped in the face. "I didn't want this! I didn't ask for this!"

If the gods hadn't stolen her powers in the first place, and cut her off from her original family, she wouldn't have had anything to do with this. She would still be the same happy Mary Marvel she was supposed to be. *It's not my fault!*

Black Adam ignored her protests. Turning away from her, he started to fly away. "Do not come to me seeking a partner in your misery."

Mary's shock at his brusque dismissal flared into anger. How dare he abandon her—just like everyone else! "Don't!" Lightning blasted from her fingertips, striking Black Adam in the back. "Do not turn your back on me! Not ever!"

The thunderbolt knocked him out of the air, causing him to crash down onto the moonlit sands. Smoke rose from his scorched uniform as he rose angrily to his feet, but still he refused to look back at her, as though she was unworthy of his notice. "I called you a child, and you reacted like one." He took off into the sky once more. "As I normally find beating children distasteful, I shall simply take my leave." She found herself staring up at the soles of his boots. "Farewell, Mary."

She was tempted to fire another blast at him, but what was the point? He had made his feelings clear. "That's right!" she shouted after him as he disappeared into the distance. "You'd better run!" She shook her fists at the heavens. "I'm Mary Marvel! I don't need you! I don't need anyone!"

Lightning erupted all around her, tearing up the desert. Billowing clouds of sand raced outward across the dunes, leaving the aggrieved heroine standing alone in the center of a smoking crater. Her tantrum over, she took a deep breath and contemplated the messy aftermath of the explosion. The extent of the damage demonstrated, once and for all, that there was still one thing she could always count on.

"I'm Mary damn Marvel," she whispered.

The rest of the world would just have to deal with that.

IVY TOWN.

"First Donna. Now you two?" Ray sulked upon his easy chair. "One more super-being sets foot in this house and I'm going to start charging rent."

"Sorry," Jimmy Olsen apologized. The carrot-topped reporter perched on the arm of the chair next to Ray. "But Forager insisted."

The insect-woman, who was wearing a restored version of her chitinous exoskeleton, was conferring in the corner with Donna, who had apparently invited them to this improvised reunion of the Challengers of the Unknown. The only consolation was that, according to Donna, Jason Todd would not be joining them.

I can live with that, Ray thought.

"But to what end?" He gazed at the alien female standing over by the entertainment center. "The gods she served, the worlds of New Genesis and Apokolips, are all gone." Superman had informed the League that the two planets had ultimately crashed together, forming a new world whose future was known only to the Source. "I can't help her find any of her own kind who might have survived."

Jimmy shrugged. "Yeah, well you tell her that."

His weary tone implied that his ardor for the exotic alien had cooled somewhat. Ray felt sorry for the younger man; it seemed that true love remained evasive no matter what planet you were on. *At least she didn't go crazy and murder your friends.*

Donna and Forager finished their private conversation and joined the two men. "We've decided," Donna announced, her hands upon her hips in a very take-charge manner. She sounded completely confident in her choice, whatever it might be.

"To leave?" Ray said hopefully. "Please?"

Donna shook her head. "We're going to monitor the Monitors—with your help."

"No way," he protested. Just because he had figured out how to traverse the Multiverse didn't mean he was planning to make a career of it. He lurched angrily from his seat. "And why would I want to do that?"

"Because you know they are right," a solemn voice declared from a sparkling column of light. The teleportation beam signaled the arrival of a Monitor, but the not one Ray first expected. Instead of the bearded Solomon, Ray recognized the clean-shaven Monitor of Earth-51, the one who had granted Ray sanctuary on his world until Solomon barged in and sent everything to hell. The one who had banished him from Earth-51 forever.

"Nix Uotan!" Donna blurted.

"Yes," the Monitor confirmed. The coruscating energies dissipated, leaving behind the looming extraterrestrial in his intimidating high-tech armor. His black hair was bound up in a ponytail. "I have heard your words and agree. Sentinels are not infallible. Mistakes are made. Hubris, arrogance . . . these are the pitfalls of those who become complacent with the responsibility they bear."

Ray was grateful that the living room drapes were drawn. The last thing the neighbors needed to see was the steadily growing alien population in his living room. "Count me out!" he insisted. "I've got a life."

"Really?" the Monitor asked. He eyed Ray dubiously. "Professor Palmer, you above all others should know the difference between living and merely existing." He looked about the crowded living room, as though he knew exactly just how lonely and forlorn this place had been before Donna had invited herself in. "Have you ever felt more alive than when you were exploring the new worlds? First in the Nanoverse, then in the Multiverse?"

He's got a point, Ray conceded. *What's really holding me here?*

He walked away from the others, trying to get a little distance from their arguments. "I tried running away before. It didn't work."

"You wouldn't be running away this time," Forager observed. "You would be serving a purpose."

"I don't know," Ray said. "I—I've got think about this. . . ."

Donna came up behind him and gently laid a hand on his shoulder. "No. You don't."

THE TIMESTREAM.

The Monitors' enormous space station, which was located at the nexus of the fifty-two universes, reminded the Atom of the Justice League's satellite headquarters. Air locks and heavy steel bulkheads protected the heavily shielded base from the formless void outside. Insulated cables snaked across the walls and ceilings. A multitude of glowing view-screens offered pictures of all the myriad realities, from the postatomic wasteland of Earth-17 to a world of anthropomorphized cartoon animals. Portholes looked out onto the swirling vapors beyond the station's walls. The air was clean and sterile. The gravity was mercifully Earth-normal.

"This is preposterous!" an indignant Monitor proclaimed. "Sheer madness!"

The Atom, Forager, and Donna occupied an elevated dais in the Monitors' central assembly hall. Dozens of the armored aliens packed bleachers and galleries facing the dais, their individual appearances reflecting the distinctive nature of their respective universes. Fangs and pointed ears betrayed the vampiric nature of one Monitor, while another sported Victorian-style muttonchops. Facial hair, scales, feathers, tattoos, skin color, and variations in size and gender distinguished the Monitors from each other. The Atom scanned the galleries, but failed to spot Solomon among the quorum. According to Nix Uotan, the rebellious Monitor was now a pariah among his kind.

Solomon could be a problem, the Atom thought. *We're going to need to keep a close eye on him.*

"They do not belong here!" another Monitor objected. Her elaborate headdress looked vaguely Kryptonian in nature. "Their presence is an insult to our eons of selfless duty!"

"And yet here we are," Donna said defiantly. Like the Atom, she had traded her civilian garb for her super-hero costume. Silver stars glittered upon her ebony leotard. "You will abide by our decisions, or you will accept our punishments."

Forager brandished a futuristic lance. "You know we do not lack the will to enforce them!"

The Monitors could barely contain themselves. They rose from their seats like an angry mob. "We are the Monitors!" someone in the first row shouted. "We answer to no one!"

"We are flawed!" Nix Uotan shouted above the uproar. He strode out onto the stage beside Donna and the others. "I sponsor these Challengers!"

"You!" another Monitor mocked him. "You could not even stop Solomon from invading your own universe!"

Uotan did not back down. "All the more proof they are needed."

"But they are anomalies!" An avian Monitor, whose scalp sported glossy black feathers instead of hair, pointed accusingly at the Challengers. "Only the being known as 'Atom' has a world!"

The Atom stepped forward. "Not anymore!" His voice was strong and without hesitation. He had made his decision and he was going to stick to it, no matter what. "There's nothing left for me in my world. I renounce my place in it." He held his palm up as though taking an oath. "From now on, I join these others to serve the Multiverse as 'border guards' for man and Monitor alike!"

The audience was not yet convinced. "This is without precedent," observed an elfin-looking Monitor whose armor bore a medieval coat of arms. "We must weigh your proposal carefully."

"You misunderstand," the Atom corrected him. "We didn't come to ask permission. We came to serve notice." He activated the controls upon his belt and brilliant atomic orbitals circled him and the two women. Harnessed white-star energies prepared to transport them away from the nexus. "We're out there . . . so watch yourselves!"

They disappeared into the Multiverse.

THE SOURCE WALL.

"Well, well." Solomon chuckled. "And so a new game begins."

The renegade Monitor watched the Challengers' departure via a miniature view-screen on his gauntlet. Although unwelcome among his fellows, he continued to track their affairs with interest. He savored their consternation at the Challengers' professed new mission.

Who knew Donna Troy and her fellow anomalies would prove so amusing?

Solomon stood astride an asteroid at the literal border of the universe. Before him rose the Source Wall, a dense barrier of incalculable size. Although it appeared to be constructed of weathered ocher stone, it was actually composed of a unique preternatural substance more durable than any mundane element. Humanoid figures, some hundreds of feet tall, were embedded in the very substance of the Wall. No mere effigies, the figures were actually the entombed remains of the ancient Promethean Giants, as well as everyone else who had ever attempted to penetrate the Wall to discover what lay beyond. The victims of their own overreaching ambitions, they stood as eternal warnings to any other reckless soul who might dare to brave the Wall's impregnable defenses. Few knew that, among other things, the Source Wall divided the fifty-two universes from each other.

"The Wall still stands," Solomon stated, recording his observations for posterity. His personal force field protected him from the vacuum of space. "Despite his every machination, Darkseid won only scattered skirmishes, not the war. The Fifth Age will dawn. The Multiverse endures."

And I too endure, he thought, *even while shunned by my fellow Monitors.* He scowled at the galling injustice of it all. His bold vision and decisive action should have raised him high among their immortal fellowship, but instead he found himself an outcast. "So be it," he spat venomously. "While they dither and debate, my plans unfold. Infinitely patient, I play for the highest stakes imaginable."

Diverting the course of the asteroid, he cruised nearer to the Wall until it was close enough to touch. Its vast immensity filled his vision as he spied a solitary ledge jutting slightly outward from its ornate surface. "Let me be the first to add to the Wall in this new age."

He reached out to lay a small object upon the ledge. Only seven inches tall, the exquisitely sculpted chessman was nearly lost amidst the colossal dimensions of the Wall.

"Darkseid would have been Creation's new architect, yet his monument is the smallest of all," Solomon gloated as he contemplated a miniature figurine fashioned in the likeness of Apokolips's once-invincible ruler. "A token reminder for anyone foolish enough to underestimate me in the future."

He vanished in a shower of sparks.

METROPOLIS.

"**Man,** oh man," Harley whispered. She perched on the fire escape of her and Holly's new apartment as she stared up at the starry night sky overhead. An oversized Gotham University T-shirt served as a nightdress. Her bare feet dangled over the nocturnal alley below. A warm breeze, holding the promise of spring, rustled her pigtails.

"You say something, Harley?" Holly climbed out onto the fire escape beside her roommate. The fresh air felt good after painting the kitchen all day. Her ratty tank top and shorts were splattered with aquamarine splotches.

Harley kept on gazing at the stars. "I was just thinking."

"Really?"

"Yeah," Harley replied. "There's so much going on here, and out there, and places we don't even know about." From where they were sitting, you could see the enormous crater where the middle of Suicide Slum used to be. The two women had managed to get a good deal on the apartment by pretending that they had lost everything when the New Gods exploded; they figured it wasn't really all *that* far from the truth. "Everything's so scary and uncertain. We never know when fate—or some wacky alien god—will shake it all up."

Tell me about it, Holly thought. She cast a wistful glance at Harley's T-shirt. Someday she hoped to return to Gotham, but that wasn't an option right now; she was still wanted for murder there. Things could be worse, though. Metropolis didn't quite feel like home yet, but at least she had a roof over her head and a friend to share it with.

"That's deep," she told Harley.

Lowering her gaze, the blonde watched the construction crews working overtime to rebuild Metropolis. Darkseid and giant-turtle Jimmy had left a hell of a mess behind. "You gotta wonder how we'll ever make it through what comes next."

Holly shrugged. "I guess we can fall back on what's gotten us this far."

"A positive attitude and lots of denial?"

Holly laughed. "Don't ever change, Harley."

THE BEGINNING.

About the Author

GREG COX is the *New York Times* best-selling author of numerous books and short stories, including the novelizations of two previous DC Comics miniseries: *Infinite Crisis* and *52*. He has also written the movie novelizations of *Daredevil, Death Defying Acts, Ghost Rider, Underworld, Underworld: Evolution,* and *Underworld: Rise of the Lycans,* as well as original books and stories based on such popular series as *Alias, Batman, Buffy, CSI, Fantastic Four, Farscape, The 4400, Iron Man, Roswell, Spider-Man, Star Trek, Underworld, Xena, X-Men,* and *Zorro.* His official website is www.gregcox-author.com.

Greg lives in Oxford, Pennsylvania.